A CRIMINAL MAGIC

For Lindsey —
Make the impossible possible!

Lee Kelly

ALSO BY LEE KELLY

City of Savages

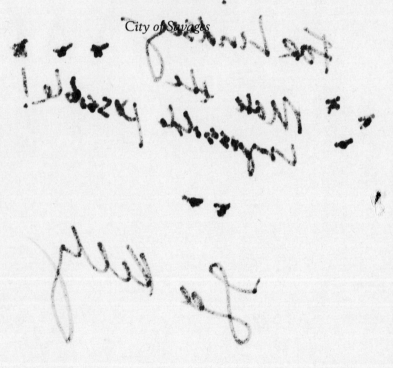

A
CRIMINAL
MAGIC

LEE
KELLY

SAGA  PRESS

LONDON SYDNEY **NEW YORK** TORONTO NEW DELHI

SAGA PRESS

AN IMPRINT OF SIMON & SCHUSTER, INC.

1230 AVENUE OF THE AMERICAS, NEW YORK, NEW YORK 10020

| Text copyright © 2016 by Lee Kelly | Front cover photo-illustration © 2016 by Steve Stone | All rights reserved, including the right to reproduce this book or portions thereof in any form whatsoever. For information address Saga Press Subsidiary Rights Department, 1230 Avenue of the Americas, New York, NY 10020 | SAGA PRESS and colophon are trademarks of Simon & Schuster, Inc. | For information about special discounts for bulk purchases, please contact Simon & Schuster Special Sales at 1-866-506-1949 or business@simonandschuster. com. | The Simon & Schuster Speakers Bureau can bring authors to your live event. For more information or to book an event, contact the Simon & Schuster Speakers Bureau at 1-866-248-3049 or visit our website at www.simonspeakers.com. | Also available in a Saga Press hardcover edition | The text for this book was set in Revival 565 BT. | Manufactured in the United States of America | First Saga Press paperback edition January 2017 | 10 9 8 7 6 5 4 3 2 1 | The Library of Congress has cataloged the hardcover edition as follows: | Kelly, Lee. | A criminal magic / Lee Kelly.—First edition. | p. cm. | Summary: "Washington, DC, 1926. While sorcery opponents have succeeded in passing the 18th Amendment, the Prohibition of magic has only invigorated the city's underworld. Smuggling rings funnel magic contraband in from the coast. Sorcerers cast illusions to aid mobsters' crime sprees. Gangs have even established secret venues called "magic havens," where the public can lose themselves in immersive magic, as well as imbibe a mind-bending and highly addictive elixir known as "the sorcerer's shine." Joan Kendrick, a young sorcerer from the back woods of Norfolk County, accepts an offer to work for DC's most notorious crime syndicate, The Shaw Gang, when her family's home is repossessed. Alex Danfrey, first-year Federal Prohibition Unit trainee with a complicated past and talents of his own, becomes tapped to go undercover and infiltrate the Shaws. Joan meets Alex at the Shaws' magic haven, and soon discovers a confidante in her fellow performer. As Alex grows closer to Joan, he begins to fall under her spell. But when a new breed of sorcerer's shine— one sorcered within the walls of the Shaws' magic haven—gets set to change the face of the underworld, Joan and Alex are forced to question their allegiances and motivations, as they become pitted against one another in a dangerous, heady game of cat-and-mouse"— Provided by publisher. | ISBN 978-1-4814-1033-5 (hardback) | ISBN 978-1-4814-1035-9 (eBook) | 1. Magic—Fiction. 2. Prohibition—Fiction. 3. Washington (D.C.)—Fiction. 4. Fantasy fiction. 5. Alternative histories (Fiction) I. Title. | PS3611. E4498C75 2016 | 813'.6—dc23 | 2015022120 | ISBN 978-4814-1034-2 (pbk)

For Jeff—you are my compass

ACKNOWLEDGMENTS

They say it takes a village to raise a child, and I'm pretty sure the same should be said of a book. Endless love and thanks to my parents, Joe and Linda Appicello, for always being there for me: as sounding boards, career managers, babysitters, beta readers. This book simply wouldn't have been possible without you. To my husband, Jeff, my best friend and biggest champion, who believes in me and encourages me even when (especially when) I most doubt myself. Thanks to my sisters, Bridget and Jill, for the late-night conference calls and virtual martinis, and for reading this book in all of its first-draft messiness, as well as to my parents-in-law, Alice and Paul Kelly, who were true lifelines during this book's revisions. And of course, to Penn and Summer, for all of the joy and for reminding me of what matters most. You guys are my village, and what an awesome village it is.

A million thanks to my brilliant and amazing agent, Adriann Ranta, for being my champion, for the constant support and encouragement, and for always making time, and to her partners-in-crime, Allison Devereux and the entire Wolf Literary family.

Endless thanks to my talented and incisive editor, Navah Wolfe—her insight and guidance helped me shape what vaguely resembled what I was trying to accomplish into a story I'm very proud of. Thank you for challenging me and for pushing me, Navah, and for those "You Can Do This" emails at the beginning of our process that meant the world.

Many thanks to the rest of the Simon & Schuster family who made this book possible, including Joe Monti, Saga Press's fearless editorial director; designer Michael McCartney, who is batting a thousand on Saga Press covers; the incredible managing editor Bridget Madsen; Jacquelynne Hudson, for her interior design savviness; wonderful production manager Elizabeth Blake-Linn; ace publicist Ksenia Winnicki; Valerie Shea, for her copyediting chops; and fabulous design coordinator Tiara Iandioro. Thanks as well to Steve Stone, who illustrated the beautiful cover on the front of this book.

Thanks to the Freshman Fifteens, the Class of 2K15, and the Fearless Fifteeners for their continued support over the past few years, particularly my friends and confidantes Chandler Baker, Virginia Boecker, Jen Brooks, Kelly Loy Gilbert, Lori Goldstein, and Kim Liggett. And much appreciation to my fantastic critique partners, Erika David and Lisa Koosis—Erika, your cheerleading meant so much on this one.

And last but perhaps most, thanks to the readers. To me, the fact that this book is in your hands is the absolute best kind of magic.

THE AMERICAN ISSUE

A Sorcery-Free Nation and a Stainless Flag

VOLUME XXVI	WESTERVILLE, OHIO, JANUARY 29, 1919	NUMBER 6

US IS FREE FROM MAGIC'S SPELL

36TH STATE RATIFIES ANTI-SORCERY AMENDMENT JAN. 16

Nebraska Noses Out Missouri for Honor of Completing Job of Writing Anti-Sorcery Act into Constitution; Wyoming, Wisconsin, and Minnesota Right on Their Heels

JANUARY 16, 1919, MOMENTOUS DAY IN WORLD'S HISTORY

September 1926

PART ONE
THE SORCERERS

BLACK WOODS

JOAN

Magic can achieve a lot of things, but it can't undo the past. I've sworn off sorcery, buried my magic with earth, blood, and tears below the ground, but I'd gladly sell my soul to use it just once more, if sorcery could find a way to bring me back in time. If it could bring me right to the edge of where I once stood and shattered my world into tiny shards, and make me walk away instead.

I've managed to trick myself from time to time. Even after all these months, I'll sometimes wake up and forget for those few hazy minutes between sleep and morning, and the world will feel different. Like all the color hasn't been stolen out of it, like she might be in her spell room mixing lavender and poppy, whispering her words of power, sneaking in some work before breakfast as dawn creeps into the windows behind her. It's such a warm and comfortable feeling, like burrowing into a blanket, and I want to snuggle in tight, burrow a little deeper, even as my mind's coming into focus, even as my heart's catching on to being duped and starts beating faster, *faster*, then double time.

And then it hits me like an avalanche of bricks.

She's gone.

But that's the problem with tricks. The world can feel even emptier, once their hold on you is over.

I start drying the load of glasses I've just rinsed, arranging the tumblers on the bar behind me like an army of clear, thin soldiers. Out the window, the gray sky of late afternoon has deepened into a sad twilight over our backyard clearing. It's almost five o'clock, and both our sham liquor bar and Uncle Jed's shining room need straightening. I don't have the luxury of running headfirst into the dark right now, of getting lost again in the black woods of the past.

There's a rattling coming from the closet near the stairs to Uncle Jed's shining room, and my cousin Ben emerges with our mop, the loop-ends so dark they look like tangled strands of a witch's wig. He slaps it on the floor, over that same spot he always cleans, where one of Jed's lightweight regulars lost control on a shot of Jed's shine last year and got sick in the corner. The government says this place won't be ours anymore in a few weeks, but Ben and I have both become experts at living in denial.

"Just forget it," I say. "That stain's never coming out."

"Gotta try, right? In case the Drummond loan officer shows up?" Ben huffs and puffs as he sends the mop slogging across the thick plank floor.

I let a tiny bubble of hope rise inside my chest, despite how smart it may be to pop it. "You got Jed to finally sign the paperwork?"

Ben doesn't meet my eyes, and the thrusts of the mop become stronger. "No, I had to forge it."

I nearly sling back what I really think of Jed, but somehow I manage to bite my tongue. Ain't Ben's fault his pop's a waste of breath and bones. Besides, the peace under our roof is delicate, something that needs to be handled with care. "I guess considering all the ways we're breaking the law, forgery's the least of our worries," I say, and start slotting the glasses underneath the bar.

"Here's hoping to God this bank man pulls through, Joan. 'Cause I don't think we've got another option."

"We'll figure it out," I say, to remind us both. "We always do." And it's the truth. We will, because we have to. Because that's my charge—to fight and scrape my family out of the hole Uncle Jed and I dug them into.

But Ben doesn't answer. Most probably 'cause everything that could be said has already been said before. We've had this conversation over a dozen times since Uncle Jed got the cabin repossession notice. Not that we know exactly when it came— Jed stumbled out one night he was half-fit enough to work and shoved the crumpled thing under Ben's nose, mumbling about not understanding the "legalese."

"I'm opening. You ready?" Ben flicks off the lock on the door across from the bar. He takes the little sign off the floor that says OPEN FOR BUSINESS and hangs it from the nail on the out-side. "Fridays always bring the best crowd. If we can get my pop downstairs on time for the early performance, we've got a chance of making a few bucks before Charlie opens."

Charlie is Charlie Newman, the only other sorcerer in Parsonage besides Jed, at least since Mama passed six months ago. Charlie's shining room is our only real competition—next one's someplace about ten miles south on the way to Drummond— and his place puts our dingy basement to shame. I've heard it has an honest-to-God performance stage with bleachers around it for his tricks, a couple cozy chairs for settling in for his sor-cerer's shine that's always served after. Not that we ever worried about Charlie before: people don't come to shining rooms for bleachers and cozy chairs. They come for magic, in and out of the bottle, and Jed used to perform circles around Charlie.

But then Jed got hooked on drinking his own shine, got all cracked up. And the night of Mama's death broke him wide open. Just like the rest of us under this roof.

"Ruby still resting?"

Ben nods. "Thought I'd let her be."

"All right, go on, straighten up downstairs," I say. "I'll be right back."

I duck under the bar and walk through the flap door that leads to the front half of our cabin. Uncle Jed's bedroom is closed off like always, his thin, grating wheeze throttling behind the door like a failing steam train. Across the stub of a hall is the room I share with Ruby and Ben. I don't knock, 'cause I don't want to startle my sister. I just crack it open and quietly slip in.

The room feels thick, hot and dark like a mouth, tastes like sweat and heavy sleeping. Our three cots swallow most of the room, so I kneel down at the corner of Ruby's and slide my way around till I can see her little face. It's slack, her breath long and deep. Ruby hasn't had a real fever in almost a month, but she still lies around here most of the day. Town doc wrote it off as the sleepy sickness, since he can't figure out what's wrong with her. But his field is science, not magic. And I know too well what magic can do, why it's even more dangerous than the lawmen touted when they got on their soapboxes about the need for the Eighteenth Amendment. How it's a living, breathing thing, something that makes ties and connections, appreciates sacrifice, a power that can have a mind of its own. It's Mama's old tracking spell that's poisoning Ruby, the last traces of Mama's blood still swimming inside of my sister, the magic that once let Mama keep close tabs on spirited Ruby's whereabouts now a foreign, powerful poison. But the blood's hold won't last forever, and Ruby's body is fighting it. She's getting better, I know it, I can see it, she'll survive.

"Ruby." I gently shake her. "Ruby, you need something to eat? Shining room's opening." She doesn't move, so I carefully touch her forehead. She's soft and warm. Six years old and sleepy, flushed perfection.

"Joan?" Ruby finally flutters her eyes.

"Did you take some of the dinner I left in the kitchen before you rested?"

"I'm not sure." She yawns. "I forget."

"Well, remember. And if not, you've got to put it in your belly."

She gives me a little smile and buries her mussed-up, tangled head back into her pillow. "Tell me the story first."

"Ruby, honey, there's no time for stories."

She gives me what we call her "silly face," which is when she presses her eyes shut tight, sticks her jaw out, and chomps up and down like a deranged shark. And then of course she has me. I sigh. "Which story?"

She smiles victoriously and rests her head on her arm. "You know which one."

"All right, but the abridged version." I clear my throat. "Long ago there was a young sorcerer who was the most powerful in the land. But when there was a terrible tragedy, the young sorcerer fell sick, and she was so important that the world became sick with her." I lean in to push back Ruby's thin, sweat-damp hair. "One day she realized how much her kingdom needed her to be well and to rule. So she found her strength, got out of bed, and ruled like the kind, strong sorcerer she was meant to be."

Ruby flashes me another smile, but then she closes her eyes. "Joan," she whispers, "I think I forgot what she looks like."

I don't answer, because her words hit me right in the gut and I can't, because any hollow words of comfort I could give her shatter before they find their way out.

"Her face is mixed up like a puzzle . . . I don't even know if it's really Mama anymore." Then Ruby looks up at me, a wild panic lighting up her eyes, and I have to keep myself from doubling over. *Long ago, an evil sorcerer broke her sister's heart, and her penance, to die trying to piece it back together.*

"Mama's with you, Ruby, always watching over you." I swallow, trying to recover as I rub her back. "She's not going anywhere, okay? You really need to eat."

Ruby finally swings her legs over the edge of the bed.

"Go on, it's on the counter, help yourself. Then read a little, all right?"

"Can't I come back there with you and Ben, and watch Uncle Jed?"

"Not tonight." I keep Ruby away from Jed at all costs. We might be under the same roof, Jed and me, but I try my damnedest to avoid even looking at the junkie. I do my part: taking care of Ruby, handling the finances, helping with the bar and the kitchen, and let Jed take care of his: which at this point, is stumbling in shined to his performances. Anything we need to say to each other, Ben says for us.

"Maybe tomorrow, all right?" I say, softening, as I help Ruby get her bearings and stand.

She sighs but says, "'Kay, Joan."

By the time I get back to the bar, there's already three shiners cozied up at one of the tables near the stairs down to Jed's shining room. I know this crowd—they're field hands out at McGarrison's farm, and some of the only regulars who still come in every Friday for Jed's early performance.

The oldest field hand, a freckled farm-boy type with dirty hands and weathered overalls, with a name like Willy or William (I never manage to remember), slaps the table and calls to Ben, "Been a long week, Kendrick. Sure as hell need me some magic."

"We always appreciate your loyalty, Mr. Sterling," Ben says, as I join him behind the bar. "Fact, my father's been practicing a new trick all week for you." Ben didn't inherit the magic touch from Jed, which is a crying shame, seeing as he's such a good performer: Jed's barely left his room this week. "Let me go get him, and get this show started."

"You fellas want anything from the bar?" I nod to our

half-empty shelves, the smattering of time-worn whiskey and rum bottles. The liquor bar's our legitimate storefront: our cover for Jed's shining room downstairs, which is our only real source of income now, since Mama passed. But if you're after the legal stuff, there are liquor bars easier to get to in Norfolk County, with better selections and better ambiance: the people who walk through our door are coming for my uncle's magic. At least, they were in droves when his magic was really something to see.

"No thanks," William says. "Don't want to muddle the shine-high."

His sidekicks shake me off too.

"Your choice." I cross over to our small black register and pull the bottom drawer open. "It's one dollar per fella for the show and the shine."

Each of the patrons starts mumbling complaints, but they all line up in front of the register and begrudgingly hand me a buck. After paying, the trio crowds around their table again, waiting. I can feel their impatience for the magic from here.

"Have you shined since Charlie's on Wednesday?" William asks his buddies.

"Nah, don't have the cash for more than twice a week, but I'm hankering right now," the guy across from him answers.

"Sorcerer's shine is so damn expensive, I'm gonna need to mortgage my home to feed the habit." William throws a glance my way as he adds, "You fellas read anything about this new magic product they're smuggling in from Ireland? Fae dust?"

The guy across from him snorts. "A trippy blue powder they're claiming they stole from a magic plane?" He shakes his head. "I ain't that gullible."

"Don't know, news is saying it's real. And somehow, it lasts—you can buy and store it, and get high whenever you want, instead of hitting up some sorcerer like a junkie a few times a week." William turns to me. "Joan, you hear anything about the dust? It's all over the papers."

"Don't get the papers here," I answer quietly.

"Guess smugglers are getting smart, since shine's impossible to transport, what with all its magic fading after a day. Apparently the coast guard's scrambling to keep up with these dust sweepers." William throws me a teasing smirk. "The Irish might put you all out of business, if you're not careful."

I don't feel like small-talking with these shiners—I'm short on patience, long on nerves that Ben can't even wake Jed right now—and besides, these junkies have no idea what they're talking about. Magic products all go down different, each have their own wild ride and risks, and there's nothing out there that gives the world a glow like sorcerer's shine.

But I force my lips to fold into a cardboard smile, to play nice for the clientele. "That's what they said about obi, sir, the island elixir folks claim is brewed with lost souls and ghosts. That it was going to put us all out on our tails in weeks. And yet we're still here, serving good old-fashioned sorcerer's shine." At least, for now.

At that, the cabin's dividing door swings open, and Ben reenters, with Uncle Jed in tow. Lord, he's *filthy*. Hair matted and sweaty, lips all crusted over from a daily diet of shine. Swear I can smell him from here.

"Ben," Uncle Jed says, his voice cracking from disuse, "get us ready." Jed doesn't look at me, which is a small blessing, since rage starts beating inside me like a dark heart every time we're this close again. He gives a yellow-toothed smile, thick with saliva, to his three patrons in the corner. "You fellas ready to have your minds blown?"

The trio hoots and hollers, and trails Jed down to the shining room cellar.

Ben joins me behind the bar, and we quickly gather the

materials Jed needs for his sorcery performance—a deck of cards, a stack of shot glasses, and a pitcher that Ben fills with twelve ounces of water from the same bucket I use to wipe down the bar. I put everything on a tray and hand it to Ben carefully. "You gonna watch him?"

"Of course."

"Make sure he gives the crowd a little bit of foreplay this time, all right? A house of cards, or maybe a midair shuffle or something."

Ben shakes his head. "I don't think these shiners care about performance magic."

"Well, Charlie's keeps getting busier as we keep losing customers, so I'm not sure if I agree with you." Then I add quietly, "And don't let Jed drink it."

Ben sighs. "You know what it's like trying to stop my pop from doing anything, but I'll try." We share a sad smile. "Scream bloody hell if anyone gives you trouble up here, all right?"

I nod. "All right."

"And send any latecomers down—here's praying for them." Ben exits the bar and scurries down the stairs to the shining room, and the door—which Jed didn't even bother to conceal with a magic manipulation—closes with a snap.

I'm about to sneak away for a second to check on Ruby, but then our entrance door slaps open again. I jump, thinking maybe Ben's prayers have been answered, and we've got a latecomer shiner who wants to throw another dollar our way. When I look up, a stranger with a chiseled face and a suit worth more than the cabin is approaching the bar. He takes a seat across from me.

He's not from around here, I know in an instant. He's dressed to the nines, with a butter-soft coat and a hat so white it's clearly never been touched by a dirty hand. I catch his stare, and then can't look anywhere else but his white-blue eyes. Cold. Unreadable.

"What can I do you for, sir?"

The stranger doesn't answer right away, just studies me, then takes in every inch of our tiny bar sham—the water-stained ceiling and blisters in the walls, the smattering of bottles that pockmark our shelves, the closed doors, one of which leads to cleaning supplies, the other to illegal magic. Finally he asks, "This Jed Kendrick's place?"

"Yes, sir."

He glances around once more. "Then where is he?"

I remember what Ben said about forging our loan application, so I grasp at that thin thread of hope and hang on. "Are you from Drummond Savings and Loan?"

The man takes off his fedora, revealing blond hair so stiff and coifed it looks like the top of a meringue pie. "Afraid not." He's about to place his white hat on the bar, but then, I guess thinking better of it, rests it in his lap. "Pour me a whiskey, will you?"

"Of course, sir."

He waits a beat before asking, "What's your name?"

"Joan." I pull out a tumbler from under the bar, but it takes three tries before I can actually open the whiskey bottle's crusty cap. "And who do I have the pleasure of serving?"

"Name's Harrison Gunn. You Kendrick's daughter?"

"Niece," I correct quickly. The notion of being Jed's daughter sends a small current of disgust rippling under my skin. "My mama was Jed's sister-in-law."

"Aren't you a little young to be tending bar?"

I set the whiskey in front of him. "I'm eighteen. Suppose I'm old enough."

Mr. Gunn fingers the glass but doesn't pick it up. "I've been told you have something . . . stronger here," he says to the tumbler, then flits his white-blue eyes up at me. "Is that right?"

I stop myself before I glance at the door to our shining room like a reflex. I try to figure out which way this fella's angling: his vague questions, his three-piece suit, his city accent. Another fear starts to sink in. "Sir, we don't want any trouble." Last thing we need is some sort of bust for sorcering, on top of the shit storm we're about to weather. "Down here, we deal with Agent Barnes," I say, despite the fact that we can't afford to pay off the local Prohibition agent anymore. "Mr. Barnes handles everything related to magic. He'll explain, set you straight—"

"Relax, I'm not with the government. Far from it." Gunn studies the doors on the far wall. "I just wanted to make sure I had my information right. I was told Jed was a first-class sorcerer. That the Kendricks were known for a special magic."

I let out a breath. "Yes, sir. Jed's shining room's downstairs. We've got two performances every Friday, Saturday, and Sunday nights, as well as by request, from reliable sources."

When he doesn't answer, I add, "It's a dollar for the performance and a shot of sorcerer's shine. Jed's no joke—the high'll last an hour, blast you to another universe." I cringe as I recite Ben's canned sales line. "I promise you won't be disappointed— the performance started a couple minutes ago. If you hurry—"

"I've come a long way to meet your uncle," Gunn interrupts. "Drove straight from DC. Think you could arrange a special solo performance?"

A solo performance. I'm about to tell this man that these days, Jed barely makes it through one show without getting lost in a shot of his own magic, but something about Gunn's coat, his hat, his stare, makes me bite my tongue. "Aren't there sorcerers up in Washington?" I say slowly. "Pity you had to make such a long drive for a shot of shine."

Gunn reaches out and touches the rim of his whiskey. "My plans concern a much grander scale." He flits a smile at me, a smile that changes his face, makes it softer, more attractive. Younger. "I've got a business proposition for your uncle."

A business proposition. Meaning dollars, more money, our

home. I don't want to sound too eager, too desperate, but I can't help but blurt out, "Involving what?"

Gunn pauses a long time before answering. "I'm something of a sorcery connoisseur," he finally says. "I believe in the power of magic. Don't have the touch myself, but I've read almost everything on magic out there. And let's just say I have a theory, one I need several sorcerers to prove."

This guy definitely doesn't look like a scholar, or a scientist. But I don't let that pierce the hope that's slowly ballooning inside me. "You mean, like an experiment?"

"Of sorts," he says tightly. "I'm scouting the entire country for the best of the best, bringing any sorcerer with strong talents, a taste for performance, and a mastery of shine transference up to Washington. I'll be keeping the ones who prove themselves a cut above the rest." His eyes flicker to our sad walls again, to my face that I'm sure reads wide and eager, to the water stains on the bar. "And if my little theory pans out, there's going to be more money floating around than any of us know what to do with."

I gulp, my heart now flying. "You think Jed could be one of these sorcerers?"

"Hard to tell without seeing his magic, or tasting his shine." Gunn shrugs. "But your uncle comes highly recommended from an acquaintance who used to come here a while back. If Jed's even half the sorcerer my source claims he is, I'd say we have a lot to talk about." Gunn shifts forward in his seat, and the sound of creaking wood fills our silence. "I can say for certain there'll be more money in it than some crook of a loan officer could ever offer you."

This feels like a gift, a dream, a chance. There's no way in hell I can let us lose this chance. "You ain't pulling my leg?"

"I never joke about business." He downs his whiskey in one gulp. "Now let me meet the man."

Panic clamps a rein on my heart, heavies my chest. Should I

bring Gunn down to Uncle Jed now, hope that Jed hasn't started brewing his shine, that Gunn can catch him before he's shot to the moon? Or am I too late? Should I stall until Jed comes down off the worst of his shine-high?

It's a crapshoot. But this needs to happen. Jed needs to be in this slick man's slick car, winding his way up to Washington. He needs to brew the strongest sorcerer's shine of his life. He needs to look clean enough to do it again, and again.

"He's . . . he's in the middle of a show."

"A show in the middle of Shitsticks, Virginia," Gunn says. "I've got a long drive back, and I guarantee the chance I'm offering your uncle is worth millions of these low-rent backwoods performances. Interrupt him."

I hurry through the door, down the shadowy flight of stairs into the dark cellar, nearly collide with Ben keeping watch on the bottom step. He stands up, looks at me curiously. I never, ever come down here.

"What's wrong?"

"There's a man here"—I catch my breath—"from Washington to see Jed. It's about an opportunity." I drop my voice as I crane my neck around the staircase to steal a glimpse at Jed's show. "Potentially loads of money."

Ben shifts uncomfortably. "You serious?"

"Dead serious."

"What is he, some big-city sorcerer? A gangster?"

"Who cares," I whisper. "He could save our skins." I take another step down to the cellar floor, nod into the darkness. "You need to get Jed."

Ben looks behind him, shakes his head. "He's already shot to Sunday, Joan."

My stomach drops, sending my hope plunging with it. But before I can think up a way to salvage this chance, footsteps clamber toward us on the stairs.

Gunn sidesteps me, offers his hand to Ben. "Harrison Gunn," he says simply, as Ben, shocked, numbly accepts his hand. "I'm here for Jed Kendrick."

And then Gunn barrels his way into Jed's shining room.

Helpless, Ben and I trail him into the tight alcove behind the stairs. The alcove is littered with lit candles, giving the scene a hazy, otherworldly glow. The three patrons and Jed sit around on four dirty cots that have been arranged into a circle. William's twitching, moaning on one in the corner, while his two buddies hug their knees tight into their chests. One empty shot glass sits in front of each of the patrons, a thin, sparkling red film still coating the inside of each glass. And farthest away, there's Jed.

He sits cross-legged like some magic Buddha, his head pressed into his hands, faint, haunting laughter escaping through his fingertips, his own empty glass in front of him. I don't think about how much I want to slap him, shake him. Instead I go into damage control, a weird, numb-like state just like I did the night of Mama's death, where I'm not really processing things as they're happening, 'cause I've already moved on to trying to undo them. *Maybe if I start talking, maybe if we can keep Jed quiet—*

But then Jed peeks out from his hands. "You're a lost man," he declares to Gunn. Then my uncle collapses back onto his thin, ratty mattress, laughs high and long, like some devil from a dream.

Gunn's face twitches, but he doesn't say a word.

I force myself to speak to Jed for the first time since that night. Even after all these months, I can still barely train my eyes on him. "Uncle Jed, this man's from Washington," I say as calmly as I can, as my mind shrieks, *Lord God, Jed, get it the hell together.* "He's impressed with your sorcery. He wants you to sorcer for him up in the big city. Tell him, Mr. Gunn."

But Gunn says nothing.

"There's money in it," I keep rambling, look around the room, to Ben, *will* him to do something not to blow this chance. "Loads of it. More money than we could ever dream—"

"Money," Jed mumbles, "funny money, silver money, silver fox . . . precious silver." He looks at me, for the first time in a long time, and with wide eyes whispers, "She was my silver. . . ."

A strange, cold rush washes over me as Gunn snaps, "He's a mess. Fucking waste of a six-hour trip." He barrels out of the alcove as Jed's three patrons start cackling like hyenas in the corner.

"He can't leave, we need to fix this," I tell Ben, but Ben's already yelling up the staircase, "Sir, wait!" We hurry up the steps after Gunn.

"Mr. Gunn, please, we're going to lose our home. I swear, if you just give us a couple days. We'll deny my pop straight, he'll be better in a week—"

"If the withdrawal doesn't kill him." Gunn shrugs Ben off and walks to the cabin's door. "I'm not taking any chances on a washed-out shiner."

"Mr. Gunn, you don't understand," I say. "We need this, Jed can make it work—"

"Save it." Gunn throws on his fedora and pushes open our screen door.

But as he crunches over the gravel, the cold, hard truth of our future starts pummeling me, raining down like sharp hail. Jed is lost. Jed is killing himself, slowly. Mama is gone. Our home will be gone in weeks. I pledged my life to Ruby and Ben in penance, but I'm going to fail. This man Gunn, our last chance, is walking out our door.

No, comes hot and relentless from deep within my core, a voice not mine, one stronger, more powerful, resilient. *No no no no no—*

"WAIT!"

Gunn stops.

But he doesn't turn around.

My body is humming, my nerves shorting out. It doesn't feel like real life right now. It feels like a dream, a dream skating right on the edge of a nightmare.

"Give me the chance," I rush. "I can sorcer. And I won't disappoint you."

At that, Gunn laughs. He slowly turns as Ben whispers, "Joan, what? Don't bluff this guy," behind me on our cabin's outside stoop. But Ben never found out that I got the magic touch. In fact, no one knows, except Jed and me—since Mama took her knowledge to her grave.

Gunn tucks his hands into his pockets. The sharp light of the moon transforms him into something otherworldly, almost ghoulish. "Prove it."

I nod, ask him to wait, and before I can second-guess myself, I race out to the yard behind our cabin.

It's started to rain. A thin twine of mist has begun to coil above the earth, but I collapse down onto the dirt, at the same spot I'd pleaded that night for relief from the treacherous magic inside me. Where I brewed all the magic I had, felt, and wished gone into a bottle of sorcerer's shine, then took a blade to my arm as I'd seen Mama do when she was demanding extraordinary things from sorcery. I begged the gods of this world, then its demons, then the magic itself, to relieve me of my magic touch and cage it away forever. Not sure what finally took pity on me, but something answered my call.

My fingers paw at the dirt, the soft mushy soil worming its way under my fingernails, up my arms. I dig until my nails scratch against something hard and rough. I quickly scoop the soil out from around the four sides and unearth the wooden box I buried that night, six inches long, one foot wide. Just on touching it, the memories come flooding back—*show me, Eve*—*Mama NO*—*all the magic in the world can't undo it*—

I shut my eyes to quiet the noise, unclasp the box's lock, and open it. With shaking hands, I take out the bottle that somehow cages my magic touch—the glass prison that prevents my toxic "gifts" from destroying anything else. I hold it, this cursed bottle. This opportunity. This chance. I close my eyes. *My magic touch is to blame for all of it—it doesn't deserve to be released.*

My magic touch is all I've got to save my family.

Heart pounding, I grip the glass and force myself to say the word, "*Release.*"

I unscrew the top of the bottle, which is smeared with my dried blood from all those nights ago, and a flaky red dust settles onto the ground. As soon as I remove the cap, my magic touch floods back into my body in a rush. I feel it consume me, flesh me out like it's pushing hard against my skin, making me whole. Lightning courses through my veins, sizzling, whispering *this is where it always belonged*. The sorcerer's shine left behind in the bottle sighs and crackles, like it's been awakened from a long sleep.

A history of distrust and fear drove America to the Prohibition of magic, but most folks still don't know the half of it. This country's got no idea how many secrets magic keeps, the darkness it can create, the possibilities that lie waiting in the shadows.

I clean off the bottle quickly with the bottom of my housedress and the rain, cap my hand over its top, and sprint back around the cabin. Gunn's still standing in the gravel, and Ben's still on the stoop. "What about this?" I collect myself, trying to keep my voice steady as I hand Gunn the bottle. "Is this impressive enough to get me to Washington?"

Gunn slowly turns the jar around, looks at the back, the front, studies the way the moonlight hits the sparkling, deep-red sorcerer's shine inside. Finally, he says quietly, "When'd you make this?"

"This morning, before the sun came up," I lie in a rush. Gunn doesn't need to know about Mama's blood-magic, and what I somehow managed to carry out on the night she died. No one does.

Gunn sticks his pinkie finger into the shine bottle and brings his finger to his lips. He winces, closes his eyes, rubs his tongue along his teeth. "Perfect aftertaste. I'd bet money that the shine's quite a ride."

"I wouldn't know. Unlike my uncle, I keep the shining to the customers."

Gunn and I stay looking at each other, my chance for our future staring me down. Slowly, something changes in his eyes—there's not warmth, but a new respect.

"Won't be easy up there," he says slowly. "We'll be culling the best sorcerers, and that means long days of dangerous magic, of pushing yourself to the brink. It'll be hard conditions, a tough run. I can't guarantee you'll come home the same way you left."

His words crack something open inside me. But this is the reason I've forced myself to survive—the reason I banished my magic in the first place. So I can protect Ben and Ruby, spend my life filling in the hole that I carved out of their lives.

"Jed's spot's still open, if you think you can handle it"—Gunn nods at my bottle of shine—"and if you're sure you can brew this again."

I'm so far from "sure" it's terrifying. Mama barely taught me *anything* before she died. In fact, caging my magic touch inside that shine bottle is the only true spell I've ever managed to cast, after the only magic manipulation I ever conjured ended in death. I brewed that shine in a surge of grief, a desperate attempt to cut off my talent like a poisoned limb, in the hopes of limping forward, moving on. I've got no idea how to brew this shine twice.

But I glance at my cousin, and at Ruby, who's managed to sneak outside and hide behind one of Ben's legs on our stoop. I think about their world before I went and gutted it in my arrogant, stupid attempt to save it. I look up to our sagging roof, the roof that's not going to be over our heads much longer if one of us doesn't do something soon. *Long ago there was a sorcerer who wanted to leave her cursed magic behind her, but the only way out was through—*

So I straighten my spine, look Gunn in the eye, and will every ounce of resolve I've got left to case my voice in steel. "Sure as hell I can brew it again, sir."

BIG MAN ON CAMPUS

ALEX

If you were inclined to use the term "magic" lightly, it's a word you might offer to describe a night like tonight. Twilight paints the grass of Georgetown's lawn in broad strokes of deep emerald and shadow, and streetlamps act like glowing alchemists, turning the campus's cobblestone walkway into gold. The sky is a slice of indigo, rich and sweet with Indian summer. And the crowd I've anchored onto? Just as beautiful—boys in tailored jackets, young women donning far too much makeup, beads, and gems.

This isn't my world. I'm borrowing it, holding on to my old chum Warren's stern as he sails through the warm waters of Georgetown University. But on nights like tonight, where the wind itself practically whistles a note of invincibility across campus, it's far too easy for me to pretend, to get lost in what could have been. So I clutch the cheap plastic badge in my pocket as a reminder: *It wasn't just his fault. He couldn't have done it without you. You ruined this for yourself.*

The group ahead of Warren and me charges out of the wrought-iron gates of campus and crosses over to O Street. And then the crowd's whispers start to grow louder, begin buzzing around us like fireflies:

"A faux shining room at Sigma Phi, can you believe it?"

"It's going to be tops. Performing sorcerers, with shine, just like the Red Den—"

"Poser, you've never been to the Red Den—"

Giggles, squeals, laughter—

For a second, it's too bright, too free, too wonderfully, painfully familiar, and I have to stop walking and collect myself. I start fumbling inside my jacket for a cigarette. It takes Warren a couple of steps to notice, and he doubles back as the crowd continues to trailblaze ahead.

"You're positive you want to come along tonight?" Warren asks, as he fishes a Lucky out of his own pocket and lights it.

"Don't worry, the badge is in my pocket, and that's where it'll stay."

"That's not what I meant." Warren shakes his head, takes a drag, and watches the crowd continue down O Street toward Sigma Phi's "criminal magic" party. "You're almost a real agent now, Alex," Warren says. "I thought . . ." He trails off.

"What? Tell me."

"You told me that you joined the Prohibition Unit because you needed to move on. That you wanted to help the Feds catch guys like your father."

I don't answer.

"But it's like you're not even trying," Warren pushes. "I mean, don't you think this isn't right? You hiding your badge, hitting up parties, chasing tail and magic like you're just another freshman?"

A flame of embarrassment lights me up inside, but I quickly pinch it out. "I'm not pretending I'm just another freshman." I throw Warren a hollow smile. "I'm hanging out with my old friend."

"I saw you in the Harbin dorm a couple days ago, Alex."

"So? I picked up some English-lit Betty at Chadwick's the other night. She invited me back to her dorm."

"It was in the middle of the afternoon," he says flatly, "in the cafeteria."

I turn away from him and give a stifled laugh to the sky. "Christ, Warren, I'm starting to think that you're the police here." I take another drag to buy myself time, to concoct another lie. I'm quick at it, dealing them out, stacking them up like a house of cards. I've had good practice.

And my father was the best of mentors.

"The Prohibition Unit had its trainee class come onto campus a few times, to hear Professor Starks's lecture about sorcerer's shine, and the magic of shine transference," I explain slowly. "I must have grabbed a soda or something afterward." At that, Warren's face softens. It almost tempts me to tell him the truth. That I want my old life back so bad it hurts. That I want to go back in time and erase what happened, erase it all.

Instead I add, "But it's nice to know you're spying on me."

"I'm not spying on you. I'm worried about you." Warren looks at the pavement, stubs the rest of his cig into it. "I'm just not sure I understand anymore," he says quietly. "I got it at first—tailing me till you got settled in the Unit, getting a taste of what could have been if your father hadn't been indicted. But Alex, it's been months since the trial."

I study my cigarette, the way the white paper surrenders to the hungry cinders. "Is this an elaborate way of trying to tell me to get lost?"

Warren waits a second, another second. "Of course not."

He looks back down O Street, which is now empty, save for an older gentleman walking his dog and a few students with bursting book satchels coming back from the library. "But tonight's important to me. Sigma Phi's going to choose their pledges this weekend, and I don't want anything messing that up."

I give him a glass smile. "Well, let's make sure our boy gets what he wants."

"I'm serious, Alex. Sigma's president isn't a joker, all right? Sam Rockaway takes his frat seriously, and he's obsessed with sorcery. He's been planning this criminal magic party since June. What happened the past few times I brought you around? That stuff can't happen again." A faint blush falls over his face as he mumbles, "Honestly, I didn't even mean to tell you about tonight. It just sort of came out."

That stings, not that I can entirely fault Warren for saying it. I don't mean to be a pain in the ass, a liability. My nights trolling Georgetown with Warren always *start* all right—I feel comfortable hitting the town at his side, almost hopeful, like I'm getting to relive a warm, wonderful dream—but then something always goes wrong. Some ass says something that rubs me the wrong way, or I hit on the wrong guy's girl. Last Friday I got into a fistfight with some arrogant junior who called me a "suit," and I was dangerously close to transforming his varsity letter into a straightjacket.

I take another cigarette out, light the new one with the stub of my last. It's a dirty habit, chain-smoking, but when I'm nervous I need to keep my hands busy. "Look, I'll handle myself tonight, I promise, okay?" I tell Warren. "I'm not going to mess Sigma up for you. I'm just along for the ride. For a break from the grind." I sigh out a flood of smoke. Then I add quietly, "Sometimes I just need to escape."

I steal a glance at Warren. I want him to understand without me explaining any more. I want my friend of over a decade to tell me that everything's okay, that no matter how many times I mess up, how desperate I seem, how dim my future's become while his just keeps burning brighter—he'll never leave me to flicker out alone.

But standing here under the streetlamps, the whispers of my life long gone disappearing like the crowd around the corner of O and 35th Streets, Warren's face only shows pity.

He sighs, pastes on a false smile, and slaps me on the back, a fast, flippant gesture. "Okay, friend," he says, "then we better hop. Sam said the performance starts at nine."

We walk without another word down to 35th Street.

"Sam said to use his back door, in the alley." Warren points us down a narrow, shadowed street behind the corner lot on 35th and O. The alley's bordered on both sides with old homes that date back centuries, each painted in faded pastels, with sleepy back lots cluttered with trash cans. There's a light on in about every third house, no noise but the sound of far-off traffic. In short, there's absolutely no indication of a legendary sorcery party anywhere in our vicinity.

"You sure the crowd went this way?" I ask.

Warren pulls out a small piece of paper from the pocket of his trousers. He checks the address, then approaches one of the squat, shabby houses on our left, a two-story with smudged windows and chipping rose-colored paint. Two wooden Greek letters have been nailed over the entrance, the only faint scent of "fraternity" on the block.

"This is the address," Warren mumbles.

I throw the stub of my cig into the dying bushes lining the little yard, then follow Warren up the set of cracked cement stairs to the house's back door.

"1312"—he looks at me—"this has to be it."

I shrug. "So try the door."

Warren reaches for the doorknob, but his hand passes right through it. "Oh, wow." He gingerly steps in, straight through the door, and I follow.

As soon as I cross the threshold, I feel it, that slow pull of walking straight through a protective force field. Like an unraveling, layer by layer, like I'm being consumed slowly by a thick, black nothing. I can't see Warren, hell, I can't even *sense* Warren—and then the void releases, the black softens into twilight, and we're standing at another door, this one identical to the last, leading to an identical house, except each window of the house is now glowing, animated with light from within. A steady flow of jazz and conversation spills from the house's interior.

"Holy shit," Warren says. "Have you ever experienced anything like that?"

Call me jaded, but this force field is amateur magic at best. "A better sorcerer would have added a tactile manipulation, an actual house around the house, instead of just a protective shield," I say. "See this little force field?" I wave my hand back through the charged, protective space. "As soon as cops or agents reach for the door, they'll know there's magic inside."

Warren rolls his eyes but doesn't argue—sorcery is the one topic I still have the upper hand on, always will. Of course I know I'm being a prick, but Warren's pathetic, almost childlike wonder over this lackluster work of sorcery bothers me. I'm angry at magic. I'm angry at my father, at those D Street gangsters who sold him out, at *myself*—

These days, I'm pretty much angry at everything.

Warren grabs the real doorknob in front of him, pushes the wooden door open, and we step into a narrow hall that's packed with college kids, whispers, and speculation. There must be dozens of frat boys idling, passing some of the legal stuff around—whiskey, rum—to warm themselves up for the main event. Dames are angling around one another, standing on their tiptoes to see the front of the line, to judge how long it's going to take to get in. The air is heavy with perfume and sweat, and conversations bounce off the walls. A line to the freaking door for a glimpse, a taste, of magic. If declaring something criminal doesn't render it sexier, then I don't know what does.

"Sigma Phi attracts a crowd, doesn't it?" I shout to Warren over the noise.

Warren throws me a self-satisfied smile. "It's the most sought-after fraternity on campus. And on a night like tonight, with live sorcering? Place is going to shoot through the roof."

"You really think you stand a shot of getting into a frat like this?" I mean it to sound curious, but it comes across like an accusation.

But Warren doesn't flinch. I wait as he shakes the hands of a group of tweed-vested chaps who've filtered in behind us. Warren puffs out his chest a little as he does it, tosses his hair in the same way I used to, when I was a guy who could pull off a hair toss. I've been noticing Warren's got a little more presence since he moved into his freshman dorm, and since I started training with the Unit this summer. It's like he's managed to grow into his own, now that he's out from under my shadow. "I better." He turns back and leans in conspiratorially. "My dad took Sam's father and two older brothers out to Saint Michaels for a golf weekend in August, to sweeten the deal."

"Thank God for fathers," I say simply.

At that, Warren's face turns beet red.

"Come on, War, I'm teasing," I add, trying to let us both off the hook. But the damage is done.

Before the awkwardness has a chance to settle in and stay, a redheaded dame comes barreling toward us from the back door, saving us from each other. She sidesteps through the back of the line, which prompts a chorus of, "Come on! Wait your turn!"

"Sorry, gents," the ginger announces, "but my fella's holding my spot for me."

As evidence, she sidles up to Warren's other side and plants the airiest of kisses onto his cheek.

"I wasn't sure if you'd make it," Warren says breathlessly, no residue at all of "big man on campus" left in his tone.

"And miss the party of the year? No thank you." The redhead straightens her skirt. She's cute—cherry mouth, cherry hair, little upturned nose. And rich, that much is obvious from her pearls and the embroidered LM on her purse. Perhaps equally as obvious, Warren is definitely not her "fella." Not in the way he wants to be, at least: I can tell from the way she's already moved on, is scanning the crowd for someone else she might know who's closer to the front. I hate this habit of mine—reading into the slightest gesture, the meaning of a smile, a pause. But since my father's indictment, I can't seem to stop. It's like I'm watching everyone, waiting for the other shoe to drop, scouting whether anyone's on the hunt for the full truth, and whether they're starting to circle in on me.

"Sam's roommate told Sasha who told Laura that Sam's having three DC sorcerers here tonight," the ginger prattles as she keeps surveying the crowd ahead. She still hasn't seen or acknowledged me. "And they're going to actually brew some sorcerer's shine! Can you believe it? Sam's auctioning off ten shots of it to raise money for the Christmas Ball."

"Are you serious?" Warren matches her enthusiasm.

"That's what I heard." She sighs loudly and dramatically. "God, it's so hot, all of it. I've been wanting to try shine so bad I've been dreaming about it. I better win one."

For a second, I'm tempted to show her a magic that will send her into a dream so thick and hot she'll never want to climb out.

"You're really a sorcerer's shine virgin?" I say instead, wedging myself right into their conversation.

The ginger turns her head, annoyed, in my direction. But then she stops, sizes me up, faintly blushes. I know she must like what she sees, they almost all do before they really get to know me. Sure enough, her cherry mouth starts to turn up like little stems.

"Lana Morgan, Alex. Alex, Lana Morgan," Warren introduces us quickly. I notice he leaves my last name out of the introduction.

"Pleasure."

Lana leans closer. "So are you a freshman too? I haven't seen you around—I'd remember." She lets her eyes linger on me. The line starts moving again, and we all take a few steps forward together. Warren uses the chance to reinsert himself between us.

"No, Alex is a friend from the old days, just along for the ride," Warren says quickly. "He works for the government."

I watch Lana's interest deflate. "The government," she says blandly. "How interesting."

"I'm actually a sorcery expert," I'm quick to add. "I'm training with the Prohibition Unit, the Domestic Magic division."

"You don't say?" Lana's smile brightens a few watts, as Warren rolls his eyes next to me. "I bet you're just chock-full of all sorts of fascinating information." Then she shoots Warren a confused, fearful glance. "Wait, if he's a Fed, what's he doing here?"

Warren laughs out something like, "My thoughts exactly," but I talk over him: "Let's just say I value fieldwork." I shoot her my smile, the cocky, off-center one, the one my last fling told me was the only reason she put up with me so long.

"So you're one of *those* Unit men, the fun kind." Lana meets my smile and wiggles her eyebrows. *The corrupt kind*, is what she means. The Unit's notorious for making more money off bribes than their government salaries. It's part of the reason I joined—the agency's messy, disorganized, an easy place to get lost and hide. "Did you ever have to take a shot of shine, you know, as part of the job? To see what it's like?"

"Absolutely."

Her eyes become liquid, hungrier. "So what's it feel like, drinking the sorcerer's shine?"

The sorcerer's shine—the magic spell without any other elements, water turned into pure magic touch inside a bottle. The primary reason the anti-sorcery activists were able to pass the Eighteenth Amendment, besides the record-high crime rate during the Great War and the media's frenzy over a slew of high-profile magic robberies, and one of the most sought-after, addictive magic drugs on the black market. A spell quite literally stumbled upon centuries ago, goes the rumor, when some sorcerer was so drunk he forgot to add his spell's other elements.

I hesitate before pulling out the little silver flask of shine that I brought, the one I made this morning before I took the streetcar into work and sat behind a desk for ten hours. I was planning on giving it to Warren as a thank-you, pawn it off as a score from the Unit's temporary evidence room, but now I'm not in the mood. Now I want Warren—with his big Sigma Phi dreams and his golf-trip-wielding father and his borrowed hair toss—to feel what it's like to lose something.

"It's different for everyone." I pull the flask out of my coat with the flourish of a true performance sorcerer. "You've got to try it for yourself."

Lana wraps her hands around mine, which are wrapped around the flask, and gasps. "Are you serious? I can have this?"

"Of course, doll. But better drink it tonight. Shine's magic only lasts a day—that flask will just be water again tomorrow."

She looks around, then takes it from me slowly, as Warren mutters, "Stealing government property now too?" But I ignore him, just relish this moment of having something to offer.

"Drink it now," I urge her, "so it'll hit you right as you walk into the party."

She nods, like I really am some unquestionable expert, and then takes the flask to her lips and downs it in one gulp.

"When will I feel it?" she whispers, giggles, as she passes the flask back to me.

"Any minute."

We're moving closer to the front, now maybe one or two

groups away. A narrow white door to what looks to be a broom closet stands half-open about ten feet ahead, and a nice if non-descript-looking man sits on a stool next to the door. As we take another collective step forward, Lana gasps, stops.

"Oh. My. God," she whispers, arching her neck back. "Holy Mother. Holy effing Mother."

She closes her eyes, licks her lips, purses them. I haven't hit the stuff myself in a long time, but I know the stages of a shine trip inside and out, from working with my father, and now the Unit—at least the stages of a trip before your body comes to need the stuff. First comes the euphoria, the flood of magic out of the bottle and into your blood. Then "the clarity," where things take on a different sheen, like the world is coming together. Like there's been a secret, evasive all your life, that's now being whispered into your ear. Then, as our Unit guidebook clinically states, comes a "heightened sense of invincibility, increased sociability, and the ecstasy of the senses." Which, in layman's terms, basically means that the world becomes enchanted.

"Good?" I ask.

Lana laughs, seductive, guttural, looks me right in the eyes, her pupils two tiny specks. "Perfection."

"You ever think these kinds of tricks could land you right alongside your old man?" Warren digs, as Lana stumbles to my other side, so now I'm in between them.

"Relax, Warren," I mutter, as Lana wraps her arm around mine. I try to focus on her, but Warren won't let it go.

"I still remember what you told me, right after his indictment, how you never wanted to be like him. Ever." Warren leans in. "Every time you ask me to take you out, I think about that, how ironic it is. 'Cause it's like you're *trying* to be him," he adds. "It's like you can't help it."

Warren's words hit me hot and quick, the shock of his jab quickly settling into angry shame. "I guess neither of us is man enough to change," I cut next to him. "Jealousy still looks bad on you, Warren."

We reach the cleaning closet, come face-to-face with the man on the stool sporting a black jacket, black pants, and a bowler hat. He gives us a smile and folds his hand out like a welcome toward the door. "Your turn, folks. Step inside."

Lana, Warren, me—we all peer into the closet out of instinct. There are cleaning supplies stashed in the dusty corners, an old broom, buckets. No light.

"But it's not a closet." Lana looks at me with those wide eyes. "It's a test."

The doorman nods with an almost cringe-worthy, put-on flourish. "Very wise." He smiles at me. "Appearances can be deceiving."

Lana takes me by the hand, and Warren and I follow her into the broom closet.

The closet is a double-sided trick, it has to be: linking two objects together through time and space, so that guests walk into one door, only to instantly walk out of another located somewhere else. Sure enough, as we pass through the broom closet, we magically exit a different door that leads into a low-lit, windowless hallway faintly smelling of mildew. My guess is that we've been transported into the cellar of the house.

A double-sided trick, a link, isn't particularly difficult—like all magic manipulations of reality, it just takes the right words of power, the right objects, and of course, the magic touch—but it's definitely a crowd-pleaser. And it's real sorcery, not one a puffer could try to fake in a pathetic attempt to flaunt himself as magic. So my guess is that Warren's buddy Sam has shelled out quite a lot of cash for this little party to go down. Sorcerers aren't the typical frat-house fare—you hear whispers of performances in higher-echelon circles, you find them in the city's shining rooms owned by the mob. And even though magic itself doesn't wow

me, the keys to it—money, influence, power—that's a bag of
tricks I still can't accept that I've lost.

"Don't leave me," Lana says dreamily. She works her hand
up to my bicep as we walk down the hall. "You're an angel,
you know that? You've brought me something amazing. You've
brought me light."

"Don't worry, I'm not going anywhere."

"That's for damn sure," Warren mutters behind me.

I ignore him, just wrap my hand around Lana's, and together
we follow the hallway until it dumps us into the main space of
the cellar, a wide, low-ceilinged, windowless den that looks like
it spans the entire length and width of the house. The ceiling is
peppered with small, blinking lights, and the floor is shiny as
a still mirror, reflecting back the lights on its glossy black surface, which creates the effect that we're walking over a field of
stars. There are a few trees lining the perimeter of the crowded
room, oaks with arms that stretch and bend like they're being
animated by a magic wind, with leaves that rustle and sway, all
tucked away in the basement of Sigma Phi.

All of this will be gone tomorrow. All pure magic is *real*, a
true manipulation of reality, but it's fleeting. From sorcerer's
shine to magic replicas, force fields, and every type of trick,
all of a sorcerer's magic is condemned to fade away after a day.
Most people think that makes sorcery even more mesmerizing:
getting a glimpse of a world that's better than our own, but one
that only lasts for a moment. But magic's taken too much from
me to see it as anything but a swindle.

"I feel like we're flying." Lana takes my face gently and
presses hers into it, her cherry lips on mine, before she pulls
away. "More magic," she says. "Take me."

I scan the room. The crowd is divided into clusters, anywhere from ten to about thirty college kids arranged in a semi-
circle around each of the three hired sorcerers on the floor. Each

holds their audience's attention with a small, space-friendly trick, performing it parlor-style for their enraptured crowd on repeat.

My eyes rest on the nearest sorcerer, a few feet away. He takes his time fanning playing cards into a rainbow above his head, and then folds them back into a perfect deck that lands softly on his outstretched hand.

"Come on"—I pull Lana toward him—"you'll love this."

She practically coos as we watch the trick once, twice, three times. I bet the show must seem even more wowing when she's on shine. She sneaks me another kiss as we stumble over to another performer, one who holds a small sphere of fire in his palm, waving it back and forth and jovially threatening to hand it over to a particularly shell-shocked dame on the sidelines. Lana whispers, "That light is so hot, so blinding, Alex."

As she leans into me, I can't help but agree; it's bright in here, warm and familiar. *If I just focus on this girl, the way she's looking at me, on the jazz music blaring and the faint scent of privilege that perfumes the cellar, I can forget. I can lose myself in the now.*

"I want to get so lost," Lana whispers into my ear, then pulls away from me suggestively. *I want to get lost too.* "Come find me."

"Wait, Lana," I laugh. But as I move to chase after her, Warren steps in my way.

"You can stop, all right?" he says flatly, yelling into my ear over the jazz. "Uncle. You want to feel like a big man? I say uncle."

I shake my head. "What are you taking about?"

"God, you're really going to make me spell it out?" He looks around uncomfortably, blushes. "I have my eye on Lana, all right, Alex?"

An electric feeling, shiny and heady, lights me up from the inside. "That's funny, 'cause it seems like she's got her eye on me."

"Yeah, as a joke, as a trip, same as the shine," Warren snaps. "She's the daughter of a freaking senator. Don't kid yourself."

And despite the blood sport we're playing, the hard daggers we've been slinging at each other, I'm still surprised silent by his cut. My eyes pinch without my permission, and I have to look at the floor.

"Jesus, what are we doing, Alex?" Warren says. "Look, I'm sorry."

"No, you're not."

"You're right, I'm not." Warren runs his fingers through his hair, gives me that infuriating, borrowed hair toss again. "I'm tired of this. It's awful what your father did, it really is, all right? And I felt bad for you. Sometimes I still do. But you're becoming poison," he says. "Happy? There's the truth." And then he turns to walk away.

The anger starts to boil, overflow inside. I need to direct it, somewhere, anywhere else, besides letting it burn me inside out. So before Warren gets away from me, before I think better of it, I take a step forward and give him a sharp shove to the back.

He stumbles forward, and a couple of chaps and dames on the edge of the nearby performance circle stop talking and stare. Warren whips around. "Are you serious?" He takes a few running steps toward me and pushes back. "Leave. Just go home, Alex."

But I shove him again, sending him off balance.

"Keep your dirty hands off me," he seethes, as he barrels back into me. I grab his neck into a headlock and send us both scrambling to the floor.

"Fight!" I hear from somewhere above us.

I grab Warren by the collar, give him a hard slap to the jaw, not enough to hurt, just enough to shock him. "You're a pathetic fighter," I say, as I grip him tighter.

"And you're just pathetic," he spits. He thrashes his hand, nails bared toward me, and manages to cut my lip. As he tries to roll over, I send my shoulder into his stomach before two pairs of hands rip us apart. It's only when I'm pulled to my feet that I realize the music has been cut, the sorcerers have stopped their tricks, and Warren and I are now the main performance.

"What the hell, Warren?" this Napoleon of a frat boy says, barreling in between us.

Warren freezes. "Sam, I—"

"Who is this guy?" Sam interrupts, nodding toward me.

"An old friend."

"Doesn't look like a friend to me." Sam studies me with wide eyes. "You even go here, chump?"

"No, I'm a trainee," I say slowly, "with the Prohibition Unit."

Sam pops a sharp, cutting laugh over the crowd's silence. "So you're fighting with a pig, Warren, at a criminal magic party?"

"I'm not a pig," I interject.

"Shut up," Warren and this Sam chap say in unison.

Sam turns his wrath back to Warren, stares him down. "It was stupid, bringing him here. And we take smart fellas at Sigma Phi—"

"No, no, he's cool," Warren interrupts with a stammer. "I mean, he's a total prick, but he won't rat on us—he can't, he's as crooked as his old man—"

At the mention of my father, my fist takes on a mind of its own, flies out from my side before I can stop it, sucker punches Warren right in the jaw.

Warren stops, sucks in his breath, in shock or pain I'm not sure. He looks at me silently, as he holds his face.

"Get these losers out of here," Sam barks at the two varsity-letter types that pulled us apart earlier. Each of them grabs one of my arms, as another frat boy comes to the rescue and restrains Warren.

Sam glares at Warren. "Don't come back here."

The frat boys take us up the back stairs, into a dark kitchen, through the side door and the force field, and into the alley behind 35th Street. And then they leave Warren and me with each other.

"I can't believe it." Warren gives a weird, almost girlish laugh as he rubs his jaw. "You just managed to ruin everything."

The high from Lana and the adrenaline from the fight are both waning, and a dull, familiar self-loathing starts taking over. "It's all right," I say softly. "Sam must have paid an arm and a leg for those sorcerers. My bet is he was already shined. He won't remember tomorrow. You'll get in."

Warren just stares at me like I'm insane. "Don't ever talk to me again, you understand?"

He turns on his heel, starts fumbling with his pack of cigarettes as he walks into the alley.

"Come on, Warren, that was as much your fault as it was mine."

He doesn't answer, and my heart starts pounding.

"Warren."

Nothing but smoke funneling over his head as he turns onto O Street. "WARREN!"

Christ, he's really serious.

"Warren, come on!"

And then the pounding gives way to a strange, searing ache in my chest. It vaguely feels like a part of me's melting.

I stand there for a long while, alone. I smoke one cigarette, then another, study the force field of the house in front of me, the dark exterior, the magic blanket of quiet draped over the raging Sigma Phi house within. I picture all those pretty dames and lucky chaps. Dolls with nothing to worry about but the shade of their lipstick. Boys with fathers who can buy them into fraternities. Boys like Warren.

Once upon a time, boys like me.

I take a long drag, focusing on that force field. And then I turn inward, wait for that huge, all-encompassing feeling of power to start coursing through my veins, fuel me with lightning. And when I feel ready, full, I flick my cigarette stub toward the force field and exhale with a whisper: *"Poof."*

The facade in front of the Sigma Phi house shatters, crumbles into dust in a flash of a moment, spirals away like it's being carried by a magic wind, and now I'm staring at the real house. Light shines from every window. The quiet back alley of Georgetown is shocked awake with the wailing jazz that thunders from within Sigma Phi. No longer cloaked in magic, it's bright as a beacon, a siren. The house practically thumps against the crisp September night.

I watch neighbors' lights go on around me, witness a woman in her nightgown thrust open her door to assess the commotion from across the street. Dogs bark and more lights blink on as I walk away, smiling, down the alley toward O Street.

And for just a second, the world feels a little fairer. Despite the fat lip that Warren just gave me, I even manage a whistle around the corner.

THE ROAD TO POSSIBILITY

JOAN

Gunn and I haven't said a word since we left Parsonage. His sleek black car keeps popping as we cut through thick woods, and every jump and stall of its engine rattles me like gunfire. I'm riding with a man I presume to be a gangster, to a foreign city to prove that I'm one of the strongest sorcerers he's ever seen, and I've got about two spells and one trick total to my name. I need to prove that I can brew sorcerer's shine along with the best of them, and I've brewed shine exactly once. On the night of my mother's death, no less. And by accident, since all I was really trying to do was banish my magic touch and bury it three feet underground. And there is no room for error; there is no option to fail. Ben and Ruby are counting on me.

It nearly killed me saying good-bye to Ruby back at the cabin. Telling her that Ben was going to watch over her, that I didn't know where I was going, and that I wasn't sure when I was coming back. Ruffling her wispy hair and leaning in close so I could take her smell with me, reminding her that she needed to believe she was strong enough to fight her "sickness" and get well. I picture her smell now, try and conjure it, wrap it around myself like a blanket. *This is my charge, to make things right*, I remind myself. *I wouldn't need to do this if I hadn't gone and blown everything apart.*

Around the signs for Richmond, Gunn breaks our silent standoff. "You learned your magic from Jed, I take it?" he says quietly.

I think about the best way to answer this and finally go with, "My mama showed me." But Mama wanted no parts of me mixed up in magic. When I confided that I'd gotten the magic touch, told her I'd woken up one morning with a near-electric feeling pulsing through my veins, she reluctantly taught me a couple spells, only ones she felt necessary to survive in the world we were living in. Dark, powerful blood-spells she inherited from her family, ones that involve a sacrifice in the casting. Severing spells, like the ones she'd have to perform in secret on desperate farmers who came stumbling to our door late at night, where she'd sever a gangrenous toe off a foot to save the rest of the leg. Tracking spells, like the ones she'd cast on Ruby, where Ruby would ingest Mama's blood so Mama could keep tabs on everywhere she went. And her caging spell, where you lock away a symbol of an evil and smear your blood over the lock in sacrifice, and ask the magic to imprison the evil forever—the same spell I somehow managed to use to banish my magic on the night that Mama died.

"Your mama was a sorcerer too?" Gunn interrupts my thoughts.

I nod. "Mama had a spells license from the government. She specialized in remedial magic—ran a spell room off our kitchen, sorcering legal antidotes and cures," I say. "It did solid business before she died."

Gunn nods, gives me the gift of not asking what happened to her. "What sorts of spells?"

"Kendrick family ones, like lavender and jasmine spells to ward off the common cold, or gingerroot spells for a mind's health and clarity. Nothing out of the ordinary, I suppose, all stuff that falls under the Volstead Act concession for remedial magic." I don't mention the blood-spells to Gunn, since Mama warned me never to tell a soul about her family's special magic, and I don't think a gangster would qualify as an exception. In a time when sorcerers are public enemies, she always said, you don't go showing the world a magic that would put the fear of God back in them.

"So you're a spells expert?"

"I picked up a few things, but spells were never my strong suit."

Gunn glances at me. "Then you must be a performer." He says it like it's a fact, not a question—though I suppose if I'm in his car, it should be a fact.

"That's right." I turn back to the window. I'm awful at lying, so I need to keep my answers short, and vague, at least till I figure out how the hell I'm going to earn a place in Washington. "Though truth be told, Mr. Gunn, I've never performed for a large audience. For as shined up as Jed always is, he's still a prima donna when it comes to sharing his stage." I stare at the dark trees on the side of the road, passing by in a streak of deep green, and add, "But sometimes I think it's better not to show the world what you can do, at least all at once."

Gunn doesn't answer, not for a long while, so long that I start to wonder if he knows that I'm playing him. But when I finally work up the nerve to steal a glance his way, I catch him smirking. "Couldn't have said it better myself."

There's a point at which your body just gets too exhausted from fear to be scared anymore, and before I realize it, I'm swimming in a shallow swamp of sleep. By the time I come to, the scenery's changed. Our two-lane road has transformed into a moonlit bridge, and then a four-lane bustling avenue. The horizon becomes crowded—short towers of man-made stars light up the sky, and row homes now line the road, pressed tight to one another like little kids heading into their lessons.

I rub my eyes and sit upright as Gunn pops a cigarette into his mouth and lights it. He rolls his window down a sliver, and a steady stream of horns, engines, and screeching wheels overwhelms the car. He rubs his temples with his thumb and middle finger, gives a wide stretch of his mouth, and a yawn escapes him.

I venture, "How long you been seeking out sorcerers?"

He glances at me, looks like he's debating whether to share. "Far too long."

Encouraged, I push, "You said you're rounding us all up for an experiment?"

Gunn doesn't respond, so I look at my hands and add, "I never see the paper unless we go into Drummond, and even then, we don't have a penny to throw away on news about other folks, but my cousin's friends have told us about Washington. About these big-city shining rooms where you can drink magic all night, and get a fancy sorcerer's performance to boot. Is that . . . is that what this is all about?"

Gunn takes a right, and now we're smack in what looks to be the middle of town. Stretches of chalk-white pavement start running next to the street like thin ribbons. Dames in big brimmed hats and cloches, short skirts and long dresses, spill out onto the bleached walkways, huddle around the outside of buildings sharing smokes. Men lean out of wide-open windows, shouting and laughing into the September night.

"This is about far more than that," Gunn answers quietly. "I have theories about magic, theories I'm quite keen to prove, theories that could turn this world upside-down. But like you, I'm a big believer in waiting for the right time." Then he looks at me. "There's something else you should know about me, Ms. Kendrick. I'm far fonder of solutions than questions. You understand me?"

A strange mix of fear and shame writhes through me. "I do, sir."

And then it's quiet. We cruise down a narrow cobblestone street, Gunn's car stumbling over the bumpy stones, and then we make another turn and pull into a small parking lot pockmarked with a couple of cars. The place looks like it's been closed for days. No lights, no music, no signs of life from the large storefront window that faces out to the corner lot.

Gunn cuts the engine. "I need to make a quick stop."

I look at the dark corner lot and say slowly, "Sir, I don't think anybody's home."

"The place is spellbound. It's just a magic manipulation." He opens his car door and steps outside. "Don't move. I'll only be a minute."

Gunn slams his door behind him, sidestepping around an old Model T. But before he can get to the door of the place, an older man just *appears*, out of thin air, like he materialized from the darkness to stroll over and greet Gunn.

Spellbound, Gunn called it. There must be some kind of large-scale force field protecting the entire property from the eyes of the law. I wonder if Jed could pull off something like this. Then again, the only magic he's cared about for a long while is the kind that's transferred into a bottle.

My nerves return again, that panicky, gut-wrenching feeling of being in way over my head. Despite the secret magic that Mama and the women in her family might have conjured in our neck of the woods, sorcerers in Washington clearly have their own tricks. Big, bold, awing sort of tricks. Makes me wonder what special magic Gunn's other sorcerers might have up their sleeves.

The older man who just appeared out of nowhere is at least twice Gunn's age, around fifty if I had to guess, with thick silver hair as shiny as a polished nickel and a suit on that manages to put Gunn's to shame.

Gunn's window's still rolled down a couple inches, so I angle closer to his driver's seat, strain to catch anything of what they're saying—maybe what the heck is going on, what's in store for me—

But I only catch bits that I can't make sense of or string together—*shutting down the Red Den for a while to switch things up, sir . . . Understood, just making my rounds. You're doing your part. Danny would have been proud of you, son. . . . Any leads for the street? . . . Just some dame . . .*

At that, the older man looks into Gunn's car, searches till he finds me inside it, then laughs and slaps Gunn on the back before turning around and sliding into a car on the other side of the lot.

I scramble away from Gunn's seat before he gets back. He plunks down next to me, settles in, and starts the engine again.

And I know Gunn's warning about too many questions, but I can't help but ask, "Who was that, sir?"

Gunn grips the steering wheel tighter as he navigates out of the lot. "The Boss," he concedes.

"*Your* boss?"

He gives another little smirk but doesn't meet my gaze. "Boss McEvoy is everyone's boss. You'll find that out soon enough."

We take a wide turn out of the lot, down a back alley, and through a quieter part of town. Whatever way we're heading— north or south, east or west—the city soon falls away and then we're over the same bridge, back on a lonely two-lane road, sur- rounded by a forest so thick and dark it swallows the moon and eats the stars. The suspense, the nerves, it all keeps rising, up my throat and through my lips, forcing me to speak.

"Mr. Gunn, you said you were taking me to DC."

Gunn doesn't answer.

"And we were in DC."

Again, nothing.

"So where . . ." I take a deep breath. "Where are we going?"

The car gives a little stutter of exhaust and then keeps chugging forward on the long stretch of forested road. All he offers: "This little theory of mine, it needs privacy, room to be tested. It's an experiment that needs to develop on its own."

Gunn throws on his turning light and drops the car into a lower gear, and we take a slow turn into the trees. In all directions, there're only twisty dark branches and black-emerald leaves. It's beyond spooky, and I keep having to remind myself to breathe.

A block of cold cement takes shape amid the forest. It looks like a prison, maybe a warehouse, with a narrow stitch of windows running like a border around the top. There's a little gravel lot surrounding the place—a small white island shining under the hazy moon—but no cars besides Gunn's.

"We're here." Gunn nods to the backseat. "Grab your things."

We crunch across the gravel lot and approach the warehouse entrance. Gunn takes off a block of wood that's barricading the door on our side, props it against the concrete wall. Then he opens the door and offers me his hand. I just think *Ruby, Ruby, Ruby, Ben, Ben, Ben,* and I force myself to grasp it, to allow this gangster to lead me by the hand into a locked warehouse in the middle of nowhere.

It's too black inside to see anything, and so I step carefully, the scuff of my work boots against the concrete floor the only sound through the dark lofted space. It takes a near minute for my eyes to adjust, and when they do, I see the floor is littered with at least a dozen occupied cots.

"Who are they?" I whisper.

"The other sorcerers," Gunn answers. "Fifteen of you in total, though only seven will be staying beyond my experiment." *Seven.* I look around at the smattering of satchels littered around each cot, each sorcerer thrown over a thin mattress like a twisted bag of flour. Old, young, men, women, from what I can make out. I wonder where they're from. I wonder what they can do. I wonder if they'll all perform circles around me in whatever "experiment" awaits us tomorrow.

Stop. You will succeed. You must *succeed.*

Gunn clutches his keys in his palm, and the sudden jangle prompts a few of the sleeping sorcerers to grunt and roll over. "I need to go. It's late, and we're starting nice and early tomorrow."

"Wait—" But the word hangs there alone. There's too many other ones to choose from—*where are you going you gonna leave me here where the heck are we*—that I can't figure out where to start.

"That one's yours." Gunn points to the one empty sunken mattress in the corner. He tips his white fedora, a cotton ghost floating in a haunted warehouse, and turns on his heel. "Get some rest."

"Mr. Gunn—" I whisper, but he's already back out the door. He closes it and gives a faint grunt as he slides the block of wood over the door to lock it on the other side.

Nerves on fire, I force myself to tiptoe around the minefield of sleeping sorcerers and lie down as quietly as possible on the empty cot. The thing's all coils and sharp edges, but I just close my eyes, wrap myself around my knapsack, and pray for a sleep as deep and dark as sleep can get.

Long ago there was a sorcerer who walked to hell for her family, and in the pits of fire, the devil saw her remorse and let her walk back—

But I can't fall asleep. I'm too wound up. One of the men a few feet away shifts with a squeak in his cot, and I give a gasp before I can help it. Another wheezes—*whispers?*—while a nearby cough nearly sends me jumping off my mattress.

I turn over, close my eyes, pinch out the warehouse. *I need to calm down. I need to cut my fear out, bottle it, and put it on a shelf.*

But then I feel something warm and soft slip up against my neck. I give a startled yelp and whip my head around. "Who's there?"

No answer. And no one has moved. But I feel it again, this time on my arm, that brush of softness like a large paintbrush. No, softer, almost—almost like *fur*, and then the quickest slap of something else, like the whip of a tiny tail.

Out of the darkness molds something half the length of my forearm and twice as wide, whiskers prickling my skin, little feet pattering over my fingers. Fur. Tail. *Rat.*

I push the animal away as hard as I can, and the thing goes squealing, flying to the border of the next cot, but it doesn't skitter away. Instead it comes back at me again, bounds forward like a hell-spawned rodent and starts climbing over my right leg. I sit up, kick at it, hear myself whimpering. *Do not cry Joan do not cry Joan—*

I attempt to push it into the fuzzy dark that swallows the back of the warehouse, but the slippery bastard manages to squirrel out of my fingers, bounds up my arm, and races over my stomach, its dirty paws pressing into my shirt as it attaches itself to my other arm. I writhe away, swat at it as it runs over my shoulder, into my hair. "Get off!" I command the small monster. As soon as I say it, I hear a soft, muffled chuckling.

And then, to my immediate right, a woman's voice: "Leave her alone, Stock."

"Mind your own business, Dune, I'm just having some fun with her. She's as jumpy as a cricket." But the rat disappears, like dust in the wind. My shoulders relax, but that creepy-crawly feeling that came with the rodent still needles me under my skin.

The woman in the cot on my right side sits up, facing away from me. "Tell me if this is fun, Stock," she says flatly. Then she whispers so soft I can barely hear her, *"Breathe and slither."*

A boy in a cot a few beds down immediately leaps out of his bed and lands bum-first on the floor, swatting and cursing. He gets onto all fours and starts scrambling away from his cot. "Knock it off, hell, Grace, *stop!*"

Under the patch of light the moon casts onto the floor, I make out something shimmery and fluid. A *snake*, three inches wide, about two feet long, slithers through the puddle of moonlight, its green and gold scales glistening under the light, before it retreats into the darkness. The snake, just like the rat, I guess, the work of sorcery. Even though the rat and snake are gone, they leave behind a larger, far more unsettling fear.

"You're such a wet blanket, Dune," says my rat-tormentor, Stock. "Skirts stick together, is that it?"

The woman—Grace Dune, I take it—says, "Just save the magic for Gunn. You keep sorcering in here, and we're all likely to blow each other up."

Some of the other sorcerers have roused awake from the hushed argument, and there starts a chorus of "Shut it," "Come on, it's late," "Enough bickering," before the whispers finally fade, like the rat and the snake, into the deep folds of the night.

I lie back down. But the quiet is loaded. I wait a little while, then whisper to Grace's back, "Thanks. But you didn't have to do that. I can take care of myself."

Grace turns slowly to face me. Thanks to the moon and the prisonlike windows at the top of the warehouse, I can make out her face just fine. Nice straight features, dark hair. Not young, but not old—somewhere around Mama's age—maybe late thirties, early forties. "That was as much for Stock as it was for you," Grace whispers. "For a boy who has a chronic fear of snakes, he's awful quick to conjure pests in the night. Living on top of each other, there's got to be rules, or we're all going to kill each other."

Her comment just brings my simmering panic to an all-out boil. I am in over my head. Drowning-water depths over my head. But I force myself to say, "Absolutely."

Grace studies me. "You're as young as Stock, aren't you? Now I understand his power play." She gives me a little lopsided smile. "Where'd Gunn bring you in from?"

"Norfolk County. Little town called Parsonage," I say. "What about you?"

"Outskirts of Alexandria. Came in with Gunn and one of his associates a couple nights back, along with a few others," Grace says. "Fifteen of us total, though I'm sure you know that only seven of us are expected to stay." Grace's smile thins out. "With those kinds of odds, you don't want to pick the wrong enemies, or the wrong allies."

I assume she's talking about me and the rat-boy. "I'm not afraid of Stock."

Grace rolls onto her back, looks at the ceiling. "Maybe you should be," she says. "Lots of sorcerers here are from families that have never shared their gifts or special strengths with the world, before now. Lots of powerful magic previously kept behind closed doors."

And of course I'm afraid—the fear is like a living thing, breathing and humming inside me. But I can't let it paralyze me. I need to focus on what I'm here for, why I can't fail. Immediately the image of Ruby, standing at our door, calling "Joan! JOAN!" as Gunn's car drove me away—it flashes like a bright, clear burst of fireworks onto my mind. "I just don't have the luxury of being scared."

"And what's her name?"

"Who?"

"The little girl in your mind," Grace says. Wait, can Grace hear my thoughts or something? So was her earlier warning about Stock, or about *her*? "You were thinking about her so clearly, I almost couldn't ignore it."

Finally I concede, "Ruby." I roll over, suddenly feeling exhausted and exposed. "Thanks again for your help, Grace, but it's been a long night."

It's quiet for a while, and I assume she's dozed off, same as the rest of them. But then I hear, "Sorry, I—I didn't mean to get you upset. I just . . . I know what it's like, to be against the odds. It's been tough for me, too, past couple days. Some of the sorcerers are small-minded, expected an all-out boys' club. They've been giving me and the other girl, Rose, a lot of heat—but Rose has her brother to stick up for her," she says. "Plus, my family's got a bit of a . . . strange reputation around northern Virginia, which doesn't help." Grace's cot squeals and squeaks as she gets comfortable. She waits a moment, then adds, "Was just trying to say this place isn't an easy corner of the world, to try and navigate alone."

There's no sound but the soft chorus of snores and wheezes as her words settle around me. Maybe I'm dreaming, but it almost sounds like Grace is offering some form of friendship, or a pact. Not completely sure why she wants to team up with the likes of me, but that's not a question I'm going to ask and give her the chance to second-guess now. Gunn's taking exactly seven of us for some reason, a little less than half. I've got a crushing amount to learn to get into the top half of this crowd. And allying with a sorcerer like Grace, who can conjure snakes and delve inside minds, can only help.

"Are you suggesting we . . . team up?" I ask hopefully, as I face her.

"My family's a superstitious lot. We specialize in signs, chance twists of fate, listen to whispers of nature," Grace answers. "I get this strong sense about you, that you and I were meant to meet. So maybe I get your back, and you get mine."

Her words are the first turn of fortune I've gotten since I stepped into Gunn's car. "I'd like that."

She throws me a sideways smile and rolls over. "Get some sleep, all right, Joan?"

I find myself breathing a little easier. "I will. You too."

My body's beyond spent from the tension, the fear, the long trek up here. So I close my eyes, ready to steal some sleep to carry me through whatever lies waiting on the other side of tomorrow. It's only when I'm a few inches away from finally falling into darkness that I realize I never actually told Grace my name.

INTERROGATION

ALEX

I walk away from the Sigma Phi house fast and purposefully. My high from exposing the fraternity party has dulled, and now I'm left with the aftermath: an intense headache and a pull of regret. I try to keep Warren's words—*it's like you're trying to be your father, it's like you can't help it, you're poison*—out of my mind, but I keep going back to them, like an itch that refuses to quit, no matter how many times I scratch at it. Because Warren's right. And no form or amount of apologizing is going to fix me, or the fragile friendship I just shattered on the ground.

Sorry I'm an asshole.

Sorry I'm not the man I'd like to be.

Sorry I can't just let the past go and move on.

I cut in and out of the lively streets of Georgetown. It's Friday night, and there's a moon wild and hazy, drawn like a messy chalk circle on a slate slab of a sky. A recklessness teases from the shadowy alleys of O Street, college parties in full swing, and shining rooms that taunt with their quiet fronts and spellbound doors. A recklessness that whispers, *Lose yourself, forget it all, if only for a night.*

I force myself to ignore the whispers, follow O Street until it dumps me onto Wisconsin Avenue. Tonight was a wake-up call.

I need to move on, let the past lie in its grave for good. Because despite how much I wish I could, there's no undoing it.

As I cut up quiet Wisconsin toward its residential section, I swear I hear a scurry on the sidewalk behind me. But when I turn to investigate, there's nothing. Just swaying trees lining the sidewalk and polished, well-kept cars parked on the road.

But then I hear it again. As I place the sound, a panic ignites in my core. It's not the wind, not the trees—it's a pair of footsteps, maybe two or three—scurrying in the shadows and over the sidewalk.

Before I can run, turn, do anything, rough hands grip my shoulders and push me forward, and I fly toward the ground. "Stop—who—what do you want?!"

I'm pushed against the sidewalk, my face imprinting into the cement. I can't turn my head, I can't make anything out, it's just a blur—dark clothes, masked faces, I—"Seriously, what's going on—"

"Quiet," a voice above me whispers.

A barrage of thoughts stampedes my mind—

Are these Sam's Sigma lackeys? A robbery? A mugging?

"Listen, you don't want to do this. I'm an officer. An officer of the law—"

"Shut him up."

A thin slip of a blindfold is tugged over my eyes. Rough fingers scratch my face as another rag is tied around my mouth. A car approaches, wheels tumbling over the smooth road. Bright headlights pulse through my blindfold like two electric hearts.

Then from somewhere behind me: "Put him in the back."

We ride in silence—minutes, maybe hours. It's impossible to keep track of time when your heart's beating like a racehorse and your eyes and mouth are sealed shut, but at some point, the car I've been shoved into slows to a stop. A few doors open and close.

"Come on, on your feet."

I mumble through my mouth gag in response, and a few brusque hands pull me out of the car. Another door opens—this one heavy and creaky. I must be inside now—the air is mustier and warmer, like it's been trapped. There's no wind. No sound.

A new voice whispers, "Sit him down."

My escorts shove me into a seat. My blindfold and gag are ripped off, and light sears my eyes. I steal a glance at a man sitting across a small table, though the aftershock of the light clouds his face. "What's all this about?" I squint. "Why am I here?"

"Thank you, boys," the man across the table says. "That'll be all."

A smack of metal rips through the room, and I jump and look behind me. Four black-clad men slither out the door and close it with a *BOOM*.

My eyes dart from corner to corner of the room, trying to find some answers. This place is clearly some kind of storage facility—boxes and overflowing bins clutter the far corners, and there are no windows. I've been seated at a cheap folding table in the middle of the mess—one lonely lightbulb hangs down over it like a glowing teardrop.

"Alexander Danfrey."

I look at the man across the table, study him, from his kempt, parted gray hair right down to his beat-up briefcase. And I relax, a little. The chap's definitely some sort of government man—he's got that tame, approachable look about him despite the dramatic introduction: cheap suit, soft features. Thanks to the late nights spent helping my father run his remedial spells scheme for D Street, I've seen enough hard-nosed gangsters to know this man most certainly isn't one.

Still, government man or not, I was just kidnapped, stuffed into a car, and shuttled to a hidden storage facility.

"Who are you?" I ask carefully. "What's all this about? Why am I here?"

The man unbuckles his briefcase, removes a single manila folder. He places it on the table but doesn't open it. "I'm Agent Frain, a captain within the Prohibition Unit." He gives me a lukewarm smile. "Apologies for the subterfuge in bringing you here, but there are bought men everywhere in the Unit. Here we're safe from prying eyes and ears."

A different fear starts to take hold. If this Frain chap is with the Unit, those men who just left are likely junior agents . . . maybe they were following me . . . maybe they saw that sorcering move I pulled outside Sam's fraternity party. . . . Christ, maybe I'm going to get kicked out of the Unit before I even truly start.

"You're a trainee, am I right, Alex, within our Domestic Magic division? You've been at the academy for around three months now. Set to graduate in a week."

I give a slow nod. "Yes, that's right, sir."

"Your superiors tell me you're smart. Good marks in your Shine Transference and Dangers of Performance classes, and you're adept in field exercises. No red flags, other than several notes about your attitude problem, in and out of training class."

I blush. "What exactly did my superiors say?"

"Despite its terrible reputation, there are still some discerning folks in the Unit, Alex. Ones that don't miss a trick." The loaded way he says this makes my insides twist and fold. He finally opens his folder. "My records indicate that you joined us in early summer, a couple months after your father's trial ended, is that correct?"

A familiar chill crops up at the top of my spine at the mention of my father, but I manage to answer, "That's correct, sir."

"My understanding is that your father's judge, Judge Hoehling, personally recommended you to the Unit, after you met with him before your father's jury deliberation. He said you asked for his advice. He said that he'd never met a, quote, 'more sorrowful son for the sins of his father,'" Frain says. "And Hoehling thought the Prohibition Unit would be the perfect answer for you. A career that allowed you to fight men like your father and atone on behalf of your family."

"Judge Hoehling was invaluable, sir," I say. "He helped me gain perspective and clarity." But my father's three-week trial for running his remedial spells scheme is nothing short of a nightmarish blur. For over a year—since my father had found out I'd gotten the magic touch—I had been his right-hand man. He took me out of the boarding program at St. Albans, and I spent most nights conjuring protective force fields for clandestine meetings and brewing my sorcerer's shine for his gangster guests. And of course, helping build the Danfreys' legacy: creating elaborate manipulations that allowed my father to break into his own Danfrey Pharma Corporation storage facilities, then flip the legal spells to D Street so the gang could move them into the black market. Our remedial magic scheme wasn't unusual, but given the access to cures my father had because of his company, it was wildly successful.

During the Spanish flu epidemic, even the most adamant of anti-sorcery activists realized there was a need for a medicinal exception to a blanket prohibition on magic, so sorcerers willing to work for the common good were eventually offered government gigs, or jobs with pharmaceutical companies to work toward breakthrough magic cures.

Of course, the underworld figured out a way to exploit this medicinal exception. Gangs get ahold of magic remedies, then cart them off to mom-and-pop operations that redistill a portion of the natural elements out of the spells in order to get them closer to pure-magic sorcerer's shine. But it's a true racket. The redistilled spells might last longer on the shelves than shine because of the residue of natural elements—a few weeks, long enough to be transportable—but the high is weak and muddled. Besides, some of the redistillers have been known to add crap like red paint to their product in an attempt to make it look closer to real-deal shine, which has led to poisonings across the city.

Not that I ever thought about what I was doing, what it meant, or hell, what I'd have to give up if my father was ever caught. I just did what he required, let my magic flow through me, reveled in being needed, powerful. No, *invincible*.

And then it all came crashing down back in March—two D Street thugs ratted to the Feds, my father was indicted, my home was sold for legal fees, and my senior year at St. Albans cut short. My father on the stand, lying about my involvement in order to save me and my mother—and in a last-ditch effort to partially redeem himself. Before I could blink, I became Poster Child Alex Danfrey, Remorseful Alex Danfrey, Just-Want-to-Make-Daddy's-Wrongs-Right Alex Danfrey.

Needless to say, I didn't know who this Alex Danfrey was—I still don't.

But convincing Judge Hoehling of who he was had been a piece of cake.

"Judge Hoehling told me that I could direct all the anger and frustration I had for my father toward the criminals of this city," I add, selling the same story I'd given to the head of the Prohibition Unit, to my lieutenant, to the guys who had questions in my training class. "He explained that I could take my hatred for magic and make it work for this country. I'm forever indebted."

Frain gives me a tight-lipped smile. "That's exactly what our notes say as well," he says. "In fact, nearly word for word."

My heart has started to push against the insides of my chest, like it's got hands, like it's ready to rumble. I'm honestly not sure which way this Frain chap is angling, which annoys as much as it scares me.

"I know your mother told the papers that you were both completely in the dark about Richard's remedial magic scheme, but I'm sure you learned some facts from his trial." Frain keeps his eyes on his file. "I take it you know the name Anthony Colletto, the D Street Outfit boss? The man your father was ultimately working for?" I nod, as the name will forever be seared like a brand in my mind. "My understanding is that your father agreed to steal his own company's government-sanctioned spells right off his shelves and funnel them to D Street, in exchange for Boss Colletto's forgiveness of some pretty exorbitant gambling debts. Maybe in late 1924, early 1925?"

It was January 1925. I remember because my father had been on a shine bender since the holidays, and after a week on the stuff was barely recognizable. He'd come home lit out of his mind on New Year's Eve, thrown me against a wall, all the while barking at me with shined-up, pinprick pupils, sputtering that our lives were over. "I'm not too familiar with the details, sir, but that all sounds right to me."

"And from your training class, I'm sure you know the name Erwin McEvoy."

I nod, still not sure where this is going. "He's Colletto's sworn enemy, has been boss of the Irish Shaw Gang for almost a decade, a position he assumed after D Street killed his predecessor and cousin, Danny the Gun. McEvoy's nickname: Jackal of the District. A nickname well-earned, from what I understand," I say. "Our Unit instructor estimated McEvoy's killed over a hundred men since he took over the Shaws."

"Very good." Frain looks me in the eye. "I also understand, from our inside sources, that McEvoy's in need of a new right-hand sorcerer."

Right-hand sorcerer. I think back to training class. "You mean his magic protector on the street, his personal sorcerer?" I ask. "What happened to his old one?"

"Homicide said it looked like a trick gone wrong, from what they could tell. Some elaborate manipulation backfired, and apparently the young man ended up half-charred." Frain pauses. "Unless, of course, McEvoy just decided to set him on fire."

I shift uncomfortably in my thin metal chair. "Sir, all due respect, what's this have to do with me?"

"As you know from the Unit, McEvoy is on our most-wanted list." Frain gives me a wan smile. "He's a man synonymous with magic, who uses sorcery in nearly every way you can to break the law. Force fields to assist in robberies. Manipulations to coerce enemies. Elaborate smuggling rings to bring the haunted island brew, obi, and this newer product, fae dust, in from overseas. He's even got his hand in performance—owns a few middling shining rooms across the city, where I'm told you can get a shot of shine and a little sorcery show any night of the week." Frain leans across the table. "We've been tracking McEvoy for a long time, but we've never had an agent worthy enough to plant by his side, who can keep us informed about the Shaws' dealings, who can help us hit them at the right time." Frain pauses. "And we want that someone to be you, Danfrey. We want to send you undercover."

Undercover. With *McEvoy?* The boss of the most dangerous gang in DC? "Sir, I'm sorry, what—how would that even be possible?"

"We'd do it nice and slow, make it look credible," Frain says. "We'd get you in at the lowest level, hook you up with someone junior, on the periphery of McEvoy's operation, and you'd work your way up the ranks. Like I said, McEvoy's looking for a new right-hand sorcerer, and someone like you, who's talented, smart, and savvy about the underworld? You'll find your way to him, I'm sure of it. Besides, McEvoy's had a vendetta for Colletto since Colletto took out his cousin, Danny the Gun. We're positive McEvoy would take you into his fold just to spite the D Street boss. It's perfect."

But I'm still stuck on Frain's description of me. *Talented.* So Frain knows I can sorcer. At least, he has a suspicion that I can sorcer. It doesn't matter, there's no way I'm doing this. For one, I despise gangsters, can't even imagine rubbing shoulders with them again, much less trying to win them over—their whole magic racket ruined my life. For another, it sounds like a death sentence.

"Sir, you just said McEvoy's last sorcerer pretty much ended up burned at the stake," I say slowly. "So thanks for the offer, but I think I'm better cut out for the field."

Frain studies me. "The field." He takes a pack of cigarettes out of his pocket and lights one. He doesn't offer one to me. "And are you proud of what you're doing with the Unit, Alex? How you're setting yourself up 'for the field'?"

Warren's words from earlier—*it's like you're trying to be your father, it's like you can't help it, you're poison*—they start gnawing at me again. But I manage to answer, "I'd like to think so, sir."

"Mmm." Frain sits back in his seat. "So hitting up illegal magic parties, serving sorcerer's shine to minors, casting prohibited magic in public . . . that's all part of your plan to end the manipulative, coercive sorcery and addiction that has cursed this country? To put men like your father behind bars?" He gives a put-on laugh. "We've got a lot of corrupt men within our ranks, Alex. But I have to say, corrupt sorcerers? You're a special breed."

The walls feel like they're closing in, the overstocked boxes and bins of this cramped storage room are slowly inching forward. So the Unit *was* following me at Sigma Phi. *Did they trail me into the party? Or is Frain bluffing?*

"If you want to accuse me of something, why don't you just

say it, Agent Frain? I've got nothing to hide." I paste on a smile and push out from my seat to stand. "I appreciate your offer, but getting myself killed isn't something I'm interested in. So with all due respect, I'd like you to take me home."

"Sit down, Danfrey." Frain's face hardens. "Let's spin this another way. The same D Street thugs who sold out your father for poaching his own company's cures? They went on record when we first brought them down to the station, claimed they saw someone else in the shadows of your father's cellar when they made that final exchange." He pauses. "Neither of them caught a face, of course. But they described him as tall, young. Not enough to build a case on, but enough to raise some eyebrows."

"Are you attempting to threaten me, sir?"

"Just stating the facts."

My facade of a smile feels even stiffer, thinner. "Sounds more like rumors to me," I manage. "You'd need more than that to even get the papers' ears."

But Frain's face stays stone. "We also pushed your father in prison, Alex. Offered him a better deal if he walked us through the process of shine transference. Even put some pressure on him. And he couldn't do it." I don't move, I don't speak, but my heart pounds like a drum inside my chest. "Can you imagine that? The country's most well-known white-collar sorcerer can't brew sorcerer's shine, a magic spell that every sorcerer's capable of," he says, "which leads me to the only real conclusion. That Richard Danfrey was obviously the mastermind behind his D Street racket, but he wasn't the magic." He leans forward, drops his voice, and says, "Now, I've got you on low-level charges, eyewitnesses to your little reveal off O Street tonight. Plus enough to go on to reopen Richard Danfrey's case—*your* case. And if I'm successful? You spend the rest of your life behind bars."

My heart is now sputtering, racing, flying. But it's not the threat of jail that's set me off, or my father getting "pushed" by the Feds. It's my mother. I think of the mania of the press when my father was indicted, the reporters banging on our door, Mom locking herself in her room, crying, sobbing at all hours of the night. Her walking into my room like a strange, tormented ghost: *He betrayed us . . . you're nothing like him, Alex, nothing. Tell me. Swear it.* Even though she knew. *She had to have known.*

I close my eyes to blink out the memory.

"I know you joined the Unit to try and escape your past." Frain uses a different, softer tone. "But sometimes fate's chips fall in the damnedest of ways. You can use what's happened to your family and put it to work for your country. You can help, Alex, and in a way that only *you* can."

I choose to focus on the trees, because the forest is too dark, too thick, too dangerous. "Sir, let's just say I was even entertaining the idea of doing this. Guys like Colletto, like McEvoy, they're smart. They've lied and cheated and killed their way to the top. I can't just be *planted* and expect it to all work out—"

"Like I said, we'd do it right, Alex," Frain interrupts gently. "Believe me, this is one shot for us, too. We'd sever your ties with the Prohibition Unit. We'd stage a bust, charge you for attempting to move some of Danfrey Pharma Corp.'s remedial magic into the black market on your own. A minor charge, but enough to look credible. We even have a cell mate lined up for you out at Lorton Reformatory, some low-life, low-rank runner in McEvoy's operation who got picked up by the coast guard a couple weeks back for smuggling fae dust. You make nice with him, he introduces you to the Shaws when you get out. Then you win them over one at a time and claw your way up to McEvoy."

I lean back in my chair. The fear is in my throat now, tastes like metal, bile. Could I even do something like this? *Do I have a choice?* "Those thugs would eat me alive."

He shakes his head. "You know how to reinvent yourself,

what it takes to stay above water, that much is clear," he says. "Think about what you've done to survive the storm surrounding your father—you've lied, manipulated, deceived your way right into the agency that should have brought *you* down. You're a survivor, Danfrey."

A *survivor*. I've never, ever thought of myself that way.

"We'll stay in contact discreetly, of course, but this is your show. *Your* game. And if you do this for us, if you excel, if you fight for your country, in a way I think you really want to, maybe even need to, I promise, all the charges, they all fall away. And I guarantee you'll be a national hero instead."

I study the top of the card table, running it all through, piece by painstaking piece. "So you hook me up with this cell mate, and I'm supposed to make sure he knows I've got it out for D Street. I use him to angle my way to Boss McEvoy." I breathe out. "I help you catch the big fish, and then I walk away."

Frain nods. "That's the deal."

I close my eyes and think through everything that's led to this moment: my father demanding that I help him, after he caught me sneaking back into my room after a night out with Warren, my magic self-replica still lying in bed as a decoy for my parents. My reluctance, then my slow acceptance of the raw, unbridled magic coursing through me. Then the feeling that my father and I were above the law, the world, that no one and nothing could touch the Danfreys, that the world was our oyster. And then the day it all came crashing, tumbling down.

What I've been doing since—following Warren like a dumb puppy, skating by in the Unit, hating everyone and everything, wanting to bring the world to its knees? Maybe Agent Frain's right. Maybe I do need this. Christ, maybe I need to own the sins of my family, walk headfirst into the underworld that ruined everything, and blow it apart, exact my true revenge, in order to fully leave the past behind.

Besides, what's the alternative? Decades, a *lifetime*, in jail?

Still, the fear, it has me, taunts me, winds it way around my throat—

"Alex," Frain adds gently, "I can't guarantee it won't be a long road, and a bumpy one, but you are truly the only one who can do this for us."

And something about his tone, his words—*the only one*—massages a tender, deep and hidden spot inside. Before I can think through it anymore, I force out a whisper. "When will it start?"

Frain reaches out and pats my hand. "I'll take you back to your place. Trust me, you're going to need some sleep."

He pulls his hand back to gather his file and close his brief-case. Then he stands. "We'll come to arrest you in the morning. You tell your mother what you have to—that you slipped up, that you're sorry," he says, as the reality of what I'm doing, what I'm owning up to, the trash I'm going to be slumming with—it all winds its way around my throat like a collar and clicks shut with a *snap*. "No one can know you're still working for me."

STICK, CARROT

JOAN

I barely dream: I'm usually so tired by the time I finish cleaning our cabin, maintaining what's left of the herb garden out back, cooking, helping with Jed's shows, and caring for Ruby, that most times my mind stops churning and surrenders to a big, blank nothing. And for that, I'm grateful—'cause the nights I have dreams, it's almost always the same one.

It starts with Mama's long, low wail from outside our cabin. In the nightmare, I get up, leave Ruby gently snoring next to me, and grip the textured walls of our bedroom, trying to find the door, trying not to wake her and Ben. Then Mama's call grows louder, and real worry starts gnawing at me. Mama's not an actress, or a yeller. If she's hollering, something's wrong.

I stumble into the moon-drenched clearing, wade through the tall grass, scan the rows of distant trees—nothing. I turn around, but there's nothing by the back side of the cabin but rake and shovels, and I don't see her by the silver lip of the brook across the yard. Then I hear rustling, from somewhere in the grass.

A white-hot panic seizes me. *This isn't right there's something wrong* blares loudly through my mind, and I start running in all directions, calling her name as her cries become more urgent—

Finally I see tall blades of grass on the far side of the clearing bend and quake. "Mama!"

I run to her. But she's not alone.

There's a man pitched on top of her, spread over her like a tent, whispering, pleading, forcing her to keep quiet—*Show me, Eve, show me what I've done for you. That's it . . .*

It takes me a full second to realize it's Uncle Jed.

In a wild, desperate moment my mind offers, *Maybe he's helping her she was out here alone she's fallen*, but it goes quiet, and the silence shatters everything I thought I knew in one furious blast.

Rage, pity, pain, my magic—the new, red-hot magic that's been burning in my veins since my magic touch ignited a couple weeks back—it's all rising up inside of me, forces its way out of my mouth, screams, "GET OFF HER! NOW!"

Jed's head whips around. Pinprick pupils, almost grotesque childlike smile, steady movements—it's obvious he's all shined up, and not in the throes of withdrawal. And the bastard has the gall to say, "You're dreaming, Joan, get back to the cabin."

Tears I didn't feel starting are running down my cheeks. "I'm warning you, Jed, I'll kill you if you don't leave her alone—"

"Joan," Mama whimpers from underneath his body, "please. Just GO."

And her fear, her careful, cautioning *pleading*, that's what does me in.

I get a running start before Jed knows what's coming. I throw myself into him, tackle him, wrestle him to the ground. I'm small but I'm fast. I get a few licks into his side, at his ears, before he tosses me off him and rolls over to recover.

"Mama, run!"

But she starts pulling me toward her. "Jed, don't you touch her, leave her be, she's got nothing to do with this, you hear, she's just scared. Joan—" She lunges to grab both my arms—

"You want this?" I wrestle away from her as Jed curses and starts clambering to his knees. I won't believe it. Mama is my hero. Mama is my salvation. Mama is my sun.

"Get back inside. He'll kill us both."

I don't move. "How long has he been using you like this?"

She doesn't answer. But her face says everything. "Better me than you," she whispers to herself, her voice breaking. "Thank God for my protection spells."

All words are silenced, stay dammed in my throat. Images flood my mind from the past, of Mama in our washroom, of her slicing a pocketknife into her thumb for a spell she wouldn't explain, rubbing her blood over my lips and eyelids, her whispers I could barely hear: *Not to be seen by him, not to be touched, when he looks at her, he sees me,* and all at once the memories crystallize, take on new meaning. I'm so livid I can't move—it's like the anger has me hostage, or under a spell—

But then I realize I can end this abuse and her pain with one desperate, powerful trick.

Slow, fearful realization settles over Mama's features, and I can tell she knows, that all the times she's told me that magic is dangerous, poisonous, that it takes as much as it gives—her words have fallen on deaf ears. 'Cause as Jed is shaking off pieces of high grass behind us, coming over to give me hell's reckoning, she reaches for me—

"NO, JOAN, DON'T!"

But I wrangle away from Mama, conjure this new, untamed magic force inside me, picture the dark, awing, invincible *something* running through my veins turning into pure lightning, command the lightning to burst out of my frame like a storm of hell, and I mutter, "*Destroy—*"

I see it too late, of course, in that split second where I throw a pitch of pure magic force, that Jed already knows what's coming too. He beats me to it, sends his own swath of wrath and sorcery toward me to swallow me and my amateur trick—

But not before Mama leaps in between us.

Long ago there was an arrogant sorcerer, a child of a sorcerer, a black hole of a sorcerer—

The wind stops, the sounds of the clearing are gone, the texture of the night is flattened into one never-ending moment, as Mama is suspended, perfect, floating in between us—

And then she turns brittle, like she's made of glass. She bursts, shatters into pieces, falls to the ground like scattered dust. A magic wind swirls her away into nothing, and then she's gone.

I hear a long, low, primal cry before I realize that I'm the one wailing. "Oh my God, no, oh my God, no I—wait, no no NO . . ."

Jed collapses on the ground beside me. But he doesn't say a word.

"No . . . no, we need to undo it," I sputter. "Jed, bring her back. Jed, you need to undo it." He doesn't answer, stares straight into the grass. "Take it back, you hear me?" The world is a melting blur of sounds and colors, my tears drowning all time and space. "We need to take it back."

Jed sighs into his hands. I don't know if he's crying. I don't care. I hate him, I hate him so much I want to break him. I want him to break me. "PLEASE, Jed!"

He doesn't move for a long time. Finally he looks at me with pink, watery eyes, more sober than I've seen him look in a long time. He whispers, a hollow sound of defeat and regret, "All the magic in the world can't undo it."

Jed's whisper sends my eyes flying open, my hands instinctively reaching around my knapsack-turned-pillow, like I'm trying to claw my way back out of the past.

And then I'm curled on a coil-riddled cot in the warehouse, the bruised sky of early dawn sneaking into its windows, face-to-face with a lightly snoring Grace.

I sit up, stare at the sad sea of sleeping bodies around me, attempt to shake off the remnants of the dream—my sputtering pulse, the few tears that trail around my ears.

All the magic in the world can't undo it.

If I keep thinking about what magic helped me to do, how it beat through my veins and told me I was strong enough, how it convinced me, enabled me, to go and destroy everything—

I'll want to banish my magic again and cage it back inside a bottle.

No. I need to put the *past* in a bottle, on a shelf, keep it all preserved but hidden in some dark corner of my mind. I don't deserve to get rid of it, but I need it out of my way right here and now. This needs to be about the future—Ruby's future, Ben's future, the ones I devoted the rest of my life to.

Magic is the only thing that can save us now.

Magic is all I got. I need to make peace with it. A *truce*.

Temporary, but necessary.

Grace gives a little sigh, flutters her eyes open, studies me. She whispers, "Did you sleep at all?"

"I did, just a bad dream." I nod to the little pool of drool on the back of her hand and smile. "Looks like you slept all right."

She gives me an embarrassed smile and sits up, wipes her hand on her pant leg. "Guess the traveling, and the nerves, it all came to a head and knocked me out." She pulls out a half-empty pack of cigarettes, takes two, lights both, and hands one to me. We sit there for a minute, just inhaling the first smoky breaths of the day, enjoying the quiet before the sleeping sorcerers around us get up and remind us why we're here.

"You see that duo over there, sharing the same cot?" Grace

whispers. She nods toward the corner, points to a burly middle-aged man with his arm wrapped around a younger woman who looks hard even in her sleep—straight brows, flat nose, grim expression as she wheezes.

"That's Rose and Tommy Briggs from Tennessee, the brother-sister act I mentioned last night." I look at the way the pair is lying all tangled up in each other, and look back curiously at Grace. "My thoughts exactly. Haven't been able to get close enough to mine their minds for what's going on, but they're famous for running some all-night secret shine orgy somewhere in the thick of the Blue Ridge Mountains," she says. "Apparently the Briggs are gifted in visual manipulations, excel in conjuring what folks call staccato tricks. You know, where a magic manipulation gives way to something permanent that then gives way to another manipulation."

Grace might as well be speaking Greek right now, but I mumble a little "Right, sure" like I'm following. I try my damnedest to keep my mind blank, so there's nothing for her to go mining for. Grace can't find out how little I know about making magic. How the more I hear about my competition, the more panic blooms inside me like a thorny rose. "And which one's Stock, the rat-conjuring jerk from last night?"

Grace points at the cot next to Tommy's. "Stock Harding, barely twenty and as arrogant as sorcerers come. Apparently Gunn was after his daddy out in West Virginia, but the pop's got the sleepy sickness. Meeting Stock, you'd think he was the first in his family with the magic touch." She rearranges herself into a cross-legged position and gives a low whistle. "If Gunn's after performers, though, Stock's a strong contender, as much as I hate to admit it. He comes from a long line of sorcerers with a special talent for living and moving manipulations, like you saw with his little rodent trick last night." She looks at me. "That ain't no easy feat, conjuring a manipulation, breathing life into it and letting it run around on its own—for as long as the magic lasts, anyway."

A few of the other sorcerers start groaning, yawning, and fighting with themselves to stay asleep.

Grace drops her voice another octave. "Over there's the five sorcerers from North and South Carolina—who others have been calling the Carolina Boys. Got a thing for fire, at least their leader, Gavin Rhodes, does. But I've been watching them, and so far I ain't impressed. Besides, I get a bad sense from Gavin—don't think he can be trusted."

I give her a knowing smile, knowing damn well that she shouldn't trust me, either, as I'm only going to disappoint her. Hell, I wonder if I should even be trusting *Grace*, or if she could be as slippery as her magic snake. But I think through my alternatives.

There aren't any.

"So you've been sizing everyone up? Do you know everyone's strongest gifts?"

"Almost everyone." Grace stubs her cigarette out. "I think it's what Gunn wants us to do, assess each other, and make magic alliances. After all, he's only planning on keeping seven of us."

"Right," I agree slowly, as Gunn had said as much last night. Still, I can't help but ask, "But why seven?"

"Guess Gunn's done his research, and knows his sorcery." Grace shrugs. "Look across cultures and religions from the beginning of time, and you'll find seven as a source of mystical importance. Seven sacraments, seven sins, seven elements in some of the most secretive, powerful spells." Grace drops her voice to a hum. "Back when the line between magic and reality was a lot more blurred, before this world started regarding sorcery with such fear and suspicion, magic was like a language among sorcerers. It was a thing to share, not a thing to hide. And for a long time, it was rumored that a worthy ring of seven sorcerers could unlock a magic within the magic. That seven was the key to strengthening gifts and surpassing weaknesses— and could even bend and flex the laws of magic itself."

A magic within the magic. Never heard of the power of seven before, but after witnessing some of Mama's dark spells, and how my prayers were answered in the clearing on the night she died, it doesn't surprise me. I've got no doubt that magic's possibilities are damn near limitless, for better or worse. "How's Gunn going to pick his seven?"

"Don't think he is."

"What do you mean? Then who's deciding?"

"I tried to mine Gunn's mind, get some answers on our car ride here, but the man keeps his thoughts locked tight. But I *was* able to amplify some of his conversations in the car with his lackey, Dawson," she whispers. "And I almost don't believe what I heard, but I swear Gunn was talking about the importance of having the sorcerers choose themselves."

Choose themselves—*meaning the group of us chooses our strongest seven, instead of Gunn?*

I want to crack open this conversation, push Grace a little more on all she knows, but Stock starts stirring across from her, his cot whining like a child in a tantrum. We grow quiet as he sits up, looks around. His eyes fall on the two of us, and he flashes me a smile that reminds me of his rodent manipulation last night.

"Aw, how precious. A little morning powwow. You lecturing New Girl on the wise ways of Dune family magic, Grace?" Stock reaches for his own pack of cigs. "Telling her all about the way you Dunes fuck cows to bring on the rain?" He laughs as he lights his smoke. "And shit in fields to make the sun come up a little earlier?"

"Eat it, Stock," Grace mutters, but a horrible flush starts to crawl around her ears.

"The Dune family is known up here as a flock of strange, strange birds, New Girl," Stock laughs. "Hate to cut off this budding friendship and all, but if you're looking for some kind of sugar daddy, I suggest a real contender." He blows a puff of smoke toward me. "Someone like me. I can take care of you. I'll make sure you've got something warm and fuzzy to hold on to," he says with a shit-eating grin. He wiggles his eyebrows. "That rat was just the beginning."

"So you conjure a rat when you're lonely at night?" I say slowly.

His smile falters a little bit. "That's not what I meant." He gives a sharp, forced laugh as he takes another drag to recover. "Your head's completely empty inside that doll-face of yours, isn't it?"

I take a deep breath, quite aware that Grace is watching, that others might be watching too. If she's right, if everyone's supposed to be judging and assessing everyone else's strengths and weaknesses, and I don't know how to use magic to earn their respect, I sure as hell better find an alternative.

"Do me a favor," I tell Stock, slow and evenly, like I'm not somebody to mess with, like I'm someone like Gunn, "don't speak to me, and don't speak to Grace, until you're ready to act like a gentleman." I steal another breath before bringing it home. "I don't care what a big man you think you are 'cause your daddy's dying and you somehow stumbled into this chance. I can see right through you." I let my eyes fall over him, from top to bottom, till I glance down at the front of his pants. I arch my eyebrow theatrically and take a chance. "And you're small, Stock Harding. *Limp.*"

Stock's face erupts red, and he instinctively puts his hand over his crotch. A few of the eavesdropping sorcerers around us start chuckling.

"You little bitch—"

"Uh, uh, uh." I raise my finger, lean forward, feel the magic coursing through me that I don't know what to do with, but whose heady hold emboldens me just the same. "Be a gentleman."

I turn around and bury my gaze in my satchel, keep my shaking hands busy by grabbing a flask of water and towel to freshen up, as Grace does the same beside me. I hear Stock shift on his cot, like he's going to move, maybe confront me, but then he stops, pauses, and mutters, "Psycho skirt."

He launches off his mattress and stomps away as the laughter of the crowd gets a little louder, a few of them lobbing catcalls after him, "Temper, temper!" "That's no way to be a gentleman!"

I can feel Grace's stare as the heckling eventually fades. "Not necessarily the way I would've handled it."

"Thought you said it was a bad idea to start slinging magic in here." I keep my eyes on my satchel. "Thought we should save the magic for Gunn."

"I did say that," Grace says. There's a smile in her voice. "You're just ballsy, Joan Kendrick. And that ain't a bad thing."

I look up and mirror her smile, a wave of relief passing through me. "Well, you got my back last night, right? So I get yours this morning."

We take our time freshening up as the other sorcerers slowly wake up around us. The sky outside the warehouse's windows rises to a pink hue, then settles into the glaring white of morning. We hear screeches from the other side of the door, the sound of wood scraping concrete. The door creaks open, and Gunn steps inside with an associate in tow.

"Showtime," Grace whispers. A rush of nerves, adrenaline, fear—it all shoots right up my spine.

"Gentlemen, ladies." Gunn crosses the large space to greet us.

Everyone scrambles to stand, eager to greet the man who holds the golden key to some of our futures.

"Today, our experiment begins." Gunn looks more polished than he did last night: three-piece suit without a wrinkle, new hat, cold-blue eyes without a bruise of a sleepless night underneath them. "You each stand among the most talented sorcerers this country has to offer, so look around." He waits for a minute as we all size one another up.

"This country thinks it's seen all that sorcery can achieve, thinks that Prohibition has already funneled all of America's magic into the underworld." Gunn pauses. "But I know better. I know that some of the most gifted sorcerers—you, your families—have kept your particular magic to yourselves." He surveys our crowd. "Each of you was smart enough to recognize this opportunity I'm giving you, and come out of hiding for it. The magic I believe we can make together will be unprecedented, will truly change the face of sorcery as this country knows it." Gunn paces in front of us as his young companion, Dawson, from what Grace had said, stands like a statue behind him.

"These next few weeks will be hard. Grueling. Sorcering all day in the clearing out back, and close quarters at night. I'm not going to pretend that you won't be pushed to the very brink, that some of you won't be swallowed whole by the pressure." Grace steals a look at me, but I keep my eyes straight ahead. "But for the troupe of sorcerers that emerges victorious at the end of this trial, the ones who show me that they've got the magic we all want to experience, to taste, to *live* in—it will all be worth it. There'll be more money in it than you could ever dream. Than you can even count."

A few of the sorcerers give hearty, hungry laughs around me, and Gunn smiles.

He gestures to Dawson. "My associate, Dawson, has food outside—there's water, fruit, and bread. Help yourselves to a quick breakfast. There's a clearing about a quarter mile deeper into the woods. We'll begin out there once you've eaten."

The sorcerers start moving as a herd toward the door, a jostle of rough elbows and shoulders. Stock passes by and flicks me and Grace off with his middle finger. Grace just ignores him, but I give it right back.

We step outside, and the morning light sears my eyes. A pickup truck is now parked in the lot, stocked with crates of glass bottles, long, crisp baguettes peeking out of sleeves of paper, oranges and apples and stacks of bananas piled high. It looks like the spoils of a market raid.

Grace and I each grab a water bottle, some bread, and a piece of fruit. We settle down next to each other on a fallen tree trunk a few feet from the truck and watch the thirteen other sorcerers mosey around, divide into their small groups and factions.

My mind's itching to relax and just enjoy this—this small sliver of calm before the day's impending storm. But Grace's words from earlier—*It's what Gunn wants, seven sorcerers is the key to stronger magic, letting the sorcerers choose*—they're starting to buzz around and bite, like a swarm of unanswered questions. Whatever we're here for, whatever this experiment is, and the end game that Gunn's calling "unprecedented" magic, it's obviously something new, rare, big. Something, my guess is, that Gunn's been planning for a long time.

My eyes settle on the man as I dig into my breakfast. He stands at the passenger side of the truck, sleeves rolled up, brow creased in concentration as he gives his orders to Dawson. He looks hard, sharp, but also, under the bright white of morning, even younger than I took him for last night. "You know a lot about this Gunn fella?"

Grace shrugs as she peels her banana. "I know his name from the papers. He's a Shaw man, practically raised by the gang from what I understand—his pop Danny Gunn even ran it once upon a time. Now he's Boss McEvoy's youngest underboss."

McEvoy. The name Gunn gave me last night. *Boss McEvoy is everyone's boss.*

"Gunn manages one of the shining rooms McEvoy owns, oversees this place in town called the Red Den, has for years. But from what I was able to gather from the car, Gunn plans to make the Den . . . bigger. More impressive than a handful of solo performances and a shot of sorcerer's shine. He talked about the place becoming jaw-dropping, and blowing away all the city's competition."

"You ever been to this Red Den?"

"Hell, I've never been to DC," Grace answers. "But I needed to get out of Alexandria. Too much history . . . and too many memories."

"That I understand." I follow Grace's gaze to Gunn's minion, Dawson, as he jumps off the back of the truck and starts making the rounds, attempting to get everyone moving to the clearing.

"What Stock was saying about my family?" Grace says slowly. "It's bullshit, but there's a sliver of truth in the lie. My family's gifted in natural forecasts, has always excelled in using magic to commune with nature. But I swear, the more we listened, the louder and scarier nature got. Magic melded our minds with superstitious, primal forces, forces that whispered what they wanted constantly, forces that started pushing us all into stranger, darker spells. I needed to get out, go somewhere new, forget all of that," she adds, then looks at me suddenly. "Sometimes the only option is walking away and starting over, you understand?"

White-hot memories of Mama's own strange, dark spells sear into my mind—*Mama bent over the farm boy Skippy McGarrison, his bottom half crushed by one of his daddy's stallions, the lanterns of her spell room casting him in a sick yellow*

glow, his howls, her steady hand carving out a graft of his skin as
a sacrifice to save his life—

I shake my head to chase away the memories before Grace
has a chance to catch them. I don't know how to answer her—
whether to say that I *do* understand in my own way, or that I
could never leave my family, or whether I trust her enough to
share my family's own special magic. But before I can sort it out,
Gunn calls out to the crowd, "Time to wrap it up!"

The sorcerers fall into silence. "Clearing's not more than a
stone's throw from here," Gunn adds. "Dawson will bring the
materials we'll need." Then he gestures to the truck. "And grab
something for later—it's going to be a long day."

We take some extra fruit and bread from the truck, follow
the snake of sorcerers through the wild brush, and soon cross
over a border of tall grass to reach a clearing. It's huge, three
times the size of the one behind our cabin back home, with a
small bordering stream and a nice, clean patch of sun in the
middle. On the far side of the clearing near the stream, there's
a structure of large, stacked stones piled waist-high, almost like
an altar.

Dawson carries a crate of mismatched water bottles over
to the side of the stone formation. Gunn takes a bottle and
places it on the altar's center, and then approaches a sorcerer
who Grace didn't point out to me in the warehouse. The sorcerer's middle-aged, with hair slicked back, greased to right above
his shoulders. The sorcerer just nods as Gunn whispers to him,
doesn't say a word.

I feel the crowd's reaction around me, the whispers and side
conversations being slowly killed by curiosity, jealousy—*why's
this fella being singled out, what's so special about him*—we all
shift uncomfortably and watch the sorcerer wrap his hands
around the glass bottle and close his eyes. Like I've seen Uncle
Jed do so many times before, this sorcerer begins to brew

sorcerer's shine, to cast a spell without any components, other than his own magic touch. Sure enough, the water inside the bottle starts hissing, steaming, and thrashes around until it's transformed into something else: something sparkling, deep and red. Sorcerer's shine.

The sorcerer releases the bottle, wipes his glistening brow with his sleeve, and wipes his palms on the side of his pants.

"Thank you, Billy," Gunn says. "That will be all for now." He looks up at the crowd. "The rest of you, come gather around the altar."

Gunn rests his hands on the slab of stone as we form a semi-circle around him. "This experiment of mine might be far different than some of you were expecting," he says. "Truth is, I'm looking for a *team*, a team only as strong as its weakest member. Of course I'm looking for sorcerers who have mastered their special talents, along with the art of transference, of making shine." He pauses, his eyes scanning the crowd. "But I also want sorcerers who are going to submit fully to my vision. What I've come to believe is the basest of truth about magic: that it is a living thing." His words bring me right back to the cabin, to Mama's words of warning, to the basest truth that I too know about magic, despite everything that I don't.

"Magic only gets stronger as it makes connections," Gunn continues. "It *wants* to form ties, to build and improve upon itself. But that's not something that this country understands or that many even remember, considering America's longtime distrust of sorcery. In fact, you all are living proof that some of this country's most powerful families have insisted on sorcering in their own silos in secret and don't accept this basic truth." Gunn gazes out at the crowd, like a preacher at his pulpit. "As always, I think actions speak louder than words. If you'll entertain a demonstration." He pauses. "Will the two strongest sorcerers please step forward?"

No one moves. Eyes begin to turn on one another.

Gunn clears his throat. "Come now, the two strongest in the lot," he says, louder. "Whose magic is so astounding that I have to witness it today? Here's your chance to stand out from the crowd."

I share a look with Grace. I'm more likely to go running and screaming for the nearest bus than I am to raise my hand right now, but if I was crazy enough to try it, Grace's small, solemn head shake tells me NO. I look around, sure as hell that that jerk-off Stock is going to step forward, but two other men beat him to it.

"Mark Saunders, from Blue Ridge," a large, middle-aged man says as he steps forward. "I believe I can out-trick and outperform any sorcerer in this lot, Mr. Gunn."

"Beg to differ," says someone else behind him. "Peter Curtin, from Charlotte. No one can rival my magic manipulations, Mr. Gunn. And my shine is like something you can't believe."

"Thank you, Mark, Peter." Gunn extends his hand, gesturing to the wide, flat stretch of clearing in front of the trees, on the left side of our crowd. "Why don't we begin?"

Mark and Peter glance at each other, once, before they follow Gunn to their makeshift performance stage.

"What do you think they're going to do?" I whisper to Grace, as Gunn guides Mark and Peter to either side of the long stretch of grass, so now they're standing face-to-face, about fifteen feet apart, like they're about to begin a magic duel.

Grace whispers back slowly, "Show Gunn what he wants to see."

Mark begins. He stretches his arms out wide, stage-whispers the words of power, "*Grow. Bloom*," and almost immediately, the grass underneath him begins to rumble. Out of the shifting green blanket, a tangle of roots emerges, like a monster's hands pushing out from the ground. As the crowd gasps, the thick roots fold open, grow longer, and wider, and then the center root erupts skyward, twists into a trunk, thick and textured and now twenty feet high. It throws a long shadow over our crowd, before it splits into limbs that race to fill out the tree. The limbs divide, splinter into branches, which bloom into a tapestry of leaves.

Uncle Jed stopped sorcering manipulations around the time he lost himself to shine, but I remember this same awed feeling creeping over me and settling in, as I watched him conjure a lemon tree or shady oak in our yard. Creating something real from nothing, or protecting something with magic, or linking and binding things that have no business being linked: pure magic might only last a day, but its hold on you lasts far longer.

But before I can fully appreciate the tree, a blinding, white-hot blast of lightning bursts right down its trunk, splitting it open with a monstrous gash.

I whip around to find Peter—the lightning manipulation must have been his. I keep watching as he waves his hands forward like a conductor, and the lightning bursts into flames, red-hot orange waves that lap at the base of the tree, then climb onto its trunk, jump to its branches—

Mark returns. He throws his arms up to the heavens, commands, *"Fall and freeze,"* and a strong burst of wind comes shrieking around the charred tree branches, blowing the orange and red flames into a thick wall of gray smoke. Snow begins to fall, not a natural flurry, but an all-out, otherworldly blizzard, buckets of white clumpy snowballs caking the tree, burying it, snuffing the fire right out—

"Rise and heat," Peter commands, and the sky erupts into a near-blinding brilliance over the clearing, as a gold, electrifying, magic-made sun takes shape. It sears the snow, and the large clumps of frozen ice that bury the remains of the tree and the clearing around it melt in an instant, trickle and run fast into the clearing grass.

"*Fall and freeze*," Mark utters, and the snow begins hammering down again—

"*Rise and heat*," Peter orders, and their stage begins to simmer once more under his magic, searing sunshine—

"*Fall and freeze!*"

"*Rise and heat!*"

And then, like the magic itself has surrendered, the mangled tree and its surroundings stop changing on a dime. The complex manipulation promptly shatters like a mirror, and tiny shards of the charred black trunk scatter across the sky like broken black glass. The shards whip into a dizzying dust so blinding that it takes me a near minute to realize that the magic swallowed Mark and Peter, and surrendered them right along with it.

"Oh my Lord," I utter, before I can stop myself.

I look at Grace, but she's already searching the crowd for Gunn, for his reaction. The entire crowd of sorcerers shifts, mumbles, gasps—surely this was a mistake—

"Arrogance," Gunn says simply, quieting us. No shock or surprise, no remorse in his voice. "Arrogance is the root of all downfall. Arrogance prevents us from working together."

Wait. Gunn was . . . Gunn was *expecting* this. Hell, Gunn orchestrated this. Let two sorcerers blow each other up, so that he could prove his point? Grace exchanges a loaded glance with me, mouths, "Holy hell," as Gunn's words from last night outside our cabin float out of the dark of my mind: *I can't guarantee you'll come home the same way you left.*

Because I might come back in a body bag. Because I might not come back at all.

I look around at the other sorcerers, the crowd of thirteen of us left. If Gunn is looking for seven, what Grace called the key to stronger magic, does that mean that six of us are expendable? That's little more than a fifty-fifty chance of surviving.

You're finished, a small voice whispers inside me. I close my eyes, imagine squashing the doubt, just like I'm killing a bug. I don't have the privilege of being scared. Not with what I've done. Not with who's depending on me—

"Now for the second part of my demonstration." Gunn shatters my thoughts. He waves forward the sorcerer who had just brewed his shine at the altar moments before. "Billy, if you can come forward again. And I'll need another volunteer." When no one moves, hell, no one breathes, Gunn adds, "A volunteer of a different sort."

It takes a while before another sorcerer's brave (or suicidal) enough to step forward. A man sidles up to Billy, nods at Gunn. He's a short, stouter fella, maybe midtwenties I'd guess just by eyeing him up. "Ral Morgan. From Birdseye, Indiana."

"Thank you Ral, and Billy, for this point of comparison." Gunn ushers them into the clearing-turned-performance stage, and then takes his place in front of our crowd. "Now, instead of showing me the strongest sorcerer, show me the strongest magic."

Ral and Billy glance at each other warily. Neither one wants to take a misstep after what we just saw go down.

"It's hard to fathom that they aren't the same thing, considering how, over centuries, our country has turned magic into a solo endeavor, into the guarded, singular work of a powerful sorcerer." Gunn takes his fedora off and wipes his forehead. "But I'm going to free you from all your preconceived notions."

As if providing incentive, Gunn folds his suit jacket back from his narrow waist. Even from here, I can see the glint of the sun reflect off a long silver pistol poking out from his holster. "Don't think of your magic as a weapon, but as a tool. Build a world together—how big, how much, up to you. But two craftsmen should be able to accomplish far more together than alone."

Both Billy and Ral cast their eyes to the grass. I don't blame them. Never in all my life do I remember Jed and Mama casting spells or attempting to perform together, and they were living under the same roof, tied by fate and family. Two strangers, standing in front of a crowd of competition, can't be feeling all that connected.

Gunn pulls his pistol out of his holster. "Shall I find two other volunteers?"

And then, like a reflex, Ral puts his hands forward, like he's pressing against an invisible door. He whispers words of power that I can't quite hear, and once again a tree begins to take root in front of us, a similar one to the one Mark had manipulated only moments before—a huge oak, with a thick, sturdy trunk erupting from the ground, writhing into strong limbs, branches dotted with robust leaves.

But then the tree begins to grow flowers. Almost tentatively at first, as if the oak isn't quite sure whether it's spring or if it's jumped the gun—a large purple orchid here, a fully bloomed rose there, a smattering of daisies. Judging by Billy's smirk and Ral's relieved laughter, I assume the mismatched flower arrangement is the work of Billy.

A slow, thick, rambling ivy begins to wrap around the trunk of the tree. A few moments later, I hear a creaking, crackling sound, like the sound of new wood being laid into the ground, and on either side of our audience, wooden, crisscrossed walls erupt out of the earth and merge together over our head as a gazebo. A sheath of the same forest-colored ivy races over its walls, and soon we're enveloped in a thick, lush, green blanket.

Before I can determine whether the ivy was sorcered by Ral or Billy, plants start to pop out of the earth around our feet—the kind of sharp-leaved, heady-smelling ones that belong in rain forests, or in dreams—and form a border around us.

And then things that don't exist, at least not yet, start appearing. Scaly, iridescent fish with wings flap over our heads, dive into the multiflowered tree. Large purple frogs with red spots croak at the base of tall grass. Laughter starts from somewhere inside the audience's folds, a warm, comfortable laughter, a few sighs. Which of these creations are Ral's? Which are Billy's?

It no longer matters; the garden's magic is now something separate, something more, than just the two of them together. It's like one of them is taking inspiration from the other, both of them pushing themselves further than they'd ever dare or think of alone. Their magic garden is now everywhere, scented, heady. And I feel a tightness, small and clenched as a fist inside me, slowly begin to loosen. . . .

"That's enough," Gunn says softly.

The two sorcerers drop their hands to their sides. The tapestry of magic that's been knitted around us is pulled apart, crumbles like dust in the wind, and spirals away. Gone. I feel a deep ache inside as it vanishes, almost like it took a part of me with it.

In front of us, Billy and Ral are panting, sweating. But there's also this glow to both of them, like something's lighting them up from within.

"If you were a customer seeking magic, which experience would you choose? Which show would keep you full but not satisfied, desperate to come back and live in it once more?" Gunn walks back over to the altar. He lifts the bottle of shine that Billy brewed a few moments before. "For the final piece of my theory brought to life, Billy, if you can please brew your shine once more."

Billy crosses to the altar, all of us hanging on every movement, as if we're still under his and Ral's spell. Billy bends down to grab another bottle, and then places his hands around the glass. The water inside the glass soon churns into something magic, red and bright—

Billy opens his eyes and places his new shine right next to his old one.

Grace and I shoot each other another look. The differences are undeniable.

Both bottles of shine are red, glistening inside the glass like liquid rubies. But Billy's final one . . . it's rosy, almost like one more lightbulb lights it up from within. It looks more alive, fuller, *richer*. No doubt it's the one I'd pick if I drank the stuff.

"That's after just one trick." Gunn addresses what everyone's thinking as we study the shines. "Imagine the changes to your shine after weeks, months, a lifetime of working together. If you were hungry for magic, for something otherworldly, which would you want?"

Gunn rounds the altar until he's directly in front of it. He leans back against it, crosses his arms across his chest, like he's about to begin another sermon. "This trial is about embracing your competition, choosing and elevating your allies so that they in turn can elevate you. It's about embracing the basest truth about magic, a truth that's taken me years of study to fully understand and accept," he says. "So see if these little demonstrations can inspire you. Team up with someone, focus on creating the strongest magic—not showcasing the strongest sorcerer."

There's a collective breath through the crowd, and then we fold into ourselves, devolve into whispers, conversations. Grace nods me forward without another word, our partnership already decided. We walk slowly across the grass together, over to Billy and Ral's old performance space, and take up residence in the far corner of the field.

The air of the clearing is loaded, changed. Gunn has shown us the game and the stakes. And while his message was partnership, the underlying one was louder: pick the right partners, or lose.

"Let's start with your strongest gift." Grace sounds as nervous as I feel.

Strongest gift. I've got no strongest gift, 'cause I came into my magic all of about a week before it ruined everything. "That's all right. Let's go with yours." I'm not sure how much longer I can stall. "You mentioned you're a whiz at amplifying sounds, right? And mining into people's minds?" Not that I would begin to know how to go about doing either of them. *What the heck am I going to do, or say, when it's my turn?*

"I think image mining's a good way to ease into connecting our magic." Grace takes a few steps back, settles three feet away from me. "Let's start with you focusing on an object. Pick anything, and then I'll—"

But I can't bury the truth anymore, and I blurt out, "Seriously, Grace, why'd you team up with me?"

She looks at me funny, glances around, like she's worried about who else might have heard. "Told you I've got my reasons."

But Gunn isn't paying any attention to us. He's busy watching two sorcerers dangle a rope above their heads with their minds and tie it into complicated knots in midair. "I—I hurt someone I cared about before I ever really grew into my magic." I drop my voice to a hum. "I don't even know what I can do. I can't promise you that I can meet you halfway, that I'm even half as strong as you are." I command myself to remember why I'm here—*I will win, I will sweat and bleed until Ruby and Ben have their corner in the world*—but I can't stop my mouth from moving. A gauntlet's been thrown down, and the words just keep rushing out. "I've accepted dying for what I need to do . . . but I've got no interest in taking someone else down with me."

Grace looks around the clearing again. A hive of debates, conversations, words of power buzzes around us as the other sorcerers settle into their exercises.

"Joan, if you're here, you deserve to be here," Grace says softly. "I told you, we Dunes, we've got the gift of forecasting.

We can see things, sense things that aren't apparent to the naked eye. And I get this real sense that you're something special."

I look up at her, silently curse myself for crying. "Please don't bullshit me."

"Joan, look around. Look where we are. What the hell is my incentive to lie?" She nods with purpose. "Come on, let's start with a simple image, all right? I'll show you by mining into your mind first. All you need to do is think of one image. Imagine it as clear and detailed as possible. Then hold it, relax, and breathe," she says. "Magic is a *skill* too, Joan. You can learn new tricks. You can practice, and get better."

I wipe my eyes with my sleeve, close them, focus. Ruby jumps into my mind almost immediately. I picture her wild blond hair, her little nose, her mouth making her silly face. . . .

"Ruby again," Grace says. "She's doing this strange thing with her mouth this time. This chomping thing."

I give a release of a laugh and open my eyes. "That's her silly face," I say, and add, "Ruby's my sister."

"I sort of figured." Grace smiles. "She's adorable. You miss her?"

"I miss her even when I'm with her."

Grace's smile becomes heavier, and she drops her gaze. "Your turn, all right? I'm going to think of an object. I want you to come searching for it inside my mind. It's easier if you close your eyes."

I shuffle-step, settle in, ready to attempt what she says.

"Everyone's got their own method," Grace whispers, "but when I mine another's mind, I picture floating over to the person on a wave, seeping into them, then flooding right around their thoughts." She gives a laugh. "And I used to think of a dam going up in my mind when I wanted to keep my family out. You can manipulate the space between us, Joan, a heck of a lot more than it seems. It just takes practice."

I concentrate, try to picture myself smaller, tiny, floating . . . like a boat in an invisible sea between us, a grain of sand in a wave.

But nothing happens.

"Just relax, be patient, Joan," Grace says. "Every sorcerer has a different way of tapping into their magic. That just works for me. Trust yourself."

So I let my mind go blank, and wait.

And then something falls over me, something tall and dark as a long shadow. It pulls me forward through a wide, charged space, like I'm walking through the pressure between two magnets. I'm led into a dark, wide, empty theater, right in front of an abandoned stage. And I realize, *somehow*, that I'm inside Grace's mind. A spotlight beams down quickly, paints a pool of light onto the center of this stage. Soon, something fuzzy and gray is birthed inside the spotlight. I wait for the image to grow bolder, crisper, fully emerge—

A toy train. Down to every last detail inside Grace's mind— the little blue caboose, tiny black wheels, detailed etchings of RAILROAD CO. along the side of it.

But then the train begins to move. It chugs slowly around the circle of light, bending and flexing at the connections between the toy cars—and chugs right into a small hand. The rest of the body connected to the hand comes into form slowly, carefully, like Grace is sketching it and I'm watching over her shoulder.

Ruby. Like some silent movie playing inside Grace's head, Ruby takes the train, smiles delightedly, and then bends down to run it in a circle around herself on the floor of Grace's mind.

I gasp, tears coming to my eyes, and the mental connection between us pinches out. I open my eyes to find Grace smiling at me.

"I've never experienced anything like that."

"Me neither. Maybe Gunn's onto something," she says. "I've never been able to imagine something like Ruby from virtually nothing. You want to try again?"

And I do. Instead of feeling stretched, exhausted, I weirdly feel invigorated. "We'll start inside your mind this time."

So after a quick break, we run through five more image volleys, finding the image in the mind of the first sorcerer and then building on it in the mind of the second, like we're creating a mental bridge, image by image, connection by connection. I'm slow to start, but by the third round, I feel comfortable walking inside Grace's theater, knowing where to find her stage. And before I know what hit me, Gunn's calling out to the crowd, "Supper time!"

"Thank God, I'm starving." Grace stretches her arms over her head. "Come on, it's been a long day."

But I'm not ready to stop. It's like someone's cracked open a long-locked door, given me a glimpse of a room that glitters inside, started a ticking clock for proving myself worthy of entering. "It's all right, you go on, I'll catch up."

"You serious?" She studies me. "Joan, you've got to give yourself a break."

"So I'll break when I deserve one." When Grace just looks at me doubtfully, I say, "I'm fine, honest. I'm not even hungry. Trust me, I just need a little more time."

"All right," Grace says. "But don't burn yourself out on the first day."

She filters out of the clearing with the rest of the crowd, past Gunn and Dawson and back into the woods. But before the gangsters turn to go, Gunn spots me, alone in the corner. He approaches, no sound but his loafers tramping over the grass. "Supper time, Joan," he reminds me.

I take a deep breath. "I thought I'd spend a little bit more time practicing alone, sir, if that's all right."

He stops in front of me. "Did my teamwork demonstration not register?"

"It did," I say slowly, remembering that this man stole two lives here in the clearing this morning. But I'm not ready to stop sorcering. I need every minute I can get. I need to become stronger, *better*. So I carefully give his words back to him. "But a team's only as strong as its weakest player."

Gunn studies me for a long time, a smile in his eyes that never quite touches his lips. "Very well."

He walks out of the clearing, and I turn back inside myself, hungry to try another trick, one that I spotted some of the Carolina Boys attempting earlier. I focus on my hand, on willing it warm, and imagine my palm heating, igniting. I close my eyes and whisper, *"Spark and fire."*

It takes a second, and then another, but then I feel a sharp, stinging burn, like a snapped match against my palm. I gasp. And there, jumping and throbbing against my palm, like a captured frog from a lake, is a small sphere of orange fire.

NEW ALLIANCES

ALEX

I've been at Lorton Reformatory for three weeks, two days, and four hours of my six-week sentence for "attempting to sell magic contraband," booked under the guise of running some of Danfrey Pharma Corp.'s remedial magic inventory around town. I'd swear it's been three years, but that's impossible, because I've been keeping track of everything. Twenty-two breakfasts staring at rows of inmates in sad gray jumpsuits hunched over metal trays. Twenty-two long mornings of making clay batter and shaping bricks in Lorton's brick-making unit. Forty-four hours toiling around in the crisp fall air in the quad, waiting for someone to offer a smoke or a handshake.

But no one does. Because I'm an island here. An island in a foreign, treacherous sea. A sea I'm constantly treading, because if I relax for a second, I might find myself with my face to the floor. It's minimum security, mind you—no one in here's doing hard time for hard crime—but that somehow makes it worse. As if everyone's out to prove to the underworld that they're on their way to bigger, badder things.

Despite how much I despise these thugs, I need to transform myself into one of them. Like Frain said, I need to embrace my story—become my father's legacy. Walk inside his underworld, turn it upside down, and destroy it.

Unfortunately, I haven't gotten the chance. The cell mate that Agent Frain arranged for me to bunk with—my supposed "door" to the Shaw Gang—hasn't looked at me twice since I was booked into his room, and he sure as hell hasn't addressed me. Guy's name is Howard Matthews, *Howie*, a second-generation Irishman prone to tall tales and grandiose ideas, one of those self-important greaser types who thinks he'd be running the Shaws already if people would just sit up and start paying attention. He's uncomfortable to look at, and in an eight-foot-by-eight-foot cell, it's impossible to look at anything else: matted hair that grows past his ears, wide eyes, a lean, jittery torso that looks like it thrives on sorcerer's shine but has been denied it for weeks. In short, someone *I* wouldn't look at twice, if the Feds weren't holding me over a barrel to do it.

Day in, day out, I hear Howie at mealtimes, holding court around the small-time Shaw men who have been busted for petty crimes and burglaries, telling different versions of the same stories about his adventures running with his bigwig cousin Win Matthews, some hard-boiled Shaw underboss, from what I can gather. Howie knows who I am, I'm sure of it, as the prison guard who brought me in made a big show of introducing us, I guess hoping that the inherent tension between Richard Danfrey's son and an up-and-coming Shaw might result in some future entertainment. But Howie didn't bite.

"You in here for running too?" I finally attempted conversation several nights ago from my bottom bunk, when the darkness and the silence between us grew so heavy, I started to feel like I was getting crushed underneath it.

Just more silence.

"You're a Shaw boy, right? Smuggling for Boss McEvoy?"

No answer from Howie but breathing.

"How long you in here for, chap—"

"What's that buzzing sound?"

My heart started hammering—*nervously? hopefully?*—at the sound of his voice. "*Buzzing* sound?"

"That right there, a buzzing, like a fly," he said.

"Sorry, chap, are you—"

"God, there it is again," he said to himself, apparently. "Sounds tinier than a fly, actually. Pesty, like a flea. *Bzzz. Bzzz. Bzzz.*"

Then it was my turn to be silent.

"Much better," Howie mock-whispered to himself. "'Cause if that flea starts flitting around again, I'll have no choice but to swat it."

That was nearly a week ago, and I haven't said another word to Howie since. Now it's back to hard eyes and sideways looks between us, awkward dances around each other for the toilet, a forced, silent fox-trot as we climb past each other into our cots.

The dull fear that's always festering inside me is starting to grow into genuine panic, gnaw at me from breakfast until bed. I'm more than halfway through my sentence with nothing to show for it: if I can't get in with Howie by the time I leave, I come out on paper as a small-time magic runner with a record. The Prohibition Unit has officially discharged me since my "arrest," and Frain's threats are always echoing in my ears.

There is no safety net in this situation.

So I need to win this Howie over soon.

I'm debating the "how" during lunchtime, the meal a variation of the one from yesterday and the day before that, a plate of potatoes, Broadway-bright carrots, and a dark, unidentifiable meat. So I look around the room, debating, watching, listening. We've separated ourselves in the long, windowless mess hall like students in a high school cafeteria: the D Street Outfit and Italian small-timers keep to the front left. There're the Mexicans and the blacks near the windows, and on the right—the first few tables nearest to the kitchen—the junior Shaws and their Irish hangers-on. Then there's a wide sea of unprotected men, who bob along like fools tossed overboard who didn't think to buy a life raft.

This is my territory. I've eaten alone every day since I got here.

I run through my options as I sit, stirring my mushy carrots. Sorcering a trick for Howie—a rabbit out of my ass with no context—seems almost juvenile, forced. Like I talked about with Agent Frain when he drove me down to the station a few weeks back, for as moronic as Howie might read on paper, he's got street smarts. And a guy showing up in his cell, trying to wow him with magic when Boss McEvoy just lost his right-hand sorcerer? Too convenient.

But provoking a fight with him, showing him I've got balls, that I'm not afraid of a rumble? That could backfire.

A voice interrupts my thoughts with, "Seat taken?"

Across from me, perched over the opposite side of the table, stands a large man in his forties. He's got a tough face that's seen far too many long days, and a head of hair that's thick and thinning in all the wrong places. I've seen him hanging on the bleachers in the prison quad with the D Street Outfit crowd: the gang that used my father up and sold him down the river. I don't recognize this goon from my days of working with my father, but it doesn't matter. My hatred for D Street doesn't discriminate.

The guy doesn't wait for my answer, just lifts one of his legs over the bench and settles in across from me. "Ronny Justi." There's no handshake with the introduction. "Don't worry, we already found out who you are."

His use of "we" prompts a thick, hard lump to form at the top of my throat. I'm not surprised D Street put two and two together, obviously—it was only a matter of time before one of those goons got wind of who I am, and what I supposedly did to land myself in here.

I just thought I'd be under the Shaws' protection by the time they put it together.

"You're Richard Danfrey's son." Ronny leans over the table, mock-whispering, like we're just a couple of chums sharing a secret. "A bunch of us heard the guards talking about you in the yard this morning. Didn't know we had a celebrity among us commoners."

I turn back to my iridescent carrots and start picking at them.

"What, cat got your tongue?"

I steady my voice. "Just not in the mood for conversation."

"Loner type, eh? I can respect that." Ronny leans in closer. "But it's a funny thing I heard those guards talking about, turns out. Some of them were saying you were in here for running magic contraband." He keeps up with his mocking tone, that dance between chummy and threatening. "But I thought, that can't be right. Because any son of Richard Danfrey would be smart enough to check in with his daddy's D Street keepers before distributing any inventory around."

Daddy's D Street keepers. As if my father was just a D Street pet, or a joke. And the worst part, the part that bugs me more than anything else, is that at the end of the day, this thug's right.

But I don't want to show Ronny that he's getting to me, so I don't even look at the bastard. I keep my eyes on my lunch, imagine becoming bigger, stronger, like I'm transforming myself into steel and nightmares, something Ronny can't touch.

"Fact, we've been over there talking about you since this morning, friend," Ronny adds. "A big debate on what we should do with you."

The mess hall has gotten a little quieter, as we're right in the middle of the room, like a goddamned circus stage. So without having to look, I can bet that Howie's table is listening. I can practically feel the Shaws' eyes on me.

But maybe that's not a bad thing—Christ, maybe *this* is the chance I've been waiting for, to show Howie where my allegiance lies, and where it doesn't. It's a risk, a huge risk, antagonizing this D Street gangster in the hopes of catching the eyes of the Shaws—but I'm running out of time, and out of options.

So I force myself into the deep, dark water, and plunge in. "'Keepers' is sort of a misnomer, isn't it?" I say slowly, finally meeting Ronny's eyes. "Because 'keepers' implies that someone's watching out for you, and taking care of you. And your D Street operation let my father get sold out to the Feds. He's in for three decades, *friend*, maybe more. So 'keepers'? That's a joke."

At this, Ronny gives a spit of a laugh. Then he raises his hands a bit—a begrudging concession. "You know what? Boss Colletto might agree with you. Hell, *I* agree with you. Our entire outfit had Loretto and Mongi's numbers for what they did—caving to the Feds, selling a prime asset like your father down the river to save themselves a couple years in jail. It was wrong. Boss Colletto wanted to make things right. *Lots* of folks wanted to make things right. Trust me," he says flatly, "things have been righted."

I don't give this thug any kind of nod or indication that I agree. I'm sure Loretto and Mongi, the two goons who rattled off my father's laundry list of crimes to the Feds this past spring when they were caught with fifty gallons of remedial spells marked DANFREY PHARMA CORP. in the back of their Model T—I'm sure they're riddled with holes right now. Stuffed into some Dumpster or floating at the bottom of the Potomac for thinking of their own skins over the future of D Street. But that doesn't do anything for me. That doesn't give my family our lives back, doesn't erase the year of pressure and threats that Colletto wielded over my father. And so even though my heart's so wound up on fear it might spring out of my chest, there's something else ticking inside me too. Relief. Maybe even excitement. Because this is a moment I've actually dreamed about—a chance to tell Colletto's gang how much I despise them. Regardless of what's for the Feds, this moment—this is also for *me*.

Ronny gives a big, put-on sigh and looks back to his table of D Street cronies in the corner. "Look, I understand your . . . hesitation to make amends, Baby Danfrey." He shifts in his seat. "But it's time to let bygones be bygones. You understand? You let the past go." He drops his voice, I assume so the guards can't hear. "You work for us until your father's debts are paid."

I stare at Ronny for a long while, way too long. It's definitely more uncomfortable for me than for him, but I make myself do it. "I'm not ready for that."

The corners of Ronny's mouth start twitching. "I urge you to rethink that, 'cause your father had an arrangement with Boss Colletto. And that final shipment of spells he owed us? That was paid for in advance, check signed, sealed, and delivered. So as far as we see it, anything you're trying to sell on your own in DC should fall back to us. And any way you slice it, you running magic is something Boss Colletto needs to know about. We own you, till you make it right."

"No."

Ronny grabs my hand across the table, ending my meal. His face has started to flush, and there's a thin coat of perspiration seeping from his patchwork hairline to his brow. "Excuse me, did I just hear a *no*? This isn't a negotiation."

I force myself to look him in the eye again. "You're right"—I wedge the words past the lump in my throat—"we're done here. I'm finished with your guinea operation."

Ronny tightens his grip around my wrist, twists his neck a bit, and slowly leans forward. "What did you just call me?"

I've gotten into tons of fights before, but nothing like this.

I'm trying to push a gangster past the brink. A gangster from a gang that kept my father drenched in sweat and nightmares. A gangster almost double my size. *Howie better be watching.*

"You heard me." I focus on keeping my voice steady and my lunch in my stomach. I pop an overcooked carrot in my mouth and push it to the side with my tongue. Then I add with a bite, "Guinea."

An odd, thick vein in Ronny's forehead starts pulsing, and his face begins to redden. He's big, but he's fast—he lets go of my wrist and grabs my tray with both hands in one jerky motion, then throws it right in my face. The dull metal edge knocks me in the chin, and the last of my potatoes hits my forehead with a thick, wet *thwap.*

I don't let myself pause to wipe my eyes.

I spring out of my seat like a jack-in-the-box, lunge for Ronnie, and grab his collar. Then I send his head crashing onto the table.

The mess hall goes wild, and the D Street boys in the corner shove away from their benches and start running toward my table to aid their man, shouting, fists up and ready. I can feel their advance, I can see them out of the corner of my eye—and if Howie and his dirty Shaw men don't decide to hop and come to my rescue, I'm going to get pulled apart.

A lukewarm shout of a warning comes from one of the prison guards in the corner. "All right, settle. Settle!"

But none of the guards have moved, and the D Street boys keep coming for me, a tidal wave in the distance approaching like a slow, steady roll.

Ronny lurches and thrashes against my grip, his hands snaking and jerking over his head, blindly trying to grab me and pull me off. I tighten my hold, pull him across the table, and throw him onto the floor at my feet.

For a second, my desire to use magic burns like an itch. I could conjure a spell quicker than this thug could blink, could try to teleport a tray right into his skull. Better yet, conjure a force field around me and slip out of the mess hall. But I can't risk it. If a guard catches me sorcering a single trick, it would double my sentence.

Besides, I don't want the help of tricks.

I want it to be my bare hands that rip this guy apart.

I sit on top of Ronny's chest, tuck my legs under me as I straddle his stomach. And then I just start pummeling him. I bring my fist down, hard, against his cheek. He keeps reaching for me with both hands, but I've got the advantage of pinning him down, so I take another jab, then another, to his jaw. Blood starts gushing from his nose, and he's stammering, playing defense with wild arms and loose fists.

But before I can take another blow, I'm lifted off him in one fell swoop and thrown headfirst into the table. I hit the ground with a thud, my lungs slapping against the hard tile of the mess hall. I roll over, but all I see are legs towering over me, a shadow splayed across my features. I close my eyes out of instinct, raise my hands to block my face—

But then the shadow's gone. I scramble to the table's bench a few feet away to steal a breath. *Who had my back?* I grip the edge of the bench, steadying myself, and stand.

And then I'm face-to-face with my cell mate, Howie Matthews.

His hands are up like a boxer's, his brow stitched, and his mouth open mid war cry, and for a second I wonder if I've somehow managed to get double-teamed—that I have *both* D Street and the Shaws after me—but then Howie turns around and starts pummeling some dark-haired greaser behind him.

The fight has ballooned, at least ten, maybe twenty, men sparring and swatting at one another, the D Street boys who flew to Ronny's side, and yes, yes, *yes*, the Shaws to mine. I take quick stock of the scene, at the smattering of brawls—two young guns locked together like wrestlers on the ground. A sinewy older man whaling on some lanky teenager. A fistfight at the nearby table.

The place is chaos.

"Goddamn it, you half-wits!" a prison guard shouts above the noise. He smacks my table with his baton, and a deep boom clangs through the mess hall. "ENOUGH!"

Everyone stops moving and turns to look at him. Everyone, except for Ronny. Ronny crawls off the floor slowly and stands. And then like a wounded dog that won't stay down, he lunges for me. I duck out of the way, as the guard steps in and shoves his baton into the thick of Ronny's stomach. Three other guards approach from my left side, guns and batons out. They surround our table, pistols drawn and pointed into the crowd.

And then you can't hear anything but deep breathing and the clanking of spoons from the mess hall workers in the nearby kitchen.

We're all filed back into our rooms, doors locked behind us, outdoor privileges forfeited for the day. I know I just painted a mark on my back for D Street's target practice, but I also know that it was worth it.

Because that night, for the first time, Howie speaks to me. He waits until we've both washed up and are in our separate cots.

"That was a hothead move, Danfrey," he says from the top bunk, "taking on that D Street prick solo."

My heart starts beating overtime. *He's talking to me. I did it. It begins.* I study the bottom of his bunk, trying to figure out the best way to play this, to use his comment as a wedge to prop open the door.

"Maybe," I say as coolly as possible. *Bring it home, win him over.* "But that thug was making claims he had no right to make. I don't owe D Street anything."

I hear Howie's bed squeak above me. "Well, that's a damn wop for you. Invite him over for dinner, he'll try to screw your wife, then have the balls to stay for breakfast."

I laugh, the laughter coming easy, a bubble of relief. "Isn't that the truth?"

It's a while before Howie speaks again. "So you really severed all ties with the D Street Outfit? 'Cause I might've thought, like father like son, even after those lowlifes sold him out to the Feds—"

"I don't care if it was a couple of no-names or Boss Colletto himself who gave up my father," I interrupt, my excitement getting the better of me. I regroup, add more quietly, "It happened under Colletto's watch, so as far as I'm concerned, it's Colletto's wrong. I'd never work for him. D Street's a big fat hole on my map."

Howie laughs—the kind of long, deep laugh I've heard him belt out in the mess hall when he's around friends. And I take it as a good sign. Not a sign to let my guard down, but a sign that things are moving in the right direction. "Hell, I understand. When someone wrongs me, I never get over it."

"Some two-bit fogey who plays lapdog to Colletto tells me that I owe them a cut of what I run?" I add. "If I had my way, each and every D Street wop would be dead."

Then there's silence for a long while. But I can hear Howie breathing.

In a panic, I wonder if I've blown my chance—I actually meant what I said, but it sounded almost pompous, and way too hard. Maybe I've laid it on too thick, and the door to the Shaws is closing just as soon as I've managed to prop it open.

But then Howie whispers, "I think certain people would like to hear that, Danfrey. Powerful people. People who could get your back like I did, and more, if you'd be open to it when we get out of here." I hear him shift again above me. "Boss McEvoy, my cousin, and the other Shaw underbosses—they've been sworn enemies of the D Street Outfit for years, since Colletto took out McEvoy's cousin, Danny the Gun. You knew that, right?"

"Not sure my father ever mentioned the bad blood," I say carefully, "and these days, I'm working alone."

"Well, you ever hear the phrase, 'If two people have the same enemies, they should team up'?"

I think Howie's going for "the enemy of my enemy is my friend," but clearly, now's not the time to correct him. "I take the point; it's wise advice."

He clucks above me on his cot. "'Course, the only guy I've got a real *in* with is my cousin, Win—but he's high up, helps run McEvoy's smuggling operation. Besides, Win promised me. He said if I took the fall on our last run, denied how I got the dust shipment in from the coast—and let the big boys walk—he'd hook me up when I get out."

Then Howie goes silent again. And I can sense it: he's waiting for something. Maybe for me to meet him halfway—some sign that I'm interested, that I need him, just like I did in the mess hall.

"You think they might be looking for other young guns on the smuggling side of things?" I say, trying to keep my voice non-committal.

"Depends." Howie looks down at me from his top bunk. There's a bit of a glimmer in his eye. "You got any other assets, other than being a hothead?"

I give him a smile, an honest one. This feels like the right time. We're alone in our cell, no guards on rotation, and they've already done their nightly room-to-room check. Besides, I'm surprised that I'm near electric over the idea of showing my magic to this chump.

Because this time the magic's for a reason.

A good reason.

Bringing all these gangsters down.

I turn away from Howie and focus on our cell door. I home in on the steel slats of the jail cell wall—twelve bars, each a few inches apart. Then I focus on the world behind those bars, the empty hallway, the flickering ceiling lamps that hang down above it, the row of other prison cells on the opposite side of the corridor.

I mumble the words of power, *"Replicate, protect,"* and in seconds, there appears a carbon copy of the jailhouse scene I've been staring at, right in front of the real one, an exact two-dimensional replica posing as a facade. My attention to detail is perfect, my father always boasted, so Howie probably doesn't even realize I've created this manipulation. In fact, the only way he'd be able to tell is if he got up and walked into it.

But I'm attempting something even trickier. A stacked trick—a trick layered on top of another trick. I return my focus to my manipulation, the jailhouse scene replica, and I imagine erasing the bars. *"One by one, erase."* And then, the bars of the cell disappear, flicker and fade one after another, like they're long beams of light turning off.

"What the hell," Howie whispers above me. "Wait, can we"—I hear his gulp from here—"can we actually get out?"

"Afraid not, my friend." I don't want Howie's wheels turning over whether I can try to unlock door after door, defeat dozens of guards, only to stage an escape from a place I've worked hard to get *in*—so I release my manipulation. The fabricated scene I've just conjured dissipates like dust in the wind, and then we're both staring at our locked cell door again. "But I've found these types of manipulations come in handy too, from time to time."

Howie matches my whisper. "So . . . you can sorcer, just like

your old man?" His tone is breathless, childlike even, like everyone else when confronted with magic.

"A little bit." I downplay it. "I've got a couple of tricks."

Howie shifts in his bed above me. "God, I've always loved
magic. My mother was a sorcerer too. I know how rare the magic
touch is and everything, but I'd always hoped that she'd give me
the gene."

"You're right, it is rare," I say softly. "Odds are over one in a
thousand. And I read somewhere that there's no rhyme or reason
to who inherits the magic touch." I didn't read this—I actually
heard it, in my Sorcering Basics class at the Unit. Firstborn, last-
born, second cousin—it's a crapshoot—all we know is that sorcery *is* genetic, and that about three times as many males as
females get the recessive trait.

"I heard that too," Howie says with a sad laugh. "Guess I've
got to settle for being ordinary."

"What you did for me in the cafeteria back there? It definitely wasn't ordinary."

There's a long, long pause. Finally Howie says, in a different
voice, "I've had to fight with my fists for everything, Danfrey."

His answer warms me, encourages me. Maybe I might actually be cut out for this line of work. Hell, maybe I'll survive
undercover. Because all the little things I can't help but read
into: all of people's tiny gestures and comments, their looks,
their sideways glances? Now I've got a reason to put them to
use. And it's beyond obvious to me what Howie wants right now.
What he always wants, I've gathered, from listening to him in
the cafeteria.

"It shows, Howie," I say softly. "You're quite the fighter."

He laughs, full and warm, and it bubbles over his cot. "Well,
you ain't so bad yourself, Danfrey. That POS was almost twice
your size." He waits another minute before he whispers, "You
know, Boss McEvoy could probably use a young street sorcerer

somewhere in his outfit. Especially a guy like you—guys like me and you. Scrappy guys willing to put their time in, and work their way up the ladder," he says. "I'm hell-bent on doing it. One day, I swear, I'm going to be sitting at McEvoy's table."

Howie leans over the edge of his bed once more, steals a peek at me, like he's making sure that I'm still down here. "And I'm just saying, we didn't make a bad team back there."

"You're right." I smile up at him. "We didn't."

"And there could be an opportunity for you—for both of us, if you want to team up on the outside, too," Howie says. "It's something to consider."

I don't want to seem too eager. But my heart is pounding, practically beating out of my chest. I nod at his upside-down face and his greasy hair hanging straight from his head like a patch of wet weeds, and I give him my most confident Alex Danfrey smile. "Then I'll consider it."

Howie rolls back onto his cot. "Good." He gives one of those long laughs again. "Christ, you're an animal, Danfrey. I mean really, who knew? Damn near got yourself killed by that half-brained guinea."

His laughter dissolves into a chuckle, and I chuckle along with him. Because I know I've just received the highest form of compliment from this lowlife.

And I also know that I'm on my way in.

BRICK BY BRICK

JOAN

The four of us are nestled deep into the woods, away from the clearing, like many days these past few weeks. Grace and I stand farther into the forest, fifteen feet apart from each other, with our other allies Ral and Billy situated closer to the clearing, fifteen feet away from us, and from each other. The four of us form a perfect square. We're in the middle of running a series of magic immersions in what Ral calls our "sanctuary"—a boxed space in the forest enclosed by a sorcered protection wall on each side of our square. Each protection wall works like a mirror, reflects back the dense, tangled wood, so that someone approaching our sanctuary would assume there was nothing but forest ahead. We use the space to try out new magic, perfect old tricks, and hide the little bumps and setbacks we don't want the other sorcerers or Gunn to see.

"I want to work on our performance transitions," Ral says. "Let's run through the seasons."

Billy groans. "My God, I can't do the seasons again."

"Our timing's off, you know it, and Grace says the end's coming soon."

"I said I got a *sense* this whole trial of Gunn's is ending soon," Grace corrects Ral. "Gunn's still tougher to read than a German paper."

"That's why we should be working through new tricks, bigger and better manipulations," Billy presses. "*That's* what Gunn wants to see."

"No, I think Ral's right," I pipe up softly, across the sanctuary. "Our transitions should be flawless. The group performance has always been what it's about for Gunn."

Billy grumbles, "Fine, whatever. Just know that I can make it snow in my sleep."

Ral shoots me a quick smile, then settles into his grassy corner. He whispers his words of power, raises his hands, and a collection of thin trees erupt out of the ground in the center of our performance sanctuary. The spindly trunks sprout into a mass of branches, then a kaleidoscope of fierce orange, deep red, and yellow leaves. Just as quick, the trees begin to kiss the leaves good-bye, sending them on a slow dance to the ground.

I'm not exactly sure when Ral passes the reins of the manipulation to Billy, but the pass-off is without a stutter. Ral's autumn trees begin to grow darker, brittle, shrink under the touch of a light, soft, falling snow. The dusky gold sky of our sanctuary hollows into a crisp, clear white, as the piles of leaves around the tree's roots wrinkle and blacken into dark corpses, and soon become buried by the thick-lying snow.

Grace steps in, and with a few whispers, she softens the sky into a light blue, rises a magic-made sun over the trees, and Billy's snow begins to melt. Green vines twist slowly out of the ground, extend their full length, and burst into bright tulip flowers.

My turn. I whisper, "*Glisten,*" as I focus on the sky over our sanctuary, watch it deepen into a piercing, brilliant shade of blue. "*Fly and sing,*" and the chirp of birds fills the space with the sweet tune of June. And then, just because I've been practicing tactile manipulations the past few evenings, I infuse a honey-scented, heavy moisture into the air. I feel it press against my skin like a warm cloth.

"Wow, Joan," Ral says.

I break my attention to find all three of my teammates staring at me. "All right?" I say hesitantly.

"Better than all right," Grace answers quietly.

But that's all. We move on. Because this isn't about any one of us, it's about all of us. Because there isn't any time to stop for praise.

Ral pinches out our manipulation, and the trees, flowers, and birds all crumble, whirl into a fine dust, and fade into nothing. Then he conjures a stone altar—identical to the one back in the clearing—that rumbles up from the ground. We file around it, two on each side, as Ral passes each of us a bottle of water from the crate we brought out to the sanctuary. "Begin," he whispers.

We've brewed sorcerer's shine every evening since we've teamed up, but each time I touch my bottle, images of Mama's final night threaten to cripple me—her remains swirling into dust, me slicing my arm open in a desperate attempt to perform a blood-spell and banish my magic. So every time I brew, I have to close my eyes and just surrender to my magic, the magic that's always hungry to make something, do something, *be* something more. Heat surges through my fingertips, and a strange cross between adrenaline and euphoria floods through my veins, rushes to where my skin touches the glass. Sure enough, the water inside starts sizzling, churning, before it relaxes under my grasp. Then, only then, do I release my bottle and take a look around.

Four bottles of shine now rest on the top of the stone altar. If you mixed them up or drank them, you wouldn't be able to tell one from the other. Rosy, glowing, sparkling, powerful. I've got no idea what the other sorcerers outside of our foursome are brewing, but they've got to be killing it to match what we're putting out.

"God, I could use a hit of this," Billy mumbles. "Been a long day." He touches the top of his own bottle. "Hell, every day here is a long, backbreaking day."

Without a word, Ral reaches over the altar, grabs Billy's bottle, and dumps its contents onto the ground.

"Hey, what the hell!" Billy protests. His shine hits a patch of grass at my feet, corrodes the earth into a shallow hole, and dries with a thin sheet of sparkling dust.

"We never drink it," Ral says solemnly.

"I *know* that, I was just messing around."

"Really?" Ral sizes Billy up. "I've caught you eyeing Stock, Rose, and Tommy at the warehouse these past couple nights, when they're riding their own shine-highs, looking all wistful."

Billy averts his gaze. "I'm just taking notes on the competition."

"I'm serious, Billy. We can't afford to get weak, not now."

"I'm tired is all, okay?" None of us can protest or argue with that. He adds with a huff, "Christ, Ral, you're like my mother."

We dump the remainder of our shine into the grass, release our four-sided sanctuary, and trek back through the thick woods to the clearing. We've practiced every day as a foursome, sometimes in the clearing, and sometimes out here in the woods, since the day after I first arrived. Grace had a strong sense that she and I would work well with Ral and Billy, after Gunn forced the pair to demonstrate their magic for the rest of us. Grace pegged them as hardworking, open, prone to collaborate—and as usual, she was right. She approached them that night at dinner, while I hung back in the clearing, trying to tease my magic into something more, and offered them an alliance. I think to both Grace's and my surprise, Ral and Billy accepted.

And we work pretty darn well together. We've found our rhythm. Ral's the closest thing we've got to a ringleader, which is a natural fit for his big-picture magic, and his role as family man back home. And for as brutish and one-way as Billy can be as a human being, he's a sensitive sorcerer, who keeps our magic stitched together when Ral's grand ideas have a couple holes in them. Grace, a master amplifier, is of course our details specialist, embellishes our magic and ensures that our manipulations sing. She also has a habit of keeping mental tabs on us, making sure we all feel heard and respected.

And me? Somehow I've become a strong jack-of-all-trades. The fact that I practice every minute I can—every chance I get to forgo sleeping and eating to make sure I'm as strong as I need to be, for Ben and Ruby, for whatever Gunn has in store—well, that sure as heck helps.

We've become a well-oiled machine, a quartet of sorcerers whose magic is more than the sum of its parts. Just like Gunn said.

We cross into the clearing, where the other two factions of sorcerers are also winding up for the day. We're down to eleven sorcerers. Besides losing Mark and Peter during Gunn's demonstration our first day in the clearing, we lost a young guy named Carson Jameson from Tennessee a couple weeks back, a loner type, to an ambitious vanishing-reappearance trick gone wrong (flying swords that disappeared and then reappeared in unfortunate places). The other, one of Gavin's Carolina Boys crowd, perished soon after. I didn't see the trick, but Grace said that Gavin forced his team to try a time-space manipulation of the clearing, some kind of elaborate "folding" of the field in half, so that taking a step forward on one end would promptly put you on the other side. But the trick combusted, and one of their members became forever lost in the fold.

Eleven sorcerers, to become seven. Our foursome, the four Carolina Boys, and Stock's trio, which consists of him and the strange brother-sister-questionable-lovers pair, Tommy and Rose Briggs. We've been like this since Carson died—three islands of sorcerers, with no bridges between us, and Gunn never giving any indication of which seven he wants to see win. The choice, apparently, is up to us, and we're at a standstill. There's an inherent distrust between Stock and me, and Gavin has a beef with partnering with women.

Grace, Billy, and Ral now plow hungrily into the clearing. Out of habit, I lag behind.

Ral sees me hesitate. "Joan, you don't need to do that anymore. You're running yourself ragged with the extra practice."

"Grace'll sneak me dinner after, she always does. Trust me, I need to keep up, stay on top of my game."

"Keep up?" Billy gives a sharp heckle. "Kendrick, I'd bet at this point, you might well be stronger than all of us put together."

"I still don't have Ral's self-sustaining magic down. Like how he creates a tree manipulation with enough magic to bloom on its own," I say to deflect the compliment, but I don't meet Billy's eye. Because I'm not telling him the truth: that practicing magic has become something of a compulsion, a superstition. That if I keep putting in my time, learn and master as much as I can, I earn the right to stay here. I earn the right to win.

"Forget the trees. Billy's right, Joan. You're the last person I'm worried about," Ral says, as Dawson shouts over the clearing, *"Supper time!"*

Stock, Tommy, and Rose, followed by the Carolina Boys, trek like hungry lumberjacks into the woods for supper near the warehouse. Our crowd moves to follow, but Ral extends his arm, holding us back. "But I *am* worried about fleshing out our ranks to seven . . . before someone else does it first. We need to figure it out, and soon."

Before any of us can answer him, we spot Gunn and Dawson watching us from the border of the forest, and we fall to a hush. Gunn signals for Dawson to go back to the truck without him, and then he crosses the clearing toward us.

"Damn it," Billy whispers. "Can't stand being close to Gunn."

Ral scolds, "Quiet, Billy."

"You all have a good day out in the woods?" Gunn says curtly, his shiny brown loafers crunching over the grass. "I didn't see you out there."

We all shift uncomfortably, until Ral answers, "That magic enclosure was my idea, sir. I hope it wasn't in poor form. We were practicing a dangerous trick, a new magic. Didn't want to risk putting anyone else in jeopardy."

Gunn smirks. "How thoughtful." Then he adds, "And a truly impressive manipulation."

Despite how Gunn keeps all of us tight, tense, and small, I feel a distinct surge of pride at his compliment. I'd bet money that the rest of my team does too.

Gunn looks at me suddenly. "And are you gracing us with your presence tonight, Ms. Kendrick? Or are you spending another night out here alone?"

I feel four pairs of eyes on me. This is the most attention Gunn's given any one sorcerer, at least since he forced Billy to be a part of his "work-together" demonstration that first day in the clearing.

"I was going to practice, sir," I say slowly. "If it's all right with you, of course."

Gunn looks at me intensely, curiously, like he's sizing up a car, trying to figure out its make, its model. "Come to dinner, Joan," he says. And then he walks away.

As soon as Gunn turns into the trees, Billy says, "Looks like someone's been noticing where you go, Kendrick."

I shrug him off, though I'm surprised too. Most times, I get the distinct feeling that we're all still interchangeable to Gunn. "He keeps tabs on all of us."

Billy stands tall and rigid, leans in with an exaggerated glare. "But he wants you to *come to dinner, Joan*," he fake-barks, in

Gunn's flat, even cadence. "Not sure any of us have ever gotten such a warm invitation."

Grace and Ral laugh as I give Billy a little punch to the arm.

I walk lockstep with them through the clearing and try to relax, to block out everything else and just enjoy the night off with my team.

After supper, we head back to the warehouse. There's no electricity, so once the sun goes down, our only lights are cigarette butts shared around the room. It looks like a field of fireflies, glowing embers blinking and burning through the wide, long space. Our days are long, *hard*, so soon after supper, most of us hit the sack, then rise along with the sun glaring through the tall warehouse windows.

But some nights, like tonight, there's a restlessness in the air—a collective charge of electricity, magic—and folks'll stay up chatting, scheming in corners, some of the shine drinkers even brewing a quick batch of sorcerer's shine with a water jug they smuggled from dinner, in an attempt to ease themselves into sleep. Me, Grace, Billy, and Ral—we play cards with Grace's faded, dog-eared deck by the light of candles we conjure for these types of occasions. As usual, we're playing poker, the only circle of ours where magic's not allowed. Found that out the first night, otherwise you're in for a tying game of royal flushes.

"Hate to bring it back to business," Ral leans in and whispers, "but we really need to figure out our next step." He looks at Grace as they exchange three cards. "You get any better sense of when the end of Gunn's 'experiment' might be? And what's in store after?"

Grace frowns as she studies her cards. "Hardly ever near enough to Gunn to mine into his thoughts," she tells Ral, "and when I am, he's hard to breach. But from what I can gather from his thug-puppy, Dawson, Gunn will end this soon. Dawson's been thinking constantly about this shining room, the Red Den. I see a wooden door sign, this two-story space with stages, a crowd where little glasses of shine are being passed around." She looks up at us. "Dawson's got a bare-bones imagination, and the images are clear, almost pushy. I'd say any day we're looking at the finish line."

Ral shows his hand. "If you're right, Gunn will need to force the issue, *force* seven of us to team up." He shakes his head. "It can't come to that. I'm not going home to Marla and my boys empty-handed. I want to approach another team and make an alliance now."

"With who?" Billy puts two queens down with a flourish, and I toss my pair of twos into the center. "Stock's trio of shine junkies and sibling-humpers? Or those quacks from the Carolinas? I don't think there's a lesser of two evils in this situation."

Ral says, "You know there has to be."

And Ral's right, of course. We need to choose. I size up our alternatives.

Stock, Tommy, and Rose sit against the back wall of the warehouse, puffing spirals of smoke to the ceiling, deep in the middle of their own hushed conversation, that dull, grayed-out, post-shine-trip haze about them. Rose quips something into Tommy's ear. Her brother laughs, low and sultry-like, which breaks me out into all sorts of uncomfortable. But on the other side of the warehouse, the Carolina Boys are playing with fire, *literally*—each of them passing a palm-sized ball of flames around their circle of four, until one of them decides to mix things up, burst the ball, and burn the hands of the passer, like a high-stakes, sadistic game of hot potato.

Ral's comment hangs there, unaddressed, and I realize

it's been silent for a while. I look back at my team. Ral, Billy, Grace—they're all looking at *me*. "What's your vote, Joan?" Ral whispers.

And something I haven't felt in a long time rises up inside me: a sense of doing well. Of mattering. Fact, it's such a warm and wonderful feeling that I force myself not to take the memories of Mama and that night down off their shelf, like I always do whenever I feel a shade of self-satisfaction.

"We go with Stock."

"Stock," Grace repeats slowly, looking at me curiously. "The Stock who's teased and taunted you from the moment you walked in the door. The guy who's been throwing insults our way every time we rub shoulders with him."

"We don't have the luxury of holding grudges," I say. "First, look at those Carolina Boys. They're *burning* themselves. That the sort of fellas you want to be teamed up with, heading into a gangster den to perform cutting-edge magic?"

"But—"

"Two, if we try for the Carolina Boys, we still have one extra man if Gunn insists on walking away with only seven to achieve the strongest troupe," I interrupt her. "What happens once we're eight? Does Gunn pick the one who goes? Do we vote?" I look around at the trio encircling me. I don't want to leave their sides. "No, we stick together. Allying with Stock's trio lets us do that. It's the only option."

Ral waits a beat, then says quietly, "I'm with Joan."

Billy nods. "Stock's a long shot on accepting. But he's better than Gavin's crowd. As always, on the bull's-eye, Kendrick," and I smile.

Grace shakes her head. "It can't be me or Joan who asks him."

"I'll do it. I'll wait for the right time," Ral whispers, as the rest of us settle into our cots around him.

"Right time better be soon," Grace whispers back. "Telling

you, I sense Gunn's gonna bring this whole thing to an end any day."

I don't want to fall asleep on that note, but nobody's arguing with Grace's forecast. So we give her the last word and surrender to the darkness.

We never make it to the morning. Sometime in the middle of the night, I hear a banging, a tear of a noise through the dark warehouse that shakes the walls. I jump up in my cot, look around, panicked, as a few of the other sorcerers sit up, jittery, anxious gray forms in the darkness.

There's a scratching sound, like the wood barrier on the other side of the warehouse entrance is being lifted, and then the door is thrust open with a *BOOM*. Footsteps shuffle toward us. I crawl forward to Grace's cot.

"Grace," I whisper. "Wake up, I don't know what's going on—"

The pair of footsteps halts at the edge of our sea of cots.

"It's time this experiment of mine ended. My patience is wearing thin. You can consider this your wake-up call." It's Gunn's voice, though he appears as a fuzzy mirage, a floating illusion in the dark. "Everyone has five minutes. Gather your things and meet Dawson outside. You won't be coming back here."

Gunn leaves, but Dawson stays hovering over us, watching as we all shake one another awake and start scrambling for our belongings. Panic has wound around the warehouse, tense whispers, mumbled prayers.

"Can you sense what's about to happen?" I ask Grace, as I shove my loose things into my satchel.

"No more than you," she whispers.

We all grab our bags, and I reach for Grace's hand hastily. We stumble out of the door, regroup with Ral and Billy on the other side. The October night is frigid, shocking. Dawson's truck headlights shine across the empty lot, slaying the pitch-black forest like a pair of swords.

"Throw your bags in my truck," Dawson orders as the rest of the sorcerers spill outside. "You all know where the clearing is by now. Gunn's waiting for you there."

We hurry through the woods, the eleven of us tripping over unseen roots, climbing over fallen branches.

"What do you think Gunn's going to do?" Ral asks us, as we cut swiftly through the trees. "Force some kind of face-off? A performance duel?"

"Whatever it is, we're going to win it, for us, and our families back home," I tell him. I close my eyes, picture Ruby in our cabin's kitchen, sitting on the counter singing as I whip up morning eggs. I focus on her, let her be a beacon. *She will keep her home I will win I have to win—*

We emerge from the forest to find Gunn waiting in the clearing. He holds a black lantern. Three identical lanterns have been placed on the ground, arranged ten feet away from one another in a long line, cutting the clearing in half. Their dim light bathes the clearing in a hazy, otherworldly glow, makes the space feel like something not of this time, or of this world. We cross over the line and join Gunn on the right side of the field.

"I've been studying each of you for weeks," Gunn's voice breaks through the silence, "learning your strengths, your shine, your magic." The eleven of us shiver in front of him, our team in the middle, Stock's trio on our left, the four Carolina Boys huddled tightly on our right side. "I told you at the beginning of this endeavor that I was looking for something groundbreaking—a troupe of sorcerers, seven men and women held together by magic, elevated and strengthened by magic. A group that is more than the sum of its members. But I'm tired of waiting for you to overcome your hesitations and insecurities for the sake of something greater. You've left me no choice but to force the issue." Gunn motions theatrically to the wide stretch of grass on the other side of the line of lanterns. "Billy, if you will, can you please create a door?"

I feel Billy flinch beside me. "What kind of door, Mr. Gunn?"

"Any door," Gunn says curtly, "the only requirement being that you can walk through it . . . and that we can close it at the end."

Billy faces the clearing space behind the lanterns, his brow stitched in confusion. But he closes his eyes, whispers his words of power, and in the middle of the field, right behind the center lantern, a thick, white wooden door materializes against the night sky. It stands there, no walls, no support. It looks eerie, like a passageway to a nightmare. Or a gateway to hell.

"Consider the space behind that door your canvas," Gunn says as he paces in front of us. "I want the eleven of you to enter that door and use your magic to create something out of nothing in the clearing behind it. There are no rules I'm going to set for this final trial—the only limits are those you and your allies conjure, and the ones in turn that your adversaries create. I don't care what happens in that clearing, honestly, once you walk through that door. The only thing I care about is that only seven of you walk back out." He stops walking. "You decide who that is, and what makes that happen."

The clearing's so quiet you can hear crickets squeak like far-away rocking chairs. My mind is racing, trying to process what Gunn is actually demanding—*only seven walking out? What happens to the rest of us?*—but before I can think it through, Gunn says in his flat, even tone, "Begin."

And then it's like a gauntlet's been thrown down, a race to get to the door, to stake an advantage in an unknown trial, me just as hopped up with adrenaline and fear as the rest of them. Stock and Tommy barrel ahead of us, with Rose trailing behind. They reach the door first. Stock grabs the handle and pulls it open. His trio bursts through the entrance and closes the door with a snap behind them.

"Let's go!" Ral grabs my forearm with one hand and Grace's with his other. He starts to pull us forward, in an effort to get a jump on Gavin's crowd. Billy falls in beside us, but the Carolina Boys are right on our heels.

"Better move fast, little girls," their leader Gavin taunts, panting as he runs behind us. "We're coming for you."

"I don't understand. What are the rules?" Grace sputters as we stop in front of the door and Ral twists its handle open. He ushers her and me inside.

"You heard Gunn, there aren't any," Ral quips.

"Then how the hell does he determine the winners?" Billy asks.

"He doesn't. The winners are the seven who survive whatever happens in here and manage to walk back out," Ral says. "No matter what, we stick together, all right?"

I take another step forward as Ral slams Billy's conjured door behind us—

But the clearing is gone. The grass, the night sky hanging over it like a swollen lid, the shadowy trees of the forest sketched like a charcoal border around it, all gone. Instead the four of us stand at the beginning of a long hallway—white walls, white ceiling, white floor—that extends in front of us like a scroll, stretching on and on for as far as I can see.

"What the hell?" Billy whispers.

"It must be Tommy and Rose's visual manipulation, a hallway to shield them and Stock as they move farther into the clearing," Grace says.

Ral nods. "Come on, let's move. Gavin's boys were right behind us."

"Don't think they're behind us anymore." Billy points back the way we came. "The door's gone."

I turn around instinctively, and my heart starts to quicken. Sure enough, the door we entered through a moment before has disappeared, and the whitewashed hallway extends for what looks to be forever in the other direction too.

"Holy hell," Grace whispers beside me.

"Gavin's team must have pierced through this manipulation already." I approach the right wall, study the mottled white plaster that looks and feels just like the wall of my cabin bedroom back home. "I bet Gavin will try to ally with Stock's trio, just like we were planning to. It's an even seven, easier. And once they shake hands, they'll start circling in on us and trap us in here to finish us off." I will my heart to stay inside my chest. "We need to find Stock's team before Gavin gets to them."

Billy says, "And how the hell do you expect us to do that, Kendrick?"

I take a deep breath. "One step at a time." I put my hands on the plaster wall, whisper the words of power, *"Out becomes in."* A dark perimeter of a door begins to carve itself into the wall, four long slashes that merge to form a rectangle. I hover my hand over the newly conjured door's left side, and the white plaster balloons until it gives birth to a silver knob.

Grace sidesteps me and grasps the doorknob.

"Decide where we're going first," Ral orders.

"Conjure atrium." And then Grace turns the doorknob and steps through my magic-made door.

I follow right on her heels, Ral on mine, Billy behind him, as we step through my door into a huge, circular, nearly three-story-high atrium. A glass ceiling above us shows the faraway stars. The rounded walls are decorated in thickly striped white-and-pink wallpaper. Burning candelabras are mounted around the atrium's perimeter. A red marble floor runs under us like a foaming sea of blood. Ral looks at Grace curiously.

Grace shrugs. "Old habits die hard. Can't help but care about details."

"You spellbind this door?" Billy calls ahead to me, pausing before closing it.

"Yeah, with a double-sided trick, in case we need it as an exit. I can link it to another door."

"Nice." Billy shuts it with a click.

We move across Grace's atrium, our shoes squeaking on the newly conjured marble. Ral takes a few more steps ahead, pauses when we're in the center of the magic-made space. He looks up to the sky. From here, in the belly of an unfolding magic manipulation, the stars look far, far away.

"This place is too visible," Ral whispers. "Either team can surround us."

"I thought we wanted to draw them out," I say, "force them to deal with us. If we keep running, making new rooms, new hallways, we could bury ourselves in here."

"Hush," Grace says, "stop talking for a sec."

We all fall silent, and I close my eyes, try to listen with my whole being.

"There's a scratching sound, right over there," Grace whispers.

"You see anybody?" Ral whips his head around.

Grace nods to the far side of the atrium. "No, but I hear a couple voices, let me amplify." She pauses. "That wall over there, that's actually not the real atrium wall. It's a force field so they can spy on us. They're right behind it."

"Who? What are they saying?" I whisper.

"It's . . . Gavin." Grace closes her eyes. "At least one other . . . they're debating . . ." Grace's eyes fly open. "They're going to drop out the center of the atrium floor."

The marble floor below us sighs, creaks, *cracks*. . . .

A boom echoes through Grace's atrium. The marble below

our feet breaks open like the spine of a book, a deep gash racing from one point of the circular floor straight across to the other side.

"*STAIRS!*" I command as the ground begins to quake. "Come on!"

My conjured set of stairs erupts out of the floor step by step, building itself like a floating set of blocks—one slate of wood stacked, teetering, on top of the other. We climb onto the staircase and follow it as it races to the top of the atrium.

"Christ," Billy near-whimpers a few steps below me. "Don't look down."

"Where's this taking us, Joan?" Ral calls ahead to me.

I carefully wave my left hand, sweep it from the left side of the atrium across to the right, and whisper my words of power. Like a giant is stitching a ribbon around the top of a hat, a five-foot runner of carpet begins to run itself around the inside of the atrium. The floating staircase carries us up to the ledge of this new balcony. The four of us clamber onto it, bend over to collect our breath—

And that's when I see Gavin and two of his cronies approaching. They're on a bridge one of them must have conjured, a bridge that arches from what's left of the floor right up to our balcony.

"Ain't no use running," Gavin calls out to us from the bridge. "My boy James is conferring with Stock's team right now, offering our alliance as you jokers play around." He smiles as he ascends the bridge. "You admit defeat now, and you'll save us all a hell of a lot of trouble."

"Bullshit," Billy spits, as a cold fear settles over me. *So Gavin's team already got to Stock?*

"Don't believe it, if you're more comfortable with denial," Gavin says. "You're dying either way."

Gavin's threesome laughs as they advance.

Billy mumbles next to me, "If Gavin's right, I'm going to send everything I've got at him. I'm going down with one hot, brilliant trick." He pulls his hands back, like he's about to center his magic, throw a ripple through the universe—

"No." I grab his wrist. "I've got another idea."

I collapse onto the balcony's floor, quickly run my finger over the carpet in the outline of a square, and whisper, "*Trapdoor emerge.*" My finger trace deepens into the carpet, cuts a perfect square out of the floor, as a silver handle forces its way out of the carpet.

"What are you doing?" Ral says as he crouches behind me.

"Sending us back to that hallway with a linked trick. *In becomes out.*" I flip the trap open, jump feetfirst inside of it—

And end up falling through the trap, magically, instantly passing through the door I'd made in the whitewashed hallway we first stepped into from the clearing. The hallway with no beginning, and no end.

"Shut the door before Gavin gets to it!" Ral orders, as the rest of my team tumbles through the same door.

Billy turns on his heel, slams the door at the same time I command, "*Vanish.*"

We watch as the frame of the door in the hall disappears, like an eraser's been taken to a chalkboard. The doorknob shrinks and then pinches into nothing. And then we're staring at a flat, limitless white wall of plaster.

Billy collapses down next to me. "This is like some devil's fun house."

I rest my elbows on my knees and breathe into my hands, trying to center myself, calm down. "The door back to the clearing has to be off this hall. It just must be disguised, hidden by Stock's team's manipulation." I look around at the blank white walls that look to extend forever in both directions.

"But it could be anywhere," Grace says, her voice cracking, "behind either of the walls, the floor, the ceiling."

Somewhere down the hallway, we hear the creak of wood, the turn of a knob.

"That has to be Gavin coming for us," Grace whispers. She looks fearfully at Ral, then Billy, then me. "I think we run."

As a door swings open down the hall, Ral turns to his right, commands the words of power, *"Door emerge, conjure hallway."* Another door etches itself into the plaster wall, and a doorknob jumps out from the wood. Ral swings the door open, steps into another long corridor, and we follow and slam the door behind us.

We race down Ral's bare-bones corridor as the hallway continues to unfurl itself, rolling forward through the clearing like a four-sided scroll. *But we can't keep running, hiding, getting lost forever—*

And then the first tendrils of an idea start curling around my mind. *If we can find Stock, Mama's caging spell, sacrificing my blood, maybe I could convince him—*

I need to stop for a second. I need to sort this out.

I fall to my hands and knees as my teammates stutter-step in front of me. I utter words of power, and a small trapdoor emerges on the ground. But this time, when I open the flap, I reveal an eight-by-eight-foot dark crawl space.

"What are you suggesting, we just crawl in there and hide?" Billy demands.

"You want to keep running until they catch us or we fall over?" I ask. "We need to come up with a better strategy."

Billy shakes his head but still lowers himself down into the crawl space. Once he's in, he lends Grace a hand, and then me. Ral closes the trap shut above all of us. I wave my hand around the perimeter of the trap to conceal it.

I crouch down, lean my head against the cool stone wall of the dark crawl space. Billy stretches his legs out as Grace and Ral slide down beside us.

Grace closes her eyes, puts her fingers to her temples, and frowns. "I hear them. They're not far away." We all fall silent, listen for Grace's amplification to reach our ears. Sure enough, in a few moments I hear the pitter-patter of footsteps. Another minute, and there's a loud chorus of approaching thuds above us. *They're close.*

"Running isn't working," I whisper into the dark.

Ral cuts in, "If you've got a better plan than trying to stay alive, I'm all ears." Ral's never snappy, never quick, and the fact that he is now just drives his fear, *my* fear, home.

"We need to get on the offensive," I say softly. "We need to find Stock, convince him to align with us." I pause. "And I think I should go alone, while you three stay here."

"*What?*" Grace whispers.

"Joan, that's suicide," Ral says.

I shake my head. What I'm going to attempt to do—what I *need* to do—I have to do alone. "I'll move faster on my own," I say, "and if I can manage to pull Stock away from the others, I might have a way to convince him."

"Please, be more vague, Kendrick," Billy huffs.

But I'm not explaining Mama's caging spell right now. I'm not sharing that thanks to my mother's dark, questionable blood-magic, I might be able to scare the hell out of Stock and save our skins. "You're going to have to trust me."

"You heard Gavin, it's over. His team already allied with Stock," Grace says.

I shake my head. "Promises can always be broken."

A second, another minute more, and the footsteps that have faded become louder, as if the crowd above us is retracing their steps, homing in on us slowly.

"Let her go," Ral finally says.

Grace balks. "What? No."

"She's strong enough to try," Ral persists, without looking at me. "If Joan can't find Stock, win him over, we're finished. And none of us want to die inside this magic."

I don't wait for an answer. I lean over and squeeze Grace's hand before scrambling into a crouched position. "Do you hear anything right now?"

She looks at me for a long while, a silent protest. Finally she shakes her head, closes her eyes, and whispers, "It's distant. Footsteps. No one's right above us now."

I exhale the breath I've been holding on to. "Stay here. If you sense anyone coming your way, make a trapdoor within the trapdoor. And keep this one. I'm gonna need it." I scramble to stand and spellbind the trapdoor with a linked trick, "*Out becomes in.*"

Then I push open the trap, close the concealed door behind me, and leave our crawl space to run back down the hall. I know where I need to get to. Somewhere visible. An open space where Stock can see me alone, where I look easily overpowered.

I race back through the hallway Ral has created, heart and feet pounding, until it dead-ends back at his magic-made door. I thrust it open, and I'm back in the main whitewashed hallway— the one where we first entered this living, breathing house of magic. I have to get back to the atrium, up to the balcony, a place where anyone looking for us can see.

I make a right, rush down the hallway and then stop, breathless, and face off with the right-side wall. "*In becomes out,*" I whisper, completing my linked trick, and setting up a future escape. A door crackles and rumbles into creation out of the plaster. I grab the door handle and open the door to the atrium.

The marble floor now has a chasm running through it from Gavin's trick. My staircase still hovers above it, floating to the balcony. A few feet away, Gavin's bridge arches from the floor to the balcony like a sad rainbow. I sidestep around the huge chasm in the floor, until I get to the bridge. Then I take it up.

I wait on the balcony, panic building inside me as I try to remember Mama's caging spell, the words I said her final night, the way I managed to lock my magic inside that bottle of sorcerer's shine. I need her powerful magic of last resort—I need her imprisoning spell to *force* Stock into an alliance with us. I close my eyes, and my pulse starts throbbing underneath my skin, like it knows what's coming—*a draw of blood, my sacrifice to the magic, blood gashed across the lock—*

Then words from the past float out of the dark of my mind like an eerie beacon. *Less of me, an offering to cage for eternity—*

There're squeaks on the floor below me, whispers. My eyes fly open, and I look to the perimeter of the chasm below.

"You lose your pack, she-wolf?" Stock calls up. He's standing on the edge of the huge gash in the floor, Tommy and Rose right behind him. One of Gavin's Carolina Boys, James, is with them. I let out a sigh of relief. They might have teamed up, like Gavin told us, but it looks like Stock's team hasn't found Gavin and the rest of his men in here—at least not yet.

"I came to talk to you," I call down.

"So talk," Stock yells.

"Alone."

"What do you think I am, stupid?"

I throw him a taunting smile. "You afraid?"

At that, Stock's face rearranges into something uglier, and he turns back to Tommy, Rose, and James, mumbles words I'm sure I don't want to hear, and begins to ascend the bridge. "Got to say I've been looking forward to this moment, Kendrick, for a long, long time," he says as he climbs. I put my left hand into my coat pocket, whisper, "*Conjure switchblade*," and cold, sharp metal presses into my hand inside the wool. With one hand, I separate the blade from the handle. *Please, let this work. Please let Mama's magic—my family's magic—save us.*

Then, before I lose my nerve, I press the blade lightly into my palm. A shock of pain pulses under my skin; then a rush of warm liquid curls around my fingers.

Stock steps off the bridge and onto the balcony. When he's only steps away from me, I begin. I whisper words of power, and a large, transparent box builds itself like a cage around us, four walls, a ceiling, and a floor, an entire box made of glass, no more than five feet long and wide, and maybe six feet tall.

"You want to be alone with me this bad?" Stock smirks. He looks through the glass and down to Tommy, Rose, and James, who stand, necks craned, staring up at us. "Kinky with the glass windows."

He raises his hands, whether to dispel the glass or end me, I'm not sure, because without another breath, I take my bleeding hand and press it against the glass, run it around the entire box like a thin, smeared, red border.

Stock gives a weird laugh. "What the hell?"

"*Less of me . . .*" I whisper the old words of Mama's caging spell, hope to God the magic answers me once more.

"What is this? What are you doing?"

"*An offering to cage for eternity . . .*"

"What are you mumbling? Some backwoods trash spell?"

"*My wish, to cage us forever, or until I release us.*"

Immediately, the space feels tighter, like all air has gone out from the box, like we're inside one big soul-crushing void.

"What just happened?" Stock says, panic creeping into his voice. He turns to the glass wall behind him, draws a finger frantically in the shape of a door—but nothing happens. *Because nothing can happen. Because Mama's dark magic worked. I made it work.* Fear, adrenaline, pride, it all thunders inside, gives me a thick, heady rush.

Stock turns to me, fear in his eyes. "What'd you do?"

"I trapped us in here," I say. "There's no way for magic to get in, and there's no way, magic or otherwise, to get out."

Stock spins around and tries to fashion another door, then throws a ball of force at the glass, but it just gives a little shudder of recognition.

Stock turns slowly toward me again, his hands still extended.

"You kill me, and you never get out," I say flatly. "I'm the only thing that can release us."

Then I lean a little bit on the side of the glass box, which already hangs a couple inches over the balcony. It creaks a bit, shuffles forward, farther off the edge. "What are you doing? STOP!"

"Got very little to lose right now, Stock. I need you to tell me you're with us."

"You lost your mind?!"

In response, I shove the glass box forward a couple inches more, push us that much farther over the edge.

Stock folds into the opposite corner, throwing his weight back onto the balcony. "Enough!"

The fear is squeezing my throat closed, and instinct is clawing at my insides, roaring to push us back to safe ground and release the spell's hold. But I can't. This is it. *They're all counting on you. Grace, Billy, Ral, Ruby, and Ben*—

I glance below to the atrium floor, to where Tommy and Rose are firing hopeless bolts of light toward our glass box. But deep down, I know as fiercely as I know my own mother, nothing can break it. Nothing can touch us, not when we're bound by my sacrifice. *The magic will keep us caged inside.* "Tell me you're with us or this entire box goes crashing to the ground."

Stock closes his eyes. "Fuck, Joan, I'm with you."

"Swear on your life. On your family's life," I say, taking another step, pushing the glass box forward another inch. The glass cage gives a little stutter and shake, like it's balancing on a blade.

"Yes, devil woman!"

"Swear it."

"Goddamn it, I swear on my life, my family—my magic, on whatever you want." His voice cracks.

"Tell them." I nod below.

Stock looks below him. Tommy and Rose won't be able to hear him, but Stock points to me and then interweaves his fingers. When Tommy and Rose shake their heads, confused, Stock grabs my hand and shakes. I watch as the Carolina Boy, James, looks guardedly at Tommy and Rose, and then runs across the atrium to conjure a way out.

"I promise you, Kendrick," Stock says. "Now get me the hell out of here."

I raise my arms. *"Release."* The blood-smeared glass disintegrates. The entire glass cage manipulation whips into a magic wind and swirls into nothing.

Stock shoots me a fearful, disgusted look as the two of us stare each other down on the balcony. "I've never seen anything like that." He gulps. "What did you do?"

"What I had to. Come on." Without another word, I head down the bridge, Stock trailing me as we approach Tommy and Rose on the floor.

"What's going on?" Tommy says.

Rose eyes me up and down suspiciously, says to Stock, "Thought you were going to finish this Southern belle."

"Change of plans," Stock says as he looks at me guiltily, fearfully. "Kendrick and I had a little heart-to-heart. She won me over."

I ignore Rose's narrowed eyes and point toward the door I used to get into the atrium. "We need to get the rest of my team. Through there—I linked the door as an escape. Where are Gavin's boys?"

"They're searching for the rest of yours," Tommy says.

"Follow me." I thrust open my spellbound door, scramble through it—

And then instantly, through my linked trick, we're all plunged headfirst into the trapdoor that leads into my team's crawl space. The four of us force our way into the cramped sanctuary, right beside Ral, Grace, and Billy.

"My God, you did it," Ral breathes out, as Billy cuts in with, "About time."

Grace throws her arms around me, gives a deep gasp of relief. "Thank God."

"Can you get us out of here?" Ral asks Stock, as I pull back from Grace.

Stock nods. "Rose made a magic link," he says. "Show them."

"It's a 'divide and seek to be completed' charm, a version of a linked trick," Rose says proudly, as she pulls out a ripped bottom half of a cigarette box. "You take an object, divide it in half, and the two sides are charmed like magnets to come back together. So you use one half"—she waves her half of the cigarette box as evidence—"to find the other like a compass. And the other half of this is lodged around the doorknob of the door to the clearing."

"Clever." Ral nods. "All right, lead the way."

We climb out of the trap, the six of us trailing Rose, as she holds her charm out in front of her. The charmed box pulls us through Ral's hallway, and back to the original hall. Rose walks down it slowly, and then stops walking, turns to her left to face the white wall.

"Right here. I feel it," she says, rubbing her hand over the plaster. "*Reveal.*" And then, like two white curtains are being pulled back, the wall's plaster peels away to reveal Billy's original door to the outside world.

Rose lunges for it, pulls it open. Tommy and Stock follow her, and our foursome trails behind them. One by one, we stumble into the soft, moon-drenched grass of the real clearing. It feels like we've been transported to another time, another space. It feels like I might not be the same person I was walking in. Billy scrambles to shut the door behind us—

"Erase the door, Billy!" Ral shouts.

Billy waves his hand, and the door to our house of manipulations crumbles and swirls into dust. But it doesn't erase the world of hell we've just created together, a giant structure with domes, enclosed hallways running around it, odd towers that shoot up three stories high over the clearing.

"Now destroy it," Gunn orders behind us.

We all turn around to face him.

"I need seven," Gunn says evenly. "And only seven. I never leave loose ends."

We all look at one another, no one saying a word. Something jabs underneath my skin—something raw, sharp, a double-edged blade of fear and shame. Did I ever want Gavin and his allies *gone*? No. But is there a choice?

Me or him, I hear from somewhere inside me, a mantra that somehow takes root and grows into a weed all on its own. *Us or them. Don't think, just do. Remember the endgame, why you're here.*

Remember what you did to get here.

And then it begins. I'm not sure who starts it, all I know for sure is that I have a hand in it too. The magic structure we've made, with all its domes and hallways, starts to extend like it's being pulled taut in both directions. The entire manipulation becomes stretched out, and thinned, like it's being pressed into one long, wide, flat piece of paper.

"We need to fold it up," Stock says hollowly.

The manipulation begins to fold in on itself, the edges of the left side of the flattened manipulation folding over like the page of a book and meeting the right. And then again, and again, and again, until the entire manipulation has been folded up into a square the size of a window. The magic keeps collapsing, folding into itself, becoming smaller and smaller, *a box, a breadbox, a block*, until it pinches out into dust.

And then there's nothing on the other side of the lanterns but a flat scroll of grass.

A strange cross between remorse, regret, and pride, beats inside me like a new heart. I look around. Grace, Billy, Ral. Stock. Tommy, Rose. Me.

Seven sorcerers.

Gunn walks toward us, slowly, carefully, like he's approaching wild animals that have been released from their cages.

"Congratulations to the future of American magic. This troupe has greatly, *greatly* exceeded my expectations." He clasps each one of us in a firm handshake. The sign of a partnership. The sign of respect. "And I promise to God that I'm going to exceed all of yours."

PART TWO

THE REHEARSAL

EASY RUN

ALEX

It starts tomorrow. My real performance. The one that takes place on a stage beyond these prison walls, the one that all this time inside Lorton Reformatory has been preparing me for. It's been a month since my cafeteria brawl, a stunt that earned me an extra week on my sentence. A solid month of listening to Howie and his Shaw brothers' never-ending stories during mealtimes. Of afternoon cigarettes in the quad outside Lorton's dormitories, just one more duck in a row of gray jumpsuits. Of nights spent scheming and self-aggrandizing with Howie, about how we're going to set ourselves up on the outside, work our way up, and take over the world.

A month of playing someone else, day in and night out.

I suppose I should be exhausted. I suppose I should be asleep right now, getting as much rest as I can before I stand in front of my parole review board tomorrow and try to convince them that I'm fit to walk the streets.

But I'm not tired. In fact, I feel almost electric. Because despite the sheer terror that pumps through my veins, walking through these halls, showering next to thieves and vagrants, eating lunch with guys who would terrify my mother if I ever brought them around—for the first time in a long time, I feel like I have a purpose. I'm working for the Feds, and not just as some bought man, some interchangeable suit who lets himself be greased by a dollar. I'm undercover, important. Hell, *essential*, to bringing down the Shaws—and I think I'm actually pretty good at the job.

So maybe I'm not damaged goods. Maybe there's more to the story for me.

"Alex," Howie whispers from the top cot. "You up?"

It's too dark to see what time it reads on our nightstand clock—all the hall lights have been turned off, the prison now a field of sleep and shadows—but I can tell it's late. I've been running everything over and through for what feels like hours: what I know about Howie's cousin, Shaw underboss Win Matthews, when I'm next going to see Agent Frain, how I'm going to break the news to my mother that I'm not coming home. So I'm surprised to hear that Howie's still up too.

"Yeah, what's up, man?" I answer softly.

"Nothing, I—" He stops. "Just had a bad dream."

"About what?"

He sighs, rolls over with a huff. "My mom," he concedes. "She was walking away. I was calling for her, but she didn't turn around."

I don't know how to answer. From what I've gathered these past few weeks, Howie's sorcering mom left him when he was little, took off with some wandering hobo sorcerer after Howie's dad died, and never looked back. It's why Howie started pick-pocketing with his cousin Win on the streets, and how eventually, they found their way in with the Shaws.

"Christ, I could really use a smoke," Howie says, as he turns over once more.

"Your pack's finished?"

"Yeah."

I dig out my cigarettes and matches from underneath my

mattress. I pull out a cig, light the thing, and then release it like a dove from my hands, let the burning stick float in the air, *up up up* to Howie's bunk, where I imagine it floating over to him like a cloud.

Howie laughs above me and grabs the cigarette, breaking my spell.

"I freaking love how you do that." I hear a sharp inhale, see a creeping puff of smoke waft away from his cot and settle over our small cell like fog. "Better," he says. "But if you weren't such a roughneck, Danfrey, I'd swear you were missing your calling as a performer."

"I think I'd rather be on the street than in some circus show."

"Eh, I don't blame you," Howie says. "Though I've heard one of the Shaws' shining rooms has become a far bigger deal since the last time I went in there." He laughs. "That it ain't so much a circus anymore as some all-night wild trip to the moon."

My ears perk up a bit. "What do you mean?"

"Guys are saying that Harrison Gunn—he's McEvoy's underboss who runs a shining joint called the Red Den, down on M Street—finally got McEvoy's blessing to clean house. That he canned all the sorcerers they used to have pulling card tricks while patrons waited for their shine, brought in all new talent." Howie sends another cloud of smoke floating over the edge of his cot. "Win always says Boss McEvoy calls the Den a failing money pit, but apparently Gunn's managed to transform the place. Now it's some big immersive show: a spellbound performance hall that changes as you walk through it, a team of sorcerers brewing shine live, a huge audience group trip at the end. Gunn's even calling the Den a 'magic haven' now. Freaking wild."

My heart starts beating a little faster with all I don't know, with all I want, *need*, to find out about Howie's underworld. "You spend a lot of time in shining rooms?"

"Whenever I can, when I'm not on the road with Win," he

says. Then he drops his voice to a hum. "Speaking of, Sanders came by when you were out at the brick-making unit. I'm up for release. Going in front of the review board on Thursday. I'll be right on your heels."

A mix of dread, fear, excitement churns around inside. "That's great, man."

"Great for both of us. I plan on getting back in the smuggling game right away," he says. "You need to meet Win. He'll break you in, set us up, get me working again."

All I need is the where and the when. "I'd owe you big-time, Howie."

Howie must be stubbing his cigarette butt on the wall, because little flakes of ash start drifting down to my cot like a cinder waterfall. "You'd do the same for me, brother. Friday at five, at the Red Den, all right? M and Sixteenth Streets. Make sure to mention Win's name or you'll never get inside."

Friday, five p.m., the Red Den. It begins. "Thanks, How. Looking forward to getting started."

But Howie doesn't give his usual boastful cackle, or jump into his laundry list of the ways we're going to take over the Shaws. Instead there's a long silence between us. A silence that begs to be broken. So I venture, "You feel ready to be out there?"

"'Course," Howie answers. But he's quiet again for a while. "But I mean, it just feels safer in here sometimes. I know that sounds crazy, but . . ." He pauses. "In here, we're big deals. Out there . . . it's going to be different."

Howie would never talk to me like this in the morning. But at night, in your cell, when it's just you and your bunk mate, you're allowed to say things you'd never admit to in the daylight. I've done it with him, too—told him things about my father. Things I only see now with hindsight, little ways he conned me, when I thought he only needed one big score of magic cures to settle his debts with D Street. Not a year of breaking the law.

"I hear you, How. I feel the same way."

"But we'll get each other's backs out there," he says.

"You and me against the world." My answer, unrehearsed, natural, surprises me on its way out. I used to say the same thing to my buddy Warren. I'm even more shocked that I mean it. "Get some sleep, Howie, okay?"

"Yeah, yeah." His bed creaks as he rolls over and flicks his cigarette stub in the vague direction of our toilet. "You too, Danfrey."

I'm in front of my parole board the next morning by nine a.m., and I hit the streets of the outside world before lunchtime. It's been less than two months, but it seems like forever since I've seen the outside of Lorton Reformatory, and the world beyond its walls feels much different than the one I left. The keys that Agent Frain must have left me through inventory thankfully have a small tag with the address of my new home: 1206 P Street. Right on the border of the old Hell's Bottom district.

1206 P Street is a sagging row home, one lonely window on one floor overlooking a narrow plank porch with more scars and holes than Frankenstein. And the inside is worse than the outside. My suitcase that I packed the night I met Frain has been placed in the corner of a sad-looking kitchenette: a slice of a room consisting of a few cupboards, an icebox, a cheap laundry stove, and a table. A single bed stands opposite the kitchen. One room. From the Danfreys' mansion on Massachusetts Avenue to one room on the edge of the slums.

Speaking of the Danfreys' fall from grace, I work up the nerve and call my mother on a nearby pay phone that afternoon. I give her the story that Agent Frain and I agreed to—that time in jail allowed me to really think. That I need some time away from home, to sort myself out, to figure out who *I* am and what

I really want. Mother barely speaks, just gives me confused, punctured gasps that I know means she's crying, and it's the first time I feel shame's sharp, familiar stab since I was booked down at Lorton. It's also the first time I've ever been tempted to blow my cover. When we hang up, I miss her so bad it hurts.

Remember, you're doing this for her, in one sense, I tell myself on the walk back home. *To clear our name. To get revenge.*

My walk to meet Howie at the Red Den on Friday is a blur of crippling nerves and adrenaline, and I find myself standing at the corner of M and 16th Streets before I realize I've arrived. The lot is a squat, two-story redbrick building with one large storefront window, and a wooden side door with a gold lettered sign, THE RED DEN. The faint whisper of jazz seeps out of the establishment's walls, like a promise of a good night to come. I collect myself and open the door.

Inside is small, quaint, not at all what I was imagining from Howie's description. There's a narrow mahogany bar with a few stools dotted around it, and stocked liquor shelves towering above. Behind the bar stands one lone bartender, young and polished-looking in his coat-tailed jacket and pressed white shirt. The whole scene, the image of legality: just another run-of-the-mill drinking establishment. A premature panic starts ticking inside me, faint but steady, like a watch. "I'm sorry. . . ." I look around. "I'm here to meet a man named Win Matthews and his cousin, Howie."

The bartender looks me up and down shamelessly. "Your name?"

"Alex Danfrey."

The bartender waits a full minute before answering, while I stand here like a chump with my hands in my pockets. "Howie Matthews is already waiting for you downstairs, sir."

"Downstairs—"

"Go ahead." The bartender gestures behind me, to a small corridor on the left side of the joint's single table. "Walk straight through that wall."

I slowly walk to the end of the hallway, to the sheet of egg-shell plaster that poses as a wall. I take another step closer and carefully reach to touch the plaster—

But my fingers pass right through it.

As I step through the wall, I'm hit with that feeling you get when you're passing through a force field—that magnetic pull at your insides, like a strong internal storm—

And then I'm standing at the top of a staircase. I take the stairs two stories down until I arrive at a set of double doors, give a thrust with my shoulder to push them both open, and walk into a performance space the size of two banquet halls.

The space is two stories high, with a cement floor, gray cinder-block walls, and two hallway exits, one on each side. Nearest to my entrance are several small performance stages, each encircled by a cluster of benches. Beyond that, there's a seating area of lounge chairs and tables, and beyond that, a long, elevated stage.

I scout around the wide space, looking for Howie, for anyone really. But it's empty. Then I spot a lone shot glass resting on an end table in the seating area. It faintly glimmers red, evidence of sorcerer's shine long gone.

I pick up the glass, as a young woman dressed in all black approaches me from one of the corridors off the performance space.

"Can I help you?" she says, pausing at the mouth of the hall a few feet away.

I take her in: raven hair, long locks not sacrificed to that blunt-bobbed style all the dames are wearing. Rail-thin frame, almond-shaped eyes that stay locked on the empty glass of shine in my hand. She's got a decent-sized basket resting on her hip.

"I'm looking for a friend, Howie Matthews. I was told he was here." I hold the glass up as evidence. "I'm thinking this is his?"

"You're thinking right." She gives me a smirk. "He's in the john, giving a shine-induced sermon to the wall on the meaning of life. You can hear him from the hallway if you're after free advice."

"Christ." I turn Howie's empty shot glass around in my hand. Having Howie high as a kite the night I meet his cousin was not the plan. Having him shot to another planet does nothing to help work Win Matthews over for me. "You know about how long ago he took this, by chance?"

She shrugs. "Maybe twenty minutes." Then she studies me the way I was studying her. "You need a shot of shine yourself, sir? We try to keep a few extra ounces of the stuff around for the Shaws and their guests, from the previous night's performance. And sorcerer's shine only lasts a day—"

"No thanks, I'm set." Remembering my manners, I put the glass back on the table and rush toward her. "Sorry, let me help you with that—"

"It's okay, it's my job." She shakes me off, a note of pride in her voice. "Besides, it's light as a feather." She tips the basket toward me as evidence. Inside are hundreds of white feathers. "Literally."

I smile. I guess she's some sort of stagehand. "So you work here?"

"Nah, I just like to wander off the street sometimes. Smuggle out random props."

I laugh. Quick, as well as cute. And more than cute, I realize, as I study her again. Pretty damn breathtaking. I find myself flustered for a minute, all my old come-ons stalling out. It's been a while. "And how's that working out for you?" I try to recover. "Tricking sorcerers?"

"It's working out just fine."

"Maybe they're just tricking you into thinking that."

As she laughs, I glance back to the door, wonder when Win's going to arrive. *I need to get Howie, run him under cold water, slap him sober.* "What's your name?"

There's a rumble of noise from the back of the performance space. Two middle-aged chaps roll a cart loaded with glass bottles to the base of the stage, which spans the entire back wall. They clamber up the stairs to the stage and call down, "Hey, Joan, Grace is looking for you. Something about the right dress?"

"I'm coming!" the girl answers, then mutters to herself, "Lord, that woman is obsessed with details."

"Joan," I repeat to her, with a smile.

"Look at you, putting two and two together." Joan gives me another smirk as she steps by me, and places her basket of feathers down in the center of one of those little performance stages near the front. Then she flits past me again on her way to the back stage. "Good luck with your friend, Alex Danfrey."

I hurry down the dim, windowless hall studded with a few wall lanterns, stop in front of the door marked GENTLEMEN, and step inside. Like Joan promised, Howie's standing at the sink, arms outstretched, pupils tiny pinpricks, smile as wide as the Potomac River. He sees me in the reflection of the mirror, and his smile breaks even wider. He turns around with a flourish.

"Alex Danfrey!" he announces loudly to the bathroom stalls. "Get the hell over here." Howie wraps me in a full body hug, holds the shaky embrace one, two, three seconds too long.

"So you're already all shined up?" I pull away and fake a smile.

"Shiny as a freaking new penny, man," he whispers.

"And that's the best idea, when we're about to meet Win and

get started?" I put my hand on his shoulder, keep on my forced, hollow smile.

"A trip like this is always a good idea." He closes his eyes. "We'll work hard, play hard. Every night, Danfrey, we're going to be partying here until dawn."

I take a deep breath. *This will work out. Howie has to be coming down soon, shine's high doesn't last more than an hour.* "Why don't we go wait outside for Win? Don't think your cousin wants to meet us in the john."

As I push Howie out the door, he gushes, "I swear, brother, you need to try this shine *now*. Your eyes—they're like, two radiant beams of light."

I lead him into the hallway. "I think you're beyond shined, How."

"*You're* shined. You're so shiny you're glowing. God, man, you're beautiful." He reaches his hands up to my face as we turn into the main performance space. I carefully take his hands and place them back by his sides. Joan and the other stagehands are gone. "Just take a seat, all right?" *Win better be late.*

Like a cruel joke, the double doors on the other side of the large room slap open, and through them barrels a monster of a man. Tall and meaty, big arms and wide chest. His loose hair hangs over his forehead like a permanent dunce cap, but it's clear this guy's no joker. He's got the look of a man you don't want to meet. He's the kind of man who should send you running.

"Cousin!" Howie cheerfully bellows through the space. He slides off the chair I've managed to sit him in and opens his arms to embrace this behemoth. But Win doesn't return the hug. He's all cold eyes, cold stare, cold shoulder. "You're high," Win tells Howie, but keeps his gaze trained on me.

"No worries, Win, I'm coming down." Howie gives an awkward laugh. He puts his hand behind my shoulder and shoves me forward. "This is Alex Danfrey. The fella I was telling you about, my Lorton cell mate." Howie reaches up to slap his cousin's back, misses. "Take a seat, we've got a lot to catch up on. Sure there's time for another shot of shine before we hit the road."

"There isn't." Win shifts. "And it's just me and you on the ride along."

I start to get a nauseating, sinking feeling as Howie shoots me a loaded glance. "I don't understand. I thought you were looking for extra men on the street—"

"Don't want the liability of a junior Danfrey." Win shakes his head, but those odd bangs of his don't budge. "It's not time to further antagonize D Street—there's too much at stake." Just Win's mention of D Street sends a flash of something heated and hungry through my frame, but I know better than to open my mouth. He looks me up and down, then adds, "Besides, I don't like the look of him."

Howie glances at me again, his anxiety weakening the hold of his high. But his nerves don't have anything on mine. *If Win says no, this is it. I'm finished before I even manage to hit the street.* "Win, I swear, the boy's solid—he stood up to a bunch of guinea chumps who were messing with him on the inside. I saw it—I saved him. The two of us, we were like a tornado at Lorton. No one fucked with us after that."

Win shows no outward signs of being impressed.

"Plus, he's got sorcery talent—I've seen his tricks—and he knows the street side of the business. He was trying to break out on his own before he landed at Lorton."

"Talent," Win repeats dubiously. His eyes crawl over me once more, searching for something I'm not sure I have. *Honesty? Presence? Loyalty?* I try my damnedest to keep my eyes locked on Win's. I try to show him whatever he's looking for.

"I'm asking you for a favor, Win," Howie coaxes, in his softer, more tentative tone—the tone he'd use only at night in our cell, when we were trading whispers about our fears in the dark. It's a last resort for Howie—I know he doesn't like showing anyone his softer underbelly—and despite all else, it actually touches me. "Danfrey and I had each other's backs. I gave him my word I'd look out for him on the other side."

Win sighs. "How—"

"Come *on*, cousin." Howie drops his voice to a low, slurring hum. "Don't make a liar out of me."

And then my warmth tips over into itchy, ugly guilt. I remind myself that Howie's just a two-bit thug who's only vouching for me because he knows I'll prove an asset in the future. That he only cares about me because he cares about himself. But right now, watching Howie plead with his cousin to take a chance on me like an eight-year-old making a case for a puppy—it's kind of hard to do.

Besides, as much as I don't want to admit it, I've actually come to like the bastard.

Win runs his fingers through his bizarre hair, walks away, leaving Howie and me unsure of where we stand. "We don't have time to talk this to death," Win calls behind him.

Howie looks at me hopefully.

"Come on," Win adds. "Might as well bring your girlfriend with you."

Howie slaps my shoulder excitedly as we trail after his cousin.

"I owe you one," I say quietly.

"That's for damn sure." Howie throws his arm around my shoulders and laughs as we head for the double doors. "You would've done the same for me. Like you said, you and me against the world, right?" he says. "Just wait till Win sees what you can do. Up, up, up we go, my friend. Together."

We settle into Win's old Model T, Howie in front, me in the back, turn out of the Red Den lot and make our way through the city. I haven't said a word to Win Matthews since I've met him, not that it's noticeable. Howie has said enough for all of us, keeps his mouth running as fast as the motor—about what he learned in prison, his plans for life on the outside, and how he's itching to meet Boss McEvoy. He's still coming down off the shine, taking in the world through magic-tinted glasses. Eventually he'll sober up, hollow out. Feel empty and hungry for more.

"That mouth has to shut when we get to the meeting point," Win finally says. He takes a right and the busy avenues fall away, and now we're following the Highway Bridge out of town.

"All right, yeah, of course," Howie says to his passenger-side window.

"I'm serious. You aren't here for anything but standing next to me quiet as church mice. This is an easy run. We've already made our own form of payment—we just need to grab twenty gallons of remedial spells Baltimore brought down from their inside man up north and drive the spells out to our shine redistillery."

So the same type of trades my father was orchestrating, before the Feds got wind and took him down: stealing legal magic cures off pharmaceutical shelves, flipping them to redistilleries who try to edge the spells closer to shine, then funneling the knockoff product to shining rooms and dealers around the city. I file it away for Agent Frain. Sounds like since my father's Danfrey Pharma Corp. has been thrown out of the remedial magic game, sources outside the city have been pinch-hitting.

Win takes the next exit, and we make another right. The slick road beneath our wheels completely falls away, and now we're just treading over stones, hopping and bumping as we make our way through a dense forest.

"Where's the pickup?" Howie asks.

"At one of our warehouses," Win answers quietly.

We park in a gravel lot surrounding a colorless building and get out. The cold of early November shocks me, forces each breath out with a startled puff. Win opens the warehouse door, and we follow him into the darkness. There's a thick, different kind of air in here—heavy, musty air that smells like it's been held captive.

I take a quick look around—the place is stacked with boxes and bins along the perimeter, and a pile of thin cots is thrown into the corner. Thanks to the slim row of windows perched high on the far wall, I see that our meet-up is already here. Three men stand in the shadows, right at the border of where the moonlight hits the dirty cement floor.

"It's Win Matthews," Win calls out. "I'm looking for Bobby Hun."

A youngish man, twenties maybe, steps into the slice of light.

"I take it all went well last night," Win says slowly. "So where's our thank-you?"

The young Baltimore thug, Bobby, I guess, stays silent for a moment. Then he glances back to his chums and sighs. "Bring the gallons in."

One of Bobby's associates turns back into the shadows. A rattling of glass echoes through the warehouse, and then a large cardboard box is pushed into the sliver of moonlit cement.

Win steps forward, bends down, and opens up the box. He pulls out one of the glass gallons inside, full of a murky pink liquid. A remedial spell—maybe the flu vaccine, or one of the magic trials they're running for the sleepy sickness. Ripped off the shelves before it can reach the world, to be repackaged for folks who are so hungry for a break from reality, they'll guzzle medicine to get high. A shame blooms inside me. My father was doing the very same thing. *I was helping him do the very same thing.*

Win screws off the cap, sticks his pinkie finger in, and puts it to his lips. He puts the cap back on the gallon and studies the contents of the box. "Where's the rest of it?"

"That's all of it."

Win barks a laugh. "That's a joke, right? Boss McEvoy and your boss made a deal," he says. "Our man Kerrigan loaned your gang twenty men for your Baltimore Equitable Bank shake-down—a loan we now expect to be paid back in full. The deal was for twenty gallons." Win shakes his head. "Not ten."

I try to put together the pieces as Bobby crosses his arms and begins to whisper to one of his associates. *Our man Kerrigan loaned your gang twenty men. . . .* The name Kerrigan rings a bell from my training days at the Unit. He's one of McEvoy's underbosses on the racketeering side, from what I remember, commands a small army of Shaw thugs to "protect" local businesses with muscle and magic (businesses that have no choice but to pay for this "protection"). Sounds like Kerrigan loaned some Shaw manpower to the Baltimore Gang, for their bank raid up north—

"You really don't know what happened last night, Matthews?" Bobby interrupts my thoughts, snaps out his own forced laughter. "Half of Kerrigan's men never showed up. And half of the ones who did? They were high. One of them even tampered with the linked-door trick that was set up as a means of escape. Whole thing was a mess, our men barely got out with the cash." Bobby takes another step toward Win. "It was definitely not the stellar Shaw service we were promised."

I can hear Win swallow from here, but his face stays stone. "Sounds like all's well that ends well to me," he says slowly. "Your men got out, you got your score." Win nods into the darkness. "Now quit screwing around, bring out the rest of the gallons."

Bobby shifts a bit, then puts his hands in his pockets, stays silent.

"Are you deaf?" Win barks.

"Ten gallons," Bobby answers. "As a lesson."

I can practically see anger radiating off Win like steam. "A *lesson?*"

"If McEvoy provides half-rate services, he's going to get half payments. Tell your boss not to fuck with us, Matthews. Baltimore's not afraid of the Shaws. And we make far better friends than enemies."

Under the moonlight, Win looks monstrous, like an animal ready to pounce. And for a moment, I'm sure as hell glad I'm standing next to him, and not on the other side. "You don't know what you're starting. I can't go back to McEvoy with ten gallons—"

"Then forget the whole thing." Bobby smiles, a hollow, crooked one.

There isn't a word, a breath, for a long time. I'm watching, waiting, my heart in my throat. If I could fly away, I would. Christ, I'm tempted to try and disappear.

Just when the tension becomes so loaded that I think the warehouse might combust from the pressure, Bobby jerks for the gun in his pocket. But Win's too quick and draws his own pistol first.

And then it happens so fast, I don't process what's occurred until my head is hitting the ground.

Two Baltimore thugs come at me from behind the storage bins, send me sprawling onto the floor. As Win turns around out of instinct, Bobby crosses over the sliver of moonlit cement and knocks Win's gun out of his hand. Howie goes to grab it, but one of the Baltimore thugs stops double-teaming me and turns to sock him in the stomach.

"Not too much, just enough to send a message," Bobby shouts.

Someone sends a fist to my ribs, a jab to my left eye—I double over, while Howie gives a wail in pain. A warning bullet flies and breaks a window in the warehouse. *I need to stop this, do something, anything—*

On reflex, I grab one of the gallons from the box a few feet away, take it out, and smash it over the Baltimore thug who's attached himself to my thigh. He goes down hard, like a bag of bricks, and now two of his buddies are coming for me. But I roll to stand, scramble to my feet, say the words *"Release and fly."* I reach my hands out—

And like synchronized trapeze artists, the guns fly from the gangsters' hands, land one in each of mine. Then I set my sights on Bobby.

A rumble emanates from the ground. Four walls, a square of thick stone slabs, erupt out of the floor of the warehouse, clamber up seven feet, and cage Bobby inside. "What the hell?" he screams, but his voice is muffled. "Get me out of here!"

It takes Win a second to process, another to breathe. He steals a quick look at me, realization taking him over, paralyzing him for an instant. But then he rips one of my newly stolen guns out of my hand. He points it at two shell-shocked Baltimore men, while I keep my gun trained on the other pair, and says, "Don't move."

The two Baltimore thugs slowly raise their hands in the air, as Howie bends down and wraps his arms around the crate of remedial spells. He lifts it with a huff.

"Not one inch or I swear, I'll end all you Baltimore trash," Win says.

"Matthews, you leave me in here and there will be hell to pay!" Bobby bellows from inside his stone cage.

But Win doesn't answer. Like a charmed snake, he, Howie, and I move slowly back out the door. As soon as we hit the parking lot, we start running for the car.

"What the *fuck*." Win peels out of the empty lot and skitters onto the makeshift road through the wood. Rocks and gravel from the parking lot jump up and knock impatiently on the doors.

My heart and my mind are both sputtering, the high of doing well, and the fear, the pride, it's all shorting inside me like a tangle of live wires—

"Is he going to die in there?" Win looks back at me and demands, and his car swerves a bit into the shoulder. "I need to know the extent of the damage on this."

I shake my head. "The stone walls will be gone tomorrow. It's real, but impermanent . . . just like all pure magic."

Win turns back around. "Christ, does Kerrigan not have his boys under control? Boss McEvoy is going to be livid if he finds out. And where'd you learn that trick, huh? Your old man?" Win looks at me through the rearview mirror. But now there's something new in his eyes. A fear—raw and unbridled.

I stay silent, just nod so he can see. No one needs to know my father has less magic in him than a brick. No one needs to know I was all the magic of his operation.

We ride the rest of the way in silence, the ominous forest finally giving way to a four-lane highway. I spend the ride running through what I've learned, trying to make connections, to weave the threads of information together: *Shaw underboss George Kerrigan fell short on McEvoy's promise of extra manpower to Baltimore, which nearly resulted in a bust up north—*

Win asks for directions to my place, and we screech in front minutes later.

I grip the door handle, ready for home, ready for sleep. I'm beat, my nerves shorted and spent. But I need to remember my endgame. I need to keep climbing, get to the next rung on the ladder. "What now, sir?" I venture, before stepping outside.

"Now I know where you live." Win gives a nod. "You'll hear from us."

SETTLED

JOAN

Our troupe of seven doesn't get much downtime, between our daily practices and our nightly shows at the Red Den, but early morning is one of those rare times we do have to ourselves. Time I'll spend lying in bed, looking out my bedroom window on the top floor of the Den, watching shiny new Buicks chug down M Street, and thinking about what Ruby and Ben are doing back home. Or sometimes I'll knock on Grace's door, and the two of us'll sneak out to spend our stipends on milky coffee and sugar cakes from Moby's Diner around the corner. Then we'll sit on my fire escape and chat about our dreams for the future, and the way we're going to take over this city, show by show.

So I'm surprised, as I'm lying here, relishing my morning, to hear a sharp, impatient rap outside my room. And after I get up from bed and open my door, I'm even more surprised to find Harrison Gunn behind it.

He stands there, dressed to kill even at this hour: crisp, narrow pinstripe pants, tight vest over a pressed shirt. He's got one forearm raised and pressed against my door frame. "Can I come in?"

The mixed-up emotions I always feel just on seeing him start battling inside me—*what's he want, what's he see when he looks at me, am I performing well enough*—and I have to shake my head to quiet the war. "'Course, sir."

I sit down right on top of my pillow as Gunn perches on the opposite end of the bed. The entire cot is between us, but it still feels too close. Gunn's talked with me alone a few times before, since he cleared his whole old staff out and moved our sorcering troupe into the Red Den a few weeks back. Some nights he's pulled me into his office off the main show space after our performance, to get my pulse on whether we're taking enough risks. And he's stopped by my room once or twice before, in that tight window between rehearsal and our actual show, to give me his last-minute embellishments on the finale—but he's never crossed the threshold.

Now, as he's sitting on my bed, I wonder if he's chatted alone like this with any other sorcerer, or if I've become some kind of face for the troupe. I've thought about asking Grace a couple of times, but I'm not sure what answer I'd prefer to hear.

And I'm sure as hell not going to ask Gunn.

"Wanted to let you know that your little parlor trick last night was a success with some of my colleagues," Gunn says. "Underbosses Kerrigan and Sullivan were raving about it in the VIP lounge. Said it took the old rabbit-in-the-hat trick to a new level."

Heat starts rising to my cheeks at the unexpected compliment, and I think about the parlor trick he's talking about, the way I turned the gangsters' handkerchiefs into a pair of doves that soared up to the rafters last night. During every show, there's an intermission between the individual performances we sorcerers put on for the first hour, and the immersive magic finale we perform together at the end—and for those twenty minutes or so, we're supposed to work the floor, cozy up to a patron, and perform an off-the-cuff parlor trick to get the audience even more excited for our finale. The little intermission is billed as "improvised," but our troupe learned pretty quick who we're supposed to target with our extra attention: wealthy regulars. Rich shine addicts. And of course, the higher-up Shaw men, on the nights they come in to see what all the fuss over Gunn's revamped club is about. "That's nice to hear, sir," I finally answer. "Glad your colleagues enjoyed it."

"It's important, that they understand the true magic inside this place. And I knew they would. It's all coming together."

Gunn stays silent for a while, until the silence between us is suffocating, until I almost scream, *Why are you really here, what do you really want?*

"Your troupe continues to surpass my expectations," he finally says. "An immersive show where people truly lose themselves in magic for a night. Sold-out performances for a hundred fifty people, six nights a week, at fifteen dollars a ticket. McEvoy laughed when I told him about my idea to transform the Den. He didn't think I'd pull it off. *No one* thought I'd pull it off." He looks at me suddenly, expectantly.

I gulp. "Well, clearly they were wrong, sir."

Gunn gives me that smile of his, the cagey one that starts at his eyes and gently touches his lips, but never quite comes together. "But as impressive as the troupe is, Joan, as seamless as the seven of you work together—there's no denying there's a star." Gunn studies me with those white-blue eyes, and his look, his words, they stun and silence. *He's clearly talking about me.*

"We're not so different, you and me," he adds slowly. "In fact, I think that's why we work well together. I've watched you out at the warehouse clearing, and here, night after night. You push yourself, hard. You run until you win, or until you fall. You do what it takes. I respect that."

I don't think I've breathed for the past minute. Somehow I manage, "Thank you, sir."

Gunn leans forward, rests his forearms on his thighs, talks

to my bureau in the corner. "When I was a boy, Joan, I thought
my life was going to turn out very differently. But then tragedy
struck, and the keys to the kingdom that I thought were in my
pocket, turns out they belonged to someone else." He throws
a glance at me. "I learned to be resourceful, patient, learned to
work for what I wanted until it was mine. In fact, I've been planning this Red Den transformation for a very long time."

He fishes in his pocket for cigarettes, lights two, and hands
one to me. He waves his match until the small flame surrenders
to milky smoke.

"I saw where you come from. I can put two and two together,"
he says slowly. "Clearly, your life didn't turn out the way you
thought it would either. You want to do right by your family, I
understand that, just like I want to do right by mine."

Gunn's never mentioned his family, or his past, or really anything about himself, ever. It feels like we've crossed into strange,
unsettling territory. You don't get personal, or even comfortable,
with Gunn—but that provides its own sort of comfort. "Your
troupe, these performances, the power of seven—this is your
shot, Joan, to transform yourself into something truly extraordinary. Just like it's mine." He stares at me, as smoke curls in
between us. "And I know it, I feel it. There's more we need to
do—in fact, I don't even think we've scratched the surface of
the magic under this roof."

I'm not sure where this conversation's headed, but I know
it's somewhere I don't want to go. I know Gunn well enough by
now to understand that he's somehow asking for *more* from me.
But I spend nearly every waking hour at the Den already, still
have this unshakable habit of practicing on my own after the
show and once the stagehands sweep the place clean, if I don't
think I nailed my piece of that night's finale. I'd never deny that
Gunn kept his promise, he pays us well—sixty dollars per week,
with a five-dollar bonus if we pack the house for that week's run,

which we've managed every week since we opened—I'm sending home twice as much money as Mama and Jed ever managed to pull in during the best of times. But I earn it, every cent. Long days, wild nights, nonstop magic. There's nothing I've got left to give.

"This arrived by post this morning," Gunn interrupts my thoughts, and pulls a ratty envelope from his pocket. He hands it to me, and then I forget everything else and hungrily reach for it with trembling fingers. I know the doily ridge of the stationery, the faded taupe color, the dash of a red seal pressed into the back. But still, I gasp out loud when I flip it over. My cousin Ben's crappy penmanship is scrawled across the front:

> Joan Kendrick c/o Mr. Harrison Gunn
> The Red Den . . .

It's been so long since I talked to Ben that my eyes start watering, blurring the ink.

"I took the liberty of wiring an extra week of salary directly to Drummond Savings and Loan, about a week after you arrived here at the Den. From what I gathered from you and your cousin back in September, time was of the essence in settling your uncle's debts." As I sit there dumbfounded, Gunn tears open the envelope for me, pulls out the folded note inside. "I suppose Ben got the news."

I finally recover. "Thank you, Mr. Gunn. That was far too kind of you, saved us weeks of delay. I won't expect my pay next week—"

But Gunn waves my response away with his hand. "Considering how you go above and beyond, let's think of it as a special bonus."

Special bonus. But I don't want to parse that out, not yet. I just want to fall headfirst into Ben's letter:

Joan,

Stopped into Drummond S&L today. They got the money, which damn well saved us. Said it came by wire from Harrison Gunn—sounds like you pulled it off up in the big city. I got Mr. Gunn's address and had to write.

Ruby says hi and that she loves you. She says she promised you she was going to beat the sickness inside her, and sure enough she's been on her feet more each day. Hell, this morning she was helping me in the kitchen, giving me orders like she owned the place. She looks healthier, Joan—weighs heavier. We're both beyond proud of you. Thank you. Love always, Ben

The relief and joy welling up inside me is so intense that for a minute, I actually think I might burst.

"This bonus doesn't have to be a one-time thing." Gunn uses a voice I barely recognize—smooth and slippery, like silk, or a snake. "I could keep wiring payments, take care of the back dues. Help pay down the rest of the mortgage. You could start using your salary for yourself, or save it to buy your family a new place. A palace."

A palace dances, slow and sultry, across my mind, but I ignore it, 'cause I'm no fool. Nothing comes without strings from Gunn. "Sir, I'm not sure what else you're asking of me, what I'd do to deserve more. . . . I'm giving everything I've got to the troupe, to the show, you said so yourself—"

"Thing is Joan, there's something I remember." He pauses, stubs the remainder of his cigarette onto my bedpost and tucks the stub in his pocket. "It's something I haven't quite been able to shake about you since we met. It's been keeping me up at night if I'm honest, thinking, running things over and through."

He glances at me, but now, all the softness in his eyes is gone. "That night I came down to Parsonage. You brought me a bottle of shine that looked like it went to hell and back."

My heart skips a beat. *Mama's spell, the blood-magic.* "Well, sir, I—"

"It was dark. But still, I noticed small traces of blood caked around the top, detected an unusual, almost rusty smell to the shine. It was old, Joan, timeworn, even though you insisted different," he says. "I know my magic. Don't tell me again that was a shine you brewed that morning."

In one swift motion Gunn moves closer, so that I can't look anywhere else but at him. "I know you're keeping things from me. I don't know what, I just know you are. I'll say it again: you and I have the chance to make both of our lives what they were meant to be." He shakes his head fiercely, slowly. "But not if you hold back from me."

My heart's clambered its way up to my throat by now. *Can I lie, dodge, say no?* "What—what exactly do you want, Mr. Gunn?"

"Everything," he says bluntly. "I want to know *everything* you can do."

Everything. I gulp, try to swallow my fear, my panic. *But some of my secrets aren't mine to share.*

Mama's blood-spells have been with the women on her side of the family for generations. Her severing spells, the tracking spells, the caging spells: her magic was, *is*, a personal magic, family blood in the truest sense. And I've committed myself to using sorcery in order to right the past—if I'm honest, some nights I've even felt this distinct surge of *rightness*, like performing magic is something I was born to do—but giving Mama's secrets away feels wholly different. Feels like delving into the oldest, truest parts of me and selling them wholesale to Gunn. *Besides, what's Gunn want with blood-magic?*

I look at the letter that's starting to crinkle around its edges from my death grip. If this is about Ruby and Ben, and only them, should it matter? Should I keep giving everything I can in exchange for making things better for them, for making things right? Besides, now that Gunn's circling in, how long can I stall? *What happens if you say no to a man like Gunn?*

"Joan." Gunn shifts on my bed, bringing me back to the here and now. "I'm not in the habit of asking twice." He stares at me with those cold, hard, almost taunting eyes. "In fact, I'm not in the habit of asking at all."

My heart hammers against my chest. And even though I swore I wouldn't let these memories haunt me, I can't help but think back to the warehouse clearing: to those two sorcerers Gunn turned on each other, to all the casualties during his little "experiment," to the way he forced us to "finish" the Carolina Boys during our final test. *This man is dangerous. This man knows where my family lives. Gunn does not stop till he gets what he wants.*

Mama might even understand. Hell, Mama might do the same thing, if Ben's and Ruby's futures were on the line.

"If you're promising to take care of our cabin back home, Mr. Gunn," I say softly, hesitantly, "there are some things that I can show you, things—things I've never shown anyone."

His eyes grow brighter, hungrier. "But you're going to show me."

And for just a second, it feels like the bottom of the world has dropped out, and I'm sitting on a bed with the devil himself. I can't say yes, or bring myself to speak what feels like a strange form of betrayal, despite how many ways I try to reason it away.

So I nod. Once.

"In my office, after rehearsal." Gunn extends his fingers onto the bed but doesn't touch mine. "Just you and me."

And then he walks to the door and closes it behind him.

As soon as Gunn's gone, I try to banish him from my mind,

think only about Ben's letter, let the world begin with Ben's scrawl of my name and end with his signature. But what I just promised, what I'm going to share with Gunn—it teases, itches, claws at me inside. *There wasn't a choice*, comes from somewhere deep within. *You're in this world to fight for Ruby and Ben with everything you've got. Just keep going. Like Gunn said, run until you win, or until you fall.*

By the time Gunn leaves, it's time for practice, so I tuck Ben's letter into my bureau drawer. The Shaws take care of the troupe's room and board in addition to our weekly pay: our entire troupe resides on the second floor of the Red Den, so there's never a good reason to be late for a rehearsal or show. I walk past Grace's room, Ral and Billy's across the hall, Stock's, and Tommy and Rose's beyond that, to the back stairs and down three flights to the cellar. I follow the cavernous, lantern-lit hall past Gunn's office and into the center show space of the Den, a two-story performance area floored with cement and walled in cinder blocks, which spans our entire corner lot.

Each day we begin practice with our solo and duo tricks— the ones we open our show with at eight p.m.—the five- or ten-minute performances that we'll run on repeat until about nine. These "warm-up" tricks are performed on the small circular stages in the front of the show space, Gunn's thought being that the audience can come in, get a drink at the bar and ease into the show, mosey around our stages and take in the tricks of their choosing. So during morning practice, we'll try new flourishes on these tricks, or sometimes we'll perform them for the rest of the troupe for a gut check or critique.

We wrap up around lunch, after which Gunn comes in to give us his latest idea on the "immersive magic finale" for that night. Sometimes the finale is an entirely new idea Gunn thought up, other times it's a fresh take or twist on a theme we've used before. We'll brainstorm how to execute the finale, practice, then run it as a dress rehearsal for Gunn, and around five or six p.m. we break for about an hour before getting ready for the actual show. Every day except Sunday we spend like this, sorcering from pretty much morning until midnight, all for a hundred fifty patrons willing to pay top dollar. Besides, Gunn says the long day serves another purpose: strengthening the bonds of our magic until they're made of steel. Sure, it makes for exhausting days. But it's good work—work I can lose myself in. Work we're all proud of.

"Nice of you to show, Kendrick," Billy calls across the show space. He stands in the center of his and Ral's stage, the one in the front right corner of the space. I hustle over to join the rest of my troupe. Billy's got a pile of about ten cards floating six inches over his outstretched palm. Ral's beside him, in the midst of stacking a square of face cards up like a thin wall above his head.

I reach the benches that encircle their stage and slide in beside Grace to sit. "Sorry—lost track of time."

Grace snaps her pack of cigarettes against her leg and offers me one. She drops her voice. "You really didn't miss anything."

I give a little smile as Ral adds, "We wanted everyone's take on our royal palace of cards trick." He points up to his wall of face cards. "Billy thinks it's getting stale."

"It was stale three days ago," Billy mutters. "Now it's moldy."

I peer across the circle to the far bench, where Stock, Tommy, and Rose sit in a row. "What do you all think?"

"Building a house of cards based on the type of card?" Stock answers with a shrug. "It's tedious, boring. If I was a patron, I'd pass."

"Sort of like being awake and counting sheep," Rose adds, and Tommy laughs.

"You know the deal," Ral says evenly. "Constructive criticism only, please."

"Constructive criticism," Stock repeats. He leans onto Tommy's shoulder. "Okay, I'd rather watch paint dry than watch you two fuckups sort cards above your heads. Constructive enough?"

Billy mumbles an obscenity and takes a step forward, but Ral holds him back, keeping him inside the perimeter of their stage.

It's like this, some mornings. We're one troupe, a ring of seven sorcerers working together, bettering one another, but the scars from stitching our factions together—Stock, Tommy, and Rose, with Ral, Billy, Grace, and me—they've never faded completely. Most times we manage to pretend they've healed. We ignore them. But some days one of us—almost always Stock—starts picking at the edges, whether 'cause he's in the throes of a shine withdrawal or 'cause he's just generally more of a prick that day than the last.

"You've got people around your stage every night, you two," I tell Ral and Billy, trying to make my voice sound warm and encouraging. "You're just tired of your own trick—hell, I'm tired of mine. I'm starting to see feathers in my dreams."

"Sure that's all you're dreaming about, Kendrick?" Stock cuts in.

"Excuse me?"

"He's been an ass since he got down here, think he's got shine withdrawal," Grace whispers beside me. "Do us all a favor and just ignore him."

But Stock persists. "Swore I saw someone *dreamy* leaving your room this morning." He gives me his ratlike smile and starts wiggling his eyebrows at me like a goon. I feel like throwing a shock of magic right into his gut, but I manage to stay focused on my cigarette. *You need to forget about Gunn in your room this morning, forget about what you promised him—and just lose yourself in the magic.*

Thankfully, Billy and Ral bring us back to their trick. After

Grace and I humbly suggest a few ways they could work in some audience participation, they're satisfied enough, and we all disperse to work on our own tricks on our respective stages.

Around noon, we break for lunch. I head out with Ral, Billy, and Grace for a quick bite at Moby's Diner, where Billy orders two slices of pie and then only eats one bite of each just "'cause he can." We've all reacted to our new lifestyles differently, but then again, we're all here for different reasons. Grace wants a new start—and she's naturally cautious, a saver—while Ral and I are taking care of people back home. But Billy's a lone wolf, and now has more money than he knows what to do with. So he splurges on dumb stuff all the time, like flashy cuff links, or this big, gaudy ring he's never even gotten to wear, since Gunn says it's too distracting to sport during our show.

We quickly wrap up lunch, hustle back to the Den, and Gunn comes in a little after one.

"I'm billing tonight's performance as the Night Sky. Dawson's already printing the tickets," Gunn says, as the seven of us trail him to the middle of the show space, where lounge chairs are clustered into little sitting areas. We call this area the "shine section," since it's where most patrons go once they take their nightcap of sorcerer's shine, after the finale. Here, or in the VIP lounge that bigwig patrons can rent along the left-side hall, when Gunn's not using it to entertain some Shaw higher-ups.

"Got the new idea last night—tonight's finale will be a worthy addition to our rotation." Gunn settles into a plush green armchair. "I'm picturing a huge moon, planets. Shooting comets through mist. I want it eerie but beautiful at the same time."

For as cold and calculating as Gunn can be when he wants something, I have to hand it to him: he's got an artist's touch, a true grasp of magic. His ideas for our finales are always elaborate, big-picture, like this new one, but he knows what our troupe is capable of, and every night, we don't fail him. "Ral, I thought you could handle the large-scale illusion, so focus on the back-drop—maybe add a slow spin to the floor to keep it unsettling. Billy, as always, you need to fill his vision in—night mist, a faint wind," he says. "Grace, I know you appreciate the details. You're on the stars."

"Understood, sir," Grace answers.

"Tommy and Rose." Gunn glances at the dark-haired pair. "I want you manipulating a moon. Get creative. Use those visual magic gifts of yours and take it through its phases slowly, a full moon until it all but pinches out at the end."

Tommy nods and turns to Rose, and the two immediately start whispering ideas.

Gunn looks up at the lofted ceiling. "And Stock, our motions expert, I need a slow orbit of planets. Have them rotating about a story high, so everyone can appreciate the full view."

Stock shoots me a snarky look as he asks, "What about Joan, sir?"

Gunn doesn't tear his gaze away from the ceiling. "Joan's the comet."

I feel a wave of embarrassment as Stock rolls his eyes and mouths to me, *Dreamy.* But he doesn't say another word as Gunn settles back in his chair.

"After the finale, lead the audience toward your stage." Gunn gestures to the raised stage in the back of the space. It's where we brew the audience their collective nightcap of sorcerer's shine, before the stagehands pass it around to the crowd to drink.

"All right." Gunn stands to leave. "I'll be back to see what you come up with."

So we work, each of us taking our favorite place along the show space's perimeter, improvising with magic until we get to a finale we're all happy with. I wait for Ral to get the floor slowly spinning, wait for the others to set the stars and the planets and the textured, smoky night. And then, in this man-made sky of possibility, I shoot the brightest, electric-orange comet from the double doors straight across to the back stage.

But I'm too distracted to enjoy it, unable to put everything else away and just relish the trick. Gunn's earlier visit, his haunting words—*you run until you win, or until you fall*—that somehow manage to flatter as much as disturb me. Ben's letter, my promise of sharing Mama's blood-magic, Stock's taunts: it's all buzzing, closing in.

Joan's the comet.

After a dry run of our new forty-five-minute finale for Gunn, we gather around him at the base of the stage to hear his final thoughts. The double doors to the show space clang open at the same time, and a team of young Shaw thugs bursts into the space.

The street urchins of the Shaws' operation rarely attend our show, but they take full advantage of the extra shine we brew during the previous night's performance. And in the slim window between our rehearsal and eight p.m., the Red Den gets handed over to the young runners and smugglers stopping in for a magic ride before their night's work. Their ringleader, Win Matthews—the underboss who runs the Shaws' smuggling operation, I've gathered—spots Gunn across the show space and waves him down.

"Be down here by seven thirty," Gunn says, dismissing us. "Wear the usual, the dresses and tuxes," he adds, referring to the wardrobe we all received as soon as the doors to our new Red Den opened. He nods to me. "And give me fifteen minutes, Joan. I'll be in my office."

I feel all eyes of the troupe fall on me, and that tug-of-war of emotions pulls underneath my skin again. I gulp and nod. "Of course, sir."

Stock gives me an arched eyebrow as Gunn takes Win into his office along the right-side hall. The tension inside our troupe circle is now palpable, so thick and bitter I can almost taste it. "You've got something to say, just say it," I finally snap at Stock.

But Ral's the one who answers. "We're all adults," he says slowly. "We're all here to do a job. I suggest we go upstairs and get ready, before we do or say anything we might regret."

"Yeah, all right," Stock says, but keeps his eyes on me. "See you all down here soon." Then he adds as he walks away, "*Comet.*"

I will my anger to fade, avoid meeting Grace's probing stare as we all filter toward the hall that leads back to our rooms. I'm sure she's going to start grilling me over why Gunn wants to meet with me as soon as we get upstairs, and I'm not looking forward to it.

But as I'm about to turn down the hall, I spot Win Matthews's new boy—the one I met a few nights back—hovering over the liquor bar in the corner. Alex Danfrey, his name was—the one who was chatting me up as his friend was lost to a shine-high. He's sitting with Howie now, and about three other Shaw young guns. And like he can sense my stare, Alex looks up and we lock eyes.

I've seen a lot of faces here at the Den, but it's hard for me to figure out if someone's a looker on first glance—there's just too much to take in at once to make any kind of decision. It's really the second chance I get that makes or breaks it.

And on this second chance, I realize Alex's face is pretty much perfect. Wide eyes that are blue from here, blond hair that's soft, unlike so many of the gangsters with their polished helmets of pomade. Straight nose, right-angle jaw. I notice he's got a nice build, too, not too big, not too slim, his long legs stretched out under the bar as his torso's rounded over its edge.

Go, Joan. Move.

Put your head down. This is no time to get distracted.

I give him a smile and force myself to keep walking down the corridor.

But when I'm halfway down the hall, I hear a hesitant, "Joan, right?"

I turn around. And there he is, Alex, no more than ten feet away, like I conjured him there myself. I don't say anything, but I get a flippy, almost sick feeling in my stomach, now that he's closer.

"Just need to use the washroom." Alex gives a big exhale when I don't answer. "Actually, I don't need to use the washroom. I just . . . wanted to say hello."

But my mind stays blank, and I keep staring like a damn fool at his pretty face.

"Anyway, probably should get going," he says, not that I blame him, seeing as he's found a weird mute in the hall. He turns back to the main space.

And then I find my nerve, my magic, and quick throw up a double-sided protective wall in front of him at the mouth of the hallway: on the show space side, a replica of an empty hall. On ours, a thin sheet of glass, so we can see the show space without being seen ourselves.

Alex turns back to me, a sparkle in his eye. "Wait . . . was that *you*?"

"Got to watch what you say in this place." I recover with a smile. "I feel a bit more comfortable talking, now that we have some privacy."

"So you're a sorcerer?"

I make a little curtsy.

He smiles. "I thought you said you were a stagehand."

"No, you *assumed* I was a stagehand."

His smile grows wider as he turns to the new wall and reaches out to touch it. "What do they see on the other side?"

"An empty hall."

He won't meet my eyes, just keeps looking at the wall I've conjured. "A double-sided trick. Impressive."

"Does that surprise you?"

"Not at all." He turns around and looks at me. "If I'm honest, I really did think there was something magic about you."

His compliment does something to my cheeks—warms them before I can stop it. "You know what a double-sided trick is," I say. "That's impressive too, for a guy working the streets."

His smile turns the slightest shade serious. "Well, you know my last name. Pretty sure that says it all."

Alex *Danfrey*. The name did sound vaguely familiar when that shiner Howie kept rambling on about him the other night, but I couldn't place why. I still can't. "Sorry, have to say I've got no idea if that's supposed to mean something to me."

He studies my face, like he's looking for a lie. "You've got to be kidding me." He clears his throat. "You don't read the news?"

I shrug. "Newspapers aren't a necessity where I'm from."

"Well, I guess that's kind of refreshing." He shifts a bit, crosses his arms in front of him, and leans against my manipulated wall, a strange game of trust. "Let's just say my family had quite a public run-in with the law."

"That's why you're here, working for this lot?" I nod behind him, out to the main show space where his running buddies are likely getting shot to Sunday. "Can't help who you are, sort of thing?"

Alex nods. "I guess you could say that."

"Got to be honest," I say, as I study him, "you don't look like the typical guy working on the smuggling end of things."

"And why's that?" He throws me a smirk as he ruffles his soft blond hair. "I'm not slick enough?"

I can't help but match his smile.

"Because I'm not sporting a fedora?" he says, and I laugh. "Not to worry, I just picked one out from the Sears, Roebuck catalog. It's on its way."

Alex laughs with me, looks down at his hands. "Hate to be

the first one to tell you, but you sort of stand out too. In a good way."

My grin grows even bigger. "Besides this whole sorcering thing, I really consider myself very ordinary." God, I'm flirting with him, and I can't stop myself.

"Oh, you're far from ordinary." He takes a step closer to me, and the movement catches me off guard, sends more of that sickening, churning, wonderful feeling thrashing around inside. "But I think it's good to be extraordinary."

And then he stares at me, not into my eyes, but right above my left ear. I can't hear what he whispers, but soon I feel the softest of pressures against my temple, and a new scent, heady and foreign, teases my nose.

I reach up and pull down the silky flower that's now tucked over my ear. It's a black, glistening orchid, red tongue, looks like some cross between a dragon and a flower you might find hidden in someone's dark dream, or growing on the moon. I'm near positive it only existed in Alex's imagination, until now.

"So you can sorcer too."

Alex gives a little bow. "They've got me pulling tricks on the road, protection walls, coast guard diversions, police code scrambling, that sort of thing." He holds his hands up, as if summoning the room. "Nothing as elaborate and big-time as your show here." He looks over his shoulder. "Speaking of, we're heading on another smuggling run soon. So unless you've found some way to stop time, I probably should go."

But I want him to stay. Something about Alex draws me in, like a magnet, makes me want to joke with him, keep him talking.

I focus on the wall behind him and force myself to say, "*Release.*" I nod. "Go on, you can pass through it now."

Alex pinches his fingers a few inches in front of his brow, and then a fully formed black fedora appears out of nothing, the brim inserting itself right in between his fingertips. Alex grins, takes off his new hat, tips it in my direction, and as his hand extends, the hat vanishes. "Till we meet again, Joan."

Then he turns, to join his gangster buddies across the Red Den.

I whip around, unable to wipe the smile off my face. I practically prance back toward the stairs. It's been a long time since something's felt easy, light, *free*.

But then I spot Gunn standing outside his office door. *How long was Gunn watching us? Watching me?*

"Our meeting, sir," I recall out loud, the feeling of freedom that Alex brought on like a summer wind all but snuffed out as I remember what I'm about to share: *Mama's secrets*, my *secrets, the dark magic that Mama never wanted me to whisper, much less sell* . . .

"That's right. I'm ready for you," he says, as Win Matthews slips out from Gunn's office. But Gunn doesn't watch him go, or move from the doorway. He just keeps staring at the orchid tucked behind my ear.

So like a reflex, I reach into my hair, find the flower, and pinch it out like it's made of air, before following Gunn into his office.

Alex's flower was just a trick. An easy manipulation, one I could do over a thousand times without a blink. But still, it pains me a little that it's gone.

BIG FISH

ALEX

"I'm hankering for the shine," Howie says beside me. "Like bad. Look at my hands."

I glance at Howie's shaky, chapped fingers as he runs them around each other. "It's just the withdrawal," I say, and turn back to the water. The moon hangs over it low and bright, casts a long thread of spun silver across the dark ocean as we cut through it on our bare-hull boat, forty knots speed, engine as large as an airplane. It's a beautiful night, an otherworldly night, the kind of night you want to be gazing at the vast, star-studded sky with a dame like Joan. Not with Howie. "If you power through it, you'll be fine by tomorrow."

"But maybe I don't want to be *fine*. Maybe I want to be electric."

"Take a break, okay, How? You've been hitting the shine hard all week. Relax."

Howie pulls his thin coat tighter around him. "What are you, my mother?"

It's dark, but I can still see the gray tint around Howie's cheekbones, the dullness to his eyes. Back in training, the Unit taught us the long-term effects of a steady shine diet: how the stuff eventually steals the color out of life, dulls it until you can't stand living without the polish of magic. But I don't think I ever fully understood what that meant until I became attached to Howie's side. Since we left Lorton, he's only happy anymore when he's high. Time in between he spends angry, restless—and clamoring for the next time he can steal a glimpse of a world that doesn't last.

I've tried to tell him he survived shine withdrawal before, and that he'll end up hollowing himself into a shell if he keeps going at this pace, but you can't reason with him. And after so many times of trying, I started worrying that too much anti-shine talk might compromise my cover. So tonight I stay silent and watch the indigo water race by the rudders.

We're several miles off the coast, on our way through the waters of the Atlantic. Win's in the front as captain, and Howie and I are shivering on the bench in the back. Late November's winds are brutal, breath-stealing, and while neither one of us is thrilled about snuggling, we're huddled next to each other for warmth.

"Even a cigarette would help," Howie mutters.

"Christ, How, why didn't you buy another pack before we left?"

Howie shrugs. "'Cause you usually bring enough for both of us."

And usually, I do take care of these little details, but I've been working overtime, exhausted. Howie's clearly exhausted too. But that's not the only reason we've been picking at each other, sparring like siblings vying for their parents' affection. There's a tension I haven't been able to shake, a thick, persistent one lodged right between us.

"Seriously, can't you do something about this?" Howie waves his hand above us to indicate the cold wind.

"It's tougher when we're moving, but I'll try." I focus, close my eyes. I picture a bubble of warm, soft air wrapping around us like a towel, command, "*Envelop.*"

After a minute, Howie stops shaking beside me.

Needless to say, we are definitely not, as Howie predicted when we first got out of Lorton, "partying until dawn." If I'm figuring right, this is our twelfth straight night of running with Win—no nights off, no breaks. Since that first night, when things went south with Baltimore out at the warehouse, we've been on the road by the start of every evening for a trade, or a redistillery run, or some other clandestine errand for the Shaws. Sometimes I don't come home until the sun's up, and other than the few times Howie and I have lingered at the Red Den waiting for Win, we're either on the road, or crashing. In fact, the couple of times I've managed to sneak out and call Agent Frain have been at noon, when I know the rest of my smuggling world will be sleeping.

We're putting our heads down, as Howie says, not asking questions, showing we're willing to pay our dues, get broken and rebuilt as slick, lethal Shaw boys. *And in turn, edging closer to Boss McEvoy*. But so far, the biggest Shaw fish has evaded me.

"We're here," Win calls back, interrupting my thoughts. He cuts the engine, and our boat gives a little jump, then sighs and floats a few feet more into the dark water.

Ahead of us, a long line of ships, boats, cruisers, and cutters blink and flash like stars peppering the black ocean.

"Wow," Howie whispers, "it's like a little city out here."

We've reached a stretch of safe waters right behind coast guard territory called "Magic Row," where dust sweepers and obi smugglers from overseas and the islands shuttle in their magic contraband, then wait for street runners like us to come trade and bring their products back to shore. Tonight we're after fae dust—an addictive, paranoia-inducing, magic blue powder that the Irish boast they stole from another reality. No one knows what the stuff really is, or where it actually comes from, but dust causes a fierce psychedelic trip, and unlike shine, transports across the sea easily. And there's a steady market for mobile magic, of any sort—even, apparently, if the high drives you crazy. My role in this smuggling venture: throwing distress signal manipulations up and down the coast, giving the coast guard false alarms to chase, as our boat evades their radios.

Win turns the boat engine on low again and we slowly churn through the waves to a two-story ship marked EMERALD JANE. Win turns the wheel, right, left, right, until we're right next to the large ship like a sidecar.

"HO! What's your business?" a man on deck calls down to us in a soft Irish lilt.

"It's Win Matthews, with the Shaws," Win calls up. "We're here for the dust."

There's a pause, then a muffled discussion as the ship hand confers with his cronies. "All right, come onboard."

Howie and I follow Win silently, each of us climbing up the rope ladder on the side of the ship. We clamber onto the deck, and we're immediately surrounded by a five-man crew, all of them cloaked in thick, salty, musty layers. The stench of weeks at sea curls around and suffocates us.

"Been out here long?" Win asks what I'm thinking.

"Near a month," the man with the lilt answers. "Long journey. Started up in Maine, if you can believe it. Heading to talk with buyers in Virginia Beach tomorrow."

The Emerald Jane, *dust deals up and down the East* Coast, I repeat silently, and file it away. I've become an expert at taking notes without a pen, at remembering small details. Everything gets stored and saved for the next time I get to talk to Agent Frain: all the ways we might manage to hook the big fish we're planning to fry.

"You have any trouble with the pigs?" the man adds. The rest of his team pats us down, takes our weapons, and puts them in a box on the boat's far side for safekeeping.

"No, ride out was smooth. We brought our street sorcerer. He never fails." Win nods to me in recognition, while Howie shifts uncomfortably at Win's compliment. "You've got the dust?"

"A hundred ounces, like we promised. You got the cash?"

"One thousand."

The smuggler nods, studies the water. "The sea has eyes and ears. Come, let's break bread below."

I swear, I almost follow them, invite myself right into the belly of this ship. My desire to find the beating heart of this underworld, so that I can wrap my hands around and destroy it—it's become my *own* sort of addiction. Of course, it's still about bringing down the types of men who broke apart my family. But there's something more now too, I can't deny it. The satisfaction of excelling at something very few people can do. The commitment to something real—something I might one day look back on and be proud of.

"You two stay here," Win tells Howie and me, and then leaves us to keep watch in the frigid midnight air.

The rest of the crew returns to their nighttime duties—ship hands finish mopping the deck, a few start tying thick knots alongside the ship—as Howie and I turn to face the water.

"You look tired, Danfrey," Howie whispers beside me.

I fake a laugh. "That's 'cause I *am* tired." I pause. "You're telling me you're not?"

"Nah, these runs light me on fire. 'Cause I want it, Danfrey, more than anything." He turns to study me. "I've been thinking, you know. About you. About this."

"Is that right?"

Howie rests his back against the boat beside me, then stretches out his legs, so he's at a perfect forty-five-degree angle facing the ship's interior. "Honestly, brother, I really don't think this street work is for you. I see how it's wearing on you."

I don't answer.

"There's no shame in it, though, you know? Admitting you're not hard enough for McEvoy's street, for running with the big boys. 'Cause someone like you, Danfrey, you could have a whole bunch of futures. Hell, you could be one of those performers the crowds flock to see at the revamped Red Den every night." He laughs. "You know, I haven't thought about that before, but I have to say that's a damned good idea. I hear Gunn managed to score quite a nice change purse to run the place. Could be a decent living. And a much safer one."

Howie waits, as if he's letting his idea settle in with me, but of course, I know the real reason for this "off-the-cuff" suggestion. Win's been relying more on me these past few weeks, and Howie less—which obviously doesn't sit well with him. Sure, Howie talks a big game, but in the end, he's sloppy, often shined or coming down from a high when he shows up for a job. Plus, he forgets things. Like when he didn't check all the rooms in a dealer's house last week, and some dust-bunny dissatisfied with his high came barging down the stairs with a loaded gun. Or when he mixed up the address of a local shine redistillery, and we ended up driving around Hell's Bottom for half an hour with ten gallons of newly lifted remedial spells in our trunk, looking for the right place.

"Besides"—Howie nudges me with his elbow—"there'd be other benefits."

I blow into my hands. "What are you talking about?"

"Oh, you know who I'm talking about." He arches one eyebrow, shoots me this exaggerated grin, and I can't help but laugh, despite the tension. "I've seen the way you've been watching that hot black-haired Betty they've got working the place."

"Who?"

"Oh, please, don't 'who' me."

He's clearly talking about Joan, and I blush, as I hadn't realized he was watching me, or rather, watching us. Sure, Howie's right—every time we're there, I try to catch her before she gets ready for her show and Howie and I head out the door. Never more than a quick flirtation, but it has me thinking about her from time to time. Joan's a warm, welcoming distraction when I need to take my mind off things, something harmless and exciting of my own. I laugh to myself. "It's that obvious?"

Howie shoots me an honest-to-God smile. "You might be a sorcerer, but you can't trick me, Alex Danfrey."

Win emerges from the boat and beckons us forward. "Howie, come on, grab the box," he calls over the ship deck. "Alex needs to focus on getting us home."

Howie's face changes immediately at the barked order, the menial task. And then I can almost see it, the faint spark between us fizzles, until there's nothing but cold, dull air. I offer to help Howie carry the goods, but that just seems to add insult to injury.

We spend the night near the coast, at some smuggler-friendly brothel-and-breakfast where I have to surround my room with a force field to sleep, considering the constant knocking bedposts and shine-induced singing blaring through the walls. Our entire next day is on the road, running our dust score to Win's local dealers across DC's sprawl, then a quick stop at the Red Den while Win shares a drink with Gunn. While Howie uses the chance to get shined in the bathroom, I manage to score a couple of minutes with Joan at the performance space's bar. We sneak in a checkers game using a board she conjures, while she teases me about wearing last night's clothes and smelling like a sailor.

When she's not looking, I leave her a conjured starfish as a souvenir.

I'm so tired that I almost can't see straight by the time Win takes us home. Still, I'm with-it enough to notice that Win makes a right onto 14th, instead of making a left up to my place. I sit straight up as we turn on F Street, drive through a neighborhood I've never seen, with shards of broken glass glistening on the curb like strange diamonds, sad row houses leaning on one another like shiners at the end of the night. We pull up to a nondescript building, three stories high, crumbling brick and mortar.

Before I can figure out what's happening, Win mumbles to Howie, "I'll stop by tomorrow."

And then I'm chilled with the significance of this situation. Win's ordering Howie out of the car. Which means that for some reason, I'm staying.

Howie steals a look back at me, then at his cousin. He laughs, the sound hard and brittle. "You two screwing each other behind my back or something?"

"I need your boy is all," Win says. "Alone. Nothing personal."

"Nothing personal," Howie repeats. He grabs the back of his headrest and turns around to look me in the eye. "You been casting spells to make this happen, Danfrey? Working with me just to work my cousin, pushing me down so you can get ahead?"

"Easy, Howie, don't be such a dame about it—" Win mutters beside him.

"You'd be nothing without me, you know that?" Howie cuts at me.

"Come on, Howie." I try to calm him down, but he barrels over me with, "Just forget it. All you Danfreys are traitors."

Heat sears my skin, blood rushes to my temples, the word "traitor" slapping me back to my father's trial. *Those D Street rats on the stand, my father in cuffs, the headline* PHARMA MOGUL BETRAYS HIS CAUSE *as reporters swarmed us on the courthouse steps*—"That was a shitty thing to say."

"And you deserve it."

I snap, "Christ, How, it's not my fault you're the family fuckup."

Howie stops moving, hell, it almost sounds like he stops breathing.

Shit. That just came out.

Howie lunges over the console, manages to box my ear with his palm. It doesn't hurt, but it does the job, makes *me* mad too, and I reach out and box him back. At that, a gauntlet's thrown, and he climbs around the front seat like he's going to dive on top of me—

"Goddamn it, you two!" Win takes his thick palms and pushes our heads apart, thrusting me against the backseat, sending Howie flying against his passenger side window. Win sighs. "Howie, seriously, get out."

Howie sits there, huffing and puffing, as I collect myself in the back. But I don't look at him. Sure, my courtship of Howie was calculated—but that doesn't mean what I feel for him isn't real. That doesn't mean I don't rely on Howie as a one-man social life more than I care to admit.

Finally Howie kicks open the flap door on Win's Model T. "Go suck each other." He spits on the ground and closes it with a *thwap.*

I want to follow him, maybe even apologize. I want to somehow tell him that he can have this world—that I'm just wearing it to turn it inside out and destroy it.

But Howie doesn't look back, and before I can figure out whether it's childish for me to call after him, Win settles his car back onto the road.

And then my guilt gives way, slowly but surely, to something else.

Finally I have to ask, "Where are we going?"

"The Boss has heard things," Win says slowly, eyes ahead.

"He's impressed. He wants to see you." He locates a crumpled box of cigarettes inside his pocket, pulls two out and lights them, then passes one to me. The car immediately becomes assaulted with thick, toxic air. The kind of air where it feels like dangerous things might just crawl out of the mist. The kind of air that lies waiting to spark a fire.

I nod, trying to keep my excitement tempered, appropriate. But inside I'm practically bursting. All the work, the nights, the smuggling runs, the magic—all of it is to meet McEvoy, learn his sins, and confess them for him. "Where's the meet?"

"Somewhere safe."

Win turns onto 13th Street, follows it through town, until the homes become stores become warehouses, until the road all but peters out. He pulls into a large abandoned lot. "McEvoy should be here soon." He cuts the engine and we both get out.

Broken glass dusts the edges of the gravel lot, and a sad, faded billboard stands tall amid the malnourished moonlit grass. The woman in the billboard's picture sports a hole where her face should be. But it feels appropriate, right in line with the ambiance.

Because this lot? It's the opposite of safe. This is a place where murders are committed.

We wait, leaning against Win's car in the cold, tearing through the last of his pack of Luckies. After waiting months to meet McEvoy, a few more minutes shouldn't rip me apart, but I can barely concentrate on the staccato small talk Win's attempting beside me about Jack Dempsey's latest fight.

Finally a black car pulls into the lot. McEvoy, I have to assume, emerges from the front seat and slowly walks toward us. He's got a fedora pulled down low, a thick, expensive-looking gray woolen coat with the collar popped up. My pulse starts to quicken, and there's a dull, almost sickening dread rising up from my core.

"Boss," Win says, "this is the boy I was telling you about. Alex Danfrey."

I gulp, trying not to choke. I wonder if McEvoy can sense it—that I'm here for him, like he's here for me.

He looks like he does in the papers, early fifties, polished, intimidating, somehow bigger—and smaller—all at the same time. "Heard a lot about you, Alex," Boss McEvoy says.

"Thank you, sir." I take a sharp inhale. "I hope all good things."

"You wouldn't be rising up otherwise," he says. "As it turns out, I'm in the market again for someone like you." He smirks and nods to Win. "But if you're going to have the honor of being my right-hand, my personal sorcerer, I need to make sure you fulfill all my needs." *Right-hand sorcerer. This is it. What the Feds planted me for, what all my work undercover comes down to.* "Go on, Win, bring out a bottle."

Win crosses back to his car, digs through his trunk, and removes a glass bottle filled with water—my best guess twelve ounces, what the black market has determined is the perfect amount for a sorcerer's shine transference. Any less water, the stuff's too potent, can cause a magic overdose. Any more, you're not getting the best high. But I'm surprised my transference skills matter at all to this man. McEvoy's king of the streets—he needs a sorcerer who can hide robberies, heists. Murders.

Win hands the bottle to McEvoy, who in turn hands it to me. "Brew for me."

It's been a long time, way too long for my first brew back to be for the Boss. "It's been a while," I softly tell McEvoy.

"I'm not a fan of excuses."

I give a little nod and wrap both hands around the glass.

I'm sure brewing shine is a little different for every sorcerer, but this is how it used to go for me: I imagined something mounting inside me—taking all my rage, desire, passion, fear, my magic—and I visualized it flowing through my veins, as tangible and real as blood. And then I pictured slicing my fingers open, letting all that pour out of me and bleed into the water inside the glass. And after it was done, for a while anyway—I actually felt wiped clean.

Sure enough, it begins. The glass starts to warm between my palms, and the water starts to boil. Sharp bursts of trapped lightning start crackling inside the bottle, sending the water crashing and swirling into something glistening, dark and red.

"Give it here," McEvoy says. He studies my sorcerer's shine, and then he smiles and hands it to Win. "Let's have a royal taster for the king."

Win looks hungrily into the bright sea of liquid rubies inside the glass. "Bottoms up."

He takes a sip of it, careful not to take more than an ounce. McEvoy and I both shift uncomfortably, waiting for the magic to settle into Win's veins, for the shine to take hold of him.

A minute later, Win gasps, "Holy . . . shit." He stumbles to sit on the ground, then flings himself on his back, his arms splayed out, his legs stretched at odd angles. And then, like he's seven, he starts making snow angels in the gravel as he lets out a childlike laughter. If I wasn't scared out of my mind, I'd laugh with him. I've never seen the man even remotely out of control.

"It's so bright," Win whispers as he stares up at the lone streetlamp in the lot.

McEvoy gives me a smirk. "Impressive." But then he turns away from me, begins to pace, like a restless tiger in a cage. "But there're a lot of impressive people in this world," he says. "And while sorcery is rare, I can afford to be choosy."

He takes a quick step toward me. Thanks to the streetlamp, I can see every detail of his face—the pores dotting his nose, the small capillaries around his eyes, the deep wrinkles etched by time and anger.

"I've been in this game a long time, Alex—and that's what it truly is, a game of power. A game that can transform people, just like magic, a game that can turn them inside out. It can make people do stupid things, dangerous things, especially if power is all they're after." Despite his aging face, McEvoy's eyes are clear, sharp, and wolfish. Like a jackal. The same Jackal who reportedly gunned down ten D Street thugs, execution-style in the street, in revenge for them killing Danny the Gun. Who runs through sorcerers almost as fast as cigarettes. Who wouldn't hesitate to skin me alive if he knew why I was really here.

"In my time leading the Shaws, I've come to understand the rules of this game intimately, Alex. And a man after nothing but power in this world is a man you can't trust." McEvoy nods at Win, who's still lying on the ground, shocked still, looking up at the streetlamp like it's the bright birth of the world's first angel. "Take Win over there. Above all else, he's working for his family." McEvoy turns his attention back to me. "That's something I'd bet the farm on. That's a man you can trust."

He cocks his head. "But my last sorcerer, the one who lasted all of a few weeks?" A gash of a frown cuts across McEvoy's face. "I could see right through him. Little prick thought he was smarter, more powerful than me, hid secrets. Thought he was tricky enough that I wouldn't find out." He stares at me, those eyes cold and piercing. "You understand what I'm trying to say to you?"

My heart is a hummingbird right now, fluttering in my chest. I swear McEvoy's so close he must hear it. "Yes, sir," I manage to say evenly.

"So I need to know, Alex, right now. What else are you after in this game? You obviously had other options, thanks to your father." He smiles, but it just makes him look even more like a wolf before it lunges. "Why are you and I here tonight?"

He's so close, I swear he can reach in and grab out what I'm thinking. I stop breathing, try to stand taller, refuse to let him see anything but what I want him to see.

"I want to serve you." Flattery, a knee-jerk instinct. "I think I can learn a lot from a man like you."

"Lie," McEvoy snaps.

"No sir, I want to be near you," I correct quickly. *Christ, I hear the desperation in my own voice.* "I want to be safe, to know I've got a bright future by your side."

"I smell bullshit again," he cuts in, slowly encircling me, sizing me up. My eyes dart to Win, who's still tripping on my magic. McEvoy could take that gun I see poking out of his holster and put a bullet in my head, right here, right now. And no one would save me. Hell, no one would even know he did it. Maybe I could manipulate the gun, the bullet—maybe I could save myself, take him down instead.

But what then?

Take out all the Shaws?

Take out the Feds?

"Alex"—McEvoy brings me back—"don't fuck with me. I'll ask you one more time. Why are you after me?"

I freeze at his word choice, *after me.* But that's not what he means. He can't know. *There's no way he can know.*

I close my eyes, try to think, but time keeps moving forward, and fear is crawling up my spine, stealing my breath, my words. I hear a sigh, and then the sound of metal on leather, a holster—

My eyes fly open to see McEvoy's gun trained inches from my forehead. Then he says softly, and not unkindly, "Afraid time's up, Alex. Pity."

Say something. Save yourself, my mind shrieks. But it's my body, my magic, that finally steps in—

A flat wall of stone erupts out of the ground in front of me, ten feet long, ten feet high, rumbles fast and furious as McEvoy's bullet sounds, the hungry pop of his gun echoing through the cold air and cracking against the rock.

The wall saved me, stopped the bullet just in time—

In an odd, dissociated moment, the first thing I feel is a pang of pride for quick magic. And then I double over. *My magic only did what it had to because McEvoy almost killed me he wanted to kill me—*

"ALEX!" McEvoy barks.

I hobble to stand, sick and twisted behind the wall. I almost run, but I force myself to focus, to remember the endgame. *Keep going you can do this you're almost there—*

I walk around my protection wall, approach McEvoy slowly to stand by his side. I need to give McEvoy the truth—at least, the version of the truth that I'm able to give him.

So I keep my eyes trained on my stone wall manipulation, the one that now cuts the parking lot in half. And then I reach down inside, channel everything I've got left, and perform a stacked trick, by conjuring a two-dimensional image of a man right onto my wall. A man I loathe—the man I know that McEvoy hates more than anyone for killing his cousin in cold blood—perhaps the one person who does bind McEvoy and me together, despite everything else.

I can draw the gangster from memory. The dark hair, large figure, creased face—

And then McEvoy's standing, gun in hand, face-to-face with a replica of the D Street boss, Boss Colletto. McEvoy gasps and raises his gun higher on instinct.

"The real reason I want to work with you?" I say beside him, and then I force myself to finish the trick. I look back to my fabrication of Colletto on the stone wall and imagine the entire wall glass, and my mind shattering it with a hammer. The replica and the wall burst into a million shards, break against the night sky, and finally swirl away like dust. "Revenge," I say numbly. "Simple as that."

McEvoy wrestles his gaze away from the last flickers of my shattered manipulation. He glances at Win, who's on the ground, dumbfounded, unsure whether what he just witnessed was a dream or real. And then Boss McEvoy lets go with a sharp cackle of a laugh, the caw of a crow across the empty lot.

"Oh, Danfrey." He slaps me on the shoulder, once, his grasp heavy and possessive. "We're going to work out just fine."

A MAGICAL STORM

JOAN

Gunn tells our troupe we're stopping rehearsal early today. He doesn't explain why, though of course I already know: there's a gathering of all the underbosses at the Red Den this December evening, but Gunn and I can't miss a day of analyzing and discussing Mama's dark blood-magic spells, so he and I need time to meet before. We've been scheming in Gunn's office every evening for weeks, since that day I first confessed that I knew a set of special spells—the day I spent over an hour locked in there after rehearsal, doing my best to answer his nonstop questions.

I don't know how much Gunn's told Boss McEvoy or the other underbosses about our little side meetings, but I know my charge—*I'm* not to tell a soul.

Right now it's almost four o'clock, and my mind's been wandering all afternoon. I try one last time to focus on rehearsal, on the heady feeling I get when I throw myself completely into performance magic and manage to forget everything else. Tonight Gunn has a new finale idea he's billing as "A Magical Storm," and it's supposed to be a true Category Five hurricane. Our visual experts Tommy and Rose are conjuring lightning, with Grace, our amplifier, on galloping thunder. Billy and Ral will send slick curtains of rain from the ceiling to a few feet over the crowd's heads, while Stock and I will work together to churn hurricane winds, meant to span from the double doors all the way to the back stage, with the storm's eye falling right over the audience in the center.

But our performance hasn't come together yet. The lightning feels off, sporadic, dangerous. Grace's amplified thunder is kind of ill-timed, and Ral slips up once and sends the rain pummeling to the floor. While I'm to bring the winds and Stock, our motions expert, is in charge of churning them, we can't find our footing together, and we end up picking at each other through the entire dress rehearsal.

There's a hum of discord in the troupe's usual melody, a tension, even in the magic. And as much as I try and deny it, instinct tells me it's got something to do with me. How I've been slowly disrupting our rhythm as I get pulled, further each day, into my own strange dance with Gunn.

Around four thirty Gunn calls it quits, despite how unready the troupe looks and feels. He mumbles, "Good luck" and heads into his office alone—but I know it's just a matter of time until he emerges and comes looking for me.

"Well, that was ugly," Billy declares to the troupe near the base of the back stage. "If tonight's show's just as hideous, I'm going to down a shot of shine to get through it."

"Don't fall down the rabbit hole. Not too much, we promised each other," Ral scolds him softly. "Drink it after the show, if you want to celebrate, not before."

I've been noticing Ral and Billy on the floor more and more each night at the end of our performances, taking a shot of shine right along with the audience. Billy doesn't surprise me, as even back at the warehouse clearing it was obvious he was often tempted to drink the stuff. But Ral does. Then again, guess he's been working hard, and I'm sure he welcomes the escape from missing his family—I just hope he really does know how much is too much, and when to slow down. Trouble is, I barely get any downtime with him or the rest of the troupe anymore, considering my side venture with Gunn. I doubt unsought advice from me would go over so well these days.

Billy shrugs and shoves his hands in his pockets. "Then I'm taking a nap."

Grace smirks. "Ral, you're in charge of waking him up on time," she says. "I'm sure as hell not trying to wake a dragon."

I give a laugh beside her as Billy and Ral head back to their room. She hops on the stage next to me, while Tommy, Rose, and Stock walk off toward the double doors, arguing about whether they've got time to sneak in a motion picture before our own show.

"We should get some air too." Grace turns to me once they've gone. "Catch a smoke and walk around the block or something. It's been a while since we've managed to sneak out of this place."

She's right—we haven't done our coffee-and-fire-escape ritual in over a week, and it would be smart for me to come up for air. Between rehearsals, my secret meetings with Gunn, and our nightly shows, I barely have a moment where I'm not focused on magic of one sort or another.

Besides, things have felt . . . different between Grace and me since I started meeting with Gunn about the blood-magic. When I first shared some of Mama's spells, when Gunn said no one could know about this magic but him and me, he mentioned, in passing, that I'd need to protect myself a little more, close my mind and keep my thoughts neutral so "certain talents don't go fishing around inside." Of course he was talking about the troupe, Grace's mining skills in particular, so when I'm around her these days I picture my mind a house, and keep all the doors locked but the breezy foyer.

Grace has to feel it. In fact, I feel *her*, trying to lock-pick her way inside, trying to use her magic to link us back together.

But Gunn's warnings, the extra payments he's funneling me for the cabin, how much I stand to win if the blood-magic comes through as Gunn hopes, or lose if it doesn't—I've got no choice but to keep her out.

That doesn't mean I don't miss her. "Let's do it." I flash her a smile. "Haven't had a smoke since this morning."

"That's 'cause you never buy your own packs." She laughs, and I laugh with her.

"That's 'cause I never step foot outside this place anymore."

"I know," she says, and her laughter falls away. "Maybe because you've been spending an awful lot of time with someone else."

"Gunn just wants a second opinion on our show sometimes," I say slowly.

"Not sometimes." She cocks her head, studies me. "You're in there every day."

"You stalking me, Grace Dune?" I try to make my tone light, but Grace's face says she's having none of it.

And of course, Gunn decides at that moment to bellow for me, like an owner calling for his dog in the hall. "Joan, come on, don't have all night."

Grace and I stare at each other, for a second, a minute.

"I'm sorry, I—I better go. Would have loved to step outside, though . . ."

"Hope you're being careful, Joan."

"Of course I am. I always am." But Lord, that sounds defensive even to me.

"I know what Stock's been teasing you about. You must know it too." Grace's eyes roam my face, like she's trying to figure out another way inside my mind. "Stock's been whispering it to all of us, saying that you're sleeping your way to the top of our troupe, trying to angle yourself as the star."

My face grows hot, flushed. But of course this isn't news—Stock's been making little comments every chance he gets since he caught Gunn a few times entering or leaving my room. Part of me almost wishes it were that simple. "And you believe him?"

"'Course not." But she doesn't sound convincing.

"You've just got to trust me, all right?" I say quickly, tugging my shirtsleeves down farther, past my hands. My shirt hides my fresh, recent blood-magic cuts, I'm sure of it, but the tug still comes fast as a reflex. I lower my voice. "I swear to you, it's not like that. I know what I'm doing."

"Just . . ." Grace pauses, sighs. "*Be careful*, Joan." Then she leaves, heads toward the double doors to the outside world.

If she turns around, I think in a desperate, impulsive moment, *maybe I'll tell her, about all of it, despite Gunn's warnings. I trust her, after all. I always have.*

But Grace doesn't look back.

I'm halfway through his office door when Gunn says, "Spellbind the door. You know the underbosses are coming by, and we're far from ready to show them anything."

Without a word, I do what he asks, cross the hallway to the men's bathroom on the other side and spellbind it with a linked trick, "*Out becomes in*." As I walk through Gunn's door, I complete the link with, "*In becomes out*," so that anyone opening Gunn's office will actually walk into the bathroom. And then I settle on the chair on the near side of his desk.

For weeks our meetings have started the same way: I brew twelve ounces of sorcerer's shine into a bottle he stores under his desk. Then I conjure Mama's caging spell again in front of him, the blood-magic spell I used to trap Stock and me in that glass cage during our final test in the clearing, and the same one

I'm pretty sure I managed to perform the night of Mama's death, to imprison my magic touch.

Now I place my newly sorcered shine on his desk. Gunn caps the bottle and hands me his letter opener without a word. I roll up my right sleeve to my elbow, expose ten tight, clustered cuts right at the center of my forearm. I lean my forearm over the capped bottle, and then, before I can flinch, I draw the blade quick and light across my arm once more. As the cut blooms red, and blood runs hot and fast over the cap, I recite clear and strong, *"With purpose and a stalwart heart, a sacrifice. Less of me, an offering to cage for eternity. My wish, to cage this shine forever, or until I release it."*

The glass bottle coated in red simmers, dances, and shudders on the desk before it sighs and stops—signaling that the caging spell is complete. *Effective.*

Gunn pulls out his notebook, the leather-bound one he keeps locked in his desk drawer. "Run me through it again, exactly how it works."

After our talk in my bedroom a few weeks back, after Gunn realized the secrets I was keeping, the deal between us has evolved. For my extra efforts and for the secrets of Mama's magic, Gunn is making weekly payments on our Parsonage cabin, like he promised. But now Gunn's given me another carrot, since he's come to think that Mama's caging spell could be a way to defy the laws of magic, a key to doing the impossible: creating a lasting sorcerer's shine, one that doesn't revert to water after a day. "All I have to do" is figure out a way around the spell's limitations—*limitations*, I might add, that are the purpose of the spell itself—and Gunn has promised me 10 percent of whatever the Shaws manage to score for the product.

Of course I feel guilty, uncomfortable, hell, even traitorous, over what I'm trying to pull off behind this door. A powerful magic like Mama's was never meant to get into the hands of a man like Gunn, which is why she swore me to secrecy in the first place. Blood-magic is meant to be a last-resort magic, a sacrifice of yourself for something extraordinary . . . not a potential way to work around magic's limits so that a mind-bending drug can turn this country upside down. 'Cause if sorcerer's shine becomes storable, like Gunn hopes? The law wouldn't be able to control it. It would no longer be rare, or confined to shining rooms—*it could be shipped into the hands of every Tom, Dick, and Harry across America*. And I saw shine's choke hold first-hand, how the more Uncle Jed downed his own shine, the more the real world lost its color. How, eventually, it was only thing that mattered to him. I'm seeing it a bit with Tommy, Stock, and Rose, even Billy—they're more restless, less satisfied until that time of the night when they can lose themselves to shine on the show space floor. Families would be destroyed. Jobs would be lost. Hell, crime might shoot through the roof.

And yet.

I also think about what Gunn's success could mean, for me, for what's left of my own family. How floored Ben would be if I bought him his own Six Coupe, how Ruby would flip over an actual doll. I picture us, playing on a carpeted floor, with bright light streaming through curtained windows, and Ben laughing behind us, smoking a nice cigar. *They'd never go hungry, never want for anything again.*

I twist myself around completely each day about it, each time I'm sitting in this chair. But the cold, hard truth, the final say in the matter?

Even if I wanted to back out, it's too late. I signed my name in blood under Gunn's. And Gunn's not the kind of man who lets you walk away from that.

"This caging spell is from a set of spells my mama's female ancestors fashioned," I answer slowly. "They've kept their blood-magic secret for generations, as it's a dark and powerful gift." *A gift never meant for a man like you.*

I keep my eyes trained on the desk, force myself to keep going, to share what I need to survive. *There is no choice here.* "The sorcerer focuses on what she wants to achieve, without regret or hesitation—with a stalwart heart—and sacrifices something of her own to achieve it."

"You mean she offers her blood." Gunn scratches notes into his notebook.

I nod. "Mama had a bunch of different blood-spells. Ones that used blood to track where we went. Ones that protected us from harm." My heart stutters a beat as I picture Mama in our washroom again, painting my lips and eyelids with her blood, keeping me safe from the leering eyes of Jed, and I swallow before my voice can catch. "The one I just showed you, the caging spell, is traditionally meant to lock away an evil, by putting something symbolic in a vessel, like in a bottle or a jar. Then you lock and seal the vessel with your blood, say your intention, and the magic guards the stated evil and keeps you safe."

But Gunn doesn't care about the spell's traditions. Just how he can exploit it now. "So this caging spell is teachable?"

"Yes. My mama taught me."

He leans over, grabs my sealed bottle of shine to inspect it.

"The shine is now trapped by the caging spell." I add. "It's no longer governed by the usual limitations of pure magic. It will stay preserved in there forever, or until I release it."

"Until *you* release it." Gunn meets my eyes. "Which means no one else will be able to open it." And of course, this is the dead end we've reached day in, day out. There's no denying that Gunn is onto something: Mama's caging spell does manage to defy the shelf life of shine. It's a way to cage an evil in a bottle forever, which means it can prevent shine's magic high from ever fading. But like I said, what Gunn wants—the linch-pin that could bring a shippable shine to pass—it's not possible. 'Cause once I seal the shine bottle with my blood, no one else can open it.

Not that Gunn accepts this.

He rests his forehead in his hands, leans his elbows on his desk. "We need to find a work-around, you understand? What I've been planning, everything I've been working toward, is finally coming together—but there's no room for error, no time to slow down." He stares at me. "This is the last piece. But this piece has to fall into place for the entire picture to come together."

This is all I ever get from Gunn. *Pieces.* Pieces to some plan I barely know anything about. Pieces that he gives me sparingly, just enough to remind me that more than I realize is at stake, but not enough that I'll ever be able to use the pieces to betray him.

"You need to figure this out soon, Joan."

Make the impossible possible.

But like always, I say what I have to, to get through today. "I know, sir." I nod. "I will."

Outside Gunn's office, we hear the turn of Gunn's doorknob, but the door doesn't open, thanks to my linked trick. Then the slamming of another door. A muffled curse, and then another.

"Someone's in the hall." Gunn quickly grabs the bottle of sealed shine, places it in his bottom drawer, and locks it away. "Figure out who."

I press my ear to the door, whisper *"Amplify,"* and hear more curses, mutterings, a muffled, *"I'm not sure, Boss—"*

"My best guess? Boss McEvoy."

"What the hell's he doing here?" Gunn's face is now a shade paler, though I swear I thought Gunn said there was a meeting of McEvoy's underbosses. "Where'd you link this door to?"

"The bathroom."

Gunn stands up. "Quick, go on, open the door."

I release the linked trick, and we open Gunn's office to a flustered Boss McEvoy barreling out of the john. My pulse quickens, just on seeing him. A man nicknamed the Jackal—a man who Shaw boys whisper collects teeth and fingernails as souvenirs—is not someone you want to trick.

"Is every door in this fucking Den spellbound?" McEvoy spits at me as he heads toward Gunn's office.

My throat closes, but Gunn saves me with, "She was demonstrating a new linked trick for our finale. Apologies, sir, I didn't realize you'd be stopping by."

"I always make my rounds, even to the far-flung corners of my empire," McEvoy digs. He throws a shoulder as he sidesteps me into Gunn's office, so I step out into the hall. "Besides, I need to talk to you, about Sullivan."

"Something happen down at the racetrack, sir?" Gunn asks.

McEvoy holds up his hand to Gunn, a sign for, *Wait a minute.* He calls into the hall, "Alex, protect the door, would you?"

Alex? I whip around. And there he is. Alex Danfrey, standing in front of the bathroom. A warm, sinking feeling takes me hostage for a second. But Alex's eyes are on McEvoy. *What's he doing with Boss McEvoy?* "Of course, sir," Alex says.

After Gunn closes his office door, Alex waves his hand, and a perfect spitting-image replica of the door crystalizes before the actual door in front of us. There's only one difference—his replica has no handle, no way inside.

"Clever." I manage to find my voice.

Alex smiles. "Well, it's no linked trick that dumps the Boss of the Shaws into the john, but it'll have to do."

I swallow. "God, I hope McEvoy doesn't hold a grudge."

Alex's smile just becomes wider. "You're tough to forget, Joan, but lucky for you, I think the Boss has other things on his mind."

I wasn't expecting to see Alex today, but now that I have, I'm almost hopped up on adrenaline. I want to stop time and break this moment open. It feels like a surprise gift, having Alex for as long as McEvoy and Gunn confer behind closed doors.

Alex paces back toward the main show space and waves for me to follow.

"So you're running with *Boss McEvoy* these days?" I jog to catch up with him.

Alex nods, looks around, whispers, "I'm his right-hand sorcerer now."

Right-hand sorcerer? I study Alex's face, trying to get a read on him, because I almost can't believe what he's said. Alex doesn't seem hard enough for McEvoy, isn't the kind of sorcerer who should be attached to the side of a man called the Jackal. I don't know how many of the rumors I've heard about the Boss are true, but if even half are, I'm terrified for him.

"An opportunity presented itself," Alex adds slowly. "It's a step up, obviously, from running for Win. Besides, McEvoy's not the kind of man you can say no to."

Well, that I understand. "You really must have some sorcering chops, if you caught McEvoy's eye." I feel my own blush coming on from paying him the compliment. "How's the new gig working out?"

Alex crosses his arms in front of his chest. "Truthfully?" He lowers his voice. "A lot of casting spells to break fingers. A lot of sleepless nights. A lot of tricking McEvoy into thinking I'm worth keeping around."

I shake my head, not sure how to answer.

"You think I'm joking." He attempts a smile. "I'm not. It's difficult magic, casting spells to convince others of your competence." Despite the smile, Alex's sadness is so real I can practically see it on him, like a thin layer of dust. It makes me want more than just this steady banter we've got going on between us. I want his whole story. I want to know what's haunting that smile—how he spends his days, what he's doing in the time between when I see him around the Den. If he's safe, if he really can handle it.

"Are you going to be all right?" I manage. "Haven't spent more than a few minutes with the man around here, but McEvoy's got a reputation for being impossible."

Alex shrugs a bit. "I've survived worse. Whatever doesn't kill you makes you stronger, right?" Then he leans in. "Hate to tell you this, but Gunn doesn't strike me as being a softie either."

I swallow, Gunn's name piercing our little cocoon in the hall-way. "I'm aware."

Something Alex must see in my face changes his, because all his pretense of humor drains, and then he's looking at me like he's trying to see through me, to figure me out like I'm trying to figure him. "Seriously, what's a girl like you doing in this place?"

I think about whether I should lie, keep everything as close to my chest as possible, but I find myself wanting to share the truth. "My family," I say quietly. "My sister, and my cousin. I want to do right by them, so I'm up here trying to make a living." I dare myself to take another step toward him, and now we're close enough to whisper. "What's a guy like you really doing mixed up with the Shaws?"

Alex gives a half laugh and looks at his feet. "I've been asking myself that same question. It started out about my family too, as some vague form of revenge. . . ." He looks at me. "You ever set out to do something for one reason, and that reason's like a firm, set compass in your hand"—he holds his hand out as evidence, and a little brass compass appears, floating above his palm—"but then the further in you get, the farther you go, the more turned upside down everything starts to seem?" He looks back to the door to Gunn's office, then at the brass compass floating in his palm. The little hand inside it starts spinning slowly, then faster, round and round, bypassing *North*, then *West, South, East. . . .* "Soon you start thinking that maybe your compass is broken, or wrong." He looks back to me as the compass disappears. "But without that damn compass, you're lost, plain and simple."

His words hit home, burrow right under my skin. Ruby and Ben are my compasses—the reasons I get up in the morning, the reasons I perform illegal magic in an illegal club for Gunn, the reasons I'm using to justify helping this volatile gangster try to change the face of the underworld with a dark, dangerous spell. Those compasses make me who I am: a devoted sister, a daughter trying to right the past, an honorable woman. But without them, Alex is right. I'm lost, plain and simple. I've been trying to hold on to them even tighter these days, as I barely get a moment to myself away from the Den. From the blood-magic I've been obsessing over with Gunn, to the performances I'm practicing, perfecting, day and night. I swear, magic's started seeping into my dreams. Even when I'm awake, sometimes it feels realer, stronger, than anything else.

"We're not so different, you and me." I look back to Gunn's office. "Some days, it's just easier to focus on what's right in front of me, on just putting one foot in front of the other. On throwing myself into my performance, the magic—on what I was made to do. And I think I might actually be good at it."

"You know you're good at it." Alex smiles.

"I suppose." I drop my gaze, deflecting his compliment. "But . . . other days, when I look at how far I've come, when I think about what I'm helping to build—about what this place is . . . I mean, there are reasons that magic's criminal, right? This haven, it's a place where we trick people, drug people, help them get so high that they want to keep living in a lie." I shake my head. "Sometimes I forget that, I'm so far in." I run my fingers around my temples in little circles. "God, I don't even think I've stepped foot outside this place for days."

"You serious?" Alex asks.

"It's pathetic, isn't it? But yeah." I raise my arms to signal the Red Den. "This is pretty much what I live and breathe, day in, day out."

Alex's little smirk is back. "Can you pull that trick you did a while ago?" He points to where the hallway meets the show space. "Where you protect the hallway?"

I look at him curiously. "Why? I don't think anyone's out there."

He takes another step toward me. "Just in case. It's a surprise. Come on, I promise, it's worth it."

I look at him curiously, then turn back toward the mouth of the hall. I whisper my words of power, wave my hand in front of me, and then a double-sided protection wall materializes at the entrance to the corridor.

"Come closer," Alex whispers, waving me forward. Then he closes his eyes.

"What are you doing?"

He opens one eye to spy on me, and arches his eyebrow above it almost too perfectly, like some villain in a motion picture. "Do you *not* like surprises?"

I roll my eyes. "Fine." I take a tentative step forward. Alex is so close, I can smell him now, a soft, textured scent of soap and cologne. If I leaned in, I could rest my head on the tweed vest that spans his chest.

Stop. Don't think about his chest.

"Close your eyes," he says.

I settle into my spot, and then I close my eyes, listen to his faint whispers.

After a couple moments, he says, "Okay, open them."

I gasp. Built around Alex and me is a small gazebo drenched

in lush green ivy, white-latticed walls, a cathedral-domed roof. Peeking in through the openings of the gazebo are all sorts of wildflowers, and if I angle my head just a few inches, I can see a brilliant, near-electric-blue sky cast over the gazebo like a warm blanket. The shadows of flowering bushes dance along the white wooden frame, their rhythm set by a soft and sweet magic wind. Alex's talent is extraordinary. A manipulation this complicated could only be pulled off by me, and maybe Ral with Billy's help.

"It's . . . breathtaking," I finally say. I realize I'm now holding on to his forearm, and I collect myself, let go. "The detail is amazing. Alex, you've got much more than chops."

There's a twinkle of satisfaction in his eyes. "If you can't go outside, I thought I'd bring outside to you," he says. "Besides, sometimes magic is far better than the real thing. Right now you're missing a cold, ugly, gray December evening."

I close my eyes once more and inhale Alex's manipulation. Even the scent of it is perfect—the faintest hint of roses, that rich, musty smell of earth.

"Do you need birds?" Alex whispers. "Because I can add birds."

I laugh. "I'll get by without birds." But then I hear the faintest chirp of sparrows in the background. It sounds like morning back in Parsonage, the spring chicks peeping outside our cabin window as I roll over and throw my arm around Ruby.

"We all need a breath of fresh air every once in a while," Alex adds. "Remember that."

And for some reason—whether 'cause I've stumbled into thinking about home, or 'cause this gangster seems to understand me more than anyone in the troupe right now, or 'cause I really did need a breath of fresh air, more than I realized, my eyes start to water.

Alex notices. "Crap, did I do something wrong? Is this okay?"

"It's better than okay." The feeling Alex brings on—warm and heady and tingly—it comes on strong again. But this time it's got an undercurrent, a distinct pang of guilt. Alex has nothing to do with why I'm here and what I need to do, I realize. Alex is just for me. And I gave up a long time ago thinking I deserved something of my own.

We both hear the click of a lock, and then muffled voices, the creak of the door. Alex quickly raises his right hand, and the entire garden starts to swirl, and then disintegrate into a powdery dust that whips and vanishes into nothing.

And then it's just the two of us, feet apart, standing in the middle of an empty hallway.

"Not a word of this," Boss McEvoy snaps, as he smacks open Gunn's office door and barrels into the hallway.

"Of course," Gunn answers behind him.

I instinctively step away as McEvoy approaches. But he doesn't even stop, just grabs Alex's shoulder and draws him forward like a horse. Before they reach the mouth of the hallway, I remember to release my manipulated wall. Alex looks back, once, before McEvoy drags him into the show space and out the double doors.

Gunn's little gift of a break before our showtime backfires. Instead of showing up looking rested and ready for the night, our troupe feels even more off than we did at rehearsal. Ral and Billy get downstairs only a few minutes before eight. Tommy and Rose are actually late, and I'd bet money they're already shined. Pinprick pupils, goofy grins. Not that they'll get spoken to for it, since Gunn isn't even on the floor—I'm not sure if the underbosses' meeting is still going on, or if Gunn's somewhere else, taking care of the rest of the "pieces" of his cryptic plan. So when the double doors burst open and the stagehands turn on the jazz and the patrons flood around our performance circles in their evening best, it's the least prepared I've ever felt for a show.

I try to relax and just focus on my solo performance. My magic manipulation starts with a bin of feathers: I take a handful and throw a ring around the border of my performance circle. And then I orchestrate the feathers like a conductor, spinning them, bringing them together like a fluid current, until out of a white blur of magic, a dove is birthed. Sometimes folks will even stay right on their benches, sip their complimentary whiskey or brandy, and watch me do it twice.

But tonight I can't even revel in it. Tonight I'm just going through the motions, my mind always somewhere else. Running through what Grace told me about Stock spreading rumors, to thinking about Alex, to worrying about the blood-spell and Gunn, and then frustration and worry eclipse everything else.

By the time the Magical Storm finale starts, I'm tight, tense. I should have gone outside. I should have demanded a break. I feel like the lofted show space is tightening, like my magic has somehow caged and trapped *me* in—and it only makes matters worse that I'm working side by side with Stock for the next hour.

We're now inches from each other on the right side of the show space, in a little alcove safe haven off the aisle. To our left, the clustered audience stands, necks craned, mouths open, taking in the tropical storm my troupe has started to conjure above them. Tommy and Rose are on the other side of the space, sending a perimeter of lightning bolts crashing down around the audience like a fence of bright white paint. But the pair is clearly coming down off their shine, because their movements are dicey, imprecise. Every time a bolt comes a little too close to the audience, the patrons gasp delightedly, like it's all part of the show.

Only we know better.

Ral and Billy work together to bring their big-picture magic to the immersive performance: a steady curtain of rain starts to fall from the ceiling, and a sweet, springy scent wafts through the show space. Some of the audience members gleefully reach their hands above their heads, to where the rain stops falling and forms shallow puddles of water in midair. And this is our cue—the time for me to come in with two strong gusts of wind, one coming from the double doors and blowing to the back stage, and an undercurrent blowing in the opposite direction. I focus on the space, imagine a thick, textured wind, speak my words of power. And as Ral and Billy's rain halts to a drizzle, my first strong gale begins to whistle over the patrons' heads.

"Haven't seen Gunn walking around tonight," Stock says beside me. "Where is he?"

I keep my eyes above the audience, getting ready to conjure the second wind. "How should I know?"

Stock laughs. "You really need me to answer that?"

"Not now, all right?" I close my eyes to regroup. *Just focus on the wind. Just focus on the magic.*

"So he's done with you, eh?" Stock whispers. "I know a scorned woman when I see one." He laughs to himself. "You had to know that was only a matter of time."

"For the last damn time, Stock, I am not, nor was I *ever*, with Gunn, so stop spreading lies about me."

As soon as I say it, Stock's face bursts into a smile, and I'm angry with myself for even entertaining him.

I sigh and turn away. "You're missing your cue, dipshit."

"You aren't the only one with a vision, Joan. I know when the time is right." Then he leans against the cinder-block wall of the show space and crosses his arms.

Lord, he's a child. "Stock, I swear, do it now or—"

"Or what?" He leans toward me as a hot burst of lightning crackles feet away, and the audience gives a surprised, collective gasp. "You'll put me in your bloody nightmare box again, seal me up nice and good?" He gives a disgusted laugh. "You think you're above us all, don't you? The Great Joan Kendrick. You did since you first showed up at the warehouse, looking like a drowned rat with a set of tricks you could count on one hand."

I look at him icily. "Seriously, Stock, *enough*. We're here to work. Get it together."

"No, you get it together." He takes a step toward me, and I take a reflexive step back. "If you're not with Gunn like that, then you're up to something else with him, that's obvious. I've seen enough. I've seen you sneaking around with him like you're his own right-hand sorcerer."

"Mind your own business," I breathe out.

"See, that's the thing, it *is* my business." Stock snaps a laugh. "It's all of our business—we're a troupe of *seven*, Kendrick, linked in a way we can't separate, even if I wanted to. So what you do? It affects all of us, not just the troupe but the magic itself. And you're poisoning us."

I don't answer him. But just to spite him, to show him how much *he* affects *me*, I turn away and look up at my winds, which are still blowing hard and fast through the lofted show space. I raise my hands forward, and then I start churning them myself.

"Hey," Stock says, as he glances up, sees his signature motion trick being stolen. "HEY!" he calls again, as Grace's thunder booms over him.

He grabs my arms, pulls them down, but I knock his hands away, and then he pushes me back. All my anger, my frustration, it all comes to a boil, and before I can help myself, think through it, I try to push him against the wall, but he grabs me first in one fluid motion and throws me on the ground.

A crowd of patrons look over, start pointing, whispering.

I stand up quickly, and my anger melts into something else, and then I can't stop the tears that insist on raining down. I turn to leave, to get my fresh air, to escape just for a minute despite what's going on above our heads, and I start running down the aisle to the hallway.

"No way. We're not done, Kendrick—" I feel Stock's fingers lightly brush my arm as he reaches for me, forcing me to deal with him, but I manage to wriggle away.

"Get off me!"

He rushes after me. "You tell Gunn, I *swear*—"

But he never finishes his sentence.

Because a blinding shot of Tommy and Rose's lightning cuts right through him.

RIGHT-HAND

ALEX

My focus should be trained on McEvoy's gun, which is aimed at the goon who's kneeling on the side of the Jefferson Davis Highway, but I can't stop thinking about Joan. I replay the two of us at the Den together in the hall yesterday evening, surrounded by my magic, hidden together inside that gazebo without another care in the world. Birds chirping, a magic sun shining on her raven hair, her laughter and relief that I helped coax right out of her. I picture us a motion picture, black and white. I run the reel again in my mind, and then watch it once more in color.

I want her. And not in the way I've "wanted" other women before, when I know I have them—when I've gotten some vague sort of satisfaction as their eyes reflect interest, then fascination, then hunger. Joan's different. She's easy and tough in all the right ways. Smart. Beautiful.

In a strange way, I almost find myself needing to see her. Not just her, I guess, but the way she sees *me*—as someone to know, maybe even someone to trust. After my blowup with Howie, working around the clock on the street at McEvoy's side, I sometimes feel less than human. I'm so far in, so committed to playing this figment-gangster Alex Danfrey, that I'm starting to feel like a manipulation myself.

"Alex," McEvoy snaps. "Where the hell are you right now?"

"Right here, sir." I banish the daydreams away, the spell Joan's starting to have on me, and focus back on the sad thug McEvoy's got at gunpoint on the side of the road.

"Your story doesn't add up, friend." McEvoy bends down, so that he's eye-to-eye with John, some low-level gambling bookie for the Shaws, and the latest object of McEvoy's wrath. "If Sullivan forced you to tell our contacts the wrong winner, that means Sullivan is lying to me." McEvoy smiles a wide, taunting smile. "Do you think my underboss would lie to me, John?"

John is shivering, convulsing, and I have to look away. Traffic whizzes by on both sides, the Jefferson Davis Highway bumper-to-bumper with weekday traffic coming in and out of the city, but no one will spot us. From either side of the road, we're protected by my sorcered walls. The passing cars see nothing but a thin grass shoulder.

"Don't have all day, John—"

"No, sir, I mean, I don't know, sir." John gasps for air. "I just do what Mr. Sullivan tells me. He was the one who heard the sorcerer's forecast about the horses, and I passed on what he told me to the list of Shaw clientele."

McEvoy nods at me, my cue, and I cast my gaze away from John's pleading eyes. I hate days like this. I have nightmares about days like this. I wish there was a way to obliterate all magic on days like this.

I whisper, *"Knife and slice,"* and a knife no larger than a switchblade appears right above John's left hand, and slashes itself in one hot burst right across the top of his knuckles before it vanishes.

"What the hell, AHHHH!" John grabs his hand.

McEvoy flicks me an approving look, and then circles around our capture.

"Well, we have a real problem, John. I told my contacts that I could deliver a sure thing. You told all those contacts that the winner was going to be Maisy-Gray. And yet, here we are, the day after the race, where my short list of very important people watched as Royal Flush took the crown." McEvoy raises his gun to John's temple once more. "Now the way I see it, the mistake is either the sorcerer's—which doesn't seem right, seeing as he's *fucking magic*—my underboss's, who knows I'd turn him inside out if he ever dared to betray me." McEvoy bends down, rests his gun on John's nose. "Or yours."

I keep my face blank as I try to connect the dots, for the next time I can sneak a call to Agent Frain. I've already got a laundry list of McEvoy's crimes and indiscretions, the many men and fingers he's—*we've*—broken on the side of the road. But this sounds like something McEvoy didn't have a hand in. Something involving Sam Sullivan, McEvoy's underboss who helps with the Shaws' gambling operation. Something happening at the race-track, from what I can piece together, a natural forecast from a sorcerer somehow getting boggled, leaving McEvoy's clients—who bet on a sure winner—empty-handed.

McEvoy's right about one thing. Sorcerers who are capable of forecasting nature—the ones who have learned to communicate with the natural world, who can *see* the fastest and strongest animals, see the way the winds blow and forecast a storm down to the hour—they're rare. Cagey, and smart. They don't come out of hiding and lend their insight to the mob unless they're damn well sure of their talents to judge the animals, the conditions, the track—and forecast the winner.

Which, of course, leads McEvoy back to the middleman.

As if sensing my turn of thoughts, McEvoy locks eyes with me, then nods toward John. This time I make the knife appear in front of the man's right shoulder, cut a swift gash across his pin-striped suit. Blood begins pouring out over the fabric. As

John reaches to grasp his shoulder, the knife disappears, and I conjure it on the other side to slash his left.

"AHHHH, you crazy micks!" John roars, and without another word, McEvoy raises his gun and finishes him off with a loud, hungry *POP*.

The bookie crumples into a ball on the grass shoulder.

McEvoy puts the gun into his holster again, loosens his tie. "Racist." He sighs, looks around at the puddle of blood now staining the grass. "Clean this up, will you?"

My hands are shaking, my pulse jumping, but I swallow, try to swallow it all down, *remember why you're doing this, remember the greater goal*— "Of course, sir."

I focus on the grass below the corpse, imagine parting it like hair, carving an indent right out of the ground. The dirt slowly divides, reveals a narrow valley, and the bookie's body falls into the ground. The earth merges back to swallow him whole.

"Remind me to pay another visit to Sullivan," McEvoy mutters, as we approach his car. He leans on the hood of his Duesenberg. "God, I need a hit."

And this is also part of our routine, a routine with its own messed-up sort of rhythm. "Why don't you get into the passenger's seat, sir? It's safer."

So we switch places, so that I can cart McEvoy back into town, once he's high as a kite on my shine. We settle in. McEvoy digs in the backseat, then hands me a bottle of water from the crate of them he keeps for just these occasions.

I take it into my hands, close my eyes, center myself, let my power flow through me, transfer it into the bottle—

The shine has barely cooled when McEvoy grabs the bottle. He gobbles down a large sip and sighs. He doesn't say a word for a minute, until the magic has him, until all the gray fades from his skin and his eyes take on that pinpricked, otherworldly shimmer. "My God, Alex, this is a shot of heaven." He leans his head against the leather passenger seat and closes his eyes. "I needed this."

I wait for a break in traffic, and then I release my protective manipulations and pull the car out onto the highway leading back into town.

We've ended every day like this—every run, errand, meet—since I was vetted in that parking lot weeks ago. I had no idea that McEvoy was a shine junkie. His habit has only bound us further together, tied my fate to his with one more knot. It makes me hate him a little more—because it's like he truly owns me, in every way. And as McEvoy sighs himself into a stupor each night, it truly drives home how dangerous this stuff is, how a habit can easily spiral into an obsession—and why the Unit needs to shut the shine racket down. The only silver lining of being McEvoy's personal shine tap? It gives me a window each day when he's vulnerable, a window I use to try and see more.

So as we cross over the Highway Bridge into the city, I ask softly, "Why do you think he did it?"

McEvoy shifts in his seat, keeps his eyes closed, says with a slight slur, "No clue. People do all kinds of shit that doesn't make sense." He smacks his lips, turns to face the window. "Swore it was the sorcerer's fault . . . since John's been with us for years . . . but Sullivan and Gunn insist his forecast record is flawless."

Gunn . . . I'm not sure how Harrison Gunn, underboss of the Red Den, has his hand in this. But then I remember how McEvoy visited Gunn yesterday evening, and how he mentioned Sullivan's name in the hall of the Den.

I steel myself, remember that for as dangerous as McEvoy is, right now he's wrapped in a cocoon of my magic. And as much as I just want to keep my mouth shut and focus on something light and warm, like Joan, I need to use every window I get. "Sir, does Gunn have something to do with what happened at the racetrack?"

"No," he says slowly. "But Gunn helped Sullivan choose his

forecast sorcerer—Sullivan asked him for some names, since Gunn knows far more than any of us about magic. Half the time now he talks like a goddamned mystic—though I guess he always had a few screws loose, just like his old man Danny," he mumbles. "Besides, I thought if anyone had ever heard of a top-notch forecaster picking a wrong horse like this, it'd be Gunn." He waits a beat, breathes into the glass bottle. "Even still. Something's wrong. Wasn't the bookie."

"Then whose fault do you think it was?"

But McEvoy's faded. He starts to purr gently.

I turn off 14th Street, thinking it all through—*a fixed race that somehow got botched, a winner forecast made by one of Sullivan's sorcerers, a sorcerer suggested by Gunn . . . John the bookie took the fall for it.* But it sounds like McEvoy doesn't think John should have, even though McEvoy just put a hole through his head.

Why?

I chase the thoughts away for right now as I pull onto Massachusetts. McEvoy's place is at the corner of 21st Street, a swanky, three-floor Queen Anne–style mansion in the heart of Dupont Circle. I parallel park his car outside his lush, overgrown gardens out front. By the time I cut the engine, McEvoy's full-out snoring in the front seat. I never wake him. I leave him in his shiny Duesenberg, put the keys into his lap like always, and then I walk the long trek home.

The next morning I hit the streets early, determined to claim a little bit of the day for myself before McEvoy comes calling, and before I dial the latest into Agent Frain. So I throw on my coat, scarf, and cap and head for the pharmacy around the corner for a paper and coffee. It's so quiet that I can hear the rustle of a tin can skitter across the blacktop.

But as I round the corner of the nearby alley, between Vermont Avenue and R Street, a car rips up beside me and stops with a screech. Before I can run, or even think, the door cracks open a few inches. Agent Frain leans across the front seat, with one hand on the door. He keeps his motor running.

"Get in."

On seeing that it's him, I relax, but my heart still pounds from residual fear. I settle next to him quickly, pull the passenger door closed with a *whap*.

"You shouldn't be picking me up on the street. The deal was that I reach out to you," I say. "This is blocks from Shaw territory. Next time, leave a note, tell me where to meet . . . out in the woods or something. Someone easily could have seen me."

"Don't worry, it's early—but of course I scouted around," Frain says. "It's all right. We'll be out of the city soon." He eases his car back onto Vermont Avenue. "I've been waiting for you."

I crouch low and rest my head against his cracked leather passenger seat. We make a left onto 14th Street, ride it over the Highway Bridge and out of town.

"Right off here should be fine." Frain steers his car off the next highway exit and follows the road until it winds through a smattering of farms. He finally pulls us onto a stretch of hay-colored grass, cuts the engine, and turns to face me. "You okay?"

It's a simple question, but a complicated answer. I'm exhausted, without a doubt, and most days feel like I'm owned by the devil. And yet, the more I see of this underworld, the more I believe in what I'm doing—and the more I think this dark world needs to come crashing down. "Guess it's been a long few months, sir."

"But you're doing well. Better than well," Frain says. "By the way, that Irish ship you tagged for us a while back, the *Emerald Jane*? We have the coast guard tracking it. Helped us learn the identities of two dozen fae dust sweepers up and down the coast. Honestly, Alex, you've managed to do more in these past few months than some of our entire Unit teams put together."

His words warm me, validate everything I've been through, guide me forward like a compass. *Just focus on why you're doing this, and the rush of being good at it. Leave McEvoy's darkness behind for now.*

"I've got more," I say, as I lean toward him. "Apparently there was a mix-up at the racetrack. Some Shaw sorcerer forecast a horse winner that was either wrong or got lost in translation. Some of McEvoy's bigwig contacts had a lot of money riding on it, whole thing was a mess. The sorcerer and the Shaws' gambling underboss, Sam Sullivan, both blamed the bookie—but the bookie swore he was just following orders."

"More mistakes," Frain says slowly.

I nod. "The Baltimore mix-up was the same sort of thing—the racketeering manpower that Boss McEvoy promised Baltimore fell short, and the Boss was left having to deal with the aftermath." I shake my head. "I haven't seen anything happen to Kerrigan, the responsible underboss, for it. Don't think McEvoy's going after Sullivan about the racetrack mishap, either—instead he took out the bookie."

"Both Kerrigan and Sullivan are underbosses, Alex," Frain says evenly. "They're higher-ups. McEvoy takes them down, and he's got a lot of people to answer to."

"But even some other punishment," I press, "something to mark his turf, show the Shaws that he rules them with an iron fist, that these kinds of mistakes won't be tolerated." Then I think back to what McEvoy mumbled in the car, about something being wrong, as I feel Frain's eyes on me.

And then a possibility slowly starts to crystallize. "Unless McEvoy's losing his iron fist," I finish.

Agent Frain gives a slight nod, shifts in his seat, and looks up at me. His face says everything.

"You really think there could be some . . . shake-up, some kind of shift in the natural Shaw order?" I almost can't believe it. Boss McEvoy—a man cut from nightmares, a man who bathes in blood—*someone would dare to challenge him?*

"I've been coming around to the same thing," Frain breathes out. "I've got a man on the outskirts of the Shaws' racketeering operation. Older brute of a fellow, a Unit informant, never really had the desire to work his way to the top. And he says that the misunderstanding with Baltimore you heard about? Apparently the mistake was intentional, at least that's what he swears to us. That Kerrigan promised twenty men, but after meeting with some of the underbosses at the Red Den, sent only half to the sting."

So one of McEvoy's underbosses purposely sabotaged a deal with Baltimore? "But . . . why?"

"That's what I need you to find out." Frain turns around, stares out his window, thinking to himself. "How much time do you spend around this Red Den?"

Images of Joan flood my mind, my flower manipulation in her hair in the hallway, in her performance circle tossing feathers around her, close enough to kiss under my magic gazebo—"Not as much as I'd like, sir."

"Place has been transformed, from what I hear. Not just the magic show that happens every night, but apparently it's become a Shaw meeting place. That there's a room where a lot of business gets done during the performance, behind closed doors."

I shrug. "I'm almost always on the road, Agent Frain. The game is playing McEvoy."

"I know," Frain says. "But the game might have changed." He looks back at me. "Did McEvoy tell you what happened at the Den a couple nights ago, Alex?"

A strange numbness begins settling over me at his cryptic, leading question. "He didn't, sir."

"One of the sorcerers who puts on the immersive magic show died pulling a trick." My heart seizes, whispers, *Please, not Joan*— "Apparently he got split right open by a lightning bolt." *He, thank God.* "Shook the crowd up good. Place has shut down for a few nights, I guess until they figure out where to go from here."

"What was the sorcerer's name?"

"Stockard Harding. Some kid they brought in from Appalachian country back in October, when the club was revamped." Frain pauses. "Alex, this could be a real opening, a chance to shift the focus of our little operation."

My eyes float up to meet his. "What do you mean, 'shift the focus'?"

"You said it yourself. There's something going on within the Shaws, some kind of shake-up. If we're right—if it somehow affects the Shaws' racketeering operation, and their gambling empire—it has to be driven by something big, the kind of score we've been waiting for. One that blows the underworld open, allows us to step in and take the lot of these thugs down. I need you where you can keep your eyes and ears on multiple players, not bound to the side of the man who's purposely being kept in the dark."

I finally piece together what he's suggesting, and I stutter a laugh. "Are you . . . are you implying that I take Stockard's place somehow? Because that's a joke. McEvoy owns me. I'm practically by his side from morning until night—"

"And I think it's time to fix that."

A small window of hope cracks open inside me at those words, despite how insane Frain's suggestion is. It'd be a way out from McEvoy's dark shadow. A way to escape the violence. *A chance to spend more time with Joan.* And she'd be an easy source, no question. Someone I don't have to fake caring about, someone who's clearly got a pulse on the place, works closely with the managing underboss, Harrison Gunn, and could keep me posted on who's meeting who behind the concealed doors of that Den.

Of course, the only problem is, McEvoy would likely kill me before I ever stepped foot in the door.

"And how would you suggest I 'fix that,' hmm?" I give a sharp exhale and lean back in my seat. "Walk up to McEvoy, tell him thanks for the opportunity, but I want to perform at his magic haven—a place he considers a circus sideshow, by the way—instead?"

"I know you're tired, Alex"—Frain keeps his tone infuriatingly even, careful—"frustrated, I get that. But you need to stop for a second and think about everything you've already managed to achieve—"

"This is different," I interrupt, my heart now pounding inside my chest. "Everything before, there was an opportunity—there was a chance within the Shaws, and I seized that chance." I hear my voice shaking. "Howie needed a buddy, I was that buddy. Win needed a runner, I was that runner. McEvoy needed a right-hand sorcerer for the street, and poof, there I was, seasoned and vetted. What you're asking me to do? Go up to my boss, the most dangerous man in the city—a man who acts like I'm his own personal shine tap, no less—and ask him to let me go? Sir, it *can't* happen."

Frain attempts to speak, but I keep going. "Now, I've done everything, *everything* you've asked of me," I say as I close my eyes. "Things I'm not proud of. Things I'd pay to take back. But I've kept my head down and stayed focused. I've done what I needed to do for our greater goal. This move is too dangerous. I deserve to say no, I've earned the right—this is over the line."

"Alex, this *is* like the other times. You need to see that." Frain rests his hand on my shoulder. "You need to get somewhere, and McEvoy needs you there more than he knows right now. You just need to convince him that he needs it."

I falter. "I don't understand."

"You said it yourself, that deep down, McEvoy suspects that something isn't right. That something has him paralyzed, otherwise he would have fully taken care of these mistakes, with no hesitation, no mercy." He adds softly, "So you play to his insecurities. You take his seed of doubt, and you grow the seed into a weed, then show McEvoy you're the only one who can pull the weed out for him."

And now I think I *do* understand. But the understanding numbs me. "So . . . so you want me to be a mole for *McEvoy*, too."

"Don't you see?" Frain says slowly. "It's perfect. You'd be able to keep tabs for him, as well as for us. But you only let him know what we want him to know."

I stay silent, but my heart—it's pounding, thrashing, beating a resounding *NO*.

"This is too good of an opportunity to waste, Alex, and it sounds from everything you're gathering that whatever's cooking could be coming to a boil soon."

"Let's say I can convince him," I say slowly, softly. "McEvoy is a *junkie*, you understand that, right? Let's pretend that in theory, he agrees to plant me as a sorcerer in the Den. Even if he saw the sense of it, he'd still come calling for the shine, day in and out, and risk jeopardizing the operation."

At that, Frain turns to face the windshield. "Leave that part to me," he says quietly. "I've got plenty of fae dust in evidence, from a local raid a week back. It's a different high, I understand, more of a racing, paranoid trip. Hallucinations, jitters, confusion, that sort of thing. But highly addictive. I'll get a bag to you, through safe channels, of course. Expect someone this afternoon.

Get McEvoy to take it a few times, so that he's hooked. The dust should work its own magic from there."

I stare at Frain, but he keeps his gaze ahead.

And it's at this moment when I finally understand that there are no limits to this game anymore. That I'm in as deep with him as I am with McEvoy. That even if I wanted to, I'm not walking away until this is done.

Frain finally looks at me, my silence the only affirmation I can manage to give, and the only one he needs. "Our contact should be kept to a minimum from now on. If you manage this, there will be eyes on you from all sides. You ever need me, you call my home number—but only in case of an absolute emergency."

When I still don't answer, because fear has me hostage, holds me by the throat, Frain starts his engine and pulls back onto the road. "It makes sense for Boss McEvoy to put someone he trusts inside that place. You'll make it work, Alex, you always do. Just do it soon."

I'm paralyzed with fear for most of the afternoon, turning my thoughts around and inside out, trying to analyze how to play this from every angle. *Should tonight be the night I convince McEvoy that he needs me inside the Den, working for him in another way?* I'm so deep in my own world that I barely mumble a hello to the street runner who delivers Agent Frain's promised bag of fae dust to my door. By the time McEvoy's car pulls up around seven p.m., I'm practically jumping out of my skin.

I slide into the new, almost sweet-smelling leather of his Duesenberg. I wonder if McEvoy can sense what I'm about to try and pull. If he can see anxiety pulsing its way through me like poison.

"Relax, Danfrey," he says. "We've got a bit of a drive."

McEvoy turns left around Iowa Circle.

"Where are we going, sir?"

"A meeting with the Voodoo Queens."

The Voodoo Queens—one of the most powerful gangs in the Bahamas, led by Satra James, quite likely the richest and most dangerous female smuggler in the world. The Queens run their own type of magic contraband called obi up the coast to the highest bidder, a syrupy elixir that renders the user almost catatonic, floating in a strange, haunting world between dreams and nightmares. I've never touched the stuff, but more adventurous Shaw boys say obi lets you see ghosts. That the product only survives the trip across the sea because Satra's gang has made a deal with death and has trapped damned souls inside their bottles. There was a day I'd laugh that off, but now my job is believing there's truth inside every rumor. McEvoy has had a corner on their US market for years, from what I learned through the Unit. I also know that the Queens won't hesitate to use dark magic in their dealings too—when the situation calls for it.

"Are some of the other Shaws joining us?" I ask quietly.

"No," McEvoy says, throwing me a glance. "It's just me and you."

Just me and you echoes through the silence of McEvoy's car on the Highway Bridge, follows me like a warning bell right out of town. *Why don't we have backup?*

Maybe McEvoy wants to flirt with death.

Or maybe that's not really where we're going.

Maybe he saw me meeting with Agent Frain.

Maybe he plans to get rid of me, nice and discreet.

The silence becomes suffocating as we take the highway past Annapolis, get off a few exits later, and the exit curves us onto a two-lane road. We follow the road until it becomes stones and dirt, and then pull down a dark drive labeled DONOVAN SHIPPING YARD. The drive soon brings us alongside shallow water. A graveyard of boats, cloaked in the shadows of their storm-beaten sails, rest like long-forgotten tombstones on the edges of the docks.

"This is where we're meeting the Queens?" I gulp the panic down, keep my eyes trained on my window.

"We all thought somewhere private was best . . . away from prying eyes."

McEvoy parks the car in one of the spaces in front of the boat shack. The place looks closed, maybe even abandoned—just a battered door and covered windows. He shuts off the engine, gets out, and I follow suit. We wait in silence in the frigid air on the nearest empty dock, which juts out a few feet into the dark water.

Finally a faint humming in the distance starts to tease at my ears.

"Must be them." McEvoy walks to the dock's edge. He pulls his coat collar around his neck, waves his other arm back and forth above his head, and then a motorized boat, maybe twenty feet long, emerges out of the gray, ropy mist like a mirage.

As the boat gets closer to the shore, its engine cuts and it begins floating toward us. Inside the boat sit three women, all long-limbed, straight-backed, poised as statues. The one in front—Satra, I'm guessing—turns the engine back on and carefully guides the boat alongside our dock. McEvoy and I lean down to tie it off. And then the two of us extend a hand to help the Queens onto the dock.

"A pleasure as always, Satra." McEvoy smiles and kisses the woman's hand.

"Likewise, Erwin." Satra is tall and thin, younger, prettier, than I imagined. She wears loose-fitting trousers, a salt-laced blouse, clothes that carry the wear and tear of a smuggler's life.

Two slight young things, her magic protection, I'm guessing, get off the boat behind her. They wear their hair in small braids, arranged and tied into complicated knots that rest like sculptures above their heads.

I've got talent, but I'm outnumbered. And island sorcerers are a different breed. Island sorcerers can call ghosts and spirits into their rituals. Rumors are that they can climb into your soul, turn you inside out, with magic.

If things go south, can I protect McEvoy?

Hell, can I protect myself?

"Apologies for picking a place in the middle of nowhere, but I'm sure you understand my desire to keep things"—McEvoy struggles to find the right word—"unassuming. You have trouble finding it?"

Satra shrugs and puts her hands in her pockets. "It was easy enough from Magic Row. The rest of my crew is still parked out there. Took the cutter in to find you." She gestures behind her. "My associates took care of evading your country's pigs."

McEvoy sniffs in the frigid air. "Well, I'm here, Satra, and it's cold." His eyes flicker to the two sorcerers standing behind Satra. "You said you needed to ask in person. So ask away."

Wait, so Satra called this meeting? Why?

"Sorry it had to come to this, Erwin. We go back a long time."

"Way back. From my days in the coast guard."

"And our history is the only reason I'm granting you this courtesy." Satra stands feet away from McEvoy, sizing him up. "Because in all that time, you've never tried to trick me, one-up me. Lie."

McEvoy nods slowly. "And I still never have. Told you, never will."

Satra drops her gaze to the water's edge. "There's an expression on my island, Erwin. That the simplest answer, the simplest solution, is often the right one." She glances back up at McEvoy. "So when the Shaws pay for a twenty-gallon obi shipment with magic counterfeit, when the shipment is signed by the Boss of the Shaws himself? The simplest answer is that the Boss authorized it. That you tried to get away with a free shipment before cutting ties." She takes a step forward. "And yet, you appear before me, ready to convince me different."

My thoughts race to follow, to make sense of Satra's accusations—

So the Shaws used magic counterfeit to pay for an obi shipment?
Magically manipulating money by replicating the real thing—the practice is only used by gang loan sharks, who flip conjured loans to gamblers and junkies in such hot water, and so desperate for any form of cash, that they don't think through the consequences of using magic counterfeit. But outside of that bunch of sad sacks, magic money has no real market, for the reasons Satra's implying. Sure, it *looks* like the real deal— but any underworld goon knows that sorcered cash disappears after a day, like all pure magic. So trying to pay a smuggler in magic counterfeit? Business-ending. And pulling a trick like that on Satra James? Suicidal.

"There's apparently a fuckup within my organization," McEvoy says with a forced smile. "As soon as I get to the bottom of it, the mistake will be taken care of." He cracks his fingers, like a tic. "Expect payment in full, plus five percent considering our history, for the annoyance."

"You really expect me to believe that this was all the mistake of some low-level gofer?" Satra takes another step forward. "You want to end our alliance? Be a man, say it to my face."

"I told you, I knew nothing about it!" McEvoy finally snaps. Then he quickly straightens his coat in an attempt to collect himself. Because that admission—that the Boss of the Shaws doesn't know what's happening within his ranks—isn't quite comforting either.

"Time to find out the truth." Satra nods, signaling to the two female sorcerers behind her. I take an instinctive step forward, to protect him, but McEvoy raises his hand, tells me to stand down.

The sorcerer behind Satra's left raises her hand slowly, almost solemnly, and then McEvoy sputters, coughs, and his head snaps back unnaturally.

"Sir—" I start.

"He's fine," Satra barks.

McEvoy's head starts lolling around, his eyes fly back in his head. And then Satra's other sorcerer takes a careful step toward him, as if her feet barely touch the dock. She approaches McEvoy like a mother approaching a sick child, lays her hand right over McEvoy's head. McEvoy's entire body quivers at her touch.

I've never seen anything like it before. It's like they have him in some kind of possessive spell, like they're ravaging his mind, digging into its corners and pillaging its pockets for the truth. This is obviously why they needed to see McEvoy in person.

Despite my charge to protect the man, like a reflex I take a small step back.

There's no way in hell they can get their magic hooks into me.

"He's telling the truth," the sorcerer says. She releases her hand from McEvoy's forehead, and her partner drops her hand behind Satra. McEvoy is released, starts hacking, doubling over next to me on the dock. I fall to his side, offer him my hand to stand.

"Sorry to doubt you." Satra waves her sorcerers back to their boat. "But considering the circumstances, Erwin, you understand why I needed to hear it this way." McEvoy is a big man, built of steel and broad shoulders, but Satra is intimidating in another, subtler way. Tall, thin, beautiful, she eclipses McEvoy like a shadow. And I'd be damned if McEvoy's not sweating under his fifty-dollar coat.

"Some advice, friend. If the simplest answer *is* often right,"

Satra whispers, "things don't bode well for you." She lets her warning fall over us as she steps onto the hull of her boat. "I'll expect that payment by the end of the month, plus the promised premium." She nods once more as she settles into her cutter. "Take care of yourself, Erwin."

McEvoy and I walk back to the car briskly, without a word. McEvoy opens his passenger-side door and slides inside. He's honest-to-God shaking. I've never seen the man rattled, and it petrifies me.

"Goddamn it," he whispers.

I get in behind the wheel. And even though my pulse is still pounding and the cold has stolen my breath, all I can think is that Agent Frain and I are onto something. There's a shift inside the Shaws, and someone has McEvoy's number. Someone's tampering with his operation, slowly but methodically, one aspect at a time.

"Sir," I try, "why did you keep it to just me and you tonight?"

"I need a hit, Alex."

"Sir—"

"NOW."

I turn to grab one of the long, thin bottles of water that rests in the crate on the backseat floor. I place it between my hands, let my magic pour through me, ignite the water, turn it into sorcerer's shine.

When I'm done, McEvoy takes a gulp, slides his head onto his headrest, and closes his eyes.

I pull out onto the road.

I wait as he falls under the spell of my shine. But I can't pass up this opportunity. McEvoy is scared. And McEvoy should be scared.

"There've been a couple . . . mix-ups these days, haven't there been, sir?" I venture. "Mistakes, as you called the mix-up with Ms. James tonight."

He doesn't answer. I focus on the highway, the shoulders of dark grass blurring past us. "Issues on the loan-sharking end . . . your gambling business, too," I persist carefully. "Are you . . . do you think this was somehow . . ." I feel my heart raging like a drum within. "Could they all somehow be related?"

McEvoy barely mumbles a response.

I take a deep breath. *I'm going to have to put this all together. I'm going to have to suggest that he's losing his iron grip on the Shaws. I need to play this very carefully—*

"People don't question you, sir," I push. "You've ruled the Shaws for nearly a decade. You're the Jackal of the District. Like you said, mistakes aren't made, because you've made very clear what the consequences are of making them."

McEvoy keeps his eyes closed. But this is my chance, my window. I need to keep pushing this conversation forward inch by painstaking inch. "But what if folks started thinking for some reason that there would be no consequences?" I continue slowly. "What if . . . what if people sense some kind of change?"

At that, McEvoy's bloodshot eyes fly open, fall on me, but he doesn't say a word. And despite the fear thundering through me, underneath it I still feel a small, thrilling hum. *I've tapped into something. Some deep, dark fear McEvoy harbors but would never willingly let see the light of day.*

I return my gaze to the road. "Maybe these aren't mistakes, sir. Maybe someone's behind all this, someone whispering, creating fractures, tarnishing your name on the street. And as on the pulse of your operation as you are, sir, you can't be everywhere at the same time," I say softly. "I've seen some of the higher-ups, in and out of the Den. Meeting in back rooms, conferring. Everyone knows that you're not a fan of performance magic, think the Den is a joke—"

"What the fuck are you trying to say right now, Alex?" McEvoy finally snaps.

"Just . . ." *Say it, Alex. Just do it, SAY IT, bring it home.* "Could it be possible, that as you're ruling, working the streets, someone's working you?"

No answer, and silence screams through the car.

"I mean, it could be anyone, sir. But if they're managing to stage these 'mistakes,' I'd have to think it's someone high up. Influential." I pause, swallow down the fear. "Maybe you need another pair of eyes and ears, someone who can keep tabs on what's happening with your underbosses, somewhere you aren't known to frequent. Someone who can keep track of every backroom meeting at that Den as you're taking care of your empire." Now my heart is beating so fast I almost can't contain it. "Who's passing through there, what's being whispered in the halls. Someone who can figure out how far this extends."

And then I force myself to do it, to take the hand of what I'm dancing around and drag it right into the spotlight. "If you go there yourself, any whispers of insurrection are going to quiet, shut down, find another way. But if you plant someone inconspicuous, who can pose as a fly on the wall, maybe they can get information for you that you'd never be able to get yourself."

"Someone *inconspicuous*," McEvoy repeats slowly.

"Someone who has the talent to work his way into the Den without any questions asked," I push. "Someone you know is loyal, who can tell you who needs to be taken care of, before it's too late."

"Someone like you." McEvoy says this matter-of-factly, turns to me, quick as a cat on the hunt. "Watching my back not good enough for you, boy? You think I'm on the way out, you want to hop on a winning ticket?"

I force myself to look him in his eyes. They're completely shined up.

Before I can think through how to answer, McEvoy leaps across the seat and grabs my collar, drags me within inches of his red eyes. I lose control of the wheel slightly, and the car squeals into the center of the highway. "You playing me, Danfrey?"

"No, sir, you've got it all wrong," I choke out. "I'd lay down my life for you." I scramble to get control of the car, and he loosens his grip just a hair. "I just want to be where you need me most. I want to make sure I'm doing everything I can to help you."

He finally releases me, then thrusts his head against his passenger seat.

We drive the rest of the way in silence, whether because McEvoy's too messed up to talk or because he doesn't want to. Hell, I'm not sure what's next, if he doesn't say yes. *Does he get rid of me? Beat me to a pulp for suggesting that someone is out to take the Jackal down? Make me an example?*

"Go to your place. I'm fine to drive home." He finally breaks our silence as we make our way over the Highway Bridge.

He doesn't speak again until we pull up in front of my house. I cut the engine to complete and deadly silence.

After a full minute of sitting in his dark car, finally McEvoy whispers, "I'll tell Win you're good. But you're too soft. That you'd be better suited somewhere else in our operation, away from the street's front lines."

Relief and surprise collide inside me, burst like a goddamned fireworks show. In a strange, dissociated moment, I think, *Howie will be thrilled.*

"You hold to that story, understand? Win won't be too surprised. He warned me you might not be able to stomach the job when he first brought up your name to me."

"Yes, sir."

"I'll let him suggest the Den. I'm sure he will. Gunn mentioned some big accident, one of his little performer monkeys getting killed by magic a few nights back." He glares at me. "You tell me *everything* you see, everything you hear, understand? Anything that looks or sounds suspicious. You don't spare any details. You don't censor yourself. *I* make the calls on what is and isn't important."

"Of course, sir."

He looks at the shine bottle hungrily. "Too bad you can't preserve this stuff." He clutches the remainder of my shine to his chest. "I'll need to figure something out, or still come calling from time to time—"

"I might be able to help with that." I nod across him, back to my home, the shabby porch, the cracked windows. I've never realized how much it looks like a magic junkie house. And I force myself to finish this. "You ever try fae dust, sir?"

McEvoy follows my gaze to my home. "That Irish psychedelic shit? Once, didn't take to it." He gives a grunt. "Have to say, never would have taken you for a dust-bunny, Alex."

"Well, some of the stuff Win's been smuggling in for your operation is hard to resist." I look at my hands, praying that he'll buy the lie. "I can vouch for the high, though it takes a few trips to really hit your stride. It's not the same as shine, obviously, but it . . . might carry you through in the meantime."

Without another word, McEvoy kicks open his car door. I let go of the air I've been holding on to and slink after him, up my own stairs and to my front porch.

Christ to hell.

This is a dangerous, dangerous game I'm playing.

PART THREE

THE
PERFORMANCE

NEW BOY

JOAN

The Red Den has been closed for days, the first hiatus we've had since Gunn moved our troupe in here. Stock's death sent a shock through the crowd—I close my eyes and can still see the faces of the nearby audience twisted in horror, hear the screams bubble up from the flying handbags and furs—but even more, it's gutted the troupe. It wasn't all love and roses with Stock, but we were a team. Maybe a fractured team. Hell, maybe a failing team—but a team just the same.

I spent two nights sleeping in Grace's room after it happened, 'cause I couldn't stand the idea of being alone. But that didn't stop the nightmares from finding me, my usual ones about Mama giving way to fresher ones—of hot white light, Stock's sizzling, crimson body in the aisle—images that sent me shooting up and gasping in the night. Even more unsettling, I've got a sickening feeling that there's a weird connection between the two dreams, a link I can't quite wrap my mind around, but one that's managed to chain itself around me just the same.

Gunn's given the rest of the troupe a few days off, since the Den is closed. My guess is they're all spending their days wandering around the city, or numbing their minds with motion picture films at the M Street theater, or catching up on a full sleep that none of us usually get to enjoy. I wouldn't know, because I'm still working, day in, day out in Gunn's office, the pause in our performances just clearing the way for more time to discuss Mama's caging spell, more time to figure out a way around its limits. Gunn and I can lock shine in a bottle forever, but we still can't find a way for a potential buyer to get it out. And I've tried every angle, all my morals and hesitations falling by the wayside as pure panic over not delivering has slowly but surely taken center stage. I've already run Mama's spell at least ten different ways, looking for a loophole. I've sat with Gunn and some of his contacts from the Bahamas, listening to how obi dealers trap ghosts inside their bottles, hoping there's some death-magic technique we could borrow to unlock the spell. Even got Gunn to grant me a rare field trip to the local library, where I feverishly scoured old magic texts as a buttoned-up librarian hawk-eyed me from the checkout desk. But none of it's helped. And Gunn isn't going to let me rest until I get him an answer.

It's Saturday, four days after Stock's death, and Gunn and I are in his office now, running through the caging blood-spell yet again. I should be focusing, brainstorming until I fashion a key to unlock the solution for Gunn, but I still can't stop thinking about the accident. I whisper, *"With purpose and a stalwart heart, a sacrifice. Less of me, an offering to cage for eternity . . ."*

But my voice catches on the words, and it tears. I'm exhausted, mixed-up, my nerves burned out. My heart, anything but stalwart.

"That's enough."

I look up guiltily. "I'm sorry—my heart, it's not in the right place, sir."

"Well, it needs to be," Gunn cuts. "I told you there's a window in which we need to accomplish this. And that window is *now*. You promised me you'd give me everything you have, that you wouldn't hold back." He leans forward. "And what I'm trying to achieve? There is no *partial* success story here, Joan. If you don't make this work, there won't be a happy ending for either of us, you understand?" He lets go of a deep exhale, shakes his head, looks more nervous than I've ever seen him. "It's too late to turn back. The only way we get out of this, the only way we win, is unlocking that bottle."

Gunn's words are quick and damning, wind their way around my throat. *Too late. No way out. We.*

We we we.

My fate is tied to this man's fate.

The fate of this sadistic, scheming enigma of a gangster.

I try to answer, but all that comes out is a gasp, and tears begin to fall.

"Christ." For a sliver of a second, Gunn looks lost, or remorseful, something I've never seen in his face before—and then he opens his top drawer and pulls out a handkerchief. "Here."

"Sorry, sir, I don't know what's come over me, I swear I'm fine." *Collect yourself, Joan. Jesus, stop crying—*

"I know I've been working you hard," he starts slowly. "Because you can handle it. I know the way you work, because it's the same way I do. You keep pushing, fighting, and eventually you'll get past the wall. And we're so close, I can feel it." Then he adds, tentatively, like a secret he's almost unwilling to share, "I believe in you." He leans back in his chair, assessing me, his eyes still never leaving mine. "Take tonight off, understand? Be ready to work tomorrow, to approach our problem with a clear head."

But a strange mix of shame, remorse, maybe even pride, all starts to churn inside. "No, sir, I don't need a break, I can do this. I know I promised I could do this—"

"Joan," he interrupts, placing his hands in prayer position on his desk. "I mean it. No catch. Take the night."

I look down at my lap.

Take the night.

I can't remember the last time I had a night off. I don't even know what to do with myself. "Thank you, Mr. Gunn," I manage. "I'll be back here in your office bright and early tomorrow morning—"

"Be ready for rehearsal tomorrow, actually." He turns to his notes. "We're reopening in two nights' time."

Rehearsal? Does that mean we're going to persist with six sorcerers, despite the lack of the extra strength of seven? What happens to our magic if the troupe isn't complete? Does our magic fade? Will we feel it? "Sir, we only have six—"

"I've already found Stock's replacement."

"His replacement."

"His replacement for now, at least," Gunn speaks to his notebook. "A young guy from the street side of our operation—Win says he has talent, but he couldn't handle the pressures of the job." A smirk plays at his lips. "Apparently the boy actually got sick one night, after McEvoy had him using extreme forms of magical torture."

Boss McEvoy. Alex. My heart skips a beat. *He has to be talking about Alex.*

"You mean McEvoy's right-hand sorcerer?"

"*Former* sorcerer. McEvoy was happy to dispose of him, when Win told him we were short a man. Better to recycle him, I suppose, than lose the asset completely."

I swallow. I've become an expert now at parsing vague gangster language. *Lose the asset.* Meaning get rid of Alex. Because there are no loose ends with the Shaws.

Gunn crosses his arms, looks at me with those searing blue eyes. "You've met him before, correct? Alex Danfrey?"

At the mention of his name, something warm and soft as butter slides down my sides and sinks into my core. "Around here, sir."

"Bit of a charmer, if I remember?" Gunn raises an eyebrow. "Cast a flower into your hair?" When Gunn sees that he's made me blush, he picks up his pen, continues to scratch away at his goddamned notebook. "I like using people I've vetted, people I know are mine completely. Besides, the boy's got a cloudy past, which could end up proving a hindrance or a bonus in our new little venture, depending on how things shake out." Gunn looks at me. "But we'll take what we can get right now—there're more important things to worry about. Just keep an eye on him, all right?"

"Yes, sir."

"And make sure the whole troupe—including Alex—is ready for reopening on Monday night. He'll be here tomorrow, ready to work."

"When are you going to tell the rest of the troupe about him?"

Gunn looks at me funny. "That's your job."

Wonderful. Now I'm Gunn's personal messenger, too.

As I move to Gunn's doorway, he calls up from his desk, "And I'll need the answer to our little blood-spell dilemma by the end of next week. I'm serious, Joan."

Panic surges back like a tide, but I refuse to let it drown my relief about a night of freedom. "Understood, sir."

I book up the three flights of stairs to our hall, run to Grace's door, and start pounding on it. "Grace!" I call out, near giddy over the idea of some real time with her, away from Gunn's watchful eyes, away from that ten-foot-square office I've spent the past few days locked inside. "Grace!"

Maybe a cigarette, hell, a pack of cigarettes outside, hitting up a dance club on M Street, going for a slice of pie at Moby's Diner around the corner—

I stop pounding after a full minute and crack open her door. Her room's empty.

I cross the hall to Billy and Ral's, try theirs. No answer. I even tentatively knock on Tommy and Rose's, that's how desperate I am, but both of them are long gone—

And my disappointment is as real and needling as a splinter.

I shake it off, try to hold on to the rush I got when I first heard about my night off, despite the fact that I'm alone. I grab my coat, hat, and gloves and hit M Street, turn down 15th Street, and soon run into a church. It's packed outside, people coming and going, the church's wide stone stairs busy and festive. A chorus of red-dressed girls and boys stand on the front lawn holding candles, all bundled up in their new coats and Sunday best, start belting out an adorable version of "Silent Night."

And it's only then that I realize it's Christmas.

An intense loneliness falls over me like a shadow. I want to call Ruby and Ben, make sure that Ben made my gingerbread for her, ask if he remembered to pick her up something from the Drummond Five and Dime. But they've got no phone. I want to find Grace, enjoy the holiday with her, but I've got no clue where she went. In an impulsive moment, I think of calling on Alex, surprising him, telling him that I'm beyond excited that he's joining our troupe, and that I couldn't wait to see him one more day. But I don't know where he lives.

And now my night off feels less like a gift, and more like a sad trick. Even more pathetic, I find myself wishing the Den was open tonight, so I could forget everything else, just throw myself headfirst into performance magic. I finally grab a hot cocoa from the meeting hall next to the church, watch the carolers for a little while longer, and try to make the most of the night.

The next morning I get up early, ready to break the news about reopening up and down our hall. I start with Grace. She opens her door to find me all smiles.

"Season's greetings," I say.

She's still got sleep on her: matted hair, long white night-gown. "Did Gunn finally let you out last night? I stayed around here as long as I could, but it was too depressing."

"Yeah, I got some time off, it was good." Like a reflex, I turn inward, erect a mental wall to keep Grace from reaching in and pulling out the truth. "But I've got some better news—we're reopening."

She shakes her head. "Are you serious? How?"

"Gunn found us a replacement sorcerer. Get ready, meet me downstairs in a few minutes." This morning actually seems more like my Christmas—getting back on the stage, performing. "We've got to train the boy," I tell her as I cross the hall, "work him in, get him up to speed!"

I round up the rest of the troupe, tell them the same, then double back to my room and quickly throw on a splash of rouge and a wipe of lipstick. I'm nervous about seeing Alex again, with no McEvoy or Gunn breathing down our necks. It kind of feels like a first date. A date five other sorcerers happen to be attending.

I head downstairs to the show space, my excitement about performing—about sharing something I love with Alex—flooding me with a warm anxiety. Soon the troupe files in and settles on the benches around my stage.

"When do we open?" Ral asks, as he sits down wearily.

I steal a longer look at him. Not sure how he spent his first Christmas away from his family, but if I had to guess from his gray face and dull eyes, I'd bet it was on an all-night shine bender with Billy. Losing Stock probably made the holiday even worse.

"Tomorrow night, and then we perform straight through the week." Then I add, "Should be enough time to get our heads on straight again," hoping Ral catches my message.

"Gunn's not worried about the patrons?" Grace asks. "About . . . about what happened keeping people away?"

Tommy and Rose exchange a loaded look at the veiled reference to Stock. None of us have been able to really talk about it. *Was it Tommy and Rose's sporadic lightning that killed him? Was it me running away?*

"Gunn thinks the show must go on," I say simply.

"Who's the replacement?" Ral asks.

"He used to be Boss McEvoy's right-hand sorcerer, on the street side of the Shaws' operation. He comes highly recommended."

"A *street sorcerer?*" Billy snaps. "Has he ever performed?"

There's no use lying. "I don't think so."

Ral and Billy start mumbling to each other on the far bench. I knew they'd be the most resistant to this. They're the biggest believers in the magic of seven, and two days to train and insert a new guy into our troupe, for our first reopening after a freak—and public—accident, is not a lot of time.

"And Gunn didn't think we should have any say in the matter?" Billy says to me.

"It came as an order, not a suggestion. You know Gunn."

"Not as well as you."

Billy's words sting—especially since I don't think I've ever felt more distant from him. Gunn's been pulling me in one direction, and Billy's loud, shine-laced lifestyle has sent him spinning in another. But the sting must be evident from my face, because Billy softens his tone. "You know this is ludicrous, Joan. How's this new boy going to keep up? I don't think this is the way the magic of seven works—if you're down a man, you can't just find some schmo and insert him as a stand-in. We've been working for *months*, months of magic ties and connections. You can't replicate that in two days. And if the show doesn't come together, there'll be hell to pay from Gunn."

I shake my head, because for some reason, I'm not worried. I've seen what Alex can do. And as crazy as it sounds, somehow

I know I've only scratched the surface. "We'll make it work. Gunn knows what he's doing. And the new boy's talented, Billy," I answer. "He's a manipulations expert, has a great eye for detail, works hard—"

Grace interrupts with, "Wait, so you've met him?"

At that, the group falls silent.

I swallow audibly. "Just around here. But I can vouch for him."

Tommy sits up straight. "So there's a big accident with Stock, and then poof, one of your gentlemen callers is on the roster."

Rose whispers to him, "Man, our girl gets around."

I feel my face flush as Grace cuts in, "This isn't the time to be eating our own."

"It's the truth, Mama Bear," Rose cuts back. "Stock would still be alive if he hadn't been working with Joan that night."

"You mean Stock would still be alive if you and Tommy hadn't been shined to the moon that night," I say. "It was your lightning."

And then Tommy stands brusquely, whether to confront me with magic or with his fists, I'll never be sure, because Alex picks that exact time to burst through the double doors. The six of us stop and turn.

"Sorry if I'm late," Alex apologizes, as we all stare him down.

His eyes find mine, and that intense, almost crippling feeling— angsty, raw—washes over me on seeing him again.

When I don't move or say anything right away, Ral crosses my stage and shakes Alex's hand. "Ral Morgan," he says. "My associates, Billy Caine, Grace Dune, Tommy and his sister Rose Briggs. And apparently, you know Joan Kendrick."

"Yes, I've met Miss Kendrick," Alex says warmly. He looks around at the crowd. "I'm Alex Danfrey. It's nice to meet you all. I'm thrilled about joining such a talented troupe, and I'm looking forward to learning from, and working with, all of you."

Billy crosses his arms in front of his chest. "Heard you worked with Boss McEvoy himself. He liked you enough to let you walk away, but not enough to keep you?"

"I protected him on the road for a little while," Alex answers slowly. "Needless to say, we weren't a good match."

"Wait, Alex *Danfrey*?" Rose cuts in. "Are you related to that big pharmaceutical spell racketeer, Richard Danfrey?"

Alex's face becomes taut. "I am. I'm his son."

"Tommy, you remember those sad headlines?" Rose tsks, her gaze never leaving Alex's, her dark catlike eyes glimmering. "Newspapers calling Richard Danfrey a traitor, saying his wife was poor and crazy now? Funny, never remember reading anything about a son."

I see a fire light behind Alex's eyes. "My family did well to keep me out of the papers."

"So your pop works for D Street, things fall apart, and you get burned . . . and then you work for his enemy, McEvoy . . . you're not good enough, and you get demoted." Tommy laughs to himself. "You ever think you Danfreys aren't cut out for magic?"

Even Grace clearly has doubts about Alex. She takes a step forward, like she's about to go delving inside Alex's mind for answers. "You really think you can keep up, Mr. Danfrey?"

"Enough, guys, this isn't an interview," I finally say, but Alex glances at me and says, "It's all right, Joan."

He runs his fingers through that silky blond hair of his, takes a big breath. "I *do* think I can keep up," he addresses my troupe. "I wouldn't be here otherwise. I'm good with visual manipulations, and I've been told that I have an eye for detail. Doesn't take me too long to learn a new trick, either."

"And he's being modest," I cut in.

"Joan mentioned you've never performed in front of an audience," Ral presses.

"No, but I'll learn what I need to learn. I won't let you down."

"And I'll help him," I blurt out. "He can work with me on my performance trick until he gets settled and we decide where it makes sense for him to go."

"You want to take the weight of training him?" Ral says, his voice a strange mix between relief and doubt.

I nod.

"All right, fine," Ral says. "Then let's get to it. We've got a lot of work ahead of us, if we're opening on Monday."

Alex stays in my performance circle with me, as the rest of the sorcerers move to their own spaces.

"Nice and tense around here," Alex says.

I shoot him a glance as I start dumping out some feathers from the bin around my stage. "The guy you replaced, he—he passed away a few nights back. I think everyone's just trying to find someone or something to blame for the mistake."

Alex flashes me a thin smile. "Easy thing to understand."

"Don't worry. The troupe's got bark but little bite. Especially Billy and Ral, they're good fellas deep down, trust me. And Grace just takes it upon herself to keep mental tabs on all of us." I give him a smile. "Just start imagining sky-high brick walls when she's nearby, and she'll take the hint and back off."

"I appreciate you vouching for me, Joan," Alex says. "I still can't believe I've never caught a show before." He looks around the space, to the rest of my troupe now practicing their own tricks in their performance circles. "Must be something, being here as a patron." He swallows. "Got to say, I'm feeling a little out of my league."

"You'll get the hang of it—you just need to immerse yourself in the troupe. You'll feel it, once the magic of our seven has you. Your set of tricks will expand, your talents will start to mature." I think back to those first nights we were practicing as seven here at the Den, when we started to understand just how strong our magic had to become to achieve Gunn's vision.

"Pretend your magic is one part of our puzzle, and have faith that it'll come together to make the big picture."

Alex smiles. "That's an interesting way of putting it."

"It's what works for me," I say. "You're going to be great, okay? I'll help you, one step at a time."

At that, Alex throws me that smirk that I'm always sort of angling for from him, the one where it almost looks like he's about to laugh at you and with you at the same time. "Seriously, Joan. Thank you."

My face flushes, so I nod and start to pace around my circle. "We practice our individual performances every day—the one-man and two-man tricks that take up the show's first hour or so—and then Gunn comes in after lunch to give us his thoughts on the night's finale," I say. "Then we'll experiment, try to run the finale a few ways, until we finally show him a dress rehearsal. After dress, we break for about an hour and come back here a little early for the real show."

Alex raises his eyebrows. "Long day."

I shrug. "It is, but you get used to it. There's a show every night but Sunday, which I usually spend sleeping."

Alex smiles again. "And the shows start at eight?"

I nod and point to the double doors. "Right through there, a hundred and fifty patrons come pouring into our show space. And trust me, the crowd is always something to see."

"Lots of crazy cats come in here?"

I grin. "Rich, eccentric, addicted to shine. Sure you can paint yourself a pretty picture." Then I tell him about some of the better finales we've conjured, and how we wrap up the show by brewing sorcerer's shine for the audience. "Win told Gunn that you're steady with transference—that you can brew your magic into a bottle, right?"

Alex nods.

"Well, we brew the shine up there, on the stage"—I point to

the back of the show space—"and the stagehands take care of pouring it and passing it around." I smirk at Alex. "And then it *really* gets insane in here."

Alex laughs. "Like how?"

"People claiming that they're seeing God, walking around like mummies, mumbling to themselves." I laugh. "Lord, some even go stripping and streaking. Once caught a little orgy in the corner over there." I feel my cheeks flush again, and look away. *Why did I just mention that to him?* "Sometimes I sneak up to my room, when Gunn's not looking, just for a little break from it."

"I hear you," Alex says, as his laughter begins to fall away. "Some nights on the road I would have given up my right hand for a ten-minute break from McEvoy." He points to my circular stage. "So what's your trick?"

"Watch and learn." And then I run through my solo performance, the one I've done over a hundred times since I arrived at the Red Den, where I take a ring of feathers, lift them until they slowly encircle me, then spin them fast as a tornado, until a live dove flies out of the chaos. I've done the trick so many times that I don't even consider it "magic" anymore, but when the bird flaps to the rafters above, Alex gives a sigh, just like a patron. "That's amazing." He looks at me. "What do you do with all the birds?"

"A stagehand rounds up the five or so I make each night into a cage," I say, as I gather more feathers from my bin. "Then I release them, to fly for one glorious night, before they're condemned to disappear." I give a little smile. "For that minute, when I lean out the window and watch them flap away, I pretend that I'm flying with them." *Lord, I can't believe I just said that out loud*. It feels weak, and sappy, and it's something I haven't even shared with Grace. Maybe 'cause it makes it sound like I want to run away. And maybe 'cause sometimes, when I'm in Gunn's office, when the walls are closing in, there's nothing closer to the truth.

But Alex doesn't flinch, and his eyes grow warmer. "Where would you go?"

If I really could fly? I'd turn Ruby, Ben, and me all into birds, let the three of us soar under the moon, without a care in the world, Ruby's laughter spellbinding the night. "I'd fly for as long as I could." I look away from him. "Why don't you try it this time?"

"I don't know if I can," he says doubtfully.

I sit on the bench next to him. "Just focus on every feather, at the same time you're imagining the bird. Your magic touch wants to make the connections."

Alex nods, turns in on himself. He dumps some more feathers around him. Then he furrows his brow, points his hands toward the floor, and the feathers begin to lift, sashay. Then they start to move together like a complicated dance. But my eyes stay on Alex. He's beautiful, standing there concentrating, his hair flopping over a strong brow that's just starting to perspire. He's exactly the kind of intriguing, handsome boy you'd want to trick you.

The feathers soon spin into a frantic white wind, and then a dove is birthed from the center of its magic cocoon. The bird flies across the show space and lands on a ceiling pipe high above the double doors.

"You're really talented, Alex."

"I'm not so sure anymore, now that I can see what you all can do." But he's clearly pleased by my compliment.

"When did you find out you could do all this, that you could sorcer?"

"At the end of puberty, same as most people who get the magic touch." He studies his hands. "Wonderful, isn't it, trying to figure out who you are right as you realize you can create lightning with your fingers?"

I nod but think back to my conversation with Gunn, how he said that Alex had a "cloudy past." From Rose and Tommy's teasing, it's clear that Alex's father ran some big, scandalous spells scheme. I wonder if Alex's pop was like my mother and tried to keep him away from magic, at least at first—or if he was the reason Alex dove headfirst into this underworld. "So did your father teach you everything he knew? About magic, and the spells racket he was running?"

He looks at me quizzically. "Thought you didn't read the papers."

I shrug, drop my gaze. "I don't, just couldn't ignore what the others were saying, is all." I give him an apologetic smile. "I'm sorry, don't mean to pry—I'm just trying to learn more about the mystery man, Alex Danfrey."

"You want to learn all my secrets?" he jokes softly, takes a couple steps closer. "Why don't you show me yours first?"

I look up, and Alex is holding a small mirror in his palm. I expect to see my reflection back in it, but in the center of the glass just floats an image of that same black orchid he gave me, all those nights ago in the hall. And then my dove trick kind of feels beside the point. An idea, hot and fast, turns me on like a switch.

"*That's* what we'll do for our performance," I say breathlessly. "Magic's better when it means something—when you let it breathe."

Alex gives a little laugh. "What are you talking about?"

"For our performance circle trick," I say, "we should do something new, something we can't accomplish alone. Forget my birds," I add, my idea fully possessing me now, lighting me up with possibility. "Stay here. I'll be back."

I grab an empty mirror stand from the prop room, and once I explain to Alex how to perform a double-sided trick, how to separate the glass down the middle and spellbind each side, we run through my idea all morning, during lunch, and into the afternoon, when Gunn shows up with a strange smile on his face.

I never used to be able to read Gunn, but after all the time I've spent across the desk from him, now I know his tells. There's a little bit more fluidness to his movements when something good happens. I wonder if it's about our secret shine venture. I'd have to think it is.

"Welcome, to our newest troupe member," he says evenly to Alex. "Hope my team is treating you well."

Alex nods, as we settle around Gunn in the shining area in the middle of the show space. "They are. Thank you, sir."

Gunn looks at our troupe. "As Joan no doubt told you, we reopen tomorrow night, and it'll be one of the most important shows of your lives. I want a full-scale, seven-sorcerer performance piece that will transform the entire atrium into a sky, from the earliest teases of morning right on through to sunrise," he says. I can feel Alex's eyes on me. "Fading stars, a blazing horizon, a hanging sun—a complete and flawless immersion. Give our regulars something worth coming back for."

The group nods and mumbles in assertion.

Gunn adds, "All right, take a spin, run it through—we've got less than two days to master this."

And then we divvy up our tasks, fill out the length of the show space, and immediately start improvising. But this rehearsal's even more exciting, 'cause Alex is right by my side. Our troupe finally breaks for the night invigorated, and I swear, I've never felt so alive after a full day of magic.

After Alex goes home and the rest of the sorcerers head upstairs, Gunn pulls me into his office. He closes the door but doesn't sit down.

"I'll be holding an important meeting in the VIP lounge tomorrow night. Some of the underbosses will be here for the show, but once the shine gets passed around, I want the hallway fully concealed, you understand?" He opens his top drawer and pulls out one of my blood-caged bottles. "Think it's time to show folks what we've been working on."

I look at him, confused. "I don't understand. You won't be able to open the bottle—"

"Which you and I will figure out," Gunn interrupts me. "It's time to take another risk. If I can't tease them with what's possible now, I'm going to start losing them." He holds the bottle up to his face, like the answer to our problem might be in the shine itself. "They'll be able to see that the shine outlasts magic's normal one-day shelf life. I'll tell them it's cursed. That it can't be opened until I have their firm support. Should buy us a few days."

Christ, I wish I knew what Gunn is up to. He better know what the hell he's doing. Ruby and Ben, our livelihood—hell, from the way he talks, *my life*—it all hangs on Gunn, just as much as it does on me figuring out this spell. "I'll make sure to conceal the meeting, sir."

"And how's the new boy working out?"

"Just fine."

"Any wrinkles, issues?"

I shake my head, still feeling the faint buzz of pride over a good day of magic. "He's a hard worker, fits in, puts his head down."

"Good," Gunn breathes out. "Tomorrow night is key, has a lot riding on it for the Red Den, and for you and me as well."

"The troupe will be ready."

Like a reflex, Gunn reaches out to pat my shoulder, but just as quickly he pulls back. He strokes his hand over his slick blond hair instead. "All right, get out of here." He opens the door with the faint trace of a smile. "And keep thinking about that spell, Joan. Your deadline's coming faster than you think."

THE SHOW

ALEX

I've been in a lot of nerve-racking situations these past few months, but none of what's come before has triggered the strange, almost surreal blur of emotions I feel walking back to the Red Den right now. Because tonight, in some weird twist of fate, the powers that be—Frain, McEvoy, me—have moved me like a pawn onto a stage. A stage that I'm sharing with Joan. A performance where I play an agent, playing a gangster, playing a sorcerer. For a packed house.

I cut through the busy streets, sidestep the rush of business suits wrapping their thick wool coats around them as they grasp their briefcases with leather gloves. Then I make my way through the throngs of families as they wait patiently, in the blistering cold, for the doors of Saint James on 15th Street to open for nightly mass.

I haven't been able to connect with McEvoy since I started up at the Den yesterday morning. I've barely been home except to sleep, and the one time I managed to sneak out of practice for a "smoke" and run to the nearest pay phone to let him know I'd been officially folded into the troupe, no one answered McEvoy's line. The past couple of days have been a blur of training next to Joan, learning her tricks, complementing them. In fact, I've been trying to enjoy this hour of downtime, of just existing and nothing else—but I can't seem to do it. If I'm not figuring out the next move that gets my Unit and me closer to our score, I get restless, like I'm just wasting time and standing still.

I walk into the liquor bar that the Shaws use as a storefront cover for their Red Den. I nod at the stagehand already settled in behind the bar, walk through the magic-made wall, down two flights of stairs and into the wide performance space. My "troupe" is already clustered in front of the bar on the left side.

They stop talking once I approach, and I wonder if they've been talking about me. Maybe whispering that I'm not ready, that I'll never fill Stock's shoes. Or maybe that they suspect something's afoot, that one of them has a *feeling*, can delve into my thoughts and mine out the truths I'm desperately trying to keep locked inside.

The troupe fans out from the bar, and Joan steps forward from the center. She gives me a huge smile, and my worries start to slip away. "Don't you clean up nice."

I feel a deep hum in my core. Because Joan doesn't just clean up nice. She looks stunning. Perfect. Her black hair falls in deep, luxurious waves around her shoulders, which are covered in an elaborate, long-sleeved lace dress, with a neckline that gives just enough away, while teasing everything else. I can't take my eyes off her, and for just a minute, I actually forget what I'm tasked with, why I'm really here.

I force myself to look down at the tuxedo Gunn tossed at me as I headed out the door, maybe an old one from the back of his closet, or an extra from the wardrobe for the troupe. "At least I *look* the part."

But it's Ral who responds. "Joan was right, Alex, you're talented," he says. "Don't doubt yourself. You're ready." He and Billy have been just as transformed as Joan, have traded their farm-friendly button-down shirts and beat-up slacks for cummerbunds and black silk vests. Grace and Rose both look dazzling too, with deep-red lips and sequined black dresses. Even Tommy, the dimwitted chap who seems to let his sister do his thinking for him, looks all polished up in a slick tuxedo with tails. He actually shoots me a begrudging smile. "Let's give them all a show they won't forget."

"It's almost eight." Joan takes my forearm lightly, my skin firing underneath her touch. *Stop it, Alex, focus.* "The stagehands are bringing in the mirror stand now. We should get ready."

The troupe exchanges words of encouragement, divides, takes their respective places around the performance space, and waits for the crowd. I follow Joan over to our circular stage, the one the audience will see first and, given our trick, no doubt flock toward to watch. Our tilting mirror stand has already been placed in the center of our performance stage, but instead of a mirror inside it, it holds a long, narrow piece of glass. Joan and I each settle on opposite sides of the glass and smile at each other through it. Waiting.

You need to make sure, in the midst of all the tricks and manipulations, that you're not fooled yourself.

Keep your eyes open—for McEvoy, for Agent Frain. Something's going down, maybe something tonight. Remember your purpose—don't get distracted.

In minutes, the doors open. The stagehands have dimmed the lights, taken their places behind the liquor bar to serve a complimentary cocktail to our patrons. A staccato-like jazz begins to waft from a phonograph next to the bar. And then, in clusters, the patrons begin to pour into the space.

They come in, dressed in their evening best—polished, powerful-looking older couples, furs and gems on the ladies, fedoras on the men. Crowds of youngish professionals and new-money gangster types, each one of them willing to throw away fifteen dollars to get lost in magic for a night. They burst through the door hungrily, flood around the bar, buzz around the stagehands. *Soon they'll be on to us.*

Joan takes a long look at me through the glass. Despite the confident smile I've managed to glue on, perspiration starts dotting my forehead, and my throat is tight. I can feel the jump of my heart through my borrowed silk vest. I've been onstage a long time in one sense, for months, played all sorts of venues. But something about being under these hot lights with the music playing and the audience closing in, it starts to turn me inside out. Almost like it's too fitting, too much.

"Alex, you're going to be great," Joan stage-whispers around the mirror stand. "The first show was hard for me, too."

"It's nerves. I'm fine." I flash her that false smile again.

But I can't seem to calm down. Working over Howie, working over Win, working over McEvoy—it was careful work, nuanced, and personal. This is a performance in the truest sense, big and bold, and with a huge audience. My eyes scan the room for the underbosses I'm here to tail, to spy on—*can anyone tell I'm here to bring this Den to its knees? Can anyone see right through me on this stage?*

Christ, I actually might vomit—

"Alex," Joan says as she walks quickly around the glass stand dividing us. Now she's inches away. Her eyes flit to the crowd at the bar. "You just need to focus, okay? Don't make this about more than it is, like proving McEvoy wrong. *You are talented.* It was his loss, letting you go." She grabs my hand and I puff out a breath. She thinks I've got stage-fright. That I'm paralyzed over what happens if McEvoy's discarded street sorcerer can't earn his way to stay working at the Den. She's as right as she is wrong.

"I understand what you're feeling"—Joan drops her voice another octave and squeezes my hand—"like you're on your last legs, like everything's riding on one night. But just focus on one step at a time, all right? Keep your focus on me, me and you, right here, right now, just like practice." Her eyes are warm, encouraging, almost needy. Like she's depending on me.

Just her and me.

Joan is right, I need to focus. Alex the agent doesn't survive another day without Alex the performer. *All I need to think about is this trick, this show.*

Joan flashes me one more encouraging look, drops my hand, and walks back across our circle. A small crowd has gathered around us, and I hear whispers, speculation about the new boy onstage with Joan, attempting a trick they've never seen before.

I can do this, just like everything I've managed to do to land me on this stage.

And then Joan and I begin. We approach the stand, stop when we're a few inches away from it, and press our palms against our respective sides of the glass. At the same time, we take a breath and whisper, "*Capture and divide, befit to enchant.*"

The glass trembles, glimmers just the slightest shade brighter before it settles, spellbound, in between us, as a double-sided trick. But unlike a double-sided trick that links two objects into one, like two doors into a passageway, this is a separation: it takes one object and divides it into two. On my side, the image of Joan is now trapped in the glass, my easel to use and manipulate, like a mirror that gives me back the wrong reflection. On her side, my image in the glass will remain fixed and provide my own replica as her canvas. The audience immediately starts murmuring, some of the polished, painted women in the front getting off their benches to make sure they see both sides.

"It's some kind of double replica—"

"He's got her, she's got him—"

"Did you see the other side?"

The excited whispers encourage me, empower me. I can no longer see Joan herself, just her replica, who smiles at me, frozen, inside my side of the glass. I slowly raise my left hand to touch the image of her hair. The thick black waves spark and then turn red as fire, her hair churning into a sea of bright auburn.

I hear the crowd gasp, laugh with delight behind me.

Joan must be meeting my move with her own embellishments to my image on the other side. I can't see what she's doing, but the crowd of women behind her look at her side of the glass, then peer around to me. "She somehow made him better," I hear the amused whispers.

I turn back to my own work in progress, touch the glass where Joan's lips are smirking at me, and with a wave, I change them to purple. Joan responds with another embellishment on her side. I carefully touch the shoulder of her replica's dress. It's just a replica, but even still, I find myself blushing with the gesture. At my touch, the replica's entire black, lacy dress transforms into a pure, sky-blue shimmer.

"Time's up," Joan says softly.

I step a few feet away from the glass, and as we've rehearsed, we switch places to see what the other has created. I laugh out loud. My replica has hair as colorful as our upcoming dawn finale—a nice touch and teaser from Joan—a shimmering purple suit, skin the color of eggplant. I look more than magical. The reflection is electric. I wonder if this is how Joan somehow sees me.

It gives me a strange and wonderful sensation, thinking about whether it is.

I look around. We have at least fifty patrons of the hundred fifty surrounding us. I get a heady surge of pride, but for the first time in a long time, I don't ground myself. Instead I just enjoy who I'm with and revel in this chance to showcase what I can do—regardless of what it's ultimately for.

Joan and I pinch out our own replicas, and then we spellbind the mirror once more, run the trick through once, twice, four more times as some of our initial patrons flitter off to other performance circles, but many stay camped right in their seats. Before I know it, the music changes, becomes more festive, lively, and the clock hanging above the double-door entrance chimes nine. Joan rounds the glass stand and joins me on my side.

"I forgot to tell you about this part," she whispers. There's excitement in her voice; she knows we've done well. "The finale will start in about twenty minutes. This is intermission, where we interact with the audience, flirt a little, get them excited for the finale."

I smirk at her, emboldened by our trick together. "Flirt how?"

"Like a little parlor trick for a patron or two, like your compass manipulation, or that flower move you pulled on me in the hall."

"That wasn't a move," I say. "That was for you."

It's the right answer, because she blushes, smiles at the floor. "Whatever you say, Alex Danfrey." She steps around the benches and makes her way into the crowd. "Go after the ladies. They'll love you. I'm sure you'll do just fine."

She disappears into the crowd of tuxes and evening gowns and is swallowed whole by hungry patrons who begin to chat her up, angling for a little magic for themselves. I take a scan around at the packed crowd of the auditorium. One hundred and fifty people move through the performance space in all directions, surrounding the sorcerers, or milling around the stages. I do a quick scan for familiar faces—for McEvoy's main men, his underbosses, for anyone I'm actually here to track—but I don't recognize a soul.

So I target my sights on an older woman, fiftyish, painted, all dolled up with money and privilege. She's got a smile on, but it doesn't reach her eyes. As I walk toward her, ready to fashion her a rose, put a real smile on that painted face, Howie Matthews appears out of nowhere, stops right in front of me, blocking my way.

I'm shocked still at seeing him. It's like a window to my past opening, sobering me, blowing in a stiff, uncomfortable breeze in the middle of this warm madness.

He grins. "You look good in a costume, Alex."

"It's good to see you, Howie," I reply, recovering. "Been a long time. Too long."

He shrugs as he looks around the performance space. "I've been busy."

"You just here for the show?" I say slowly. The pull of my hunt is now back in full force, tugging inside me once more. *Howie's a small-time player, just another guy on Win's ride-alongs. He wouldn't be in on anything involving the higher-ups . . . would he?* "Nice to see you get a night off."

"I'm moving up in the world, Danfrey," he says with an annoying little pedantic smirk. He gives me a long, exaggerated once-over. "Too bad I can't say the same for both of us."

Like a reflex from a phantom limb, I almost tell him that despite what he thinks he knows about me, it doesn't scratch the surface—I'm not the half-rate gangster chump he thinks McEvoy has discarded, who he needs to believe he's eclipsed.

But I manage to quash the urge. Because those days, of making sure the world knows how important Alex Danfrey is, they're over. There's just too much at stake. I can't afford to have any enemies lurking in the corners of this place.

"Listen, How, I'm sorry, about what I said before, that night in the car with Win," I say softly. "About you, and your family. I didn't mean it."

"Water under the bridge, Danfrey." But his eyes stay hard as diamonds. He flashes me a wolfish smile. "Anyway, that's your MO, right? Come on strong, then fizzle out?"

I swallow. "Thought you just said it was water under the bridge."

Howie slaps me, hard, on the back. "Can't two friends still mess around?"

"'Course."

Howie looks around. A crowd's starting to gather in the center of the performance space for the impending finale. "Don't you owe me a little trick or something, Danfrey?"

I burrow into my pocket, pull out my pack of Luckies, light one, and then float it over the space between us. Howie reaches for the cig, then takes a pull. "Always did love how you did that."

It's getting late—the other sorcerers have started to move to their positions around the space's perimeter. I should go, but I feel like there's something Howie's hiding, something he wants to rub my face in but knows he shouldn't—*if I take another minute, push him, maybe I can trick him into it*—but then I glance at Joan. When she catches me watching her, a huge grin lights up her face.

"Well, at least you got the girl, man." Howie follows my gaze and slaps my back once more before leaving me. "Have fun with your tricks."

I sidestep the patrons who are now crowded in the middle of the floor, arranging themselves into ten- to fifteen-person rows across the performance space. I take my place beside Joan on the right of the crowd, off the aisle. "Grace is about to start," Joan says nervously. "Remember, wait for my cue."

I shake off Howie's taunting, try to settle back into light, flirtatious, performer Alex. Joan's Alex. "Yes, boss."

She smiles. "Seriously, don't get too trigger-happy. This has to be just right."

I give her an exaggerated bow. "Your wish is my command."

She rolls her eyes, but her smile only grows wider as she looks away from me and up to the lofted ceiling above the audience. And as we stand here beside each other, waiting, I take the opportunity and whisper, "Is Gunn working the floor tonight?"

She keeps her eyes on the ceiling. "He's getting ready for a meeting."

"Here, you mean? With who?" I look around pointedly. "I didn't see any of the other head honchos here." I flash her a grin. "You're making me even more nervous."

"Don't be nervous, you're a natural. Everything's going better than I hoped it would."

Before I can press her anymore, Grace starts blinking out all the lights that hang in rows over the space, and soon the entire room is coated in a thick darkness. There are gasps, murmurs from the crowd.

The darkness begins to fade, slowly but surely, like someone's taken a bucket of midnight and mixed in a steady drip of light. Black, to a rich gray, to a fading silver—

At some point, Ral and Billy finish painting their night canvas. They hand the reins over to Tommy and Rose, who send billowing clouds drifting across the space and splatter shocks of yellow, deep purple, and electric pink above the audience's heads. The colors begin to deepen and run together. I try to imagine what it must feel like, to have this world of magic hit you all at once, for the first time, not slowly during hours of careful rehearsal and improvisation to make it happen. It must truly feel out of this world.

"Our turn," Joan whispers.

She sparks to life a small sphere of light, maybe the size of a globe, right above the audience's heads. And then she breathes life into it, slowly expanding it, like she's blowing up the world's most brilliant, glimmering balloon.

I whisper beside her, "Incredible." Because despite how dangerous magic can be—how it's been used to hide murders, cover up robberies, send people spiraling into the throes of addiction—there's just no denying that it is.

Joan smiles, her eyes still on her bright globe, which keeps expanding. Men and women, young and old, they all arch their necks up, watching Joan's woman-made sun bask them in a warm light. And then she lifts it higher, the sun rising, *rising*—

And now it's my turn. I take her sun manipulation and slowly crack it open like an egg, watch the brilliant yellow run like a yolk across the lofted space, bleed into a huge, vast, spectacular morning. Tommy and Rose step in once again, bring their full and bulbous clouds drifting under the ceiling, and the audience bursts into applause.

The world's first enclosed sunrise.

After our magic immersion, the crowd is now even hungrier, wants to ingest and swim inside the magic that has bewitched them. We sorcerers all climb the stage, as our team of stagehands gathers around the base, waiting patiently with trays of empty shot glasses to fill and hand out to the patrons.

Each of us takes our place in front of the seven bottles on the altar. In unison, we wrap our hands around our glasses, each channel our magic touch right into our bottle. We do this one more time, two tricks of twelve ounces of sorcerer's shine, before the stagehands pour our bottles into shot glasses and hand the patrons their elixirs.

Soon the entire crowd falls under our shine, and as Joan warned, the place erupts into a strange mix of insanity and abandon. People dash across the space and spin around like children. Some dance, others sing, still others hopscotch through the performance space. Some drag lovers into dark corners, letting the shine speak for them, maybe in ways they hadn't had the courage to do on their own before—

Not that everything's so sensual, or freeing. A stagehand rushes a young girl into the corridor toward the bathroom as she sputters and chokes—my guess, an overdose, despite the Den's firm rules of one ounce per patron. A few feet away from the mouth of that hall, I spot that same older lady—the one with the painted face I was going to charm—crying away her makeup, pleading and pounding on the cinder-block wall of the performance space. It brings me back, to strange, terrifying nights working with my father when he was high. Because as invincible as shine can make you feel, it doesn't let you escape yourself forever. In fact, eventually, it just makes everything worse. *This is why you're doing what you're doing, why places like this need to come crashing down.*

"You did wonderfully, Alex," Joan interrupts my thoughts—like always, bringing me back to her, to the now.

"Thanks to you," I say, as she falls in line beside me. "You saved me earlier. And our replica trick you came up with is something special. You heard the crowd. They were wild for it."

Under the bright lights that highlight our stage, Joan positively glistens. "My mama used to always say that magic is alive. That if you want things from it, you need to respect it, listen to what it has to say." She looks away from me, back to the crowd, drops her voice to a seductive hum. "And there was real magic on our stage tonight, Alex."

And for one quick, hot moment, I almost reach out and grab her, pull her into me, make her mine like I do in that trick. "I think your mother was right. And I even think we did one better." I throw her a wink but fold my hands on the altar, forcing them to stay where they are. "I actually think we went and spellbound the magic itself."

She looks at me strangely, like I've said the wrong thing. But then she laughs, a big, freeing, bold laugh. Her smile grows wide, her eyes expectant. "I think you're righter than you know, Mr. Danfrey."

By this point, Tommy, Rose, Billy, and Ral have all left our stage and angled the stagehands for their own glasses of shine, so Grace crosses the empty space and sidles up to Joan and me.

"That little mirror trick of yours is going to run the rest of us out of town," she shouts to both of us over the jumpy jazz. Her voice is warm, but even still, she takes a step closer. I swear I can almost *feel* the pressure from Grace trying to mine her way in and figure me out. Thank God Joan warned me about Grace's special gift, and every time she gets close enough to burrow her way into my mind, I picture a fortress, sky-high and insurmountable.

On the surface, of course, I flash her a grin and wiggle my thumb playfully toward Joan. "That trick was all Joan's idea."

Grace mentally retreats. Maybe she senses she's not getting in. Or maybe she's decided to trust Joan, who's now shooting Grace a pleased, loaded look over my compliment.

I can't help but smile too, as I glance back to the main space—

And then my heart leaps, just for an instant, over who I spot at the back of the crowd. There's a cluster of mob men—I recognize their faces, all of them, some from my time running with McEvoy, some from black-and-white photos that were pinned to the Prohibition Unit's board of wanted Shaw men. Harrison Gunn, Win Matthews, and George Kerrigan, McEvoy's underboss from the racketeering side, plus a few others I don't know well enough to connect with a name. And they're all heading with their little glasses of sorcerer's shine into the left corridor off the main space.

"I better get going," I say to Joan, a little too briskly. So I force a yawn. "Long night, and it's going to be a longer week." I look around quickly. "But should I stay? Is there a post-performance meeting or anything?"

Joan gives me a canned smile. I can't read her—I'm not sure if she looks more anxious or disappointed. "No, of course, you're free to go."

I grab her hand, give it a little squeeze. "I'll see you tomorrow."

I angle my way through the sea of shiners and to the mouth of the hallway. I wait until a small crowd of half-crazed dancers surges forward, a perfect cover while I sneak down the hall after the underbosses. I reach for the cinder-block corner of the hallway, ready to round it—

But my fingers are stopped short, smack against a hard surface as smooth and strong as glass.

I step back a few feet, take in the perfect manipulation—a flat facade of an empty hall closing off the actual corridor. A protection wall, just like the ones Joan used to create, to keep our hallway conversations secret from prying eyes.

Is this Joan's handiwork too?

On instinct, I look back to the stage, wonder if she's watching me, and if I can somehow conjure a door straight through her replica without being detected. She and Grace are still up there, scanning the crowd slowly, talking in hushed whispers, both of their faces creased, concerned.

It's not worth the risk. Not yet.

I bound up the two flights of stairs to the first-floor liquor bar, dart through the small space, needle my way out the door. I walk home quickly, only stop when I reach Iowa Circle, collapse onto a park bench to catch my breath. *Plans are cooking inside the Red Den, maybe something involving Harrison Gunn, Win, others. Joan at least knows enough to protect them, to keep their meetings hidden behind magic walls.*

I need to get more out of her, push her, figure out all I can.

But it pains me a little, thinking about actually doing it.

I'm so lost in my own thoughts that when I finally round onto P Street, I almost walk right by the black car sitting in front of my house. The window rolls down a crack, and a pair of feral, bloodshot eyes peer out over the glass.

"About goddamned time, Alex," McEvoy's voice bellows from inside. "Get in."

My heart nearly stops. *The last thing I want to do right now is get inside this man's car.*

I reluctantly slide into the passenger seat. Between McEvoy's seat and mine, a small mirror lies facing up. It's dusted with blue powder, and a rolled dollar bill lies on top of it. *So McEvoy must have tried the dust—tried it many times, from the looks of him right now. Which means he's paranoid, unpredictable.*

Even more dangerous than usual.

"You're supposed to check in every day with me."

"I tried you last night, sir, but it was late," I say slowly. "They have me there all day practicing, and nights are at the show. If I sneak out, it might arouse suspicion—"

"You're there *for me*, you understand?" He roughly pinches his nose, sniffs loudly. "If you arouse suspicion, you find a way to deal with it."

"Of course, sir, that's not what I meant—"

"You've been there two days already. I need information, Alex."

I steal a better look at him. McEvoy's hand is itching over the pistol tucked into his holster, like he's just waiting for a reason to use it. *Now's not the time to tell him that at least three underbosses were meeting behind a concealed door. Now is not the time to tell him that instead of somebody after him, it might be a goddamned coup.* I need an answer that buys me as much time as possible at the Den, without McEvoy barreling through its doors before my Unit can. "Harrison Gunn wasn't on the floor." I give him the name of his youngest underboss. "He's been more absent from the performances, seems a little distracted. Could be nothing. But whatever's going down, my best guess is that he knows about it. I think I need to start homing in on Gunn, paying him a little more attention, tailing him."

"Gunn." McEvoy shakes his head, starts his car's engine. "Time for a chat with Gunn—"

"Sir, wait, I'm not even sure if he's involved," I rush to say, "or if he's just providing the meeting place. You go after him now, you might never find out the truth, or how far any of this extends." I steal a breath. "Let me find out more, get to the heart of it, find my way inside the meetings at the Den."

McEvoy stares at the window as his engine hums. My fate, the Feds's sting, it all hangs in the balance.

"You start ringing *every* night, Alex," he says. "You don't reach me? I expect you to come calling, sit on my fucking door-step till you find me and loop me in. Or I'll find myself a new little rat to burrow in there. We clear?"

"Yes, I will. I'm sorry, sir." I nod, relief coming out in a small gasp as I push my door open. "Of course I'll find a way."

WHILE THE CAT'S AWAY

JOAN

At midnight, after the crowd has left the show space and as the stagehands clean the place, I finally release the protective wall I sorcered to hide Gunn's meeting. None of the troupe even notices—my manipulation was flawless, only noticeable if you went ahead and walked straight into it, which none of them are likely to do, seeing as no one uses that hall but Gunn—and besides, everyone is exhausted at this hour, or coming down from shine. Not at their sharpest.

I head upstairs with the rest of the sorcerers, share a whiskey nightcap with Grace on my fire escape—ten minutes she spends grilling me over what I really think about Alex. But her questions are warm, and teasing, and it feels good to talk with her about something real, instead of dancing and sidestepping around my business with Gunn.

Still, as soon as she leaves, my nerves return. I sit in my room, counting the minutes until I'm sure everyone's asleep. I need to talk with Gunn as soon as I can, and his meeting in the VIP lounge has to be wrapping up soon. This can't wait. I might have an answer, the solution he's been waiting for, the missing piece in his plan that will determine both our futures. Alex, of all people, might have managed to help me crack the riddle of the caging spell—

I think we went and spellbound the magic itself.

These simple words of his set off an idea, one that grew strong and fast and stubborn as a weed. *Trick the magic.* That's what we need to do, to get around the problems with the caging spell, make a long-lasting shine feasible, and let a buyer open the damn jar.

Trick the magic itself.

I walk down my upstairs hall carefully, quietly, round the two flights downstairs, then knock on Gunn's office door, barely able to contain the nerves and excitement flowing through me. Then I knock again. It's not like me to be so impatient, but I need to pass this on, and I see a faint light from Gunn's office lamp filtering out through the bottom crack of the door. This caging spell riddle has been a thorn in my side, sharp and relentless. So relentless, in fact, that somewhere along the way of trying to solve Gunn's puzzle, I stopped worrying about the hypothetical people in their hypothetical homes across America—the ones who might get hurt if a shippable shine comes to pass—and focused all my worry on me and mine. What would happen if I didn't deliver, what would happen to Ben and Ruby—

I close my eyes. *But you* are *delivering. Their world is only going to get better. Not just the money from your work in the show, but payments on the cabin. And when Gunn rolls this shine out to the world, ten percent of whatever flows back in—*

The door clicks open, interrupts my thoughts, and I jump back to find that weaselly-looking fella I used to see with Alex when he was still working the street: one of Win Matthews's junior guys, always on the sidelines but never in the spotlight, and almost always shined. Howie Matthews.

"Joan," he says too warmly, with big shined-up eyes, like we're long-lost soul mates. "Sorry for the wait, doll." He glances back to Gunn and throws him this disgusting, suggestive grin. "Man's all yours."

Howie shoves his hands in his pockets as he angles past me. He starts whistling down the hall after he leaves, and I close the door behind him. What the heck is a bottom-feeder like Howie doing with Gunn's ear?

"What is it, Joan?"

"That shiner Howie's working for you now, sir?" I say slowly, as I settle into the chair across from Gunn. He's hunched over a large map. If I squint, I can see the vague cursive of *Potomac* scrawled down the sky-blue river that runs right down the middle.

"He has information on Alex Danfrey." Gunn traces his finger down the left border of the Potomac. "Information I felt compelled to hear."

I freeze at the mention of Alex's name. "Is something wrong? I told you I'd keep an eye on Alex, sir. And he did great tonight."

"I keep tabs on everyone, Joan." His eyes glance up to me briefly. "It's nothing for you to concern yourself with."

Everyone. Including me. When I don't answer right away, Gunn pushes, "You had something to tell me?"

But my twisty, almost electric anxiety has given way to a dull hum. "I might have come up with a solution, to our shine problem," I say flatly.

At that, Gunn stops looking at the map.

I take a deep breath. "It was something Alex said, in passing, about our double-sided trick tonight. The one we use to enchant the glass stand." I lean forward a few inches. "You know how you've talked about magic being alive, that it needs and wants things, same as the rest of us?"

"And?"

I study my hands. "What if we . . . what if we somehow spellbound the blood-spell? What if we tricked the magic itself?"

Gunn's face stays stone, unimpressed. I lose some of my nerve but stumble forward. "Before I brew the shine, we'll spellbind the top of the bottle with a double-sided trick. Like our glass stand manipulation, or a protective wall that shows two different things to those on each side." I try to think this through once more. "The bottle will appear closed on the inside but will be a pass-through on the outside," I say. "And then I conjure the blood-spell over this double-sided trick."

I practically see his mind's wheels turning. "Can someone besides you release it?"

I nod. "They should be able to. Because it will only be blood-caged from the inside out, and not the outside in." I pick up the bottle of water on his desk. "Imagine a stopper sitting right here"—I point to the neck of the bottle—"a stopper that's separated into two manipulations: the one facing the liquid inside is a closed container, and the manipulation that faces upward is an open container. I conjure the blood-spell over this stopper"—I point again to the neck of the bottle—"but we seal the bottle with a cap up here." I slap the top of the bottle. "A buyer can open the real cap, because the magic inside is none the wiser. It still thinks it's trapped, blood-caged. It has no idea it's been tricked."

The beginnings of a smile slowly start to pull at Gunn's face. "But the shine would still be bound—"

"It wouldn't be bound, it'd be released," I interrupt. And then I stop, take a breath. *You don't talk over Gunn.* "Just because the magic doesn't know it's been tricked," I start again, more tentatively this time, "doesn't mean it hasn't been. The bottle would be open. The shine's shelf life would begin."

Gunn doesn't say anything for a long time. Then he simply says, "Show me."

He leans over, takes off the cap of the water bottle in front of me, and leans back, waiting for my demonstration.

I swallow down the nerves, the fear, the doubt. *You can do this. It will work. It has to work.* I take the bottle into my hands, keep my right on the glass, wave my left over the top. "*Conjure and split—to the bottom enclose, to the top release.*" A small glass stopper sparks alive at the mouth of the bottle. And then I close my eyes, brew my shine into the bottle, letting my magic touch flood into the glass, and transform the water into a pure red shine.

I steal a glance at Gunn. "Moment of truth." He passes me his letter opener without a word. I pause, then draw it quick across my arm. A flash of blood pulses out of the cut, trails over my skin, drops into the bottle and around the glass stopper I've just conjured. Then I slowly place the real cap on top, right over the bloodstained stopper wedged into the bottle's mouth. "*With purpose and a stalwart heart, a sacrifice.*" I chant the spell. "*Less of me, an offering to cage for eternity. My wish, to cage this shine forever, or until I release it.*"

The bottle trembles, accepts my sacrifice, and shudders once more before it stops.

"When will we know if it works?" Gunn says.

"After at least a full day. We need to make sure the caging spell has preserved the shine beyond the magic's shelf life." I pause. "And then someone else has to try to open it."

Gunn leans back in his chair again, pensive, begins to bite his cuticles. He takes a long look at the bottle. "If this works, it will blow the market apart," he says simply.

But I can't let myself think about that "market," about all the folks who could get hooked on shine if this comes to pass—their homes that might get broken, their families who might get left behind. And maybe that's gutless, but I never tricked myself into thinking I was a hero. I'm here to do right by one small corner of the world. *Besides, Gunn didn't give you a choice. This is the warehouse clearing all over again, the house of magic manipulations. You or them.*

"If you teach the troupe, and they in turn each teach a team of hired sorcerers"—Gunn thinks through it—"we'll be able to churn out larger shipments. We hire even more magic gofers, and we can mass-produce it." He gives a sigh. "Ship as much of this as we can manage, anytime, anywhere. The only limitation being, as I understand it, that as soon as you open the bottle, you'll need to drink its contents within a day."

I chase away my guilt and answer, "Which will still keep people coming back to us and wanting more."

At that Gunn pops a hard, hungry laugh. "Here's hoping to God, Joan." He leans forward, opens his notebook, and says, "All right. I'll let you know."

I walk to the door feeling like I've been released from a set of shackles, and my shoulders actually feel *lighter*. I might have done it. Given Gunn what he wanted, secured Ruby and Ben's future by doing what I needed to do—

"Joan, there's one more thing. You were asking about Alex Danfrey." I turn back to Gunn, who's still focused on his notebook. "Don't get mixed up with him, you understand?"

"I'm sorry?"

"You heard me." He pauses. "Besides," a smug little smile teases his features, "you need to keep that stalwart heart."

And just like that, I feel caged again, but by a whole different set of chains.

Gunn's got no right. He might control everything else, but he's got no right to control my heart.

"Go on, Joan," Gunn says when I don't move, can't bring myself to answer. "That'll be all."

I'm a ball of nerves that my solution might fail, so I try my best to focus on other things: on throwing myself into my performance, on our show, on my crowd-pleasing trick with Alex. Alex and I just keep improving it. On Wednesday, Alex gets the idea to change my replica's *scenery*, and sends my image on a swim through a lake. The next night I win over the crowd by having his replica trek through a snowstorm. Thankfully, between our heady, nightly performances and the long but delicious days of practicing side by side, the week manages to pass in its own magic flurry—and by the end of it, I've somehow shelved my worries about Gunn.

But Friday morning he comes knocking on my bedroom door. "Mr. Gunn."

Gunn's eyes are electric, his hands practically shaking. He shuts the door behind him, burrows through the satchel that's thrown across his body, and pulls out my blood-caged shine. My glass bottle from Monday night is still capped, with a blood-stained glass topper wedged into the mouth. And the shine is still a brilliant, glistening, full-bodied red.

He twists off the top easily, and then places it back on again. "It worked," I breathe out.

Gunn turns the bottle over carefully to its side. "Oh, it worked all right. I already tested a drop of the product this morning, too. Joan, it's flawless." We did it. *I did it*. "Some of the higher-ups are already on board. It's real, this is happening. With their support, I'm meeting a distributor tonight, so I'll need you to make another bottle," he rushes, "see if we can't get him committed to a partnership."

I exhale loudly, the words, "ten percent," flashing like a stoplight in my mind.

Gunn tucks the bottle of shine back into his satchel. "Might be a long night of breaking bread, ironing out details. So you need to manage the troupe tonight—pick the finale, run the floor. It's New Year's Eve, should be a festive crowd."

I swallow. "Excuse me, sir? You mean your meeting isn't here?"

He shakes his head. "It's at Colletto's shining room, out near Union Station—too risky to do it here."

Wait, Colletto—as in the D Street boss, Colletto? I might not know all of the Shaws' inner workings, but I know that a meeting between Gunn and Colletto is far more than *risky*, the gangs are sworn enemies—

"The troupe will be fine, you'll be fine," Gunn interrupts my thoughts, mistaking the worry that I'm sure is all over my face as concern over running the Den tonight. "Just don't burn the house down, all right?"

"Sir—" I leap forward to get more details, but Gunn's already closed my door.

I run my fingers through my hair, pace back to my bed, flop down onto it. I'm managing the troupe tonight. The show is my show. An eternal shine might be possible, shippable. D Street, the Shaws' enemy, is somehow involved.

Then a thought strums and rings out over all the others, a thought that refuses to be quieted: *Ten percent. Ben and Ruby will be taken care of for the rest of their lives.*

You run until you win, or until you fall, Gunn had said of me, all those mornings ago, in this very room. At the time, the words felt almost like a shaming, especially coming from a man like him. But I'm committed to seeing the other side of them. I've given everything I have, things I didn't want to give, things that weren't mine in the first place—but I've done what I came here to do. I'm taking care of Ben and Ruby, changing their lives for the better, in a way me and my family never could have dreamed of before. And for once, I give myself permission to feel pride over that—not regret, or shame or fear.

I let myself relish the victory.

The day only gets better. I go down to practice expecting a heap of hell from some of the troupe for playing boss, but when I announce that Gunn's on the road and they're going to need to deal with *me*,

I barely get a grumble, not even from Tommy or Rose. Our practice even reminds me a little of our days back in the clearing, when our only real worry was figuring out how to make our magic all it could be. No blood, no back-office deals, no secrets.

So in honor of the troupe, I suggest our immersive finale be a garden, like the one that Billy and Ral built in the clearing, on that first day Gunn was testing us.

Because there're some things that you can't speak, but that magic can say.

"The finale is perfect, Joan," Ral says, after we break a little early, all share a smoke outside the Den's door, the winter breeze a welcome change from the trapped air of the show space. His smile has returned, as has his normal olive skin, the aftereffects of his shine bender gone. It relieves me, and I nod and touch his shoulder. I guess we all need to escape once in a while.

"The garden might be one of our best finales yet. It's beautiful." Grace blows a steady train of smoke circles that she somehow enchants into a parade of smoky flowers. I laugh as I attempt to grab them.

"They're right," Alex whispers beside me. He's so close our arms are touching, his forearm putting the slightest pressure on my recent blood-magic scars. He looks up at me with his perfect smirk. "The crowd's lucky that Gunn got called away—that it's you at the helm. Tonight's going to be extraordinary."

And when the doors open tonight, I taste things I've never tasted so exactly before, though of course I've gotten whiffs of them—pride, and ownership. Like the Red Den really could be my show. Like I was made to dazzle and win over a crowd, and make them fall in love.

"Let's light this place on fire, Joan," Alex says, as the first wave of patrons in their black-tie best and dazzling dresses floods the cocktail bar.

I match his smile. Not going to lie: when he came back to the show space wearing a tux, I almost wrapped myself right around him. Alex reminds me of what magic can feel like. He reminds me of the best kind of performance, one that taunts and teases and slowly sneaks up on you, until it has you completely.

"I'm ready," I say. "Just hope you can keep up."

"Getting a little cocky, aren't we, considering last night I had sixty-three percent of the crowd on my side of the mirror?"

"Sixty-three percent? You're sure about that?"

"Positive," he teases, as he takes his place on his side of the glass stand. "You might need to step up your performance, Joan. I daresay the pupil is eclipsing the master."

A group of older women dressed to the nines in furs and red lipstick settle into the front row on my left, while a few couples in matching silky black sit down on my right.

"Put your magic where your mouth is, Danfrey." I nod to my side of the glass stand. "Prediction: I've got the whole crowd by the end of the show."

He gives a put-on, theatrical gasp. "She raises the stakes," he says. "Challenge accepted."

Alex warms the crowd up with a manipulation of my replica that must be impressive, but not jaw-dropping. I can tell by the whispers of the ladies on the front bench, the ones ogling and whispering about *Alex*, instead of his magic.

When it's my turn, I go for broke and light Alex's replica up from the inside, as if I'm turning him on like a jack-o'-lantern. His face, suit, skin—they glisten. He looks otherworldly as he glows from the glass. A few audience members on his side actually stand up because of the whispers on my side and angle around to see. Alex even breaks our protocol, takes a few steps toward me instead of returning my trick with another of his own, and peers around to spy on what I've done.

"You're supposed to wait until the end of the round," I stage-whisper, and the patrons closest to us laugh.

"I couldn't." His actual face looks almost as radiant as his replica's.

We're flirting, sparring, pushing each other with our magic— we both know it. I want to beat him so badly. A very small part of me wants him to beat me.

Truth be told, I want us both to soar.

And then I block out Gunn's warnings about Alex with everything I've got. Because Gunn's not here right now. For once, I focus not on what I should do, but on what I want. And maybe, just tonight, I deserve that. *I want to lose myself in this. . . . I want to lose myself in him.*

We run through it again and again, and before I feel like I've fully settled into the trick, the clock chimes its hourly bell, nine chimes for nine o'-clock, marking the end of the performance hour.

"I'll meet you over by our spot on the right after the intermission, okay?" I say to Alex, once I reach him.

"Where are you going?"

"I'm working the floor tonight, remember?" I wink at him. "Pretending to be Gunn? I need to check in with the rest of the team."

Alex folds into the crowd for the parlor trick intermission, and I start making the rounds, checking in on the troupe, making sure everyone has their part to play in the finale. To me, it sort of feels like our first show.

"I know you're nervous, but this is going like clockwork, Joan," Grace says when I find her near the front. "And I'd sure as hell rather answer to you than Gunn."

"Billy and Ral all right?"

She smiles. "Think they're honored about the tribute to their garden."

I feel myself beaming. "And Tommy and Rose?"

She throws a glance across the show space, where Tommy

leans over Rose in the corner, whispering. "As hard to read as ever." She laughs. "I think they're fine."

I laugh with her, squeeze her hand. I'm grateful for her, for everything, and for just one minute I let myself pretend that this really is my place, that there is no Gunn.

I walk with purpose, *confidence*, through the crowd, excited to get back to Alex and begin the finale. But then I spot him on the other side of the show space—and I realize he's been pulled aside by Boss McEvoy.

I can't hear them from here, even if I attempted to use magic, but Alex looks upset. His brow is creased, and he's using hand gestures, speaking to the floor, as McEvoy keeps interrupting him heatedly, like he's barking. Even from halfway across the room, I see the deep-purple bruises underneath McEvoy's eyes, the dull-gray polish to his skin. He's either hankering for something magic, or he's coming down. Then he grabs Alex's collar and yanks him closer.

Panic grabs me and I start cutting through the crowd, though I'm not sure what the heck I'm going to do when I reach Alex. Tell the boss of the Shaws to calm down? Get some air? Gunn's not here, none of the higher-ups are here to calm McEvoy down—

Thankfully, before I reach them, McEvoy stumbles away from Alex, swimming upstream against a crowd now gathering in the center for our finale.

I tap Alex on the shoulder.

He whips around, looks like he's just seen a ghost.

"What was that about?" I say breathlessly.

"It's fine, it's nothing," Alex says slowly, runs a hand through his blond hair. "He's just taking the night off, and he's all hopped up on dust. I've seen him like this before. I'm used to him taking it out on me."

But I don't know how someone like Alex can ever get used to being treated like that, can learn to accept it. It makes me hate

McEvoy just a little bit more. It also makes me wonder what Alex's father was like, if this wonderful boy has learned to smile in the face of being browbeaten. "Was it strange seeing him here, in this world, instead of out on the street?"

"Strange, but in a good way," Alex says. "Reminds me how lucky I was to get out from under his shadow."

"Come on." I take his hand, pull it gently. "I think it's time we got you your own breath of fresh air."

And our magic immersion finale is just that. Trees sprout up and bloom along the aisle. A huge crisscrossed lattice of ivy runs one story above the floor, from the double doors to the back stage. Birds fly, darting across the two-story space, and grass begins to grow up from the cement floor. And as we watch our troupe's magic unfold around the audience, Alex takes my hand and squeezes. *Long ago there was a sorcerer who met her match, who finally understood all that magic could be—*

And just like magic, Alex taps into something raw and pure and electric inside me. I feel . . . light, *free*, by his side, like I'm riding my own personal high, and without Gunn here to tether and weigh me down, I get an idea, wild and unlike me. A chance to celebrate my recent turn of fate, to reward myself just a little, live a little bolder and bigger in the now. Honestly, I'm not even sure if I want to do it or if I *need* to do it, if the desire to let go—to forget my charge, my past, *myself*—has become so strong that it's taken on a mind of its own. And despite my complicated past with it, I know shine is the only thing that will actually let me get as lost as I want to.

So when we approach the stage to brew our sorcerer's shine for the audience, I whip around and sputter to Alex, "When we're done, I think—I think we should join the crowd tonight, on the floor."

Alex studies me, confused, as we approach the stage stairs. "What do you mean, take sorcerer's shine?"

I blush and turn away. *What if he doesn't want to? What then?* "Tommy and Rose do it every night—and Billy and Ral join the crowd on their fair share of evenings. Only one time, like a celebration. Just once. I thought, I mean, if you don't want to—"

I let my garbled sentence hang there, watch a storm of emotions cloud Alex's face. We arrange ourselves onstage, each take a glass bottle that's been left for us.

Then Alex leans in and whispers, "I want to."

We brew our magic touch into our bottles, and then once more to ensure we've got enough for the audience. The stagehands take the bottles of shine, pour them into shot glasses, and start to pass the glasses around to the crowd. And then the place explodes into a beautiful chaos, and the rest of my troupe, sans Grace, begins to descend into the madness themselves, each grabbing a shot of shine from a nearby stagehand's tray.

This time Alex and I go with them. I don't meet Grace's eyes as I move with Alex to the floor, even though I hear her call after me as I move to the stairs, "Joan, wait, where are you going?" Because I'm kind of as surprised as she is that I'm actually going through with this, and yet I also don't want to stop.

Alex looks around. "Do you want to stay on the floor with the audience?"

No, I want you for myself. "The underbosses aren't using the VIP lounge tonight, since Gunn's on the road. We could go there."

"How gracious of Gunn." Alex smiles. But I can tell he's nervous, maybe as nervous as I am. "Lead the way."

As soon as we get to the small lounge along the left corridor, I close the door behind me and spellbind it, lock it tight. The room's cozy: a few chairs, a little round table, and a sofa. A room meant to serve as a clandestine meeting spot, for Gunn's bigwig guests and the underbosses who trade schemes behind magic concealments. But right now the room is ours. And it feels charged, dangerous. Alex and I have been alone before, but not like this.

"You sure you want to go through with this?" Alex raises his shot glass of shine.

Shine will always have dark edges, thanks to Uncle Jed and the way he ended up losing himself in the bottle. And yet, I want so much more from Alex, and I know shine is the only thing that will let me escape myself, let me have him, in the here and the now. "I think so." *But I know so. I want to wrap a cocoon around us. Just for one night, I want to know you in a way I can't form words around, in a way that I'm positive only magic can say.* "Have you ever tried it before?"

Alex peers into his glass. "A few times. In darker days." When he next looks up, his eyes hold a strange mix of warmth and hunger. "I have a feeling it will be different with you." He touches his shot glass to mine. "If you want to jump, I'll jump with you."

And then, before I get cold feet, I take the shine and swallow it.

It burns a bit on the way down, feels like I'm drinking pop heated over a stove, but when it hits the center of my gut, it spreads across my loins like warm honey. And then the warmth rushes up from my core to my throat and spreads around my mind. The world sparks to life, dances, tilts, and I stumble and collapse into the corner. There's hysterical laughter pawing at my ears before I realize it's mine.

"Whoa," I whisper, then laugh and look at Alex, who's stumbling into a seated position on the floor next to me. I laugh again. "The word 'whoa' is so strange-sounding, isn't it? W . . . H . . . O . . . A . . ." and then I can literally see the letters, *W, H, O, A,* come floating out of my mouth like little word balloons.

"Here." I grasp at the air, giggling, trying to wrap my fingers around the *A* that continues to float up from my mouth to the ceiling. "An *A*, for Alex."

I keep the little letter trapped in my hand like a firefly and try to hand it to Alex. But he's already collapsed onto the floor, back to the ground, sprawled out and looking up at the ceiling of the lounge, like the shine has somehow broken it open to the heavens.

Wait, it *has*.

"Oh my God." I lie down, straighten myself out beside him, and look up at a thick swirling constellation, a dusty, bright collection of moving, blinking stars.

"This is insane," Alex whispers next to me. He glances over at me, his eyes as bright and wild as the stars. "Do you think this is what shine feels like for people without the magic touch?"

"Shine's probably even more intense for them," I say. "Because we see a world that's full of the *possibility* of magic"—it feels very important that I explain this to him—"but normal people, well, they just see the world."

"Wow," Alex deadpans. "That's deep, Joan."

He laughs, and I go to punch him playfully, but he ducks away from me and scrambles to his feet. And then he pulls me up, folds me into a foxtrot pose beside him. "We need music," he whispers.

A nonexistent phonograph jumps to life, crackles through our sanctuary in the middle of the Shaws' VIP lounge, and then the sultry voice of an unknown crooner wails through the space. Both of us burst out laughing, and then we begin to dance. The foxtrot, then the Charleston, then Alex begins some complicated tap maneuver he somehow continues halfway up one of the walls, before he collapses into a fit of laughter on the floor.

The music's tempo becomes slower.

Then Alex stands up, approaches me. He takes my hand and pulls me closer. And this time I don't just smell his trademark scent of soap and that almost spicy cologne—I smell something heady and fresh, all-encompassing: the scent of possibility.

"We got lucky that the room isn't being used tonight," Alex says. "It's better being here, alone with you, than sharing you with the entire crowd on the floor."

I smile into his shoulder. "I feel lucky too."

Alex's chest rises and falls underneath my cheek. "Why's the room empty, anyway? Where'd Gunn run off to tonight?"

Just the mention of Gunn's name is like an alarm, threatening to end a perfect dream. I give a deep exhale. "I'm not sure. He said he had some business on the road."

"Right." Alex nods, rubs his chin softly against my hair. "But he only manages the Den, from what I understand. Where else would he be?"

Despite the throb of the shine inside me, Gunn's warnings push through it, wrap around my mind like rope. *No one can know about the shine, about the deal.* "Probably on a run for McEvoy or something."

"Strange, because McEvoy was looking for him—"

"Hey, Alex?" I say softly. "I don't want to think about Gunn right now."

He nods, pulls me tighter, and the music's singer starts to croon, "Time stops when you're in love. . . ."

And then Alex opens his mouth beside me, and somehow the woman's voice starts to pour from his lips, "As timeless as the stars above . . ."

I laugh, lean my head against his shoulder. "I don't know how you're doing that, but please stop. It's kind of creepy."

He laughs with me, but stops singing, and pulls me closer too. And then the music fades away and it's just our heartbeats jumping, beating like a pair of drums.

BUM. BUM. BUM.

"This is nice, Joan." He puts his hand on the back of my hair, lets his fingers wrap around the nape of my neck. And then he whispers, "No, this is wonderful. *You* are wonderful."

I burrow a little more into his shoulder. The way Alex looks at me is almost as intoxicating as the shine. The way he sees me makes me feel like I *do* deserve him, that I might even deserve another chance—not just this chance to do right by my family. But a chance, maybe, to leave the past behind.

"What past, Joan?" Alex says softly.

"Wait. Was I talking out loud?" I practically whimper.

"I don't know . . . but either way, I can hear it."

Out of the corner of my eye, I see a flash of white—a nightgown, hands grasping for me, a worried, strained face watching me from the corner.

I gasp, pull back from Alex—

And then the image is gone.

"You okay?"

"Yeah, yeah, I'm fine."

But on the other side of the room appears a thin, haunting-looking girl standing at the door, reaching for me, crying, "Joan, I can't see her. Joan, I'sm losing her—"

The high is suddenly too much, too intense, too loud, and I crawl onto the floor, pull myself into a ball, my back to the edge of the sofa. I close my eyes.

But all I see is blood curling around wrists—

"Make it stop." But the voice that comes out of my mouth is Ruby's. "Oh my God." I push my hands into my eyes. Stop. *Stop stop stop stop stop—*

"What is it? What happened?" Alex sputters as he sits down beside me.

I don't look at him. "The shine's getting intense. I can't tell what's real and what's in my head anymore."

"I think that's the point." I open my eyes, and Lord, I can *see* Alex's whisper slink around my shoulders like a rich, gray mist. *Like the mist behind the cabin that night, Mama's pleading, her cries, show me, Eve, show me—*

"I'm not who you think I am," I blurt out.

Alex falters, pulls back a little bit. "Joan, it's all right, you're high."

"It's not the shine, it's me." I squeeze my eyes shut tight again. "There's something wrong with me."

The words open a dam inside me, and a river of tears starts running over my cheeks, winding salt into my mouth. And then I know I'm going to say the words I've never been able to say, not out loud at least, the words that make me loathe myself as much as I loathe Jed. Even as I'm thinking, *Stop, Joan, don't don't don't say it don't make it real*, I blurt out, "I killed my mother."

Alex looks at me, confusion—*fear? repulsion?*—stitched across his features. "What are you talking about?"

"Nine months ago," I whisper, "right around the time I was coming into my magic. I was scared of it, a late bloomer, hadn't expected that I was going to get the magic touch at all. Mama was the only one who knew I even had the 'gift' until that night." I try to stop the crashing rush of blood to my head, but I can't. And even still, my mouth keeps moving. "I found my uncle abusing her, using her—I tried to fight him—but instead I ruined everything."

When Alex doesn't say anything, I rush on, "Sometimes I feel like if I give everything I've got, work myself into the ground to help my sister and my cousin, maybe then I'll make it right. I'll earn the right to leave the past behind."

I gasp, trying to collect myself. I must look a mess. I feel the dull ache of snot and tears, the heaviness of bawling. "But I don't deserve that. I don't deserve you."

"Joan, stop. It was a *mistake*, an awful, gut-wrenching mistake," he says slowly. "And you're doing everything you can to help your family."

I wipe my eyes with the back of my hand. *How did I just take this and ruin it, take something bright and eclipse it with the dark?* "You must think I'm a monster."

"You're not a monster. You're a good person." He pulls me into him. "I see it. I see you. And I understand, maybe more than you could ever know."

I want to ask him what he means, what he *sees*. I want more, like always from him, I want more. He wraps both arms around me. It's the first time I've been held in a long, long time.

"Sometimes I don't know who I am anymore, Alex," I whisper. "What I am."

"I know the feeling." He begins to stroke my hair, edges closer. "I . . . hurt my family too, in a different way," he says slowly, as he rests his chin on my head. "The news said it was all my father." His breath catches. "But it was *my* magic that let him pull that racket, that ended with those D Street bastards selling him down the river. Without me, none of it would have ever happened." He pulls me a little more into his lap, so he can look at me. "I have to believe we get another chance, Joan, a chance to do things differently, be somebody else—better versions of ourselves. That's why I found myself here, working with you." He shakes his head. "I've never told anyone that."

"I've never told anyone about my mama, either."

Alex lays me down, gently, on something soft. And in the starry space between consciousness and unconsciousness, I pat the soft blanket below me. "Did you just sorcer this?"

"Just rest, Joan. I'll be right beside you."

I think I'm asleep, but then I feel the softest of pressures on my forehead, the smell of Alex's soap and cologne, a beacon through all the sensory noise of the shine. A kiss, above the bridge of my nose. "I do know you, Joan," he says, once he's pulled away. "I see you. I know who you are. Maybe not everything, but the important things."

I want to tell him that I see him, too. But my thoughts are too heavy, my mouth sealed shut. I'm no longer aware if I'm in the throes of the shine, or if I've survived. I close my eyes and let the dark creeping around my mind finally up and swallow me.

DUST-BUNNIES

ALEX

Joan's hair is splayed out on the pillow I conjured earlier, the dark tendrils cascading around its edges. A soft white blanket—another manipulation I vaguely remember sorcering—is spread out underneath us. Joan's beside me, eyes closed, curled tight, like even in her sleep she somehow protects herself and keeps everything locked up inside.

I sit up, realizing that we're still in the VIP lounge, my head throbbing with a dull, shine-induced headache as I arrange myself into a seating position. I have no idea what time it is. *When did we finally pass out?*

I take out my pack of cigarettes, dislodge one, and turn away from Joan as I light it. I think about us last night, guards thrown down, her telling me about her dark secret, me blubbering to her about mine.

Christ. Last night was dangerous, taking that shine with her, dangerous bordering on reckless. I remember the convoluted logic I used to justify doing it: *Joan is my strongest contact at the Den, and you do what you need to, to please that contact. Get her shined. Get her vulnerable, angle her, get more out of her, push your hunt forward.*

But the truth? I wanted to, because she wanted me to. Joan

has me under some kind of spell. She's at the center of this whole affair, is right in the line of my hunt. She's the most talented sorcerer at the Red Den, some suspicious sort of confidante of one of the gangsters I'm spying on for the Feds *and* for McEvoy, and yet, she somehow feels separate from all of this.

This whole night has been reckless, from my little tryst in this lounge to McEvoy showing up shot out of his skull, shouting that he caught his underboss Kerrigan in some convoluted lie about a job tonight. Threatening that he was going to confront Kerrigan, confront all his underbosses, and if the night ended in a bloodbath, so be it. Thank God none of them were here, and I could talk McEvoy down, tell him the dust was just making him extra paranoid, get him to sleep it off. In fact, that's what *I* need to do: sneak out before anyone sees me, go home, get some rest.

But I don't want to leave Joan like this.

I stare at her, beautiful, formidable, even as she's sleeping. And the secret that I've been tricking myself into not believing flashes across my mind: I'm completely falling for this girl.

Being with Joan might be the only time I feel like I'm not performing. In this house of lies and magic manipulations, she might be the only thing that makes me feel like a shade of my old self anymore.

"Joan." I shake her awake, gently. "Joan, you fell asleep. You need to get upstairs, get some rest, all right?"

She comes to slowly, and then as soon as she sees me hovering over her, she gives a little start. "Where are we?"

"The VIP lounge, off the performance space."

"Gunn," she says in a panic, and then collapses back down when I say, "He's on the road tonight, remember?"

She shakes herself awake. "Wait, but—"

"You don't remember our little shine experiment?" I say.

"Watching the ceiling break open into stars? Dancing? Passing out on the floor?" I give her my best smile. "All your idea, for the record."

I watch realization sink into her, even as I'm trying to joke. She remembers what she told me. She remembers how she cut herself open and showed me all her darkness inside. I wonder if she regrets it. God, I hope she doesn't.

"Alex." She puts her hands over her face. "My Lord, I was such a mess. I can't believe . . . those things I told you . . ."

I reach out tentatively, begin to stroke the top of her hair. "I'm glad you told me about your past. I'm glad I told you, too." And I realize, above all else, that I am. It felt *right*, coming clean to her about how essential I was to my father's crimes. Cathartic, and freeing. Like a last confession, before I can fully leave it all behind.

Joan sits up next to me, leans her head against the soft green fabric of the couch behind us. The heady dance of before, the shine stripping off our inhibitions, the electric feeling of possibility at being alone with her: that's all passed. It's left us with something more honest maybe, but also more uncomfortable. I still want to kiss her, obviously, wrap her up in my arms so bad it almost hurts—

But not right now. Not like this. "You want me to help you get upstairs?"

She gives me a wan smile. "Probably a good idea."

I help her up, take her arm around mine, and walk her across the main performance space, which is now dark and abandoned, pristine from the stagehands' nightly cleanup. I glance at the clock hanging above the double doors: almost two a.m.

"Happy New Year," I whisper.

She smiles up at me. "Happy New Year."

We cross the space to the other hall, walk quietly side by side. When we pass Gunn's office, we both notice a dim light reaching out from underneath the door, and Joan's eyes go wide. She puts her finger to her lips.

That quick, there's a different energy between us, as if Joan's awareness of Gunn inside the Den has set her to a new gear. *Is she just his best sorcerer? Something more? Is she really involved in the score I'm circling in on, or is there something else—something* personal—*going on between them?*

She pulls me past the door swiftly, to the bottom of the stairs. She mumbles a good-bye and begins to climb the steps quickly, like now she can't get out of the hall fast enough.

Then, like a second thought, she turns around, descends just as fast. She throws her arms around me. "Thank you," she whispers.

But before I can figure out how to answer her, she's gone, and I'm left alone at the base of the stairs.

I wait, look back anxiously to Gunn's door. This is a gift, a stroke of fortune finding his office closed without one of his sorcerers around to spellbind and protect it. I approach it quickly but quietly, lean in, whisper the word, *"Amplify,"* and the muffled voices behind the door louden into audible exchanges.

"You really think the troupe can pull off fifty gallons in a few days?" The voice is familiar, low and gravelly. Win Matthews. *Win must somehow be involved in whatever's shaking down too. And fifty gallons . . . fifty gallons of shine? That's fifty times the amount that we brew for a show. Why?*

"They'll have to. Anything less looks like an amateur operation." Low, flat, even tone—definitely Gunn. A pause. "Before we go any further, I need each of your words that if this goes through, I have your backing."

Another pause, a longer one this time.

"You have it," a third man answers slowly. *How many gangsters are behind this door?*

"And mine," another voice, this one higher, tighter, chimes

in. "You make this deal happen with Colletto? I can convince O'Donnell to fully step on board too."

O'Donnell—*McEvoy's underboss who works on the loan-sharking side. Win Matthews and Gunn. My guess is, the rest of the men behind this door must be Shaw higher-ups too.* And a deal with *Boss Colletto?* Just the man's name sends a familiar, hungry rush of vengeance surging through me. *The Shaw underbosses are breaking bread with* D Street?

"You've got the support of the majority of the underbosses," Win says softly. "This will happen, Gunn."

"Hell, you ask me, this is your birthright, Harrison," the third gangster adds.

There are mumblings of agreement. "We shouldn't go after McEvoy until we have D Street fully signed on," Gunn says. "Once we shake hands with Colletto, then we'll deal with the loose ends, and make the changing of the guard official."

Go after McEvoy, loose ends, changing of the guard. Christ, Gunn really plans to take McEvoy out—

"When do you want to hold the demonstration?" Win asks.

"It needs to be here. I want Colletto to see the full scale of everything we can do. I want him to buy into all of it, taste and crave all of it. It's the only way he'll sign on."

I close my eyes, pray for another clue as to what this demonstration is about, whether it's of our troupe's immersive magic, or something else altogether.

"A live demonstration is going to be tricky, though—we'll need to close, and that could arouse suspicion," Gunn adds.

"There's always Sunday," the third gangster chimes back in. "You're closed that night, right? Plus, the Bahama Boys say there's a smuggling party out on Magic Row: some four-night spirit-raising voodoo bender on the water, right behind the coast guard border. McEvoy, all his top dogs on the smuggling side, they're all invited."

The fourth answers, "So we need McEvoy, Baker, and Murphy on that boat, and out of your way." *Baker and Murphy*—the names are familiar. They're two of McEvoy's underbosses—Murphy's in trafficking, Baker manages a few middling shining clubs somewhere in the city. They're likely McEvoy's last two remaining loyal underbosses, from what I'm gathering.

As the men give a round of nervous laughter, I try to figure out my next move. McEvoy's going to expect my daily check-in—maybe I can avoid him tonight, but there's no avoiding him for long. *Do I tell him, warn him about this somehow?* I can't. He could take matters into his own hands, bring this whole place crashing down, blow this monumental score before Gunn can bring it home and the Unit can bust it.

I agree with Gunn and Win on one thing—McEvoy needs to be out of sight, on that voodoo party cruiser, and out of my and the Unit's way.

"Well done, Harrison. Never thought I'd see the day, but you've proven yourself. You've delivered." I hear the clinking of glasses, the squeak of leather. "To Sunday. To the Gunn legacy."

They're wrapping up. I back away from the door quickly, run back through the hall, out of the performance space, and hit the street.

It's far too late to dial Frain, so I take the walk home to run everything over and through again: *Gunn is challenging McEvoy as top dog and already has the support of the majority of the Shaw underbosses. But it all rides on some unprecedented deal with D Street happening, and there'll be a demonstration to ensure that it all goes down.*

But a demonstration of what? The troupe's performance?
And why D Street?

I stumble to a pay phone, put my obligatory call into Boss

McEvoy, pray that he doesn't answer his phone at this hour, since I've got no idea what I'm going to say if he does. I let the phone ring four times, and then I hang up, relieved, and head home to sleep everything off. I'll sort out what I'm going to tell him, and stop by his house as soon as I wake up. I won't make it through the day without some rest.

I dream about Joan. But instead of warm, or even seductive dreams, they're disorienting. Her teasing me, racing ahead of me, and then turning into a raven right before I can hold her. In one, I follow her through a strange house of illusions until I think she's around a corner, but instead of finding her, I find Gunn. Needless to say, when I wake to a loud, insistent *"Mister, Mister!"* outside my door a couple of hours later, I'm not happy. It's not even seven a.m.

I open the door to find a young boy standing on my crumbling front stoop. He's in a cap, no more than nine or ten, scrawny and hard in that street-rat sort of way. No coat, despite the weather. He holds a piece of folded stationery, which I take and read:

Be in the back alley in exactly one hour.

After he hands it to me, he bounds down my stairs and runs away.

I study the note again. I'm playing so many parts that I'm not certain who to expect is coming to call. *McEvoy? Frain? Joan?*

I take a quick bath, get changed, make a cup of coffee, hit the back alley right at the hour mark. A black car pulls up minutes later. The passenger door cracks open two or three inches, and McEvoy calls through it, "Get in."

Nerves on fire, I settle in beside McEvoy and steal a quick

glance at him. And then my anxiety doubles. He looks even worse than he did at the Den: faded gray skin, wild, wet eyes, hair that looks like it needs to be washed. I'm not positive, but I think the suit he's wearing is the one from last night. "I tried calling you," I say quickly. "I was going to stop by first thing this morning. Have you been up all night, sir?"

"There's someone behind every door. Watching me, waiting for me, changing the locks," he rambles. "I need to be all eyes, all ears, all the time." His hands shake as they grip the wheel. "Can't sleep. Not with them watching me."

Christ, he's high as a kite. He shouldn't be driving. He's unraveling, dangerous, a liability at this point. The conversation I overheard between Gunn and the underbosses last night flashes across my mind. *The boat party out on Magic Row—*

McEvoy starts his engine.

"Sir—"

"I trusted you, Alex." McEvoy slams on the gas and screeches into the alley full throttle. "You told me you could get to the bottom of this, you could find the monsters for me, but you're a liar."

"I *am* getting to the bottom of this, sir, just like you asked—"

"NAMES, Alex! I need names!" He swerves his car onto P Street, nearly crashing into a Buick as his car rights itself on the road, and a barrage of beeps and honks blare through his half-open window. "Who's after me? Who thinks they can take me down? Time's up, Alex. I'm tired of twiddling my goddamned thumbs. Is it Gunn?"

But I can't confirm Gunn's involved, not for sure. If I give him Gunn, or hell, Win, or any of the underbosses planning to take him down, then McEvoy's likely to start a war in this state. *And all my work, for nothing. No, I want all these animals behind bars. I want to stand right beside Frain as we lock these monsters away—*

McEvoy digs under his seat hastily. He pulls out a gun, snaps it hard against my left temple, and the car goes skidding out.

"Sir, the road!" We nearly jump the curve, drive right into the park at Iowa Circle, but McEvoy manages to swerve back onto the boulevard with one hand. He presses his pistol harder against my skull.

I close my eyes, try and stay as calm as I can as the boss of the Shaws holds me at gunpoint, on a drugged-up joyride through town. *Don't use magic don't take him down you need to stay in control. Think about the endgame—*

"Know what, Alex? I think you're in on this." McEvoy spits his words at me.

"That's not true, sir."

"I think it is. I'm thinking *you* orchestrated all of this, that you're the one working me."

I steal a quick look at him, see the dust practically pumping through his veins, the paranoia that has him in a choke hold. *He's going to kill me if I don't give him something, he's going to shoot, right here right now—*

"No, I got a lead last night!" I sputter in a rush. *Get him out of the city, out of your way, give him a new scent to track, one of his loyal underbosses—* "Apparently Murphy has been working on the side with the Bahama Boys smugglers. He's going to try and make some kind of deal at a big voodoo party out on the water. He got word you aren't planning to be there, thinks he can land a score while the big fish is away." I shoot McEvoy a look and raise my arms higher. "He thinks he'll get away with it, sir."

"*Murphy.*"

I gulp, but keep my eyes trained on him. I remind myself that handing Murphy to McEvoy is only speeding up the inevitable. That the Unit will get all these thugs, for one crime or another. Besides, Paul Murphy's no angel. Murphy's smuggled thousands of gallons of obi—a haunted elixir that's actually scared people insane—into this country. Murphy's claim to fame is bashing a young smuggler's face in when the kid decided to sample the island brew himself and came up a little short on a delivery. Murphy deserves no mercy—*none* of these thugs deserve mercy.

"That's right. Murphy. Sir, you—you might want to consider being on that boat."

But McEvoy doesn't lower his gun. Instead he puts it under my chin, snaps my head back. "A monster's coming for you, too, Alex. It's been watching you, waiting for the right time. You think you're safer than me?" He leans over, his day-old breath wrapping its noxious scent around me. "I go down, I'm taking you with me."

His dust-haunted words pierce right through my skin. "You get on that boat, sir, and you catch the deal as it happens." I try to sound convincing. "And then you make a public example of Murphy. *He's* the one who arranged for half of Kerrigan's men to stand down in that Baltimore mix-up. *He's* the one who bought the sorcerer off to tell him his real horse forecast at the tracks. I heard it all. I amplified a late-night meeting at the Den."

McEvoy finally, slowly, lowers his gun. He puts both hands on the wheel, mutters, "Going to rip Murphy's eyes out."

He pulls over on some random corner in the heart of Hell's Bottom—sagging town houses, smashed windows, shouts from inside broken homes. I must be miles from my own place at this point. I don't know if McEvoy's so high he doesn't realize that we're in one of the most dangerous pockets of the city, or if he doesn't care.

"Get out," he says flatly. "Apparently, I have a party to attend."

My heart is stuttering, clawing up my chest, wants to fly. I barely manage, "Good luck, Boss," as he screeches away with my car door still half-open, flapping like a doomed bird against the wind.

I breathe, collapse in half, breathe again.

I haven't prayed in a long time, but here and now, on this corner of hell, I pray that McEvoy does get on that boat. And if the monsters out there don't get him, that me and my Unit will.

A NIGHT OF CHANCES

JOAN

In the morning, right before practice, Gunn pulls me into his office and shuts the door. His eyes are so bright, they're practically glowing. "It's happening, Joan," he says. "I won them over. All of them. And Colletto's ready to initiate a deal for our new shine—all we need to do is show him that the product is real, and everything falls into place."

Colletto, D Street—I still don't fully understand, but I've never seen Gunn so lit up before. My relief, my nerves, it all comes to a head, compounds the shine-induced high I've been trying to ignore all morning. "When, what's the deal?"

"Colletto wants fifty gallons by next Thursday."

I gasp before I can help it. Fifty gallons means fifty sacrifices of blood, fifty blood-spells—and that's assuming D Street wants the shine stored in gallons. "Sir, that's a lot, in not a lot of time. I'm going to need to train the troupe to perform the caging spell too, and the double-edged trick, of course, so we can divide and conquer and get this done. There's no guarantee all of them will be able to pull it off, either. Blood-spells require a particular mindset, absolute control—"

"That's why you're doing this entire round," Gunn says flatly. "I don't want any mistakes. Our entire future rides on this shipment. The troupe will brew the shine, and you'll bind each container. You'll get relief after this, I promise you."

I'm doing all the spellbinding. Fifty spells, fifty sacrifices. If not more. My body shrinks away in response. It's too much.

"McEvoy has poisoned relations between the Shaws and D Street these past few years, so naturally, I understand Colletto's insistence that he see our magic happen in the flesh." Gunn looks up at me. "So he's bringing his underbosses in for a demonstration tomorrow. I'll have my top men too." *My* top men. Not McEvoy's, I notice. And yet, that doesn't surprise me, not when I think back to all the little jagged pieces Gunn gave me to the puzzle. Of course this isn't about a huge deal for McEvoy. This is about a huge deal that lets Gunn take everything away from him—though how D Street plays into this, and why, I still don't know. *My God, when I think about the risk Gunn took with this deal, the risk I was forced to take just by working with him, what would have happened had either of us failed—*

"The deal I offered Colletto is a complete partnership, so we're giving them a demonstration of everything we have to offer," Gunn cuts through my thoughts. "I want you to put on the immersive performance of your lives, show him the strength of the troupe's shine, and then you'll blood-cage one of the bottles to make it last. His team will take the sample, confirm that it survives magic's shelf life, make sure we're legitimate," he says. "When they come back to shake hands, our fifty gallons will already be waiting for him. I want this to be flawless. I want us to wow him, just like we've wowed and surprised everyone else. And nothing, *no one*, is standing in my way anymore."

Gunn really managed to pull this all off. You *pulled this off.* The deal is real. The deal is happening.

"Perform the caging spell *discreetly*, Joan, so Colletto doesn't get any funny ideas like going off to replicate it on his own." Gunn puts his hand on his desk, inches from mine. "But if he tries to claim our magic without paying for it, he knows he's starting another war. I've got almost all the Shaw underbosses backing me, ensuring that this deal gets done."

But Gunn's scheming, his secrets, how he's managed to turn a failing shining room into a chance to play boss of the Shaws, all of that pales in light of his word choice, *our magic*. The words are simple ones, but they drive home just how far I've come, how much I've given away, how in bed with Gunn I am. *Long ago there was a family magic, a mother's magic, a secret to keep from the world—*

"And our deal, sir, your promise if this all comes to pass?" I scrub my mind clean of what's been done, what can't be changed, force myself to focus only on the future. "You promised me ten percent."

Gunn crosses his arms over his chest and gives me that faint smile of his, the one that barely manages to break through his smooth, cold facade. "You've become quite the deal maker yourself, haven't you?" he says slowly. "I keep my promises, Joan." Then he clears his throat, adds in a softer tone, his eyes never leaving mine, "And I'd like to think there would be other promises, if this all works out like I intend."

Something about his guarded, double-edged words, his tone, that gentler look to his eyes—it all comes together. And with a slap of realization, I know. *Stock was right all along, about Gunn and me—or at least about Gunn.*

I turn away from the man, my chest constricting, like I need air. The walls of my room feel too close, the space suffocating. *How do you say no to a man like Gunn?*

Maybe in another life, if I was a different kind of girl, I could fall for a man like Gunn—maybe if I hadn't already met a boy who showed me the freest, truest sort of magic—

You need to stop, just focus on the next step. Just get through this demonstration.

I give a small nod in acknowledgment to the floor while I compose myself, and then I meet Gunn's watchful gaze. "Should I tell the troupe about the demonstration, sir?"

"Not yet. I don't want a word of this breathed to anyone until Colletto's walking through our doors tomorrow." He moves to my door. "It's business as usual today. Pick an easy finale, one we've done before, just get the show over with, get us to tomorrow," he says, like it's a new concept, even though I've been running the troupe and our shows more with each passing day. And even more, we've been doing just fine without Gunn. "And tell them all I want a meeting tomorrow afternoon, to be ready to work at three p.m."

"Yes, sir." I can already hear the griping I'm going to get from the team about working tomorrow, on a Sunday.

I'm rattled and distracted during practice. I try to focus, but my thoughts keep mutinying, between worrying about the demonstration tomorrow, the fifty gallons Gunn promised to D Street, and what needs to take place in between to make it all come together. Of course the troupe can tell something's up—I can feel Grace probing me, reaching out with her magic to delve inside my mind, mine my secrets right out of me—but I've become an expert at defending against her advances. Even Billy quips twice that I look completely out of it. But I blame my spaciness on my shine hangover, do what Gunn says, tell them nothing. After all, I've become pretty darn good at keeping things inside.

There's one thing I know I can't do for Gunn, though, and that's stay away from Alex. Unlike the rest of the troupe, Alex doesn't push me on what's wrong, doesn't question me. Instead he just nods when I explain that we're going to run the Magical Dawn performance again, doesn't talk back like the others, who say the immersion is too stale for a Saturday night crowd. Part of me wonders if what I told him last night, about Mama and my past, might have scared him off. But that all falls away at the end of rehearsal. Because as the rest of the troupe labors upstairs to get ready for our performance, Alex lingers by the double doors.

"I'm not going to ask if you're okay, because it's obvious you're not," he says quietly, when I approach him.

I just stand there, staring at him, not sure how to answer.

"I'm also not going to ask you what's going on, Joan. If you've got secrets you need to keep, I respect that."

He walks over to me slowly, and my body actually starts to hum. "But if you need someone to lean on, to help you get through whatever it is you're clearly struggling with, I hope I can be that person for you." He brushes my hair off my shoulder, studies me intensely with those clear blue eyes. Then he drops his voice to a whisper. "You must know how much I want to be that person."

I nod slowly. The skin at the nape of my neck, where his fingers gently rest, is needles and sparks, now positively sings.

"Just don't get too lost on your own, Joan." Then Alex drops his hand and walks out the doors.

Eight p.m. comes on hot and fast. The crowd comes pouring in for our show, the jazz shrieks through the show space, and the stagehands start shaking their mixed drinks in silver shakers. As Alex and I arrange ourselves on either side of our glass stand for our trick, I think, *If tomorrow goes as planned, this might be the last time Alex looks at me this way. This might be the last time we're equals.* And fear, anxiety, sadness—they all tug inside, threatening to unravel me—

"Joan," Alex calls from the other side of the stage. Through the glass, he smiles. "Remember—*don't get too lost.*"

I mirror his nod as we both approach the glass stand. I can practically feel Alex's concern beat through it. I want to let him in. I want him to be my person too. But every time I think about holding on tight to him, letting him share the load of everything that waits on the other side of tomorrow for me, I think again of Gunn.

We each place one of our hands on the glass, whisper the words of power that divide the glass stand into two parts, and capture each other's replicas. And then we begin our performance.

I study my replica of Alex, want a way to show him how much he's come to mean to me. And then, I remember our conversation from weeks ago, in the hall, when he was still working for McEvoy and I was just starting my secret venture with Gunn. When he conjured that little brass compass in his hand and told me that we all needed one, to keep us going in the right direction, and to prevent us from getting lost.

I touch his replica's forehead, and a gold cursive *N* appears over Alex's skin. I move to the left shoulder of his tux, etch a gold *W* into it, and then move across his broad shoulders and paint the other side with an *E*. I draw a loopy *S* right into the center of his chest, and then a line from the *N* to the *S*, a needle, which wavers from side to side. I take a step back, admire my work, the truth of it pricking my eyes. Alex. Alex has become my compass, right along with Ruby and Ben. In an indulgent flash, I try to imagine what the two of them would think of him. Ruby would be head over heels, that much is certain. Ben might keep Alex at arm's distance at first, but I think he'd fall in love with him too.

Alex interrupts my thoughts by beginning his manipulation on the other side of the glass. The crowd exchanges whispers, nods, leans in to admire his magic. I take a few steps to the left side of the glass stand, watching Alex work, his hand moving quickly as he sketches over the canvas of my replica. He looks up and finds me. We switch places to judge the other's magic.

Staring back at me on his side of the glass is myself, of course. But over my black lacy dress, there now rests above my left bosom a gold, glistening heart. The four chambers glow and sparkle as the dim lights of the show space reflect off the replica.

Joan Kendrick. With a literal heart of gold.

The way he sees me is as sad as it is empowering.

The audience gives knowing, almost tender sighs. But tonight, our double-sided trick feels less of a performance for them, and more of a conversation between the two of us. We keep running the trick, until the clock hanging above the doors chimes nine. And by the time I settle next to Alex on the right side of the show space, and Grace begins to pinch out the lights for our Magical Dawn finale, I've already made my choice.

"That manipulation I pulled earlier? It was real for me," I say softly to him. "You are my compass in this place."

He stops looking at the ceiling and meets my eyes. "It was beautiful, Joan. I remember our conversation so many nights ago, in the hall." He runs his fingers along my palm. "You've become mine, too."

I want to be the girl with the heart of gold. I want to be the girl who deserves to be loved as much as she wants to love. I want to hold on to Alex, despite what happens, no matter what Gunn wants or expects.

"This place can be tough, and lonely, Alex, despite how packed it is each night. And it sure as hell was a tough road to get here." I watch Ral and Billy start to fade the textured darkness, slowly kneading the space above the audience's heads, like they're scrubbing it against a washboard and washing all the color out. "Last night, when I told you what happened back in Parsonage that brought me here?" I look at him. "It felt freeing, Alex. You do that for me. You make me feel light . . . and yet somehow you still anchor me to the person I want to be."

Alex takes my hand. "I feel the same way about you, Joan."

"This place is so tricky. Everyone's out for themselves, no one trusts anyone. I even feel it from the troupe. But I trust you. I want you to trust me." I give a little laugh. "I don't know what I'd do in this place without you."

Trust him. Protect him. Give him all of it. "Gunn wants me to tell you that there's a rehearsal tomorrow afternoon." I drop my voice. "But it's not a rehearsal. There's going to be a demonstration of our finale, along with a new product Gunn's been working on. He doesn't want any of the troupe knowing, thinks it could get out, back to McEvoy or the street."

"A demonstration?"

"Of a new shine. And it's a game changer, Alex, it's going to light this world on fire." I look at him. "I'm telling you because I trust you. And because the audience is D Street. And I think you need to know that before you walk in there." I watch his face become creased with worry, but he keeps his mouth shut. "I couldn't believe it either when I heard from Gunn, but it's true. And I know your complicated past with them, but Gunn doesn't miss a trick. If he thinks you've got a problem with them, he'll take care of it." *He'll take care of you.* I look away, hoping Alex has become as fluent in the vague threats of this world as I have. "So show Gunn, tomorrow and going forward, that you're completely in this. That you're willing to do whatever it takes. He'll respect that."

Alex lets his fingers dance on the underside of my arm. "Does he know about us?"

"No. In fact, Gunn doesn't want me anywhere near you."

"Because he wants you for himself," Alex says matter-of-factly. But there's a distinct note of jealousy.

The memory of Gunn in my room, his loaded words, that look in his eyes—I don't deny what Alex says, but I sure as hell can't bring myself to confirm it either. "It doesn't matter what Gunn wants," I whisper. "After this deal, I'm telling him about us. He can't control my heart. He can't do anything about it. Gunn needs me, same as I need you."

"Why exactly does he need you, Joan?" Alex says softly.

But I don't want to get into the caging spell with Alex, not right now. I can't think about what I've given to Gunn, what I've yanked out of the past and sold like a door prize. I only want to focus on the future, a future that I can't imagine without Alex in it.

"All you need to know is that we're going to be rich, Alex," I say it for him as much as I say it for myself. "Over the moon. You'll see. You just need to do what it takes to make that happen. You need to show Gunn what he wants to see, and we'll have a future together here."

Alex takes my chin in his hand, rubs my jawline softly. Above us, Tommy and Rose's clouds float by like pockets full of dawn.

"I promise I'll do what it takes," he says. "And thank you for trusting me."

We both turn our attention back to the finale and begin our own indoor sunrise.

CALLING IT IN

ALEX

I don't want to leave Joan, for a number of reasons, not just because I don't want to arouse her suspicion. *But because the time we have together never feels like enough. Because the act of taking what she just shared with me and running with it like a prize to the Feds feels like the purest form of betrayal, whether I'm right in doing so or not.*

"Tomorrow's a big day. Lots to iron out," Joan says to me after we've brewed our group shine on the stage. "I should check in with Gunn." Then she pauses. "But I'd rather sneak away again with you."

She wants me, like I want her. She needs me, like I need her. She trusts me, and as much as I want her to, Joan shouldn't trust me, shouldn't choose me, not at all.

I turn around, lean my back against the altar, and look her in the eyes. "Our troupe's performance is going to wow D Street, especially with you at the helm more these days. You know this troupe better than anyone, can get things out of us that Gunn never could. And all of us know it, whether they tell you that or not."

She gives me an embarrassed smile and looks at the floor.

And then, before I let this go any further, make me feel any guiltier, I squeeze her hand and walk away.

I burst out the double doors, wind up the stairs, hit the street, and walk a few blocks before I begin frantically searching for a phone. I spot one on the corner of M and 19th Streets and duck inside the booth. I dial Frain's home number, the one I've memorized, my only link to the outside world. My fingers move fast around the dial, because I have a strange feeling that if I slow down, I'm going to do something insane, like turn around and walk right out.

This is about you, your job, your purpose. Months and months leading to this deal—think about all the monsters you'll put away, the safer streets, the win for you and the Unit. Now bring it home.

Frain picks up on the third ring. "Frain here."

"It's Alex."

Sleepy, strained whispers are exchanged in the background. "Alex, what's the word?"

The significance of what I'm about to pass along finally and fully settles over me. If all goes well, this might be the biggest score in Prohibition Unit *history*. We nail this deal, and we take two of DC's largest crime rings down.

"Tomorrow." I keep my eyes trained on the abandoned street in front of me. "What we've been waiting for, working for— Agent Frain, it's all coming to a head. Apparently there's some new type of shine, something that the Shaws and D Street are actually breaking bread over. And if Harrison Gunn manages to secure the deal, he's got the support of most of the Shaw underbosses to confirm him as boss," I say in a rush. "If all goes according to his plan, they'll take McEvoy and anyone left by his side out."

"My God, wait, but Colletto murdered Gunn's father, Danny the Gun—the murder set off a war between the gangs,"

Agent Frain sputters. "You're sure about D Street? You're serious?"

"Dead serious. I heard some of it directly, and the rest is
straight from a reliable source." And then I pause. Because
"source" is such a tricky word. Because somewhere deep and
sober inside me, of course I know that Joan has to be the source
of more than a tip. She has to play some crucial part in this: she's
the head of the troupe, has Gunn's ear, somehow knew about
the deal and that D Street's on the other side of it, and knows far
more than she's giving me in pieces, of that I'm sure. But I can't
think about her being so essential to all of this, that to protect
her would be to cut some of the heart out of the score. *Even if
she's got a hand to play in this, it's not her game,* I remind myself.
*Joan's a pawn, nothing more. There's no need to give her up right
now. Focus on one step at a time.*

I turn back to the phone. "I don't have details on the shine
yet, but I will. There's a demonstration for Colletto and D Street
tomorrow. I'll report back after."

"And McEvoy? Is he right on your tail? Can you shake him?"

I think about my last joyride with McEvoy, the Jackal lit up
with paranoia from the dust. "I managed to sidetrack him. I told
him that one of his loyals was staging a secret deal with an island
gang at some bender of theirs out on Magic Row," I explain. "I
think he bit. He should be out of the city and out of our way for
a few days."

"I'll loop the coast guard in"—I hear the scratching of Frain's
pen in the background—"and we'll take McEvoy down on his
way back to the city. Alex, if this comes together, it's a hell of a
win you've managed to set up for us." Agent Frain's words, his
support, they ignite me, center me—remind me of everything
I've sacrificed, but also everything I've managed to achieve.
"Right after the demonstration, find a way to reach me," Frain
pushes. "You do what you need to do, get me the details of

what's going down between the gangs, and I'll take care of the rest."

"Understood. I'll get it done."

"We're so close, Alex," Frain says, his voice near ecstatic, crackling with electricity through the phone wire, "all thanks to you. Now bring us home."

DEMONSTRATION

JOAN

Sunday morning. The beginning of a new era with Gunn at the helm of the Shaws. An era that promises to be full, red, and rich. An era of shine. *My* shine.

Instead of telling the troupe last night about today's practice, I waited until this morning. Less time for questions that way. Besides, I wanted to enjoy our last show before the demonstration together, and not ruin it by bringing it all back to Gunn.

"What do you mean, we've got a practice today?" Billy cuts in, after I do a round-robin and knock on everyone's doors along the hall around ten. "Today's the day of rest," he adds with a mumble. "We get one day off. Already sold my soul to the man, Gunn sure as hell doesn't deserve my Sunday."

"You sure this isn't about something else, Joan?" Ral says.

Grace leans against her own door frame. "You don't have to keep it all on your shoulders, you know," she presses, looks at me with almost pleading eyes. It's been a long, long time since I confided in her. "You can trust us. We're your team."

"Once upon a time, anyway," Billy digs, as Tommy and Rose slowly saunter out, half-clothed, into the hall.

"What's all the commotion about?" Tommy says as he rubs his eyes.

I close mine to collect myself, and remind myself that in part, this demonstration is for them. That if today goes off without a hitch, there's going to be more money funneled into this place than any of us can imagine. From what I figure, I'm the only troupe member who will get a cut of the deal, but I won't forget who helped make it possible. I'll make sure they're all taken care of somehow, in some way. Not that I can share any of this—at least not now.

"Gunn's calling a mandatory meeting, a practice," I say. "Be downstairs before three. And wear something nice, but plain, if you can."

Everyone mumbles annoyances but turns back to their rooms. As I'm about to do the same, Grace steps out of her doorway and grabs my arm.

"Joan, come on. It's me you're talking to here—enough dodging. Is this related to what you've been doing, during all your time with Gunn?"

"Grace, I seriously can't talk about it, all right? You'll see soon enough."

"It's not something dangerous, is it?" She tightens her grip. Her eyes flick down the hall, then back to me. "I'm worried about you. You barely come up for air anymore."

Grace's forehead is creased, her hand still wrapped around my forearm. I know she's trying to help. I know she wants to make sure I'm not in over my head. But the questions are too much, feel more like persistent jabs than a helping hand. Even more, I feel the pressure of her trying to mine inside again, pluck my thoughts right out of my head. And right now, I'm too tired to keep my walls high enough to block her out.

"Grace." I take her hand and gently pry it off my arm. I step back, making sure I break our connection. "If you really are concerned about me, please stop trying to worm your way inside."

I don't mean it to sound harsh, but it must, 'cause she takes a few steps back too, as if I've slapped her. "Hell, Joan. I'll stop worrying about you, if that's what you want."

"I swear, I'm not trying to keep things from you. Trust me, you'll understand—"

"Oh, I understand. You're doing what you need to do," she says flatly. A pause as we stare each other down. "You've always done what you needed to do, though, right? That's been crystal clear from the beginning."

"Grace, come on."

"By the way, for the record? You're now as hard to mine as he is." And then she turns around and slams her door.

My morning passes by in a flurry of strategy sessions with Gunn and underboss Win Matthews. Some of the conversations I can weigh in on (*Which finale is the troupe's strongest and most impressive? Should I spellbind all the sorcerers' shines, or just my own? Where should the celebratory toast take place after our performance?*). And of course, a lot I can't (*Where should the dividing line between gang territories fall? Will it really be profitable if D Street gets a monopoly on distributing our product?*). But still, I stay behind closed doors with them for hours. They manage to iron everything out around two thirty, and then Gunn and I leave Win and wait for the troupe in the show space.

Grace, Billy and Ral, Tommy and Rose all file in from the hall. Alex comes through the double doors a couple minutes later. My heart starts fluttering on seeing him, and so I look away, focus on Gunn. He's studying our troupe one by one, giving us each a little approving nod. The staff of stagehands has already filtered in too and begins to prep trays of shot glasses for our shine demonstration. A few of them start to rearrange the room into a seating area of benches in front of our stage.

The troupe shifts around me uncomfortably. I can almost

feel their panic, over the not knowing, over being part of a performance they've never rehearsed.

"I apologize for the subterfuge to get you here," Gunn finally addresses our troupe when the room is set, "but when you realize what today is all about, I believe you'll appreciate my decision to be cautious." He pauses. "In a few moments' time, a man named Anthony Colletto will come through that door with some of his men, and he'll be looking for an unparalleled performance, and an even wilder shine."

There's a tiny gasp from Grace, mumblings between Ral and Billy. Of course they all know the name Anthony Colletto. Of course they realize Gunn's saying that we're performing for the Shaws' sworn enemy tonight. The troupe's faces are pinched with concern, and confusion, but either Gunn doesn't see them, or doesn't care.

"And we're going to show Colletto a shine that's not only the highest-grade, strongest magic contraband available . . . we're going to seal it, use magic to work around the limitations of sorcery, and let him ship it around the country for us. And together, we're going to take over the goddamned world." Again gasps, sideways looks. I close my eyes as I feel Grace trying to meet my gaze—

"This is possible, in part, because of all of you," Gunn persists over their reactions. "I knew, back in that clearing in the middle of nowhere, that through the magic of seven—the magic of *you*—we were going to achieve extraordinary things."

And like always, despite the fear and confusion that has taken hold of the crowd, with Gunn's words, something else starts to churn within the troupe. An undercurrent of pride. Despite having been left in the dark, Gunn's assured them they *matter*.

He always knows just what to say. Gunn's good, far too good, at getting what he wants.

As Gunn walks toward the back stage, he says, "I want you to perform the finale that you ran last night, the Magical Dawn, for Colletto and his men. And then I want you to stand up here"— he points to the back-stage altar—"and brew your heart into your shine. Joan will take it from there."

My cheeks flush, just a bit, as all eyes glance to me, wondering, judging.

"Everything is riding on this deal—your future, my future, the future of the Shaws. So give me everything you have." Gunn lets his gaze fall on each of us again, those ice-blue eyes never wavering, blinking, or doubting that we—that *he*—could fail. "Take your places."

Without another word, the troupe whispers and divides. The energy pulsing through the show space is anxious, electric.

Alex comes up to me without a word. I feel his tension, his desire to speak, to compare notes with me.

But there's no time. Because as soon as we're settled, like a stage cue, the double doors to the show space open.

PERFORMANCE

ALEX

And there he is. The man who brought my father to his knees with his constant threats and promises. The man who took my future into his hands and gutted it. The man who, in another time, another place, I'd take my magic to and break apart.

I'll never forget his face. I wonder if he recognizes mine.

"Mr. Colletto!" Gunn booms across the hall, with more warmth in his voice than all the times I've heard him speak put together. He crosses the performance space and takes the hand of the man who haunted my father's nightmares, who served as a compass for why I first agreed to help bring the underworld down. *Why D Street? Why on earth would Gunn go after D Street, especially considering what they did to Gunn's father, and the ensuing decade of bad blood?*

The only silver lining in all this: if we're taking the Shaws down, we're taking D Street down with them.

"Big place you've got here," Colletto muses as he looks around. "Would never know it from the outside."

"That's the point, of course." Gunn smiles as Colletto's small army—gangsters, young and old, a crowd of about ten—filters into the performance space from the double doors. I recognize several of the faces from my days working by my father's side.

Moments later more Shaw men arrive—faces I can't all necessarily connect with names, but they're important, familiar faces.
Powerful faces.

"You know my underbosses, Val Appicello and Chris Moretti."
Colletto nods to two middle-aged goons on his left side.

Gunn nods. "My colleagues, Win Matthews, Sam Sullivan,
George Kerrigan, Calvin O'Donnell." *Underbosses, all of them.
McEvoy's right hands, now pledged to Gunn.*

The handshaking and name swapping continue as the seven
of us watch and stare, like the hired hands we are, around the
perimeter of the performance space.

"I want to show you everything we can give you, everything
you'll be a part of if we decide to move forward." Gunn ushers
his audience forward, toward the benches that the stagehands
have arranged in front of the back stage like a makeshift theater. "Based on years of study, a dedication to finding and culling the best talent, and a strict regimen of training, I've taken
seven sorcerers and elevated them into something extraordinary. There's no one across either of our organizations who
knows what I know. There's no one in this city—hell, this
country—who's managed to do what I've done," Gunn says, as
Colletto's men make their way to seats. "And I can do it again,
and again."

Again and again . . . so is this demonstration about Gunn
opening up more magic havens . . . or transforming some of the
other half-rate shining rooms in the city, like he did with the
Red Den?

Is Gunn going to ask for a monopoly on the city's performance business, in exchange for flipping some of the profits to
D Street?

*What's Gunn's play here? What's the angle? And what does
shine have to do with it?*

Colletto sits, unbuttons his vest, and takes out a cigarette.

"I'm looking forward to every aspect of this demonstration." And then, it might be my imagination, but I swear his eyes find and rest on me. It churns something thick and poisonous around inside.

"Without further delay." Gunn gestures to the aisles around the audience, to us, his troupe of sorcerers.

My heart starts hammering inside my chest, the nerves and expectation pounding like a pulse. Whatever lies on the other side of this performance is what I've been trying to uncover for the Feds, what all the lying and sneaking around and sleepless nights have been for. In our pocket off the right-side aisle, I watch Joan, studying her. *How much does she know about what's happening today? What's her real role in all of this? Does she have any clue that her mob bosses are going to be taken down?*

I take a deep breath.

Just get through this performance.

One step at a time.

BREW

JOAN

Grace begins by turning off the lights, one by one, and then Billy and Ral step in, fade the dark of the show space into a textured gray. Then it's Tommy and Rose's turn: the pair paints a burst of color onto the canvas above Colletto's crowd and sends thick clouds, gray and purple, lined and scaly like floating fish, over the heads of the mobsters, teasing the space from early dawn into sunrise.

And that's my cue. I conjure my sun manipulation, the glowing globe, breathe life into it, make it fuller, until Alex takes over and breaks my sun open, letting the sunrise fall like a sideways waterfall over the crowd.

I can't help but steal a glance at Boss Colletto, to see what he's thinking. His head is angled up, his eyes are wide and childlike. He's enchanted. They all are—just like any audience on any night—looking up as a sorcerer-made sky sizzles, cracks, and breaks open just for them. Rendered children by our magic, our magic that wraps around and hugs them tight.

When the immersion's over, Grace turns only a few of the space's lights back on, keeps the mood sexy, seductive, and we step up, one by one, onto the back stage. But unlike other nights, I'm going to have the final word. *I'm* going to be the finale.

Thanks to the stagehands, seven bottles of water already rest on the altar in the center of the stage. We line up behind them, left to right: Ral, Billy, Grace, me, Alex, Tommy, and Rose. By this point, we have our rhythm down—there are no pauses. Together we reach for our bottles, and the water inside each jumps in response. Whirls of cherry-red tendrils swirl inside each bottle, the water surrendering quickly to the magic, the hisses and pops of the shine echoing through an otherwise silent show space.

On a normal night, in a normal show, this would be the cue for the stagehands to head up the stairs with trays of shot glasses, pour our shine into them, and pass them out to the crowd. But tonight is different.

Almost like he's finishing my thoughts, Gunn interrupts the nearly hour-long silence. "On a regular night, it's at this point in the performance that our stagehands pass around my sorcerers' shine. The sorcerers brew the shine live every night, of course, and just enough, because up until now, shine, like all pure magic, doesn't last more than a day."

Colletto grunts in assertion and shifts in his seat below us.

Gunn ascends the stairs to the stage, angles himself next to me and picks up my bottle of shine. "Shine's the highest trip on the black market. Euphoric. Transcendent. Lets you see the magic in the world. Some say that it lets you see God. Rendered even more rare and coveted because it's impermanent, and fleeting." Gunn looks up. "Until now."

He nods to the three sorcerers on my left, and then the three on my right. "Please step away from the altar," he tells them. But I don't look at my troupe, especially not at Alex. I'll just get more nervous. So I stare straight ahead and wait for my cue.

"Now, the full extent of the magic I can give you, if we find a way to put the past behind us and join forces. A shine that can be stored, and shipped, and transported all over the world. Joan, if you please."

ETERNAL SHINE

ALEX

The rest of the troupe takes a step back, completely in the dark about what Joan's going to do, as she holds the spotlight. And the dread I've managed to dam, as I've played the dutiful cop playing the dutiful troupe member during the performance, starts flooding in. *There's a shine that defies the laws of magic, a shine being sold by a gangster who wants to take over the underworld—*

And the girl I'm falling in love with is taking the stage to somehow bring it home.

The room falls completely, deathly quiet, as Joan places both of her hands back on her bottle of shine. She mumbles words of power, words I can't quite hear, even this close to her, but in seconds, a glass stopper appears and lodges itself right into the mouth of her bottle. Colletto and his men shift below us, mumble speculation.

Then Joan takes one of her hands off the glass, digs around the shelf under the altar, and pulls a switchblade out from it. As she pushes up the right sleeve of her dress, I have to stop myself from reaching out and grabbing her hand, telling her that whatever she's about to do, it's not worth it, not for them. Grace gasps on Joan's other side, and her hand flies to her mouth, while a strange, deep regret floods through me and settles into my skin.

On Joan's forearm is a patchwork of scars, some fresh and red, some pink, older. She leans her arm over the bottle, and with a calm precision, presses the blade right into her arm.

After a trickle of blood wraps around her skin and drips into the stoppered bottle, she caps the bottle and begins another spell. Again I can't hear the words, but this time I strain to: "*Less of me . . . offering . . . eternity . . .*"

Her bottle begins to tremble, quake, then settle, just like it's alive. *What did she just do? Some dark sorcery, a spell of blood? Devil's magic?*

As Joan backs away from her new creation, again Gunn goes to her side. He takes Joan's bottle into his hands, lifts it up for the crowd to assess: a bottle of glistening shine, stoppered with a cork of bloodstained glass.

"An eternal shine," Gunn says to the audience. "A bottle of pure, liquid magic, caged by magic. An old and secret magic that we have perfected, that would not have seen the light of day without the power of this magic haven." Gunn hands the bottle back to Joan. "Or of course, without a powerful, resourceful sorcerer."

Colletto stands up slowly and walks to the front of the stage. "May I see the bottle?" he asks Joan.

"Go on," Gunn tells her.

Joan heads down the stairs to hand the bottle to Colletto, while I get a strong, overwhelming urge to gut Gunn, right here and now. He's standing so close, I could wrap my fingers around his neck. I could conjure a thousand knives, incise him with cuts just like Joan's, let him bleed out slowly.

"That's yours to keep," Gunn tells Colletto, once Joan takes her place back among us. "I knew you wanted to make sure there was no tampering with the sample I showed you last time. You saw this one brewed and bottled yourself—so take it back with you, confirm its shelf life, and open it in a few days. When you see it's real, I expect we'll have a deal."

As Colletto studies the glass bottle, the room buzzes around him. The air is tense, expectant, excited—and my mind is buzzing right along with it. Because everything I've been shelving . . . *Joan's relationship with Gunn, her caginess, her secrets, her unparalleled power* . . . there's no ignoring it anymore. It's impossible not to bring this deal down without bringing Joan down with it. Because Joan is the magic behind the largest score in Unit history. *Joan is the eternal shine.*

Colletto says, "Tell me exactly how it's done."

Gunn shakes his head. "If we're going to embark on this road together, there needs to be a foundation of trust, of partnership. I assured you that I can make this product, again and again. Now leave the magic to me," he says. "Our history of hate has lasted far too long. It's time to put the past behind us."

Gunn is a cold, ruthless bastard, but even still, I can't wrap my head around his decision to team up with Colletto. He's shaking hands with the gangster who gunned down his father, Danny the Gun. He's delivering the death blow to his mentor McEvoy, to align with the enemy. This bastard deserves everything that's coming to him.

Colletto looks up at Gunn on his stage, nods. "How much?"

"You give me two hundred and fifty dollars for every gallon. You charge double on the street, and the difference of course will fall to you. We shake hands, and you'll have our word that you'll be our sole distributor, on the only shippable shine known to man," Gunn says slowly. "And in exchange, you give up the shining room business—my Shaws get a complete monopoly on performance magic in the city."

Colletto keeps his eyes on the glistening red bottle. "And the rest of our operations? Gambling, racketeering, loans?"

"The rest of our proposed agreement would go immediately into action. We reorganize the district. Everything west of Fourteenth Street is ours. You take the east. A smooth criminal empire, as I believe my father once called it," Gunn says tightly. "Before lesser men took a hammer to his vision."

A true deal between the Shaws and their enemies. A deal across all operations, no less—hell, a partnership. Agent Frain is going to flip.

Colletto turns the bottle over once more in his hand. "Thursday," he finally answers. "I'll give you ten thousand for fifty gallons. You throw in the sweeteners we talked about, and we've got a deal."

Gunn breaks into an uncharacteristically wide smile, a smile that almost makes him look boyish—reminds me of just how young this mongrel is, and just how high he's managed to claw. He gestures for our troupe to descend the stage. "I think this calls for a toast."

On cue, stagehands file into the performance space with large silver trays loaded with shot glasses, ascend the stairs, and grab the remaining six bottles of shine from the stage. And with that, the vibe of the room shifts. Shine is being poured. The deal is going forward. Foes have turned into allies, and an almost festive air settles over the crowd. *I need to pass this on to Frain, all of it—*

"But first, how about a round of applause for our performers?" Gunn says.

Colletto claps a full, long applause, and his team of thugs joins in. We bow slightly, as Joan, the star, takes a full curtsy in front of their benches. *Does she realize that all eyes are on her now? Does she understand that these gangsters see her as a commodity, a valuable asset that could be sold, or stolen?*

Another reason why I need to shut this operation down.

Another reason why this whole magic racket is wrong—because of sorcerers like her, and once upon a time sorcerers like *me*: sorcerers who get used, turned around, and forced right into the line of fire.

As the crowd moves toward the VIP lounge, Joan edges beside me and whispers, "Go up the fire escape to my room when this is done. Wait for me. Gunn's giving everyone a celebratory shot of shine—they'll be in the lounge for at least an hour, I'm sure." She flashes me a heady smile. She's clearly emboldened by what she's done, empowered, not ashamed. She's exactly where I was a year ago: being manipulated, *handled*, tricked into thinking she's invincible. Before I can think through it, I give her a discreet little nod. She breaks away and goes back to Gunn's side.

As the stagehands lead Colletto and his men to the VIP lounge, Gunn lingers and surveys our troupe. "You all did spectacularly. But I won't lie: there're going to be long, tough days ahead. I expect you all at eight a.m. tomorrow, ready to live and breathe brewing shine until Thursday, to ensure that our first shipment's on time. So enjoy your night." Then he drops his voice, addresses Joan. "I'm sure Colletto wants to meet you."

Joan nods, but as she trails him, she throws a glance at me behind her shoulder.

I can't meet her on her fire escape. I can't have Joan, even if I want her. This is about far more than her and me—

But as she turns down the hall, these thoughts are strongarmed by a greater truth: this can't be the last time I watch her walk away.

"So that's what she's been hiding," Rose says as soon as Gunn, Colletto, and their respective teams of thugs turn down the hall toward the VIP lounge.

"Stock warned us so many times about her." Tommy shakes his head. "We saw it that night in the house of magic manipulations, remember? Something evil was going on up there."

Rose nods as she plays with her dark, knotty hair. "Stock thought she was working for the devil."

"Did you know Joan was in on this?" Ral demands of Grace.

But I'm half listening at best, inside my own head. *Joan's in deeper than she realizes. Maybe her allegiance to her family and Gunn's promises have turned her around so much, she's got no sense of which way's up. Maybe I can stop her, reason with her, before it's too late for her, without compromising my score.*

"Alex," Grace says, and when I look at her, I can tell this isn't the first time she's said my name. "Did you know about any of this?"

I shake my head. "No," I say sadly, "Joan tricked us all." I clear my throat. "Excuse me, I think I'm going to leave while I can, get some rest."

Grace gives me a sympathetic smile as the rest of the troupe devolves back into their whispers and accusations.

I burst through the double doors, hit the shock-cold January air. Part of me is fully aware that I should keep walking right out to M Street, find a phone and call Frain, tell him the deal particulars that are as good as done, and not look back. *You know what Joan's room means. You shouldn't get mixed up with her like that. It will complicate things even further—*

But the other part of me is already climbing up her fire escape.

DANCE

JOAN

I burst through my bedroom door, electric, ecstatic. *I pulled it off.* I used my magic to trick shine into lasting forever, in front of some of the most dangerous gangsters in DC. I cemented my place as a partner in the largest shine venture in history. I ensured that Ruby and Ben aren't going to worry about money or a roof over their heads for the rest of their lives.

The future is bright, the future is running red with magic, and the now—

The now is Alex Danfrey on my fire escape.

He's sitting outside, enclosed by one of his own manipulations, warm as he sits there in the January air, like he doesn't have a care in the world. I run to my window, thrust it open, and back up to let him inside. He climbs over my bed and stands right in front of me.

And just looking at him, arms crossed, furrowed brow over that perfect face, it dulls all my jitters and relief into a hungry ache. Fate has spun this boy into my orbit and given me something I never would have dreamed of. And regardless of whether I deserve him or not, I'm not going to let him go.

"It's done," I say, relieved. "Thank God it's done."

Before I can stop myself, I wind my hands up his shoulders, to his neck, into his hair, and then I pull him into me.

Alex kisses me back, but it's hesitant, unsure—"Joan," he mumbles, "wait . . . stop." He pulls away. And then he won't meet my eyes.

It feels like I've been sucker punched. "What, what's wrong? Have you changed your mind about me . . . about us?"

"No. No, just the opposite, I—Christ." He starts pacing. "This is all just a lot to take in at once. I mean, how long have you known about what you could do?" He steals a breath. "How long have you been planning this with Gunn?"

"A while," I say. "I told you what I could last night, but I couldn't tell you all of it. Gunn's been so damn cagey about the whole thing, I've been scared to breathe a word."

Alex looks at me strangely for a second. "Joan, are you really sure you want to go through with this?"

Like a reflex, I tell him what I've been telling myself. "Don't you know what this deal could do for someone like me, for my family? For *you*?"

Alex looks to the door, drops his voice to a whisper. "I know you think you're a player in this game, that you have control. That you're making your own choices. But I was once *just* like you, Joan—my father started working me slowly, carefully. And he had me so far under his thumb by the end, I didn't even realize I was trapped until I was suffocating."

"Alex, this isn't like that." Although in some ways, of course it is. But it's for good reason. And I'm not trapped if I accept why I'm in the cage. I've made peace with what I'm doing, and why I'm doing it.

"Don't you wonder what happens if Boss McEvoy gets wind of this, if he realizes his underbosses are planning to cut him out, and he manages to get to Gunn first? What's he going to do?" Alex glances at me, a fire in his eyes. "Take you out, or steal you. And if it isn't McEvoy, it'll be Colletto. Only a matter of time before something goes wrong between him and Gunn—the gangs have hated each other for years."

Alex is getting cold feet. I know it, I can sense it. It's nothing I don't understand, but I'm beyond it. I just need to coax him, steer him back in. "You don't understand. This isn't about just me—it's about all of us. I'm going to teach all of you the spell, Alex, once this first shipment is taken care of. That's the point of the troupe, don't you see? And then we'll teach other sorcerers, until we can produce a shipment overnight. This deal is going to be the beginning of a goddamned *empire*. This is an opportunity for all of us, to change our lives, to make something of ourselves."

Alex stops pacing. "And did you ever think that something this big could attract *other* attention?" Then he takes slow, careful steps toward me, like he's approaching a lion in a cage. "It's one thing to perform in a magic haven—we get busted one night, you do a few weeks' time for sorcering, and you come out the wiser. But to be the key sorcerer behind the world's first eternal shine? Helping to produce and distribute it nationally? You could end up behind bars *for life*, Joan. What about Ruby and Ben then? You said this is about your family."

"Of course it's about them, but I'm not walking away 'cause I'm scared, Alex." I give a nervous laugh. "I don't have that luxury. Besides, I'm not going to get caught."

He presses his hands into his forehead. "Christ, then what about other people's families, Joan? People with fathers and mothers and uncles who are going to get hooked on this stuff, break their family apart just like your uncle did to yours? You want that on your conscience? It's not, it's not . . ."

"What? It's not *right*?" I complete his sentence. "Alex, I've spent most of the past year hating my magic with every fiber of my soul, cursing and burying it. But the truth? That night wasn't magic's fault. It was *mine*." I feel the hot push of tears coming on, so I look at the floor. "*I've* got to live with the terrible choice I made back in Parsonage. To blame the magic is the easy way out. And you and I, we were *made* to do this. There's nothing wrong about that," I say, the truth coating my words with something warm and strong. "Besides, what people do with our magic once we make it? That's not in our control."

"You're telling yourself what you want to hear."

"And you're so scared you're talking crazy," I cut in. Lord, maybe my performance really spooked him, maybe the stakes have been raised higher than Alex ever wanted to bet. But I can't let him walk away. I can't—*won't*—do this without him. "Is this about Colletto, about working for the man who brought your father down?" I take another step toward him. "Of course I understand your problem with that. But if you're in this world, you do what you need to do to survive. You take comfort in the fact that you're using him, just like he's using us. Just like I'm using Gunn, and Gunn's using me."

"So that's what you really want?" We're so close, a foot away. "A world where everyone's just playing and using each other? A world of tricks and lies?"

"Hell, I can survive it. Especially if I have you in it," I say. "I told you, you're my compass through this slippery world, Alex. Just like Ruby and Ben."

I study his cast-down eyes, the way he's biting his lip mercilessly. I feel like I almost have him. Besides, I can't imagine how it would gut me if he walked away.

"I don't want anything happening to you."

"So don't let it. Stay by my side, for our biggest performance yet."

He doesn't answer, just tentatively reaches out and rubs his fingers along my jaw.

"Maybe I trained you under this roof," I add slowly, "but the truth? *You're* the one who showed me all that magic can really do. When we're together, we're so much more than ourselves— we're extraordinary. You have to feel that too."

He drops his hand, takes a sudden step back. "I really shouldn't be here, Joan."

"Why, because of Gunn?" I blurt out, my heart hammering. "Don't think about Gunn right now."

Alex shakes his head. "Because of everything. I need—I need to think." He quickly climbs over the bed, pulls the window open to leave. *No. No no no no no—*

Before he can climb through it, I focus my magic on the glass pane. The window seals closed with a slow, satisfying snap in front of him. Alex doesn't turn around.

"You're lying to yourself, Alex," I flounder. "Maybe you got into this game for revenge, or for an easy way of making a living after your father burned your old life to the ground. But that can't be all it's about for you anymore. I *know* you feel this too."

He doesn't answer; his fingers dance on the window's edge.

"We don't have to punish ourselves forever. We deserve this. We deserve each other."

Alex turns, studies me, waits a beat, a second that feels as long as forever. "You think you know me, Joan," he finally says quietly.

"I *do* know you," I tell him, believing it with every fiber of my being. "Maybe I don't know everything"—I give his words from the other night back to him—"but I know the important things."

There's a second, a moment, a minute more. Silence, where the air becomes more charged, tense with almost an electric energy in between us. Alex stares at me. I stare back at him. He doesn't speak, doesn't move. I'm just as sure he's going to turn and go as I am that he's going to stay.

I'm not positive who first gives in to the pull, the magnetic force drawing us together, but once it starts it's like a train barreling through the wall, and we're going so fast, so intense, *flying*, that I can't slow down, can't get off, even if I wanted to.

Alex's fingers are in my hair—not tentatively, but rough and assured, and he presses into me, his lips on my lips, and over them, under them.

His arms pull around my waist, the warmth of his hands presses against my back, and then he lifts me off the floor and onto my knees on the bed, facing him. Eye-to-eye with him.

We tear off each other's clothes, me pulling his shirt over his head and throwing it onto the floor, him unbuttoning my dress and letting it fall down around me like a shiny black puddle. It's then that he sees my arm, red and marked and naked under the low lights of my room. He grips it, pulls it closer. As he holds it, I don't move, don't breathe.

But then he takes the field of scars to his lips, kisses them, lets his mouth move up to my shoulder, to my lips, enveloping me completely, accepting me completely. I guide him next to me, and then we're lying together, horizontal, like the sea and sky merging into a hazy slice of morning.

"God, I've wanted this," he whispers. "So much. Too much."

He flips me under him quickly, and then he's staring down at me, hovering over me. I study him, his hard jaw, his face, that thick, perfect hair that right now is hanging down like a curtain. He's more than perfect—he's magic, addictive. In fact, maybe right now, this is what it's like, to have an addiction—to want something even more as you're consuming it, to dread the high wearing off even as you're at the peak of it.

I lean up to kiss him, and then grab his neck and pull him into me.

Alex takes his time, teasing me, moving his mouth down to the hollow of my breastbone, and when I can't stand the waiting anymore, I make it known. I sigh and bite on his shoulder, and he kisses me, long and deep, muffles my moans.

We're standing on a precipice, right at the start of a performance, and then the magic takes over and for one perfect stretch of a moment we are one, we are exactly the same—

As soon as it's over, I want him back, want to live in the spell all over again.

Alex collapses, gently, tenderly curls himself into me. His soft, slippery skin presses against mine. My body feels spent and sore and full in all the right ways—

I close my eyes and revel in the warm, textured silence. "I'm so glad I found you," I whisper after a while. I reach out, run my finger along the side of his face, down to his jaw. I don't want to let him go, to break the connection. "I can't imagine what this world would look like right now without you in it."

He takes a long time to answer, and when he does, his voice is fading, soft, balanced on the edge of sleep. "Have you really ever pictured the two of us, away from all this?" he whispers, letting his hand rest above my hip. "Somewhere else?"

I smile, rest my head in the crook of his armpit. "You dreaming, Alex Danfrey?"

"I mean it. Somewhere new, that we could be together," he mumbles. "Maybe I could help you . . . help your family . . . you could leave all this, for me."

But I can't imagine a future like that. I'm so far in, so tangled up in this web of magic and secrets, that even imagining a world without it feels like an empty trick. "We're together right here, right now, Alex," I say softly, as I play with the ends of his hair. "Just focus on right now."

"Right now," he whispers. I watch his face become a little slacker, his breath start to deepen. He's inches from sleep.

But I'm not ready for the now to end, not yet, and so I gently place my hand on his chest, and then slide it down, farther, *farther*—

Alex's eyes are closed, but he smiles a sleepy, heavy version of that half smirk of his. He leans over and kisses me once more. And then he's pressing against me again, and I dive headfirst into the deep, dark, warm pool of abandon.

I jump at the sound of a knock, a hard swift rap that soon becomes an all-out pound. I've got no idea what time it is. Alex is gone, must have slipped out while I was sleeping—I see the imprinted sheets beside me and feel a warm, dull ache. Outside, the parking lot of the Red Den is as dark and quiet as a graveyard, Gunn's Six Coupe the only car in the far corner of the lot.

The knocker raps again, and the door practically bursts from its hinges. I unravel myself from the covers and stand.

"Joan," I hear on the other side of the door. "JOAN!"

Lord. It's Gunn.

I throw on the cotton pajamas that rest in my top dresser drawer, as a sharp panic lodges itself in my throat.

"Mr. Gunn," I say, after I open the door to find him leaning against its frame. "It's mighty late."

"It's eleven, Joan." Gunn's got that loose, shined look about him, and I'm positive he's on something magical. I don't think I've ever seen Gunn out of control, not in full, frightening command of himself and everyone else. It's terrifying, seeing him unhinged, this close, in the doorway of my room. Especially when I think back to that strange, loaded conversation we had yesterday morning.

"I was asleep."

"I was shouting." Gunn stares at me, unwavering, unflinching. Like if he looks long enough, he can see right through me, to everything I might be hiding inside. "Was someone here?"

I give a jumpy laugh. "No."

He sidesteps his way into my bedroom. The faint brush of

his suit jacket on my arm sends something near electric jumping through my skin. *Fear.*

No. More complicated, tangled, mixed-up than fear.

"Is there anything wrong, sir?"

But Gunn just pushes my door closed behind him. The hairs on my arms stand up on end. "I know you're lying."

Before I can mumble another lie, he cups my face with one hand, arching my neck back. It's the first time he's touched me since that night he shook my hand in the clearing, and once more it sets off that complicated, uncomfortable stirring inside. *I wonder if he'd have the gall to place his hand on me right now if he hadn't been lit up with magic.*

Gunn releases his hold on me just as quick and walks to my bureau. "I have an awful habit, when I fall hard for something, of not noticing its imperfections, Joan." He runs his hands along the top of the chest. "Sometimes I never catch them, and I'm none the wiser." He flits those white-blue eyes back to me. "But sometimes I find these flaws. And I get so angry at myself for being blind to them, *weak*, that I go too far in trying to correct my mistake."

Quick as a reflex, he grabs a thin splinter sticking out of the bureau top and yanks. It leaves a long, bleached scar along the top of the stained wood. My heart jumps, starts racing—

Correcting my mistake—

"I gave you an order, Joan, an order I have my reasons for." *Alex. He has to be talking about Alex.* But how can he know? Besides, no matter how turned around this man's got me, hell, how much I've turned around *myself*, I know that Gunn's got no right to be talking about Alex. A hot throb of anger starts jumping with my pulse.

"You disobey my order, and I start wondering: if you're lying about one thing, maybe you're lying about others."

"I'm not lying."

"Problem is, I don't believe you," Gunn taunts. "I think it's time to remind you of your priorities. I think it's time to remind you of everything that's on the line here."

Everything on the line? I almost scream. *I know everything that's on the line. I know my life, my family's welfare, the future of this place all ride on whether I win or I fall. And you here, taunting me with it, having the gall to tell me who's allowed in my room between the days and nights of sweating and bleeding for you, it's too much.*

Gunn's studying me with that look again—the one that gives too much away, if only for a second. And all his veiled threats and twisted words, the cage he's built around me with his secrets and warnings, I let myself forget it exists, just for now. Because I need *him* to feel what it's like to be this trapped, to feel this small. "And that's why you're here at this hour? To remind me of my priorities?"

I take a bold step toward him, lift my chin, keep my eyes hard and unforgiving, like I'm showing him back himself. I add with a whisper, "Why are you really in my room, Mr. Gunn?"

Gunn doesn't speak for a long while. Finally he takes a quick inhale, shakes his head. Then he snaps a disgusted, put-on laugh and briskly turns to leave—like he's realized he's shown his hand, when he's supposed to have full command of our game.

But before I can breathe, calm down, regroup, he says icily, "Everyone has a blind spot, Joan." He grabs the door handle and gives me that penetrating stare once more. "Don't disappoint me. Don't crash and burn because of yours."

THE SKINNY

ALEX

What was I really expecting when I went to Joan's room? A confession of her sorcery sins, right after she performed them for her gangster-studded audience? To convince her with a few words and kisses that she's thinking about this all wrong? To get her to abandon her magic and jump into my arms, and together we'll ride a white horse out of the Red Den?

Joan doesn't want to be saved. She's worked herself up the ranks, is now standing at the forefront of the Shaws' sorcery troupe, with a dark unparalleled trick that will change the face of the underworld. Joan is Gunn's right-hand girl, not a damsel in distress, but the fucking distress itself. And I know my charge, despite how much I'd give for it to be different, despite how much I wish to God it was *anyone* else conjuring that dark magic on Gunn's stage.

Joan needs to be taken down, same as the rest of them.

Despite my feelings for her.

Despite her feelings for me.

It's over—she made her decision. You know she can never really be yours.

I keep to the shadows of M Street, walk a block, take a right, walk another block, get as lost as I can in this dark city. I focus on my next move, on dialing the details in to Frain. There's a monumental deal going down between two warring tribes for all of DC, and to top it off, Harrison Gunn is staging a coup, taking McEvoy down as he rolls out an unprecedented, shippable sorcerer's shine. A product so unbelievable, so impossible, that I wouldn't have believed it if I hadn't seen it myself. But it's real. And the magic behind it clearly needs to be contained, because according to Joan, it's teachable. Shutting Gunn down won't do the trick by itself. We need to arrest the entire troupe, before that spell ever sees the light of day.

I force myself to focus on how I'm closing in, how the score is near, and how I've exceeded my and the Unit's expectations, instead of the girl I just left behind. The girl I already miss. The girl who's still lying tangled up in those covers. The girl who brings on a sharp ache when I even think about losing her.

Don't do this. You can't lose something that wasn't yours to begin with. Now. Let. Her. Go.

I duck into a red phone booth on the corner of K and 16th Streets, scan the roads to make sure I'm alone, and grab the receiver. I dial Frain's home number. The phone cuts to static and then rings.

"Frain here."

I let Frain's voice be a calming spell, a reminder of what's most important, what I'm doing all this for. "It's Danfrey."

"Did the demonstration happen? Did you get the details of the deal?"

I try to catch my breath, calm my nerves. "Yes, Colletto came in tonight, with some of his top D Street men. Gunn was there with the majority of the Shaw underbosses—Kerrigan, Sullivan, Matthews, O'Donnell—he's won over most of the Shaw leadership."

"So D Street and the Shaws are really working together?" Frain asks incredulously. "I almost—I can't believe it. Gunn, going after D Street, after Colletto put a hit on his father? The man's inhuman."

"And the deal he's attempting? It's huge," I breathe into the phone. "It divides up the whole city between the gangs. The Shaws will control street operations west of Fourteenth Street, D Street will run all gambling, racketeering, and other business to the east."

"Like a partnership? Why? I don't understand—"

"The whole thing rests on a shine that Gunn has managed to make shippable," I interrupt, excitement getting the better of me. "Agent Frain, he's managed to do the impossible, and make shine last inside a bottle."

"*What?*"

"It—I—they use magic to bind the bottle somehow. It prevents shine from turning back into water, somehow preserves its magic, so that it can be shipped up and down the coast."

For a second I don't hear anything on the other end of the line but Frain's frantic scratching of fountain pen on paper. "My God, Alex, this is huge."

"The first exchange is fifty gallons for ten thousand. And going forward, Gunn's prepared to give D Street a monopoly on distributing the product, in exchange for D Street walking away from performance magic altogether," I continue in a rush. "The Shaws will control all shining rooms in the city. They'll produce the world's only eternal shine, and D Street will be the sole distributor. A win-win."

"Tell me more about this product, Alex, the shine that lasts." Frain's voice is almost quivering. And he should be scared. A product like this will take the underworld by storm. A product like this could turn this country upside down, if we don't stop it first. *But we will.* "How's it done?"

"Through magic, naturally—magic somehow spellbinding other magic," I say. "From what I could gather, the shine gets cursed somehow by a spell, and the bottle gets locked." I shake my head, trying to chase away the image of Joan on that stage, whispering, harming herself for the sake of the deal. "Gunn claims the dark spell is teachable, given certain considerations. Honestly, I've never heard of anything like it, sir."

"If the spell is teachable," Frain says slowly, "it's imperative that we contain it, shut it all down now. Indict the entire troupe working in that Den." He says what I was assuming he'd say. Then he pauses, and the scratching of his pen stops. "Is there a key sorcerer?"

You planned to give Joan up. You need to give her up. And yet as Joan's name bubbles up from my core, my throat closes, and competing thoughts whisper, *You were once as headstrong as Joan, thought the world couldn't touch you. If someone had tried to stop you when you were working with your father, would you have listened? Or would you have needed a stronger sort of persuasion?*

I picture Joan on our performance stage, under the magic-made stars of our performance space. In the Den's dark corridors, and then in her bed, the moonlight stretching long across her limbs, that seductive smile of hers teasing me, all the while inviting me in. *Am I really going to give up on her, and take her down, without a fight?*

A plan comes to me, quick and loose, like a tangled knot of thoughts and images that I need to unravel: *Gunn, Joan, her family, getting her out, walking away—*

And I realize, right here and now, that despite everything else that I'm committed to doing, despite my mission, I have to find a way to save Joan too. I have to believe what we have will survive this somehow, that it won't crumble despite the lies it might have been built upon. The Unit and I will still get our victory—but Joan and I can have each other, too.

"Alex, you still on the line?"

"Gunn's smart, and cautious." I close my eyes and plunge in before I can second-guess myself. "He explained the shine's magic, but then he dismissed the crowd to keep the identity of his key sorcerer secret. I assume he took Colletto aside for a personal demonstration." *This is the last time I play outside the rules, regardless of who's depending on me to do it. Besides, all I'm doing is stalling, just giving Joan a little more time to come around. It doesn't change the endgame.* "But it has to be a sorcerer from the Den. And everything I'm seeing, feeling, says there's serious duress involved."

"You mean he's forcing the sorcerer to work for him?"

"I believe so, sir." *The last time—your days of lying, hiding, scheming—they've been over for a long time.* "I was told to report to the Den tomorrow and be prepared to stay until the shipment is ready. I think the entire troupe is at Gunn's mercy, that he's using personal threats and violence to get his deal done. The sorcerers are pawns, sir, could even prove Unit assets going forward if we cut them deals."

"My God, Alex, the man has no limits."

"Colletto mentioned Thursday for the deal, as soon as the gallons are ready," I continue. "So get a team prepared, be ready to bust the Den. I'll call you as soon as I know more, and then I'll get you inside. If we move in right at the exchange, we'll get Gunn and his team, as well as Colletto and all of D Street. You make that call to the coast guard, too, and you'll pluck McEvoy coming back from Magic Row."

Frain pops a nervous laugh. "A hell of a win," he says. "I'll wait for your call, and be ready to move in. And Christ, well done, Alex."

"Thank you, sir."

I hang up, regroup. *This will work out. And you have done well. Don't forget that.*

And I try not to. I imagine the day I can let my mother

know what I've really been up to these past few months, see the relief—the *pride*—wash over her face. I picture the headlines that will scream that the Unit has managed a huge score, that the city's been rendered safer because of our operation. I try to focus on the deck I've stacked for Agent Frain, on the winning hand I've dealt to the Unit—

Instead of the one card I've tucked under my sleeve.

PART FOUR

THE SHINE

TIES THAT BIND

JOAN

It's been two nights and three days since I've talked to Alex. First thing Monday morning, he and the troupe were funneled into the VIP lounge, tasked with the job of brewing sorcerer's shine again and again, so that Gunn has his shipment of fifty gallons by Thursday—and the troupe isn't allowed to leave until it's done. Me? I'm in Gunn's office, toggling between thinking through the logistics of bottling and transporting the shine, and sealing each and every quart-sized bottle. Which means sacrificing far more than any one person should have to sacrifice to a spell.

But Gunn wants me, and *only* me, handling the caging spells for this shipment. He says now's not the time to be training and opening ourselves up to mistakes. He also says I should stay back here alone to rest in between. So that my focus isn't compromised. So I can *keep my stalwart heart*. But after that night he came to my room, it's obvious—I think to both of us—that he's got other concerns with my heart. Him calling on me in the throes of his shine-high, me standing up to him, at least in a way I never have before: it's like an elephant in his office (that of course neither of us has addressed) and just adds one more dreaded question mark to how all this is going to play out.

Stock, and the troupe, their rumors and whispers—they were right all along.

My mind drifts again to the troupe, and what they're talking about in there. I wonder if Alex has mentioned me, if the troupe is poisoning him with more rumors about me and Gunn. I want to see Alex, talk to him, the way we ended things leaving my stomach twisted in an ever-tightening, delicious knot. Hell, I want to see all of them, especially Grace. Apologize for how I refused to trust her, or let her in—

"Joan," Gunn interrupts my thoughts, "your take?"

I look up from my self-induced stupor to find Gunn across his desk, and Win Matthews on my right side, staring at me.

"We're talking about realistic shipments, Joan," Gunn says evenly.

"I know, I'm following, sir."

Gunn leans across his desk, and his leather chair squeaks in protest. "You told me you deserved to be a partner for your efforts. If so, your place is here with us, thinking big picture." He looks at me, head cocked, eyes narrowing slightly. "But maybe you were wrong."

I shake my head. "No, sir, I can do this. I'm sorry, I think the blood-spell is taking its toll." But it's not the magic that has a hold on me. Alex has been on my mind for three days straight, and I'm starting to think I'm never going to kick the addiction.

"Are we on target for tomorrow night?" Gunn turns his focus to Win.

Win looks at the paper of scribbles in front of him. "Since you closed the Den till Friday, we've now got all six sorcerers brewing around the clock. So if each of them brew twelve ounces a trick to ensure the optimal high, and can manage four tricks an hour, give or take, twelve-hour days . . ."

Gunn writes the calculations into his own notebook, pauses. "Oh, we'll be more than ready." His smile breaks open wide, and he and Win start laughing. They're beyond excited. They're electrified. And understandably so. We'll be rolling in cash by the end of the week, and based on what Gunn said at the demonstration on Sunday, it sounds like money is just going to keep pouring into the Den. I should be laughing too—this means even more opportunity, a chance to give my family everything.

Instead it feels empty, and *sad*, like even though it's a party, I'm in the wrong room, celebrating with the wrong people. And I just can't ignore all the question marks still surrounding the deal. From what Gunn told Colletto, it sounds like these shine shipments are going to continue getting brewed. But who's going to be brewing them around the clock? I sure as hell don't want it to be me, or the troupe. Gunn also mentioned a monopoly on performance magic—does that mean he's going to open other magic havens? So will we have competition? *Will the Red Den not be the main show? What really waits for me on the other side of Thursday? Am I looking at a future of "thinking big picture" and helping Gunn build a shine empire—being attached to his side forever?*

I've always focused on one step at a time—never really let myself think past the spell, then cracking the puzzle of our eternal shine . . . and then the D Street deal. Now that all our schemes are coming to fruition, cold, hard reality is settling in. I don't want to be here, with Gunn, separate and apart from what I've come to love. I just want to keep performing. I want to keep making magic with my troupe.

You need to talk to Gunn. It's time for some answers on what your future's going to look like, regardless of whether he thinks you deserve them.

Gunn folds his map up. "Why don't you check on the troupe, Win?" he says, like he can somehow read my thoughts. "I need a word alone with Joan."

Win gives Gunn a knowing smirk, and then he leaves.

"I have something to show you." Gunn flashes me one of those shifty half smiles, and stands.

"Mr. Gunn, I think we need to talk," I say carefully, "for a minute, about some of the things that are happening. I want to know what's next—"

"Later," he interrupts. "There's a surprise in your room. And it's too important to wait."

A surprise. From Gunn. In my room.

I'm always living on a razor blade of fear with Gunn, but something about his fake excitement right now feels extra cutting.

We head out of his office without another word. Gunn locks the door behind him, whistles a haunting little tune as we walk down the hall and up the stairs. When we get to my room's door, he pauses. "Why don't you do the honors?"

I have no clue what's waiting for me in here—dread, nerves, anxiety, it's all mixing inside me like a scalding stew. Still, my fingers find the door, I twist the handle open—

And I gasp.

Ben and Ruby. My cousin and my sister sitting on my bed. Like some mirage. Like someone plucked them out of my dreams and conjured them real.

"Oh my God." I run to them, pull Ruby into a huge embrace, grab Ben's hand and drag him in.

"What are you doing here? How did you, how—"

"Mr. Gunn sent for us." Ben wraps his arms around me. He pulls away and takes a good look at me, and his face folds into a relieved smile. "Got us a big fancy town car, pulled right in front of the cabin, and carted us up here like movie stars."

"It was crazy, Joan," Ruby says, beaming. "We got new clothes and everything." Ruby strokes the flapper dress that pulls tight over the little bulging belly she's now sporting. She's well. She managed to overcome Mama's blood-spell. *She's well.*

I pull her into another hug. "It's so good to see you," I whisper, my words catching.

Ruby pulls away from me, sizes me up like a parent sizing up her child, and then pulls me back in, like she, too, is making sure I'm real.

"So Jed's back at the cabin?" I ask Ben slowly.

"Wasn't up for the trip. He needs his rest." Ben averts his eyes. "But Mr. Stone is gonna divide his time between his farm and our cabin for the next few weeks, make sure he takes care of Pop's bills. I gave Stone a little of the cash you've been sending. He promised to keep the place up till we figure out where to go from here."

I nod, grateful for our nearest neighbor, Mr. Stone. Even though I don't give a rat's ass about Jed's welfare, I worked too hard for him to run that cabin into the ground.

"Thanks to you and Mr. Gunn here, the house is ours, though, free and clear." Ben throws a huge smile back to Gunn.

"You're here," I say again. "I can't—I can't believe you're both really here."

I crawl my fingers into Ruby's armpits and tickle lightly like I used to do when she was younger, and she blushes in front of Gunn, but laughs and squirms just the same. Then she collapses into me with a simple whisper, "Joan, you did it. You're my hero forever."

Gunn's still standing in my doorway, leaning sideways against its frame with his arms crossed. If I didn't know him better, I'd think he even looked somewhat touched.

"Thank you," I tell him, regardless of everything else.

"Of course. DC is your home now." He drops his arms and walks over to us, places his hand lightly on Ben's shoulder. "It's important to have what grounds you close by." He puts his hand on Ruby's cheek. The gesture isn't tender, though, it's almost possessive. "Nothing good comes about when people forget why they do what they do, what it's all for."

Gunn's words pull something tight inside me, and then everything clicks into place like an engine. Of course.

This isn't some kind gesture.

This is just another veiled threat, another way to keep me careful, watched, *tethered*. Gunn releases Ruby, who rubs her cheek and gives me a look like, *What a strange bird*.

But I just smile and ruffle her straw-colored hair. Gunn can think whatever he wants right now.

Because he's given me this. Because I have my family.

"Why don't you take an hour break, get them comfortable in here?" Gunn says, then looks at Ben. "Joan's told me how adept you are working at your father's shining room, but I bet you've never seen a full-scale magic haven before."

Ben's as helpless against magic's spell as anyone else. He shakes his head fervently. "I haven't, sir."

"Well, after you get settled, tell Joan to come find me and I'll give you a tour."

Ben's face lights up. "Yes, sir. Thank you, I will."

Alex's words from a few nights back, when we were lying in this very room, tangled up and twisted, come floating into my mind like some conjured ghost: *Something this big could attract other attention . . . you could end up behind bars for life . . .*

It's one thing to take risky moves, to burn fast and bright as a comet against this dark underworld when I've only got myself to worry about. It's another when my family, the ones I'm fighting for, pledged to die for, have entered the game.

And seeing Ruby and Ben here, standing next to Gunn, in this dangerous, slippery world where someone can kill you just as quick as trick you, makes me wonder if my strategy somehow needs to change.

TIGHT QUARTERS

ALEX

I'm in the Red Den's VIP lounge. My best guess is it's Wednesday afternoon, but I can't be entirely sure, because the only chances I get to see the clock above the performance space's double doors are when I need to use the john. Meals are brought in by the stagehands. Cigarette breaks are taken in here, or in the hall right outside. If we're too tired to brew another round of shine at the moment—you can power through a couple of rounds of brewing, but after a while you and your magic begin to fade— there are lounge chairs and sofas for taking short catnaps before raising up the sorcering flag once more.

Ral, Billy, Grace, Tommy, Rose, and me. Brew after brew, sorcerer's shine after shine, every trick of twelve ounces we brew to be poured into two hundred glass quart jugs that Joan will bind with her blood and trickery, so each jug can last forever on a shelf. Fifty gallons of a magical, wildly addictive drug that will mark the first shipment of shine ever to grace the black market, earmarked for Colletto's D Street gang to take and distribute up and down the coast and out to smugglers waiting on Magic Row. Fifty gallons that, if Gunn and Win—and Joan—have their way, will be the first of many shipments.

I've been trying to get Joan alone—I need to tell her

everything, including what she'll need to do to walk away from this mess, and the only alibi that might save her from prison, once my Unit charges in. But Gunn is keeping her on a short leash. The few times I've managed to sneak a spin around the Den, or climb the fire escape to her room, her lights were off, and she was gone. I've heard her voice, though, muffled behind Gunn's office door. It makes me sick, thinking about how for every quart we're complaining about filling, Joan's matching it in drops of blood.

"I'm starving," Billy says, as he collapses into a chair in the corner of the room. They're the first words anyone has said for hours.

"Me too," I say quietly.

Billy looks up. "They never brought in lunch, am I right?"

"No. What time is it?" I glance at Ral, the only one of us with a wristwatch.

"Jesus, the hours, the days, are starting to bleed together." Ral looks at his watch. "It's nearly three. How long do they intend to keep us going like this?" I assume it's a rhetorical question, but Ral looks pointedly at me. "Have you spoken to her, Alex, since the night of the demonstration?"

We all know who *her* is. "I haven't."

"I just wish I knew what was in store for us after this deal is done," Ral says slowly. "I mean, is this our new reality, working around the clock in a tight, windowless room, dumping our magic into a bottle? It can't be, right?"

"Not what I signed up for," Tommy grunts from the far corner.

"I don't know how much longer I can stand it. We're like prisoners in here." Grace sits down in another one of the armchairs. She puts her hands over her eyes, like she's going to attempt a catnap in the middle of this conversation. I can't blame her.

"Wonder what the princess is doing right now," Rose mutters, "but I'm sure it's not this."

Grace separates her fingers like a peephole and shoots Rose a loaded glance.

Rose just gives her a little smirk. "You know I'm right, Mama Bear."

"We wouldn't be in here if it wasn't for Joan," Tommy piggybacks. "She's cursed us, in more ways than one. She has us doing grunt work while she plays partners with Gunn."

And then I can't help but step in. "Enough. She's doing her part, same as you. You saw her on the stage."

"Yeah, but how'd she get such a leading role, you understand what I'm saying?" Tommy says, as Rose laughs. He takes a step closer to me. "You two were thick as thieves, partners in your little circle, am I right?" he says. "Did you really not know about any of this?"

I keep my eyes on the newly conjured shine between my hands, will my pulse to slow. "I didn't."

"She could have told us about the spell," Rose presses, "it could have been a team effort. Instead she kept it to herself to cozy up to Gunn. She played all of us." She raises one eyebrow at me. "Especially you, Alex."

Tommy adds, "Yeah, she's all yours, until you find her in bed with Gunn."

Like a reflex, my fingers tighten around my shine bottle and squeeze. The red, glistening shine explodes and splatters onto the folding table.

"Alex!" Ral rushes to my side to help clean up the mess. "Get some towels from the bar," he tells Grace and Billy.

"Christ, I'm sorry." I take off my sweater and throw it on the shine, which is now seeping into the carpet and soaking its fibers red.

Grace comes back quickly with some towels. She bends down next to me. "Pat it. There you go."

No one says anything for a long time. We don't have the

luxury of sparring in a twelve-by-twelve room, with our gangster keepers down the hall, and we all know it. Especially me. I'm too close, there's too much at stake to lose control.

"Tommy, take a break, grab a smoke," Ral says quietly. "Alex, why don't you get washed up, use my room. I'll cover for you if Win comes checking."

I nod slowly in thanks.

But as I head down the opposite hall and to the back stairs leading up to the sorcerers' rooms, I can't help but stop, right in front of Gunn's office door. I can almost *feel* Joan behind it. I'm sure Gunn's in there too. I want to break down the door, insert myself right in between them. I want to tell Joan the truth, get it over with, have her forgive me, so that we can move forward and put Gunn and the rest of his thugs where they belong.

Tonight's my last chance. Tomorrow is Thursday, when Colletto is due to arrive.

I'm going to need to get to Joan and explain things another way.

CONFESSION

JOAN

I'm in my performance circle, surrounded by feathers. The club has been closed for the better part of the week so we can focus on Colletto's shipment, but tonight there's a special performance. Tonight, Harrison Gunn sits with my baby sister and cousin on the benches around my old stage to watch me like a circus act. The rest of my troupe? Down the hall, brewing shine in a dark, windowless lounge.

I'm not sure who has the better deal.

"What's she going to do with those feathers?" Ruby says.

Ben shushes her. "Don't talk so loud. You'll break her concentration."

I hear Gunn answer in a low, almost seductive hum, "This was your sister's signature performance trick. She used to have half the crowd around her stage, clamoring for a glimpse of her magic."

"Really?" Ruby whispers.

"Indeed. Joan is our magic haven's most talented sorcerer. It's why I need her here." Gunn nods toward me. "Watch and learn."

I know Gunn wants me to look at him and give him some kind of acknowledgment, but I can't bring myself to do it. Instead I focus on the feathers that line the edge of my stage, and not my sister chatting with a gangster. I focus on the trick, instead of thinking about the message Gunn is trying to send me by taking my family under his wing.

It's not that I don't *want* Ruby and Ben here—it hurts as bad as a cut sometimes, when I wake up and forget that Ruby isn't sleeping by my side. But it turns everything around. It makes me ashamed of all this, angry with it, makes the truth of what I've managed to justify and shelf—turning shine into a shippable product, allowing the underworld to deliver it across America, ruining families like mine—inescapable.

Magic is what you were made *to do,* I remind myself. *Everything you're doing, the caging spell, the shine, the deal, it's all for them.*

But the reminder isn't loud enough, isn't strong enough to banish Alex's words: *What about Ruby and Ben . . . You could end up behind bars for life. . . .*

They tease me, taunt me, keep poking at me from the inside.

"Something wrong, Joan?" Gunn calls from the benches.

"No, sir."

I concentrate back on the feathers, until I can actually feel my mind reaching out like a hand and lifting them. One by one, the feathers dance a few inches off the ground until they form a slow, spinning circle above my head. They spin fast as the wind, then a tornado, then start to bleed into one long trail of white. And out of the swirling madness, a dove flaps its wings and flies up to the rafters.

Ruby leaps to her feet and claps. "Oh my goodness, Joan, that was wonderful!"

"Holy smokes," Ben gasps. "Pop could never manage that in a million years."

I wipe away the small beads of sweat that have collected along my hairline. "I've just been practicing."

"She's being humble," Gunn says evenly. "I've seen a lot of

sorcerers in my line of work, have searched for the strongest and the best. Your cousin is a rare breed."

A thick lump forms at the base of my throat. This time I manage to answer, "Thank you, Mr. Gunn."

"You should really see this place when it's open during a performance," Gunn says to Ben and Ruby in this secretive little voice, like they're old pals. He studies my dove, now perched in the rafters. "It's unlike anything you've ever imagined."

"I can't believe we're really here," Ben says dreamily. "Thank you, Mr. Gunn. I hope I get to stay long enough to see one of your performances."

Gunn throws a look my way. "Well, we're working on something major right now, but when it's over, the Den will be open again, and I always need good stagehands."

Ben, in this world, working under this roof? Not on your life. "Mr. Gunn—"

"It's a low-level job, I know," Gunn talks over me, "but if you prove yourself, Ben, you'll work your way up, just like your cousin. I'm a firm believer in rewarding those who deserve it." Gunn shoots another glance at me. "And keeping good people once I find them."

Another veiled threat, another two-sided message, like a double-sided trick.

I've been attached to Gunn pretty much morning through night this past week, trying to ensure his deal with Colletto goes down without a hitch. I need time away from him, with just my family. I need to remember who it's all for.

I glance pointedly at the clock. "It's almost ten, sir, and they've had a long day. Think it's time we all turned in."

"Aw, not yet, Joan, one more trick. Please?" Ruby cries.

Ben laughs. "I'm with Ruby."

Gunn stares at me for a while. "Come on, Joan knows best," he tells Ruby. "We've got plenty of time for tricks."

The four of us cross the show space together, walk down the hallway to the back stairs that lead to my room. Gunn stops in front of his office. "You want a nightcap?" he asks Ben suddenly. "Maybe a shot of shine, to chase away the day's cobwebs?"

As Ben's eyes grow wide as saucers, I cut in with, "He's fine, Mr. Gunn, thank you. Again, it's been a long day."

"Some other time then." Gunn opens the door to his office, throws me a triumphant look. "Good night."

"Good night, Mr. Gunn," Ruby and Ben say in unison.

When we get into my room, I immediately push Ben and Ruby back from the door and focus on its wooden frame. I hold out my hand, and the door's wood crackles. The frame begins to disappear, the white wood bleeding into the plaster of the wall—and then there's only one thick sheet of white in front of us, studded with the doorknob.

"Did you just lock us in?" Ben says.

"I don't want you going downstairs, and I don't want Gunn coming up." I rustle through my bureau, pull out Ruby's sole pair of pajamas. "This place isn't safe. *He* isn't safe."

"You know, I don't get you," Ben says. "I know you've made your own way here, but Gunn's the one who gave you the chance. He practically saved us. Besides, he's treating us like royalty. Treats you like a queen."

"Well, appearances can be deceiving, Ben." I kneel down and help Ruby into her pajamas. "He's dangerous. If you don't see that, you're a fool."

"I'd rather be a fool than paranoid and ungrateful."

"And just who's being ungrateful here?" I snap, before I can stop myself.

Ruby worms her little arms through her pajamas. "We don't have to leave, do we, Joan?" she whispers. "I don't want to leave you again."

I sigh, collect myself. The last thing I want is them thinking they're a burden being around. "I don't want you to leave either." I ruffle the top of Ruby's hair, then steal a glance back at Ben. "But Gunn is not what he seems, all right? I need you to remember that. I need you to be careful, keep your head about you— don't go getting all mixed up with magic and shine so you forget where we came from, and who we are."

"Like you have?" Ben says softly as he plays with the edges of my cotton sheets.

His words cut right through me. "Excuse me?"

He closes his eyes and lies back on the bed. "Parsonage was as much a prison for me as it had been for you, Joan. I never want to go back. I want what you have, I want a new start."

I can't fault him for that, can I? "Then you get a real job, outside of this hellhole. There's plenty of honest places to work up here in DC, plenty of opportunity."

"For someone who's worked in a shining room since he was nine?" Ben says. "If this place is good enough for you, it's good enough for me."

I put one hand over my eyes and take a deep breath. I don't want to snap again. I don't want to fight.

"You okay?" Ruby whispers. She bends down and pushes my fingers away from each other, creates a little window to my left eye.

I manage a laugh, stand and swing her onto the bed. "I'm too tired to argue with you anymore," I tell Ben. "We'll start sparring nice and early tomorrow."

"But I want to see more magic," Ruby says as she kneels on the mattress. "Can you do another trick? Jed never does any tricks at home."

"You want magic?" I face the little side lantern on the end table next to Ben. I point at it, close my eyes, and whisper, "*Off,*" and the lantern flickers out.

Ruby just giggles. "Too wild."

She climbs over Ben as he grunts from the pressure. He steals a pillow and slides down to get comfortable on the rug on my floor, as I settle in on Ruby's right side, into the sliver of space between her and the wall. It would almost feel like our cabin back home, except the window above my bed glows with light from the outside streetlamps, and the horns and engines on M Street chug a steady hum.

After a few minutes of silence, once Ruby burrows into her pillow and starts to lightly snore, Ben says from the floor, "You can't protect us forever, Joan, you know that, right?"

I wait a minute before I answer, "Doesn't mean I can't try."

Ben sighs. "I'm more grateful to you than words will ever do justice. But I need to make my own way in the world too." I hear him turn over. "I can't go back there, Joan. I can't keep watching my father spiral into nothing."

Of course I understand that. But even still, there's no way in hell I want him working for Gunn. So I give him the line I've been giving him all my life, when we were smaller and in charge of watching the bar with nothing but Jed's rifle as protection, when Jed showed up a few years back with a knife poking out of his left calf and was blubbering in fits and mumbles—even after Mama died, and I put that hard shell around myself, determined to keep moving forward, to use the future to right the past. "We'll figure this all out, Ben," I whisper. "We'll get through it. We always do."

But there's no answer, except a small sigh from the floor.

I can't sleep. I'm so worked up about all of it—our exchange with D Street tomorrow, my family, Gunn's slow, careful needling, and Alex—that my stomach just keeps tying itself into one long, complicated knot. I feel trapped, even more so as my back is literally up against my bedroom wall. I get a vague, almost primal urge to jump out the window, run and never look back.

So I turn to face Ruby, to remind myself of who it's all been for.

Her face is so soft, peach and plump under the light coming in from the street, and I can't help but put my hand on her cheek, feel her still-baby softness, her perfection that the world hasn't stolen away.

I am doing the right thing, aren't I?

Ruby stirs a bit, smiles back at me. "I forgot what your smell was like."

I smile. "I smell?"

"You good-smell smell," she says. "I've really missed you, Joan."

"I've really missed you, too."

She looks at me a little longer, her eyes heavy and dreamy. A sudden shadow falls across her face and she stirs, gasps. "Who's that man outside?"

I turn around, give a little gasp of my own.

"Is he real?" Ruby whispers.

"Hush, don't wake Ben." I move quietly to kneel, then press my face against the window. Alex Danfrey is on my fire escape, only an inch of glass between us. He looks like he hasn't slept since I last saw him. Ruffled hair, shirt a mass of wrinkles, deep bags under his eyes that look almost purple.

Still, just seeing his face sends a current right through me, lights up every inch.

"He's real," I whisper back.

Alex finds my eyes through the shaded glass of the window and smiles. He waves me outside.

"Ruby, don't say a word, don't move, you hear?" I say.

"You're going out there?"

"I'll be right back."

I unlock the glass pane and climb out onto the fire escape, and then close the window behind me.

"Is someone in there with you?" Alex asks as soon as I turn around.

"My cousin, and my little sister Ruby. Gunn brought them up here, to help remind me of my 'priorities.'" Then I look away, 'cause I know how that sounds: exactly how Alex pegged it— that Gunn's manipulating me, has me all turned around. "What are you doing here?"

"We need to talk." Alex takes my hand, sits me down on the fire escape. The air is frigid, has to be below zero. My body tenses as I sit, and I wrap my cotton-pajama arms around myself.

"Close your eyes," he says.

I do what he says. It takes a moment, but then I feel it, the icy fingers of January giving way to a warm breeze. The sun grazing my face, my shoulders. The smell of fresh-cut grass. I open my eyes to see the same gazebo Alex conjured for me all those weeks ago, when it was just the two of us in the hall, tricking and flirting with our magic. His manipulation is perfect, so warm and reminiscent, that I find my eyes starting to water.

"Do you remember this?" he says.

"Of course I do." I stare down at the wide wooden planks of Alex's gazebo, which now run underneath us. "I've missed you," I blurt out. "I haven't seen you since that night."

He wraps his hands around mine. "I've been thinking about you too much in that lounge. I'm constantly distracted."

My face warms. "I know the feeling."

Alex stares at me, like he's waiting for something, unsure of himself. And then in a rush, he leans in, kisses me deeply, desperate and tender all at once. It's like a spell, a heady, warm, wonderful spell of its own, and it almost makes the world outside his magic feel like a distant dream.

He pulls back and sighs. "It's been a rough few days, Joan."

I nod, thinking about all of Gunn's veiled warnings, my

family floating through this place, running my caging spell over and over—"On my end too."

"You having second thoughts about the deal?" he says slowly. "About all this?"

"No," I say instinctively. I steal a look at him. "Maybe. It just—it doesn't feel like I expected it would." I look at my hands. "How am I supposed to do what I'm doing when my little sister's right upstairs, you know?" I shake my head. "It's just gotten more complicated. And I have no idea what's in store for us after tomorrow. I'm trying to get it out of Gunn."

Alex runs his fingers through his hair, then inhales real big, like he's gearing up to sprint. "Joan . . . I need to tell you something."

I have no idea what he's about to say, but his face tells me that I don't want to hear it. "What's wrong, Alex?"

"Before I do this," he says quietly into his lap, "I need to know that despite all the lies for Gunn, the manipulations we've conjured under this roof, that this is real." He points to me, then to himself. His hands are shaking a little as he does it, which sort of scares the crap out of me. "If you trust me," he adds with a breath, "just like I trust you."

"Alex, seriously, what's this about?"

He looks at me sideways. There's so much brewing in his eyes. "It's important."

"Yes. I trust you, maybe more than anyone," I say, without even needing to think about it. "Hell, these days I might trust you more than I trust myself."

A slow smile breaks across Alex's face. But he still looks nervous.

Wildly, jumpy, out-of-his-skin nervous.

He starts rubbing the inside of my palm. "I know you think you need to do this, that this shine deal is the answer for you and your family," he says, "that there's no other way out but working alongside Gunn. But you'll be no good to your family rotting behind bars." He pauses. "Tomorrow night—it isn't going to happen. The Feds are onto it. The deal might start, but it's going to end with the largest Prohibition Unit bust in history. You need to get out now, while there's still time."

I shake my head. What Alex is saying is so far-fetched, it sounds like a story, one of the fairy tales I used to ramble on about to Ruby at night. "Alex, why are you . . . what—how would you even know this?"

"And I have a way," he talks over me. He starts breathing heavier and slower. He lets go of my hand, and then his words come out in a rush: "Colletto's gang is due here sometime tomorrow. The troupe's to make sure that all the shine we've brewed over the past few days, the glass quarts that you've been binding, are packed and ready for loading in the VIP lounge. That's where the deal is going down," he keeps talking, "but before D Street walks out of there, we clue in the rest of the troupe to what's going on and spellbind the room. If we time it perfectly—not too early to risk betrayal, not too late that we miss our chance— we force the troupe on board. And then we lock both gangs in like sitting ducks for the Feds."

"Alex." I finally find my voice. *Lord, he's really starting to unravel, to lose it.* "What's gotten into you, how on earth would the Feds—"

"I promise the Unit will cut a deal with you. I'll make sure of it." His words are soft, but now assured, and he keeps his eyes trained on a random spot to the left of my head. "We say that Gunn was the mastermind, that he had you and the rest of his sorcerers working like dogs for him, that he was blackmailing you—at the end, that's what it's been like, it's not too much of a stretch from the truth. We'll tell the troupe the same—have them corroborate the story. They all think there's something else going on between you and Gunn anyway."

He steals another breath as my head starts spinning. "If you give up Gunn and his team and everything you know, you'll walk. But it needs to be all of it, Joan—everything about the eternal shine, anything Gunn's said about his plan for expansion, plus D Street's distribution routes. And that spell, Joan—it can't get out, you need to tell the Unit everything, we need to contain it. You give all that up, and I promise your family will stay safe. I'll make sure the cabin stays yours if that's what you want. Maybe the Feds will keep you under surveillance, but you'll be free." He pauses, then adds in a more tentative voice, "Or you and your family could stay here in DC with me."

I can't speak. The world feels like it's opening up underneath me, and that I'm falling, unable to hold on to any of his words, descending *down down down*. "What are you—Alex," I stutter, "how the hell do you know this?"

He shakes his head.

He looks pitiful. Repentant. Afraid.

And then the pieces start falling into place.

Or maybe the picture has always been completed, and I've just been too blind—too willfully blind—to see it.

"Are you . . ." I close my eyes. I can't look at him anymore. "Are you a cop?"

"They had me, Joan, over a barrel," he rushes, squeezing my hands, "all my old crimes. At first I was doing it because I had to. But then I started to understand everything that magic is capable of, all the darkness of this underworld, and I met you, and—" He stops. "I believe in what I'm doing now, more than ever. I want to end Gunn and the rest of them. I want to save you. Please, please let me do both."

A cop.

Alex is a fucking cop.

Of course, this all makes sense, looking back at the full picture. His cloudy past, his questions about Gunn, the way he kept burning bright, right through the Shaws. But even still, it feels like the greatest magic—the one I've come to know as real, the one I've come to build my hopes and dreams on top of—it all teeters, then comes spiraling, crashing down.

"You piece of shit." I close my eyes. The tears come hot, fast, and overwhelming. "You liar. You've been playing me this *whole time?*"

"I never played you." Alex rushes to grab my hand again, but I jerk away from him, stumble to the edge of his gazebo manipulation. I want to tear it down with my nails. *Alex. Alex is a cop.*

"Please, Joan, me and you—that's the only thing that's always been real." His voice cracks. "I can't deny that I lied about some things—I had to in order to survive—but there're some things that you just can't lie about. You know that's true."

I don't look at him. Alex tries to angle around, force me to, but I turn away. But he gently grabs my hand and pulls me around to face him. I want to resist again. I want to tell him to leave me alone. But his look, his face. *This*, right here, right now, there's no trick.

"I've made sure the Feds don't know your name yet, but they know about the eternal shine," he says slowly. "I told you, I've got it all figured out. We'll get ahead of it, and spin your story—we'll tell them that you were coerced, that Gunn forced you to use your blood-magic. Like I said, we'll use the troupe to back it up. If they cooperate, they get off easy. Besides, we've always been after the gangsters, not the sorcerers—Gunn and Colletto are the masterminds."

When I don't answer, because I can't, because everything I might say is stuck like a thick, knotted ball in my throat, he leans in and whispers, "I would never give you up, don't you see that? You were right, Joan. We're the same, we deserve this—we deserve each other."

Those words. They're the right words.

Maybe, despite all things, they're the only words that matter.

"Please, Joan," he says. "Think of your family, of yourself. Hell, think of me." He takes my other hand, so that both of mine are wrapped in his. "This is the only way you get out of this. Please. Please tell me you're with me."

I study Alex Danfrey, this man I know intimately and yet apparently, don't know at all. This expert sorcerer who's about to take down everyone I've worked with, everything I've worked for, all in one night. One bust. This double agent who's crossing his own agency just to carve a path that lets me walk away.

We'll get ahead of this—the only way you get out—we deserve each other.

Maybe . . . maybe we *could* start over, in another city—Alex, me, Ruby, and Ben. And once we clear our names with the Feds and move on, maybe . . . maybe we bury the caging spell like Alex said, keep it a secret as Mama always meant for it to be, and we get back to our performance. Alex and I had true magic on our stage, that's something you can't walk away from. We could open our own place. A *different* place—without the violence, without the Gunns of the world breathing down our necks—just a place to make magic together. Alex says he's working for the Feds, but I've seen him in action. And I know what he can do, what he won't be able to live without forever, despite how much he's turned himself around otherwise.

We'll work it out, we'll figure it all out, together.

"Promise me you'll take care of my family after all this is through?" I say slowly, as I wipe a tear from my eye. "And my name is never tied to any of it. As far as the papers, *anyone* is concerned—Joan Kendrick never existed."

Alex rests his hands on my shoulders. "I will, Joan. I promise. It's what I want." He glances toward the window. "Stay up here, get some rest if you can. I'll be in the lounge with the others tomorrow, finishing up our shipments, just to avoid tipping Gunn off that anything's wrong. You do the same. You act like everything he's been planning is finally coming together. Soon as I know when Colletto's coming, I'll phone it in to the Feds," he says. "And when the gangsters exchange the cash and the goods, we pull our final trick—we clue in the troupe, and lock those thugs in the VIP lounge. Then the Unit arrives to take them down."

I nod slowly, wipe my eyes with the back of my hand. "I understand."

He presses his lips gently to my forehead and pulls me into him. And I smell his scent again, that mix of soap and cologne. I breathe it in. "We're in this together, Joan," he whispers. "We always have been."

We both climb through the window, Alex angling around Ruby to make his way to the foot of the bed. "Until tomorrow," he says, after I break my spell on the door.

And then he's gone.

I lie back down. I toss and turn, running it all through, praying to God that Gunn doesn't get a whiff of this and break Alex apart, only to break me next. I'm angry, more scared than I've been in a long time, so twisted around that sleep is now a dream. But there's one thing I know deeper and truer than anything:

Alex was right.

Even though we didn't know why, or how, or what it was all for, Alex and I have always been in this together.

DEAL SWEETENER

ALEX

I leave Joan's room and creep downstairs, settle onto the sofa in the lounge, determined to catch a little rest before tomorrow breaks wide open. There's no way I'm going to be able to sleep—my nerves are shot, my heart is beating so fast that I'm surprised it hasn't taken off—but I should try. Tomorrow is going to be a long, backbreaking day of finishing up the shine shipment for Gunn, making sure Agent Frain is ready for our score, and then all the paperwork I'm sure will take place at the Unit, after.

Of course it was a huge risk, coming clean to Joan. A huge, potential career- and life-ending risk. But I trust her. Regardless of whether I should, I do. And I can't leave her behind. No matter how much I try to lie or trick myself, the truth remains. I'm in love with her.

What's left of the night passes by in a fit of strange dreams, and tossing and turning on the lounge's sofa. When Ral and Billy show up in the morning, they look me up and down, and Ral actually asks if I'm strung out.

"I'm fine," I say, as I stand and light a cigarette. "Just tired is all."

"After tonight, Gunn sure as hell better give us a night off." Billy picks up one of the jugs of water resting in the corner and pours the optimum twelve ounces into an empty bottle. "Can't take much more of this."

"I'm with you," I say.

Once the rest of the troupe arrives, we slowly get to work, dig our heels in, and we all keep a steady pace for a few hours, working as a team. Around late afternoon, we each brew our last trick of shine, and fill the final quart container. Despite the collective exhaustion, the air in the lounge becomes festive, excited. Win comes in a few minutes later, and when he sees the finished shipment, he calls for Gunn.

Gunn paces around the glass quarts of eternal shine, the 180 bottles that have already been caged by blood and sealed, plus the twenty that will still need to go to Joan to be finished this afternoon, and then brought back here to await Colletto.

He looks up and nods. "Excellent. As always, you've exceeded my expectations." He moves toward the door. "Everyone should get freshened up, be down to greet Colletto's men before eight." *Eight o'clock. So that's when the deal takes place. I need to call this in to Agent Frain.* "I'm not sure what Colletto expects, if he'll want another celebratory shine toast, or a magic performance, so be ready for anything." Gunn looks back to me. "Alex, I know you've been carting yourself back and forth each night, running yourself ragged between here and home. Win, drive him home to get changed, will you?"

But I need this sliver of a window to get to a pay phone, to call the Prohibition Unit— "I'm okay with walking, sir. I know you both have a lot on your plate."

"Relax, I'll drive you." Win stubs his cigarette into an ashtray on the end table.

"Thanks." I force a smile. "I'd appreciate it. It's gotten awful cold."

I follow Win numbly down the hall, to the stairs and out the bar front. Adrenaline has me flying. I need to shake Win somehow, get through to Frain, give him the details so he can get set to move in.

Should I pretend I'm sick? There's a pharmacy on P Street with a telephone—

"Where you headed?" someone says from across the lot.

I turn to see one of Gunn's minions, Dawson, strolling toward us.

"Running Danfrey home," Win says. "Want to come along?"

A gangster ride-along would be somewhat comical if I wasn't so pressed for time.

Dawson smiles. "Sure, what the hell, if you lend me a smoke."

Win opens the front door to his car and nods to the back of his old Model T. "You don't mind riding in the back, do you, Danfrey?"

"Not at all."

I settle into the beige leather, the seat squeaking in protest, as Dawson and Win climb into their seats in front of me.

We rumble down M Street a few blocks and then stop at a traffic light. Before the light changes, two cars roll up next to ours simultaneously, one on each side. That's my first warning bell, since M Street is only four lanes wide, two lanes in each direction, which means the car on our right has had to use the shoulder to stop beside us. But I don't really process this. I'm still inside my own head, figuring out timing: how to get changed, sneak out to call Frain, whether my plan with Joan is bulletproof.

Then the doors to the cars bookending us open.

One man hops out from the car on the shoulder, and one hops out from the black Model T on our left. They each run to our car, open the respective backseat doors, and slide in next to me, surrounding me. Caging me, in seconds.

I look up. The guy on my right side is Howie Matthews. He gives me a knowing smile. "Heya, pal."

My stomach starts to lurch as the two cars on either side of us screech away through the red light. When the light turns green, Win steps on the gas, and we go flying, the roar of the engine shattering the silence. The mixed scents of aftershave suffocate me, the steel of my captors' holstered guns starts poking at my hips.

I don't recognize the guy on my left, but he's a young thug, maybe my age, average build but with a face you don't want to mess with. He catches me looking at him, flashes me a crooked grin, and simply says, "Sorry, Charlie."

"Win?" My voice is high, so high and strangled that I don't recognize it on its way out. The heat inside my stomach is starting to reach a fever pitch, and I can barely hear my own words over my heart. We make a right on 14th Street instead of a left. "You just passed the turn, we missed my turn—"

"Change of plans, Danfrey," Win says. "Turns out Colletto had a problem with the son of his old spells distributor turning his back on him and attempting to go his own way. Turns out your hothead moves in jail didn't sit so well with D Street."

I can't process, I'm not sure what's happening, my mind is scrambling, my thoughts stumbling to keep up. *Am I . . . am I part of the deal? This whole time, has Colletto been harboring a grudge against me, same as I have against him?*

"But then again, we were all tricking each other, weren't we, Alex?" Win flashes me a smile through his rearview mirror. "When we got ahold of McEvoy on that boat, he sure had some interesting tales to tell in his final hour."

They went to the voodoo party. They already got to McEvoy.
McEvoy must have confessed that he used me as a mole.
Time's up, Alex.
Jesus. Effing. Christ.

I can't catch my breath, can't slow my heart, as Win starts weaving in and out of the 14th Street traffic. He throws a glance back at me, and the car does a little swerve into the closest lane. "What did you think would happen? That you'd just burrow your little rat face into the Den and keep McEvoy apprised? That he'd protect you when push came to shove?" Win laughs. "He's a junkie, and moreover a jackal. He's never known what loyalty is, and he treats his people like trash. Which is why he's at the bottom of the Potomac, floating alone right now."

"Well," Dawson says, "not alone for long," and the entire crowd starts laughing.

I'm going to be sick.

"Howie," I whisper to my old cell mate. "Howie, you don't want to do this."

"Oh, but I do, Alex." Howie puts his arm around my shoulder, maybe for the last time. He looks around the car, then drops his voice to a whisper, "You always thought you were so much better than me. So when I found out you were a rat for McEvoy, spying on my cousin and Mr. Gunn?" As he leans in, his greasy hair brushes my shoulders. "I *begged* them to let me ride along." Howie stretches his thin legs out long under the seat in front of him, while I just get tighter and tighter. Then he leans in and adds, "Traitor."

I turn away from him, blood pounding against my skull, my fear so intense I start seeing bright-white spots against the leather seats of Win's car. *Have they already told Gunn about me spying for McEvoy? They must have. Will Gunn think Joan knew about it? Will he punish her because of it?*

I close my eyes. I can't think about that. She has to survive this.

She has to walk away.

Win slows at another traffic light. I look past Howie, out the window and a few blocks ahead. We're almost at the edge of town. There are about five more blocks until we're on the Highway Bridge, on a long road to an endless nothing.

I can't think, all my thoughts are just one long silent cry—*I'm going to die this is it this is real—*

But my fingers start to twitch, and my will to go down fighting takes over. *Should I take them out with magic? Conjure knives, and send them flying? If Gunn found out, would he hurt me by hurting Joan?*

I can't take the risk. Besides, I'm not a murderer, or a criminal—I'm charged with taking guys like these animals down.

So I focus on the window, watch the traffic light from the other direction flip from green to yellow to red. "Duck, Howie," I whisper.

"What?"

"*Shatter.*"

Our car begins moving, while Howie's window breaks into a million pieces, shards of glass flying into his face, his hair. He closes his eyes, burrows his head—

"What the hell!" he screams.

I send a sharp elbow into the eye of the guy on my left, and then I turn and jab my fist into Howie's face. Blood starts gushing out of Howie's nose as he doubles over.

"What's going on back there?!" Win keeps his hands on the wheel but whips his head around to look at me as Dawson scrambles to grab my shirt. I shrug Dawon off, kick him in the stomach, and send him careening back—

People start beeping behind us, and Win turns back to the wheel and steps on the gas.

I focus on the road ahead, conjure a thick brick wall to stack itself five feet tall in front of us. Before Win can brake, the car smashes into it, and we all snap back against our seats—

And that's when I scramble over Howie.

"Grab him, Howie! Just do it now!" Win barks. He throws his

car into reverse, but before Howie can get a clear hold on me, I jump through the open window.

A rush of pain and cold wind snaps at my body as cars beep and drivers scream. Tires screech as Win pulls his car over to the shoulder ahead of me. I pick myself off the road, hip throbbing, face pounding, and dash between two cars just as Win's jumping out of his. I trip over a set of trash cans that line a row of storefronts on the other side of the National Mall, and cut into the alley behind them.

"I just heard him!"

"Over there."

"Behind the alley, move!"

Footsteps pound the cement behind me, a chorus of angry shouts—"Get back here, you little shit!"

"It's worse if you run!"

The sound of bullets roars through the sky.

I sprint down the alley, turn a sharp bend around a brick corner grocery, push myself inside, and conjure the door to lock behind me. I nearly collide with the dodgy storekeeper, a large, tired-looking man who jumps out of my way.

"Stay back!" The grocer backs away, hands up, face frozen with fear, toward the counter. "I don't serve no sorcerers, you hear? I want no trouble."

"Is there a roof?" I gasp, as I steady myself on one of his shelves for a second.

"Don't speak to me, hell spawn!" The grocer covers his ears.

I lunge toward him, grab his collar. "I need you to focus." I nod to the stairs on the side of the store, behind neat aisles of Campbell's Soup and olive oil. "Do those stairs lead to a roof?"

He nods quickly, gasps, "Please, don't hurt me."

I release him, stumble up the staircase, dart across a dingy, cluttered second floor. I climb another staircase until the steps dead-end into a door. I heave my shoulder against it—*one, two, three*—and stumble out onto the roof of the grocery.

The brilliant colors of the oncoming sunset blind me for a second, but I get my bearings, dash to the edge of the store's blacktop roof, and peer out to the main drag of 14th Street. Win and his men are shouting, cursing, firing bullets into the alley, peering around every corner.

"Check the stores," Win's steely voice echoes through the abandoned alley. "Every one. We can't lose him."

As they stop to catch a breath in the front of the grocery, Dawson points to a drop of my blood that must have smeared across the window.

"Blood," Win says, then surveys the grocery's door. "In. Open it."

Panic starts to thrum again, my short burst of relief pinching out like a flame. I hear the breaking of glass, the smack of a door underneath me, then hurried footsteps echoing through the grocery's thin walls and shoddy floors.

They're coming.

Surrounding me is a smattering of rooftops, a patchwork of three-story town homes and squat two-story stores. And then an idea starts to take hold.

They need me dead. They're not going to rest until I'm dead.

I limp to the edge of the building, take a look below. There's a three-story drop-off, but about ten feet away, there's a building with a dangling fire escape on its second floor. My ribs, sore and bruised from the fall, are now aching, maybe broken. *This is the only way out*, I tell myself. *You need to jump.* I look across the alleyway, to the fire escape that shines like a beacon in the sun. *And they need to think you fell.*

I take a few steps back, close my eyes, and wait for them, and when I hear the trapdoor to the ceiling flap open, hear Win shout, "There he is, fire!" I dig in and run as fast as I can toward the edge of the building. I don't falter. I don't stutter-step, and I jump, my legs propelling me like a windmill, *up around up around—*

I reach, lurch in midair for the base of the fire escape, desperate to reach it, to hang on . . .

My fingers find the steel, whiplash shoots through my shoulders, the heady rush of jumping causing my nose to gush blood. *Move, Alex, before they reach the roof's edge.* I scramble onto the fire-escape landing, whisper, *"Replicate and conceal."* A force field, a replica of the scene behind me—the brick wall, and the zigzag cut of the fire escape—appears like a flat wall of camouflage in front of me.

I peer down at the alley two stories below and complete the ruse. On the ground of the alley, emerging just as Win and his men sprint to the edge of the roof one floor above me on the other side, is a facedown replica of Alex Danfrey, splayed out and broken on the alleyway ground.

"Son of a bitch tried to jump," Howie says, his voice cracking a bit as he studies my body from the third-floor roof.

"Make sure he's really gone," Win says quietly.

Howie and Dawson and Win's other thug, they pause only for a moment. Then, one after the other, they take their pistols from their pockets, aim at my replica, fire three floors down, the cold, hard bursts of gunfire rattling me, *POP POP POP*, as I watch from above. *I need to match their gunfire with magic. This needs to look real.* So I focus on my replica on the alley floor, say the words of power. And then three deep, black marks of blood bloom like nightmarish roses across my replica below.

The gunfire stops.

"That was close. Too close," Win sighs out. "Come on, we need to get back. Tell Gunn it's done."

I wait until they back away from the edge of the building across the alley. I take a minute, and then another, to collect myself on the cramped landing of the fire escape, to revel in being alive, as Win and his goons climb into their car and drive themselves back to the Red Den.

I was part of the deal. I was always part of the D Street deal. Boss McEvoy and me, Gunn's thoughtful little deal sweeteners for D Street. His loose ends.

My body is cut and bruised and pleading for rest, but I limp down from the fire escape, through the back alley to 14th Street, hobble over to the corner where a large streetcar is about to pull away from the curb. I flag the driver down, shove a few coins from my pocket into his hand, and slide onto a seat near the front. The crowd of middle-aged women and flustered mothers with small children angles away from me, but I just tilt my head back and close my eyes.

I need the next stop and a phone—Frain needs to be at the Den by eight and has no idea how all of this has just imploded. But this can't be over, we need to salvage this, and Joan—

I need to get to Joan. I promised her. I have to save her.

We have to save each other.

CHANGE OF PLANS

JOAN

I've been in Gunn's office all day, trying to finish my spellbinding of the final quarts. My nerves are eating me alive, over everything that's about to happen tonight, and worrying about my family and Alex. *Everything will work out*, I repeat like a prayer. *This is all almost over.*

I'm done around half past six. I've never wanted to see my family more than at this moment. My plan is for Ben and Ruby to stay upstairs, wait behind my locked bedroom door for me and Alex to execute our sting, for the Feds to come, before we get them out and leave this house of tricks behind.

So when Gunn comes in a little while later, I stand up from my chair. I try to remember that he has no idea what's about to happen, that he's in the dark, that Alex and I are the sorcerers behind this elaborate performance. So I say as confidently as I can, "I think it's time I see my family, Mr. Gunn. The shipment is ready. And D Street should be arriving soon, so I better get on upstairs." He doesn't answer, just stares. "It's important to me, before the deal goes down, to see them. As motivation, like you said."

"How interesting," Gunn finally answers, slowly, "that you listen to some things I have to say, but not others." I know Gunn and his loaded meanings too well, and a chill starts to crawl up my spine.

He shuts his office door. And then he takes a step closer, rests his hand on his desk, and looks up at me with those searing eyes. "Do you know why I'm partnering with D Street, Joan?"

His question catches me by surprise, but he doesn't wait for me to answer.

"My father, Danny Gunn, once ran the Shaws. His cousin was his right-hand man. This cousin was a hothead, a quick trigger, the antithesis of coolheaded Danny. They disagreed often, more often than not behind closed doors. Doors, of course, that as a small child, I was often behind as well." Gunn uses a low, even, patient tone, like he's telling me a story. "For example, McEvoy— he was my father's right-hand man—never agreed with my father's shaky peace with the Italian gang on the other side of town. McEvoy thought D Street constantly overstepped their bounds, and he started threatening violence when a group of Colletto's thugs supposedly robbed a bank on the wrong side of gang lines," he says. "Without consulting my father, McEvoy made an example out of a young D Street associate. Shot him down like a dog, right on 14th Street." Gunn pauses. "Unfortunately, this young associate turned out to be the nephew of Boss Colletto."

He shakes his head. "My father was livid, knew he had to punish McEvoy for acting out. But before he could, in retaliation for the Shaws' murder of Colletto's nephew, my father was killed in a street shootout orchestrated by D Street. McEvoy was unanimously voted in as boss, seeing as Danny's son—yours truly—was a mere fifteen years old."

Gunn turns to face me. "But instead of grooming me as a protégé, Boss McEvoy treated me like a threat. When I came of age, he gave me a figurehead title and a job running some half-rate shining room, which at the time was the lowest-earning operation the Shaws had a hand in," he says. "And if things had gone just a bit differently, maybe I could have accepted my fate as low-level gofer, even been grateful for the chance McEvoy threw my way. Thing is, Joan, I knew all along that D Street hadn't executed my father."

This is the most Gunn has ever shared with me. And while I've got a clear sense of where the story's going, I'm petrified over what it has to do with me.

"I was a young, slippery thing, never trusted McEvoy. I kept tabs on him—who he was meeting with, what he was scheming behind my father's back. I tried to warn my father, but it was tough to get his ear." Gunn looks at the floor. "Before his memorial service, I went to the morgue. I had to know for sure if my suspicions were right. The coroner confirmed my father's head had been ripped open back to front. A near-range, personal kill. McEvoy's kill, blamed on D Street, and he was left holding the keys to the Shaws."

Gunn's eyes get wider, brighter. "I acted like I knew nothing, of course. I put my head down, secretly planned my revenge. But do you know what that's like, to live under the thumb of a man you despise? To live out each day in the shadow of someone who stole your life away?"

Immediately, I think of Mama and Uncle Jed. And I almost say, *Of course I do*. And maybe in another life, on another roll of fate's dice, this story of Gunn's would have bound us together, made us a formidable team.

But not in this one.

In this one, all I see is a shadow of a man. A ruthless, cunning killer.

"But I've won, Joan. I've taken it all back from McEvoy." He laughs. "And you know how? Because I'm a *survivor*. Because I never. Miss. A trick."

Something has shifted between us, something monumental, and Gunn no longer hesitates as he reaches out, touches me.

He pushes my hair off my shoulder as I stay shocked still, then cups his fingers around my shoulder.

"How many times have I told you, subtly and not so subtly, to stay away from Alex, Joan?" He turns and gently presses me against the edge of the desk, until I have no choice but to back into it.

What's he doing, why's he mentioning Alex, what does he know—

"Don't get mixed up with him, Joan," Gunn mock-whispers into my ear. There's no space left in between us, his chest presses into my own. "Don't trust him. Stay focused. Keep that stalwart heart." Our faces are inches apart from each other, and his white-blue eyes, expectant, hungry, blaze through mine. I can't—I can't think, I can't look anywhere else—

"After a while, it almost felt like . . . jealousy. But do I seem like a man who accepts not getting what he wants?"

Before I can even think how to answer, Gunn grabs the back of my head in one swift motion, and I flinch. "Believe it or not, I was trying to *protect* you from getting hurt, since Alex was always part of my deal with D Street, from the beginning."

He releases me, turns away, as my mind sputters, *The deal, part of the deal—*

But my thoughts stop cold when Gunn looks back at me. Because now there's only rage, white fire burning behind his eyes.

"Then I find out that not only were you lying to my face about Alex, but that he was a mole for McEvoy. A mole you were confiding in, passing little secrets over the pillow to, secrets that little two-faced shit passed right on to my enemy. My target."

I start stammering, "Wait, no, Mr. Gunn, you've got it wrong—"

"Could've been really disastrous, Joan, your decision to keep things from me," he interrupts in that mocking tone.

"Fortunately, I've always been one step ahead of McEvoy. Always one step ahead of you."

Does Gunn know Alex is a cop? Does he know about me working with him? I can't, I don't know how to play this—

"Mr. Gunn, I swear, I'm not keeping things from you—"

Quick as a snake about to strike, Gunn whips his gun from his holster, thrusts it right against my temple. "Lie to me one more time and I promise you, I'll go straight to where I'm keeping your sister and break her little neck."

At that, I snap. *Crack*, and my hands fly up on their own, like they're possessed, like my magic has circumvented my mind and taken control of my body. I barrel a wave of force and power toward Gunn. He flies backward and slaps against his door.

It's quiet for a second. And then he actually laughs.

"Where's my family?" I force out. "Answer me or I'll rip you in half."

Gunn stands up slowly, walks toward me like a wolf on the hunt, slow, assured, in control. He towers over me. "No, Joan. No more working together. I call the shots. You sit in here and wait, until I make sure everything goes exactly according to plan. After this deal goes off without a hitch, you'll spend as long as it takes ensuring that the troupe can perform your caging spell. You do that, and maybe you'll see Ben and Ruby again," he says. "But you try anything at all—if you move from this room—my men will end your family. Are we clear?"

My heart is pounding, the magic inside me throbbing, near desperate to rip him apart. "No, you promised me things, you promised my family things—"

"And promises can be broken. I think you've been fooling yourself into thinking that you hold the power here," Gunn says, then smiles, a big, bold one I rarely see. "Fortunately, there's no Alex Danfrey around to trick you anymore."

My eyes fly to his. "What are you talking about?"

"I told you, Danfrey was always part of my deal." There's a new glimmer to Gunn's eyes. "Colletto considered him a traitor, thought the boy should have been working for him, only found out he was still running through a few low-level thugs who just got out of prison. So Danfrey was a *gift*, signed, sealed, and delivered, as another symbol of my good faith to D Street. A sign I want to start over and make amends." My breath catches. "But you didn't listen. You insisted on breaking that heart." Gunn looks down, smooths his suit. "Then again, guess we both know you're quite the masochist."

Alex was always part of the deal. Now I understand, and the understanding guts me—

Alex. Alex is gone.

I collapse onto the chair, and a little sob escapes me before I can trap it inside.

No. No no no no no—

"My boys took him out to the streets, shot him down." Gunn takes a step back. "Cross me again, and Ben will be next. Win's outside, guarding this door in case you get any crazy ideas like running." He opens his door. "Stay, *heel*, Joan. As soon as this is all over, you and me, we're done. And maybe you and your family get to walk out of here—final offer."

The world's spinning, crashing—

And then Gunn shuts his office door.

Lord, I think I'm hyperventilating.

Alex is gone.

Gunn has my family.

The Feds are moving in.

There's no way out of this.

A tight pop of air winds its way up my throat and comes out again in a strangled sigh. I close my eyes and see Alex's face. *Alex, who trusted me, who believed in me, who made me better than I ever could have been alone.*

I push out of my chair, spend the next minutes frantically pacing, anger, rage, my *family* . . . guilt . . . longing . . . *Alex*.

Something snaps inside me—no, *breaks*.

Like a gauntlet's being thrown down.

Gunn will pay for this, for all of it.

A man like him deserves to lose everything.

I close my eyes, like I can literally snuff out the rage and the pain, and let cold, hard reason rise from the ashes. Gunn said Alex was working for McEvoy. He never mentioned the Feds.

Which means he still doesn't know they're coming.

I think about Alex's sting, the plan we made in his cocoon of magic, perched on that fire escape like we were looking out on a whole new world. *Get D Street and Gunn in the same room*, he said. *Lock them up until the Feds arrive and take them down.* I think through it, carefully, calmly, and detached, surveying it for holes.

Because I don't want the Feds taking Gunn and his gangsters down.

I want them gone.

I want it to be *my* hands that do it, that strangle the life out of Gunn.

The beginnings of an idea start to tease at the corners of my mind. And then it all comes together quickly, in images that I don't seem to conjure but that conjure themselves, like a trick that's sorcering on its own, in the dark folds of my nature.

The last time I let my magic take the wheel, steer me where it thought I needed to go, I ruined everything. But I've grown since that cursed night in our cabin's clearing. I'm in control of my power. And I'd rather die than go down without a fight for my family, for Alex.

For me.

I straighten up and walk out of Gunn's office with my head held high. Win Matthews is in a chair outside in the hall just like

Gunn promised, watching Gunn's office with a long, lean pistol in his hands. The gun's now pointed right at me.

"What do you need?"

"Bathroom."

He waits a minute before he starts to rise and says, "Afraid not."

But as he stands, he drops his gun, just a *sliver*, and I thrust out my hand and command his weapon. The silver pistol flies out from his fingers, and I wrap both of my hands around it and call to the ends of the hall, "*Surround*." Two thick sheets of glass erupt out of the floor, block both entrances to the hall.

Win quickly spins around, takes in his cage—the two long cinder-block walls of the hall and my two manipulations trapping us inside the corridor. He looks at me, slowly raises his hands. "What do you want?"

"Show me where my family is."

"That's not possible."

I thrust the pistol toward him. "Now. I'm not playing."

Win shakes his head but raises his hands a little higher in surrender. "Gunn would kill me."

I take the safety off the pistol with a click. "At least you'll be alive to worry about it."

"They're upstairs," he finally concedes, "in Tommy's room. The door is spellbound."

"Take me."

Win walks slowly in front of me toward the back stairs, as I train his gun at the back of his head. When we're a few feet away from my manipulated wall, I release it, spiral it away into dust.

"Move," I whisper. "It's safe."

We take quiet steps up the stairs, then follow the upstairs hallway. Win nods to a door on the left. "This is it." But the door has no handle.

"Damn it, Tommy." I keep one hand on the gun trained on

Win's forehead, and with the other, reach out to where a door-knob should be. Like a cat raising its back to be petted, the door-knob arches out of the wood and appears, and I grab it.

But as I begin to turn the knob, Win lunges for me in one hot rush, fumbles for the gun, brings us both crashing to the floor. The pistol goes flying between us, and Win dives on top of it, his hands fumbling with the trigger as I crawl away from him, scramble backward toward the door. He points the gun at me—

"*Flip and fire!*"

Win's gun twists around in his hands, wrangles out of his grip like a wild animal, and shoots him in the face.

I collapse back on the ground, panting, turn away from the red gory mess in front of me. *Lord, I think I actually might get sick.*

I close my eyes, whisper my words of power, and slowly lower my hand. The floor planks below me answer my magic, curl up like pieces of ribbon, and slowly accept Win's body into the floorboards.

I rush to open Tommy's door, and find Ben and Ruby huddled on one of the beds along the wall.

"Joan!" Ruby leaps off the bed and runs to me. I kneel down, and she throws her arms around my neck. "Is everything okay? What was that noise?"

"Nothing, honey." I swallow. "It's all right."

"I've been so scared," Ruby stammers. "I kept asking Ben why we're in here, but he just said everything was fine."

I look at Ben, who's sitting cross-legged on the bed. His face says he knows damn well that everything is not fine.

I grab Ruby's hands in mine. "I need you to be brave, you understand?"

Ruby gulps. "I can be brave."

"Then I need you to go with Ben to the train station and wait for me there," I say slowly. "We'll grab your things, sneak you out the fire escape. You go as fast as you can to Union Station. Take some of the pocket money I gave you when you arrived, all right? Jump in a taxi."

"What happened?" Ben says softly.

"There's no time," I say. "Later." I stand and move back to the entrance. "Not a word," I tell them, as I open the door.

We move down the hall quickly, quietly, and I burst back into my bedroom, spellbind it behind me, start throwing all our things in the drawers into Ben's suitcase.

"Where do you want to go?" I ask Ben and Ruby as I buckle the suitcase up. "Anywhere in the world."

"Joan, please," Ben says. "Tell me what's going on."

"This is all falling apart. The deal, my promise from Gunn—everything."

Ben's jaw drops. "What are you going to do?"

"What needs to be done." I hand him the bag. "Pick any city."

"Jesus, I don't know, Joan. Baltimore, Philly—"

"Philly," I repeat. It holds the sound of freedom in it. "By nine o'clock, be at the departure board waiting for me, all right? I'll find you and we'll go to Philadelphia."

Ruby starts whimpering. "But Joan, I don't want to leave you, we just got here—"

"I don't want to leave you, either, but it's not safe." I bend down to meet her eye-to-eye. "Ben's going to get you out of here, and then in a little over an hour I'm going to meet you and we're going to start a new life. We're going to make our own magic kingdom in Philadelphia."

"Joan, no." Ruby starts crying, and it nearly breaks me, "I can't say good-bye again."

I wrap my arms around her. "I'll be with you soon. I just have a few things to take care of, and then it'll all be over. Then we'll never worry about anything again."

I climb over the cot and open the window.

"Hurry," I tell Ben, "there's carloads of men pulling up any minute—you need to be out of here before they do."

Ben's eyes are wide, but he nods and says, "Be careful, Joan. Whatever you need to do, do it quickly. We'll be at Union Station, waiting."

I watch them both slip out the window, climb onto the fire escape, jump down onto the side awning, and sneak across to the alley. A few black cars roll up moments later. D Street.

It begins.

Harrison Gunn, we are going to battle.

And only one of us is going to survive the war.

END OF THE LINE

ALEX

I'm a bloody, sweaty mess as I ride the streetcar up 14th Street, trying to calm myself down despite the glares and disturbed whispers of the other patrons, who've left a ring of empty seats around mine. It's nearly quarter to eight. I'm running out of time. The streetcar finally stops on K Street, and I dash off.

It takes about three painful blocks, but I limp as fast as I can to find a pay phone and duck inside the booth. When the Bureau of Internal Revenue operator comes on, I ask for Agent Frain.

"Alex?" Frain says in under a minute. "I've been waiting all day—"

"I'm sorry, they chased me through the whole goddamned city. They nearly had me, but I managed to escape."

"What? Who chased you? Are you all right?"

"Win Matthews, on Gunn's order," I sputter. "McEvoy's dead, and they found out he planted me." I catch my breath. "But this score still needs to happen. I can get you into the Red Den— we'll need a team of twenty, at least. The deal goes down around eight p.m. And there're the hostages we need to consider—"

"Alex, where are you?"

"K and Seventeenth Streets, in a phone booth right off the intersection." I close my eyes, very conscious that every minute

Frain dallies is an extra minute where Joan is alone in that magic haven, dealing with Gunn. "How soon can you be here?"

"Ten minutes."

"Good. Bring every honest agent you can muster."

Frain pulls up with a four-car parade minutes later. "Come on"—he waves me toward him—"hop in."

I hobble around the front and slide into his passenger seat. He studies me out of the corner of his eye as he pulls back onto 17th Street, with the caravan of squad cards trailing behind.

"Jesus, Alex," Frain says. "You look awful."

I wince as I stretch out to sit. "I jumped out of a moving car. It could be worse."

"How many do you think we're looking at?"

"Gunn will probably have his closest team of five or six, Colletto about the same. Then there are the Den's six sorcerers, but they're not going to give you any pushback," I lie. I pray to God that Joan sticks with our plan, even if Gunn told her I'm gone. I have no choice but to count on it.

So I gear up to give him the story that Joan and I agreed to, the only story that will let her and her family walk away from this unscathed. "The sorcerers in question, they've been kept in a cage for days, forced to sorcer for Harrison Gunn. And the heavy hitter—the one with the magic to make the eternal shine? Gunn's holding her whole family hostage. You need to get her out of there." I keep my eyes on the road as I spin the tale for Frain, but I can feel him watching me. "I found out that Gunn was using her right before I got pulled into Win's car—there was no time to tell you. They were driving me away before I could dial it in."

But if Frain suspects anything, he gives no indication. He gives a little grunt as he pulls a left. "Harrison Gunn." He shakes his head. "We'll get him, Alex, and all of those Shaw and D Street bastards. We're taking them all down."

We approach from N Street, pull into the alley perpendic-
ular to the Red Den lot, out of sight, and cut the engine. The
other agency cars slowly roll in behind us. Frain jumps out to
round up his manpower, but I give myself another second in the
car and lean my head against the passenger seat headrest.

I close my eyes and take a deep breath, and then another. This
will all be over soon, and then all the lies and betrayals, they're
all going to be done. I'll get folded back into the Unit's Domestic
Magic division, hopefully still working for Agent Frain. I'll have
a true second start, doing something that I excel in—something
I believe in. And Joan and I will be together, away and safe from
all of this. After some questioning and a short custody, I can get
her and her family set up here with me in DC. Her problems
will become my problems. It's what I want to do. It's what I *need*
to do. I can't imagine life without her.

I push the passenger door open and limp back to Frain's trunk,
where Unit men are digging out their weapons and ammunition.

SHOWDOWN

JOAN

I watch from my small bedroom window, as Gunn and Dawson cross the parking lot of the Red Den to greet the three town cars that have just pulled in. The engines cut, one after another. The D Street men get out of their cars, all crisp fedoras, big camel-colored coats, and black gloves. And then from the back of the car nearest to my window emerges their boss, Colletto. Gunn shakes his hand, pulls him into a half embrace, and gestures back to the Den.

They'll be downstairs in no time, and so I ignore the panic that's been rising inside me like a steady tide and force myself to focus on the next step in my plan. If the Feds are still coming, like Alex promised, they'll be here soon. First step: I need to appeal to the rest of the sorcerers. I need a cover for what happened to Win. I also need an excuse for getting inside that lounge. And I have to warn the troupe that the Feds are coming—they all deserve to get out of this unharmed. Despite what they might think of me, I still have nothing but respect for them.

The Shaws and D Street are still outside, closing car doors, sharing smokes, laughing as the night sky hums with possibility. I run down the two flights of stairs and cross the show space to the hall on the other side.

The door to the sorcerers' new home—the VIP lounge where they've been brewing around the clock—is locked, not that it would stop any sorcerer who truly wanted to break out. No, what's keeping them here is the same thing that kept me tethered to Gunn—a promise of a better future. A constant, unsettling feeling that if we step out too much, fall too far behind, one morning we might not wake up at all.

My hand wraps around the doorknob, and I conjure it open. The five troupe members stop and stare.

"What are you doing here?" Rose cuts in. "Thought you were above us now."

"Do you have a message from Gunn?" Ral says, as Billy adds eagerly, "Is D Street here? Is this goddamned nightmare over?"

"Alex never came back," Grace says softly. "Do you know where he is?"

It's like an attack, all the questions, the cold shoulders, and finally I utter, "Alex is dead."

The room becomes shocked still. Ral and Billy shift uncomfortably, Tommy starts muttering obscenities to Rose, but Grace just looks at me. "Are you all right?"

And that—the note of kindness, of concern, in her voice, after everything—it's what causes me to lose it. "No, I'm not." My eyes start to water.

"Joan, you're serious." Grace rushes toward me. "What happened?"

"Gunn had Win and his thugs put a hit on Alex. Drove him out of here and killed him in cold blood for Colletto, as some form of payback for Alex turning his back on D Street." I stop. "But I'm planning on making Gunn pay, for all of it."

The room falls silent once more.

"Is this really what you signed up for?" I press, gesturing to the room. "Is this what you want, being under the heel of a man like Gunn, a man who'll just discard us when his plans for us are done?" I shake my head. "He's been using all of us."

"Don't trust her," Tommy blurts out. "This must be some weird perverted test for Gunn."

I look around at my five troupe members, people I was once more than connected to, and finally give them the full story. "Listen, someone's dialed in the Feds—"

"The *Feds*?" Billy repeats.

"They're moving in tonight," I tell them. "But I'm going to end this before that, take what's ours, and get away."

"End *this*?" Ral asks.

"End Gunn. End all these gangsters. Finish it."

Ral and Billy exchange a look with each other, and then with Grace.

"I know we haven't been seeing eye-to-eye recently," Ral says slowly, "but Joan, that plan is insane—"

"Why?" I push. "If the Feds bust us, we're all getting locked up for sorcering for a hell of a long time. And if the gangsters manage to take out the Feds, we're looking at a lifetime of living under their thumbs." I nod to the room. "I've made up my mind. I'm doing this. And you're either with me or against me."

No one speaks, no one moves, until Grace shifts uncomfortably and asks, "What exactly do you want from us, Joan?"

"I need a cover. Tell Gunn that Win came in here searching for boxes a couple minutes ago, and that he ran out for supplies. Gunn will be looking for him," I say. Then I nod to the two hundred shine quarts on the floor. "And tamper with one of the bottles, make it look like an overlooked quart hasn't been blood-caged. I need a reason to force Gunn into bringing me back into this room. But as soon as I step inside here with Gunn, I want you all to run, and not look back. Get out of here before the Feds come in." Then I give them the final piece—the idea that's been circling, buzzing around my mind. An idea that thrills. "But there's something else, too."

The room stays quiet, the tension charged, sizzling like a live wire. With shaking hands, I grab a round metal coaster sitting on the edge of a nearby end table. I place my hands on each side of it and recite the charm I learned from Rose so many nights ago in the warehouse clearing: "*Divide . . . and seek to be completed.*"

The coaster sizzles and snaps in half. "I'm taking the next train after nine o'clock to Philly with D Street's payment for the shine shipment. I plan on starting over up there, in more ways than one." I hand one half of the metal coaster to Grace and keep the other. "And I hope you'll consider joining me."

Grace shakes her head. "What do you mean, *joining* you?"

"Once upon a time, we were good together. We trusted each other, and we made some of the finest magic this city has ever seen." As the words come out, I realize how much I still believe in us, how badly I want them to believe in us too. "Gunn turned me around—hell, he turned us all around, kept us afraid, thinking small. But I'd like to think that without his heel above us we can grow, become what we're meant to be, together," I say. "We can start our own magic haven up there, and just focus on our performance. We can leave all this behind."

The sorcerers don't move, don't say a word, my offer hanging there full and ripe for picking. *Would they ever trust me, want to work with me again? Will they track me down solely for the money?* I'm willing to take that chance. I can't imagine my life now without our magic in it.

Finally Grace tucks the piece of metal inside her blouse, her eyes never leaving mine.

"You know the offer doesn't last long." I point to her blouse, reminding her of the short shelf life of the charm. "If you want a cut of Gunn's loot, the money Colletto's handing over for our blood, sweat, and tears, if you want a chance to perform again—decide soon. And use that charm to find me in Philadelphia tomorrow morning." I pause. "They should be down any minute. I need to go."

As I slip out the door, Grace calls, "Joan!"

I duck my head back in.

She gives me a wary glance. "Be careful."

I nod, hoping with everything I've got that this isn't good-bye.

I sneak back into Gunn's office just as the double doors to the show space burst open. I close his office door, throw myself into my chair on the near side of the desk, my nerves on fire. But there's something else burning underneath my skin. Excitement. A desire to make thing right, to make Gunn hurt, to take from him like he's taken from me, an anticipation that has my thoughts racing together—

Will the troupe come through, if Gunn catches on can I destroy him, run as fast as I can as the Feds close in, will we have a chance to start over together—

After what feels like an eternity sitting there, stewing in my own fears and worst-case scenarios, the doorknob twists open.

Gunn stands at the threshold. I study him, in an odd detached moment, like he's somebody I don't know. Somebody I'm never going to see again. He looks tall and lean in his three-piece suit, a thin gray pinstripe number that matches his hat. In another life, it might have been easy to fall for a man like Gunn, hard looks, hard-edged, a man of power and persuasion.

But in this one, I want to watch the life slowly leak out from his eyes. I want to watch his long, thin fingers grasp for relief that never comes.

"Turns out I need you once more tonight," he says curtly. "Win must have missed one of the bottles, and now Colletto's excited to see you cast the caging spell again." He offers his hand. "If you do this, and you train the rest of the troupe in that dark magic, you and I will be square." He pauses, no longer meets my eyes. "I'll even be generous and give you some cash to help you and your family get home."

Bullshit. Gunn murdered Alex. Gunn will probably end up murdering me after this deal. But I don't speak, I don't nod. Because I'm going to take his cash, *all of it.* And because Gunn's going to die long before I do.

He takes my hand, pulls me out of my seat, and through his door. As we turn down the hall, Gunn's eyes flit over to the empty chair where Win sat guard outside his office, but he doesn't comment. I choose to believe that this means Grace and the troupe covered for me on this as well. I'm so nervous my entire body is shaking.

We cross the show space, where the clock hanging above the double doors reads ten to eight. If the Feds are still planning to bust the deal, I've got ten, maybe fifteen minutes to get this done—assuming I can pull it off—and walk away before we all go to jail. Before Ruby and Ben are waiting for a sister and a cousin who never meets them under that train departure sign.

The sorcerers stand outside the lounge door, lined up like a true cast of servants. Gunn barely glances at them as he roughly ushers me into the lounge, though before I cross the threshold I find Grace's eyes and mouth to her, "Go." But I can't catch her reaction, because Gunn's already closed the door behind me.

The lounge has been rearranged from a few moments ago, all the chairs and sofas now pushed into one large ring around a card table, which I assume is meant to serve as my stage. Every seat is taken—Colletto in the large armchair directly opposite the door, three of his minions on his left side occupying the long sofa, and two more standing behind them. Dawson and some of the Shaw underbosses—Kerrigan, O'Donnell, Sullivan—that I recognize from around the Den are on his right in armchairs and folding chairs, not to mention that scum-sucking shiner, Howie, who gives me this fat, shit-eating grin. Gunn's surveying the room, same as me, and with a dissatisfied huff, he leans over Dawson. I hear him ask, "Why isn't Win back yet?"

Dawson mumbles back, "Not sure, sir."

"Ah, the beautiful Joan Kendrick," Colletto says from his chair. "I was wondering when you were going to grace us with your presence."

This is the man who ruined Alex's family, the man who kept Alex cloaked in hate and nightmares, the man who arranged for his murder. Colletto will go down, same as the rest of them.

"Nice to see you, sir," I say, and add a small curtsy as a flourish.

"I don't think we should wait any longer." Gunn nods toward the door. "Dawson, why don't you bring the last quart forward?"

Dawson stands up, turns, and picks up a glass quart of red shine from the corner of the room. He sets it on the card table in front of me. The cap, naturally, has been busted. *Thank you, troupe.*

"Joan, if you please," Gunn says through gritted teeth, "show these gentlemen once more how we elevate something magic . . . into something even more extraordinary."

Colletto clasps his hands together and laughs. "I have dealers up and down the coast already signed on," he says. "Can't wait to see it again."

And as he continues to smack his hands, I take out my switchblade, hold it right against my forearm above the glass bottle, feign like I'm about to begin the caging spell. But instead of pressing it into my flesh, I close my eyes.

After a moment, a minute, I hear Colletto laugh uncomfortably. "What's she doing?"

"Joan," Gunn says carefully.

"Gunn, what's going on?" Colletto demands.

And then I open my eyes.

Time has slowed, almost stopped, shows me a world now rich with color, every gesture and glance shaded and textured.

Gunn must know my tells by now, senses what I'm about to do, because he reaches for his pistol, a fast, fluid motion. But I thrust my hand forward, and Gunn's weapon flits from his fingertips like a freed dove, flies into mine, and then I quickly throw up a force field in front of me, a thick, protective, transparent wall. In response, Dawson jumps to his feet, he and Howie whipping out their pistols to fire on me. But I enchant their weapons too.

Dawson's gun goes off, but its bullet has a mind of its own now, darts across the room in the other direction, lands in the folds of Colletto's stomach, and he gasps, falls over. Dawson's gun fires again, shoots Colletto's minion beside him, as well as the two standing above him. Howie grabs Dawson's arm, shouting in his ear for him to stop, to stand down.

But it's too late.

The two remaining D Street thugs leap to their feet in response, pull out their guns, and fire. They take out Kerrigan, then Sullivan, then O'Donnell left to right. And then they take down Howie, who falls into a pool of crimson. Dawson's head splatters, a burst of red against the green-striped wallpaper of the far wall. A rogue bullet lodges into Gunn's leg from the cross fire and sends him crumpling to the ground as he screams, "You bitch!"

The two standing D Street men turn their pistols on Gunn on the ground, but he rolls over and grabs Howie's fallen gun. With two hot bullets, he takes the pair down. Both bodies slump and collapse like dead weight onto the couch.

I wait a moment, and then another, my heart pounding in my chest, blood surging to my ears.

Gunn still has Howie's pistol in his hand. He keeps it trained on me as he looks down at his wound. It's high, a shot right into his thigh, and the blood is thick and black as it seeps through that gray pinstripe suit. He presses his hand into his leg, trying to stop the flow, and gasps from the pain. I almost feel bad for him, until I remember it's Gunn.

I focus on the pistol half-propped on his leg, loosely held in my direction with his trembling fingers, and whisper, "*Fly.*" The pistol floats like a cloud above his head and flings itself into the corner, as Gunn gasps again, winces from his pain.

I decide that I'm safe, release my protective wall, and cross the room for the money. Colletto's near-overflowing bag of cash is lying half-open, discarded on the floor beside his chair, and I grab it and throw it over my shoulder, ignoring how a splash of blood oozes from the strap onto my shirt. *Just go. Leave him.*

But I turn to face Gunn. He's now wrapped around his leg, shaking, sweating, those white-blue eyes as haunting as ever.

"You'll pay for this," he mutters between heavy breaths, but still manages to look me in the eyes. "I'm going to make you pay—"

I bend down in front of him. "Something tells me that's not happening."

"You're nothing but backwoods trash," he roars, but then devolves into a series of hacks. "I could have given you everything, and you threw it all away." He stops, his flailing lungs trumping his angry mouth.

I stare at him, the man who has driven me to the brink, who turned me around so much that I forgot which way was up. Murdered Alex, threatened me and my family, disposed of anyone and anything that stood in front of him.

Not that it's all his fault. I was far too willing to lose my way.

"Because you're a terrible human being," I say. "Because you're a monster."

At that, Gunn snaps a laugh. "If I'm a monster, Joan," he says bitterly, "then what the hell are you?"

And then I can't keep my anger in check anymore. I lunge for his face, grab his jaw, and push up his chin, just like he did to me in his office, when he thought the world couldn't touch him. I spit his own words from before right back to him. "A *survivor*."

I release him, go to the corner, grab his pistol, and toss it onto the couch, giving him an easy way out, an alternative to bleeding to death. And then I rush to the door, open it, and look back to Gunn once more. "Good-bye, Mr. Gunn."

I close the door with a click, peer at Gunn through the little glass window in the door. And then, quick as lightning, I take my switchblade, hold my breath, and dash it quick across my palm. I press my hand into the wall, run it slowly over the door, from one side of the frame to the other, and whisper those words from the night Mama died, those words that saved me in the clearing, the words that will always be a part of my being—of blood, intention, and sacrifice: "*Less of me, an offering to cage for eternity . . .*"

I feel the pressure underneath my touch, a deep, thrumming pulse, like the throb of a phonograph turned up too loud. The door locks with a hard, unforgiving snap, and then the walls begin to hum and settle in.

Gunn realizes what I've done, I see him, I watch it all sink in. He looks around at his tomb, his face contorting with confusion, rage, panic—and then he spies me watching him through the door's glass window. His scream is silent, his mouth pulled into one long O as he silently bellows, "JOAN!"

But I turn away and leave him.

I run across the show space, to the back stairs, up to my room, out to the fire escape. I will get out of this. I will survive this fire. Ruby, Ben, and I will start a new life from the ashes. I just need to run, *fast fast fast* as I've ever run.

I clamber down the rickety metal of the fire escape, think of Alex whispering promises to me in this very spot, in those early hours of this morning when it felt like anything was possible.

And now he's gone.

But Alex has given me something that no one can take from me, something I'll always love him for. Something I will hold on to when the days grow dark and the nights grow long. I'm someone who has made mistakes, far too many of them, I know that. I'm someone who might have as much darkness as she has light.

But I'm capable of love, and being loved—the truest, barest, most magical kind of love, regardless of what I've done. I'm capable of starting over, embracing who I am and what I was meant to do.

The past can't be undone. I know it's too late, that I'll never be able to undo what happened that night in our cabin's clearing. I can't save her, I can't save any of us from that awful, gut-wrenching mistake—

But I can let the past go.

I close my eyes, steel myself as I sprint toward my future.

And I can sure as hell save myself.

AFTERMATH

ALEX

I start pacing in the alley across from the Red Den, waiting for the other agents to unload their weapons, to suit up before we break into Gunn's magic haven. *God, Joan better be all right. She better walk away from all of this.*

Agent Frain tucks his pistol into his holster and trots toward me. "You ready?"

"I'm ready."

"Don't shoot unless fired upon, you got that?" Frain orders his team of agents. "The point is to take them all alive. Lock these suckers up for the rest of their miserable lives." He looks at me and nods. "It all comes down to this, Alex," he says. "Take us in."

We head down the alley, Frain and me in front, more than a dozen Unit men behind us. We cross M Street, walk briskly across the parking lot, gather at the base of the wooden door that promises the Red Den's inside.

Frain leans into the door. "I don't hear anything. You're sure?"

I nod. "The bar's just a cover for the magic haven two floors below." I conjure open the lock, and we filter into the quiet bar-front. "They'll be downstairs, in a lounge off the main performance space," I tell the crowd. "We'll need to stick to the shadows, surprise them. There'll be a troupe of powerful sorcerers roaming around, but I can reason with them." *Because Joan already should have talked to them, won them over.*

A dissenting thought flares in my mind. *That's if she knows you're still coming for her, if Gunn didn't get to her first,* but I smother it. *This will still work. This will all work out. It has to.*

"All right, Alex," Frain says, "lead the way."

I lead them down the short hallway. The Unit men start whispering as I stick my hand right into the wall, feel the pressure of the force field, that intense, dark magnetic space where you can feel the fabric of the real world giving way to the magic. I walk right through the wall as the agents murmur in surprise behind me.

There's a reason sorcerers aren't caught easily, a reason the Unit needs a man like me on their side.

One by one the agents take their time, pass through the wall, and then we take the stairs to the lower level.

"There's a hallway on the right, first door on the left," I whisper at the base of the stairs. "They're in the VIP lounge."

We shuffle into the main performance space, guns out, footsteps light, past the circular stage where Joan and I made our magic together for so many nights. It feels like another time, another world.

But when we get to the first door along the corridor, Frain halts in front of it. There's a streak of blood, still wet and red, gashed across the door.

Frain looks into the small glass window of the lounge door and gasps. "Holy Christ."

"Agent Frain?"

But he doesn't answer. So I angle around to steal a better look.

I can't . . . I almost can't process it. A heap of bodies lie around the center of the floor, like jigsaw pieces. Jigsaw pieces to a puzzle of death. Pools of blood pockmark the carpet, gather at the edges, and soak it in an almost otherworldly red. Each body is riddled with bullets, lies twisted, folded, and arranged into an unnatural pose. It looks like a group execution, some mass suicide even, the bodies collapsed into a ring around a cardboard table posing as some cheap altar in the middle.

"Open the door," Frain whispers.

A panic, a premature pang of loss and guilt is already creeping up my spine as the officer on my left twists the handle. I frantically search through the window as he attempts to pick the lock. I look for Joan's face, for her perfect face—

But I don't see her, thank God, she's not here. *Did she escape? Did someone take her?*

"Sir, it won't budge."

"So try again, Agent Brennan," Frain orders.

Brennan mumbles a "Yes, sir" and tries the lock again. And again, as I scan the faces to see who's been taken down—

They're familiar faces, all of them—Colletto, and the men he was here with the other night. And the Shaw men, Kerrigan, O'Donnell, Sullivan, Dawson, Howie—

But no Joan. No troupe. The sorcerers, gone like magic dust in the wind.

And then I spot Gunn.

Gunn, the invincible.

Gunn, the man who stood between Joan and me, who kept her in a cage. Gunn, chest rising, falling, the life inside him slowly bleeding out.

"Sir," Brennan whispers, at the same time as I put it together, "one of the men in there—he's still alive."

"You need to open that door," Frain snaps.

"I'm trying, Agent Frain, but it's—it's like it's cursed."

As confusion and disappointment set in, a deep, dark, unsettling possibility starts pawing at my mind as well. It toys with me, just scratches at the surface—but I refuse to let it do any real damage. Not yet.

Frain surveys the door frame. "Kick it in."

Brennan tries, then three agents attack the door, then five Unit men are running at it like an army, ready to take it down. It doesn't budge.

"Alex, we need you," Frain says impatiently.

So I try in vain to open it with magic, attempt trick after trick—

Frain stops us with a raise of his hand. He crouches in front of the entrance, studying it, the lock, the window, the blood dashed across the door like a warning. "Where the hell are the sorcerers?" he says to me.

I give him the only answer I have. "I'm not sure, sir."

Frain looks to Agent Brennan again. "Call this in to the station," he says softly. "Papers are going to have a field day with this."

Then Frain grabs my arm, pulls me away from the rest of the Unit, down the corridor toward the main performance space. He sets his mouth into a hard line. "This main sorcerer of yours, Alex," he says slowly. "You believe she was kidnapped, held against her will by Harrison Gunn."

I look back to the door marked in blood, in dark magic. I feel like I've been cut right in half, divided like a double-sided trick. Part of me wants to tell Frain what I think might be true, what I'm terrified might be true. The other part refuses to believe she could have done this. I swallow. "All signs pointed to that, sir."

"Did she strike you as headstrong? Volatile? Violent?"

Yes, maybe, I'm not sure. I don't look him in the eye. "Not particularly."

"Alex, Christ," he whispers, "was she dangerous?" *Far too dangerous, in more ways than one.*

But Frain doesn't wait for my response, just paces back toward the lounge, like the answer must be in the puzzle of bodies on the other side of the door.

"We need to find the sorcerers," he commands to the force, "all of them. *Now*. Dial the names in to the station. Alex, I want a full list of names," he calls back to me. "And get a backup team in here. I want that gangster taken out alive, along with the evidence."

I stand there, nodding, mind reeling. *Could Joan really have done this?*

Did all of them do this, one highly orchestrated execution? A blood-drenched escape?

As the Unit men take notes, confer, study the bodies through the little glass window, another truth starts to itch, and in moments it's crawling all over me—

I might have actually lost her, I might never see her again—

Joan might be gone for good.

As realization sets in, I blurt out, "Agent Frain, stay here, I've got a lead." I start sprinting for the double doors. "I'll circle up with you after!"

"Wait, stop, Alex, talk to me!"

But by the time I hear Frain's hurried footsteps behind me, I'm halfway out the double doors.

I sprint up the stairs, into the lot, dash across M Street and into the back alley toward Frain's car, with some vague plan to search the city for her. But as I pass the Unit's black cars, something catches my eye, just the slightest bend of reality, and I stop.

I run toward the brick siding of the town home on the alley's other side. The closer I get, the more the wall of the structure seems to distort, bend, almost looks like there's a flat replica of the brick in front of the actual brick wall. I touch the replica, feel my way to where it drops off, grab the edge of the manipulation and step around it. Sitting behind it, watching her old world crumble to the ground, is Grace.

"Where is she?" I demand.

Grace doesn't look me in the eye. But I can see how tired she is, how beaten down. Purple circles under her eyes, shaking hands as she lifts a cigarette to chapped lips. "She thought you were dead. We all did."

I crouch down, force her to look at me. "I need to find her."

"Are you a cop?" she asks. "I see the black cars in the alley, I heard your voice. In one way, that makes you as bad for her as Gunn."

"Regardless of what she's done or what she's about to do, Grace, I have to see her, before it's too late. Please, if you know where she is—"

Grace doesn't flinch, doesn't say a word.

"This isn't about what happened, this isn't about the cops." I close my eyes. "Please. This is about her and me."

And then, for the first time since I met her, since Joan told me that Grace can burrow into a mind as quick and cunning as a mole, I let my guard down. I welcome Grace in—pray she can find, *see*, my feelings for Joan.

Right when I'm about to give up, Grace stands briskly. At the sudden movement, something strange—shiny and metallic—slides up from her blouse, but she quickly tucks it back under the fabric of her shirt.

"She's taking a train to Philadelphia around nine p.m.," she says reluctantly. "If you want a shot at seeing her again, you better hurry."

I round her wall manipulation, jump into Frain's car, grab the keys from the top visor, and shove them into the ignition with trembling hands.

I screech Frain's car out onto N Street, cut in and out of

traffic, tear around the circle that puts me onto Massachusetts with Frain's headlights cutting through the foggy January night.

I need to get to Union Station. Catch her. Stop her. *It's not too late.*

I nearly drive onto the curb as I pull in front of the station twenty minutes later, grab the keys, and hobble out the door. I run into the huge, atrium-like entrance, follow it to a long, marble-floored hall, and frantically search the DEPARTURES board at the end of it. I read the block letters: PHILADELPHIA 9:16 P.M. ALL ABOARD etched in white type. Boarding, but not departed. She's on platform three.

I'm not too late. . . . I'm not too late.

I cut through the crowds, sidestepping my way to a teller for a ticket, throw some cash at him, and dart through the entrance to platform three. The thick clutter of overcoats and suitcases swarming the platform nearly swallows me, but I fight my way through it, using elbows and shoulders as I move forward, determined to find her. I search the windows of the train, each face I'm barreling past, each onlooker on the benches in the middle of the platform. My heart's pounding, my chest's heaving. *We can't end it like this—*

And then, about thirty feet away, I spot a little girl and a young man, both oddly familiar, like two characters plucked from a dream, stepping onto the train. Joan's right behind them. She's sporting slacks, a coat, her hair pulled back and a broad hat disguising those doll-like features. A bubble of relief and hope and longing rises, grows, bursts inside me.

"JOAN!" I shout. "Joan, wait, Joan!"

She stops. She spots me across the platform, and her face says it all. Grace was right. Joan thought I was dead. She thought I was gone, and her own relief floods through her, breaks her right open. "ALEX!" she cries. "Oh my God."

She bursts forward into a run, a clip-clop of her heels, and for a split second, everything else is forgotten. *This is it, this is our happy ending, I will have her, hold her—*

And then reality sets in. Joan stops running as her hand flies to her mouth. Her eyes grow big, wild—a storm of emotions clouding her face all at once. Longing, pain, triumph, regret. Her eyes flicker up to the train, and then I watch her hold out her hand.

I can't see everything, can't hear her words from here, but it looks like she points to where her wrist meets her palm, then points to the tip of her middle finger. She closes her hand, and the two points meet. And then she takes a step forward—

And in one step, somehow bridges the gap between us, through some kind of folding of the platform—a type of linked trick across space and time.

But I've never seen anything like it.

I gasp, my heart pounding, soaring, as Joan leaps into me. I wrap my arms around her, inhaling her, taking her in.

"I thought you were dead." Her voice is cracked, soft and muffled by my shirt.

"Joan, God, I'm so glad I got here in time."

She pulls away, looks at me with wild eyes. "Oh, Alex—" she gasps. "You don't know what I've done."

And then I know for sure: it was her. There's no denying it anymore, and images from that lounge flood my mind—*the blood-soaked carpet, the twisted bodies, Gunn left for dead—*

"I went to the Red Den to find you. I saw it all," I say slowly.

"And you're still here."

I swallow. "Joan, you can't run."

She glances back to the train and wipes her eyes. "What happens if I stay?"

I don't know, I don't know how I can spin any of this, if I have any more lies left in me—"We'll work it out, together," I push. "Joan, it's not too late for us."

The conductor comes to the front of the train and shouts, "ALL ABOARD!"

Joan shakes her head. "I'm not living behind bars, Alex. And for tonight, there's no pardon."

She's right, of course she's right, but I can't watch her—the Joan I've come to love, to trust—go. I tighten my hold on her slightly. "Joan—"

"There're certain things that can't be undone." She shakes her head, her voice breaking. "And I accept that." She looks at her hands, then up at me, her eyes now wide and resolute. "But you could leave the Unit behind. You could come with me."

"What? Where—you mean just run? Joan, we'd be fugitives—"

"We'd be free," she says, determined. "A new city, a new start for you, no Unit, no McEvoy, no Gunn. Just the chance to make magic together. A chance to embrace what we were meant to do, Alex."

"Joan, think about this, before it's too late," I press. "You could explain it was self-defense, maybe even cut a plea bargain, if you give up your blood-spell—"

"I don't need saving, Alex." Joan shakes her head. "In fact, I think *you're* the one who needs saving. I think when you were on our stage with me it was the most awing, wondrous feeling you've ever felt, because it was for me, too. I'm not ready to give that up. And I don't think you are either."

I stare into her dark almond-shaped eyes, and for one hot, desperate moment, I nearly agree with her. I don't know if I can watch her go. Maybe I *could* turn my back on everything I've worked for—the broken man I've managed to somehow piece back together. The charge I've come to own. The person I've become proud of.

"Joan, I'm not my father." The words almost say themselves, escape before I have a chance to think them through. But as soon as they're out in the world, I know they're true. Despite how much I want Joan, *need* her, my allegiance, first and foremost, has to be to myself. "I'm different than I was before." I wrap my hands around her wrists. "I won't hide. I believe in what I'm doing now, and I just can't run away."

"So that's it?" she whispers. "We say good-bye? Go our separate ways?"

"It doesn't have to be this way, Joan. Please, think through this—"

"But that's the thing, I have." She moves her hand over to my right ear, and I feel something soft and sweet-scented bloom beside my temple. I carefully pluck the newly sorcered flower from my hair. A black, red-tongued orchid, a spitting image of the one I made for her so many nights ago at the Den, when things, as complicated as they were, were also simpler. "If you're honest with yourself, Alex, you've always known the truth of me."

I shake my head. She can't go. If she goes, she's a fugitive, a criminal. "If you run, when we meet again, Joan . . . Christ, it's not going to be like this."

She gives me a sad, loaded smile. "That's assuming you can catch me, Mr. Danfrey." Quick as a cat, she leans in, places her lips onto mine. "I will never, ever forget you, Alex," she adds, a whisper. "You helped me become who I was meant to be."

Of course, I know she's right, because in a strange, twisted way, her words are just as true for me. And yet the feeling of having Joan so close again is thrilling, addictive. Instinctively, I reach to keep her with me just a little while longer, but that fast she slips away, turns and darts back the way she came. One more step and she disappears for an instant, and through her magic fold, her linked trick, she emerges again near the stairs of the train, down the platform, thirty feet away. "Wait, Joan—"

The train begins to move.

"Joan, wait, STOP—!"

But there's no stopping her, that becomes immediately, painfully clear. She grabs the handle up the train car stairs, gives me this teasing little curtsy, a nod that this is our final performance together, that the world was once our stage. She flashes me that heady smile once more, and despite everything, despite *all reason*, I find myself smiling with her.

Joan steps onto the moving train, and then just like magic, *poof*—

She's gone.